SEX & SOURS

DANI MCLEAN

SET THE MOOD PUBLISHING

SEX & SOURS

DANI MCLEAN

SEX & SOURS

Book 2 of The Cocktail Series

Print ISBN: 978-0-6451624-3-1

Ebook ISBN: 978-0-6451624-2-4

www.danimclean.com

Cover Design by Bailey Designs Books

Edited by Olivia Kalb

Proofread by Aimee Walker

Author photo by Rachael Munro Photography

ALSO BY DANI MCLEAN

The Cocktail Series:

Love & Rum

Sex & Sours

Risks & Whiskey

***

The Movie Magic Novella Series:

Midnight, Repeated

Not My Love Story

A Missing Connection

It Has To Be You

The Forces of Love - Out July 2023

Love yourself.
Be kind to all.
Swear to your heart's content.

1
———

TIFF

W ho the hell organizes a bar staff meeting at …
10 a.m.

On a fucking Monday?

Harry Cooper had been many things: quiet, sentimental, perennially stressed, occasionally surly.

What he had never been was a cruel bastard.

Apparently, his brother was.

As the new owner of The Basement, the other Cooper brother had ordered every single staff member to be at the bar first thing so he could introduce himself.

I didn't know a single thing about Harry's brother (was he younger or older? Was he another paper pusher? Most importantly, was he going to be in my way?), but what I did know was that I already had very strong opinions about this very early and very ridiculous meeting.

I bumped into Devon on my way North Side, three stops from the bar. We'd both closed the bar last night at midnight, and now the smug bastard taunted me with his hot coffee and still steaming croissant. Devon was the best of the bar staff—he worked hard, was trustworthy, and weathered stress like nobody's business. He was probably a little wasted at The

Basement, although the one time I suggested he pick the cocktail for our weekly special, he just regarded me like I was a lost puppy and told me he was good.

"You look ready to murder someone," Devon said, his warm smile curling around his cup as he took a sip. Damn him for looking so well-rested. His brown skin was practically glowing. "Is it sleep, or do you just hate the idea of someone else taking over your bar?"

Mid yawn, I huffed a laugh in response. "I could still fire you, you know."

"We'll see."

The train's vibrations rattled through my bones, almost lulling me back to sleep. Devon wasn't entirely off the mark. Four and a half years of working for Harry, and most of those spent running the place, could I really be blamed for feeling like The Basement was a little bit mine? And this new guy. His name might be on the lease, but this team? They were my team. My friends (well, mostly).

I wasn't about to let anybody come in and push any of us around.

"You know anything about this guy?" Devon asked as we walked from the station.

Another yawn escaped me. I was used to a messed-up sleep schedule thanks to years of night shifts, but I hadn't had a night off all week, and I was struggling to catch up. Another tick against Harry's brother. "Not a thing."

"Strange that Harry never mentioned him before."

When we reached the bar, I was surprised to discover the front door was unlocked. It looked like the new owner was already here. Fuck. He was going to be a morning person, wasn't he? I was not nearly caffeinated enough for this. "Is it, though? It's not like he was here all that often. Or talked that much about himself."

Devon shrugged and made his way behind the bar to get a head start on tonight's prep. He really was the best.

As though our presence had kicked off a domino effect, the next five minutes were a steady stream of the rest of the staff arriving, but still no new guy. Curiosity was eating at me, so I poked my head into the back office, where Harry had always spent his time. Nothing. Where was he?

I bristled. It was beyond rude to get us all here at ass o'clock and then make us wait for him. I added it to my list of grievances.

Of course, like an omen, I found him greeting the team, shaking hands and smiling like a congressional candidate when I exited the office. I swear, if there had been a baby in the room, he'd probably have been kissing its forehead.

I crossed my arms across my chest and grumbled to myself. It wasn't like I had woken up this morning planning to hate him, but something about his perfectly coiffed hair and pressed shirt made my skin itch. I'd met plenty of owners like this before, ego's bigger than their brains (which wasn't a high bar, to be honest), and I knew immediately he was going to be a problem.

Objectively, I could see the family resemblance. Same tall stature, same dark hair, same weirdly patchy stubble (was beard growth hereditary?). But everything about his manner was Harry's opposite. Where Harry had been reserved, his brother was practically a spotlight.

Younger, too. Had to be. All bright eyes and a lopsided smile. A jawline that could cut glass. He stood completely at ease, despite wearing a suit amid a room full of t-shirts and jeans. Dark blue and paired with a crisp, open-necked white shirt. It must have been tailored from the way it fit him. And expensive.

God. Dammit.

I was absolutely not caffeinated enough for this.

He was shaking Devon's hand as I approached. "Thank you, Devon. My brother told me you were his best employee."

Jealousy lanced through me. I mean, he wasn't wrong.

Hell, I'd been the one to tell Harry that. So, why did it bother me so much to hear it?

"And I apologize. I didn't catch your name." He turned to face me, eyes quickly taking in my appearance. Jutting my chin up, I held myself straight, happy to find he only had a few inches of height on me.

Let him judge. I was used to the looks by now. People always made assumptions about my appearance; tight jeans and tees that accentuated my overly slender frame, thick blonde hair that trailed past my breasts, an exposed side shave which was currently decorated by a gold chain ear cuff.

"Tiff. Head bartender and manager." I held out my hand.

"Our commander in chief," Devon joked.

Whatever he thought, it didn't show. "Ah, yes, Tiffany. I've heard about you." His grip was firm, his skin surprisingly soft when I shook his hand. "Sam Cooper."

My brain halted. He had "heard about me"? And what the hell was that tone?

At least I had a name now.

"'Sam," although I still had half a mind to call him "asshole," got the room's attention.

"Thank you all for coming in this morning. I understand that Harry ran things differently, but I wanted to make it clear that I will be making some considerable changes. First of all, I will be taking over all management duties starting immediately. This includes scheduling and inventory. If there are any days or times that you are unable to work, please let me know so that I can see how we might accommodate it. Additionally, I plan on being much more involved than Harry was, and I need you to understand that I am your boss and my word is final."

What the hell was this guy's problem? I was used to Harry being a bit of a stick in the mud, but his brother? That stick was shoved so far up his ...

"Is there a problem?" Sam's steely eyes were on me.

I jutted my chin in challenge. "No problem."

"I apologize if I'm keeping you from something, Miss Young."

Miss Young? I forced a smile.

Breathe. Do not punch your new boss.

"Not at all, Mr. Cooper."

"Then I would appreciate your full attention."

Do not, I repeat. *Do not* punch your new boss.

I never thought I'd miss Harry.

"Now, I would like to speak with each of you individually, so I will need everyone to please stay until I have gotten to everyone." There was no avoiding his pointed nod in my direction.

It had been years since I'd been in church, and I was not what anyone would call religious (to my poor mama's long-lasting disappointment), but Jesus, Mary, and Joseph, if this asshole thought he could walk in here and take over my bar, he was in for a rude awakening.

This was going to be a long-ass day.

"Asshole" moved into his office and started talking to people one by one. It became apparent that this was a calculated move, the new guy establishing his ownership of the bar like he was swinging his dick around.

Aware that my growing disdain for him was not good workplace policy, I texted Audrey, who, as my best friend for many years, had long since been on the receiving end of my tirades and would not blame me for complaining to her at this time of the morning.

Me: *I hate him so much already*

Auds: *That bad?!*

Me: *The. WORST.*

It didn't scratch the surface of my irritation, but it helped.

Auds: *Are you working tonight? I need to offload some elderflower gin from my new account.*

Me: *No and hell yes. In that order. Plus we can start wedding planning.*

Auds: *I only just got engaged, there's plenty of time*

Me: *Only because you haven't set a date yet! Also, not taking no for an answer*

Auds: *Fine. See you tonight. Take it easy on the new guy.*

Easy. Hah. Right.

Devon nudged my shoulder.

"How are things with Hannah?"

I smiled; my girlfriend was a much better topic of conversation. "Good. She wants me to meet her parents."

"Wow. Big step. Are you nervous?"

"I think Hannah is more nervous than I am."

"Are you the first girlfriend to meet them?"

"No, that's what's strange. She's been dating girls for years, but for some reason, she's worried." I'd tried to get Hannah to explain why last night, but she'd shrugged and changed the subject.

"Maybe because it's more serious this time?"

And that thought shouldn't be as worrying as it was. Because, while we'd been dating for four months now, would I call us "serious?" It was the longest relationship I'd been in for, shit, too long, and I cared for Hannah, but … But.

I couldn't even pinpoint exactly what was stopping me from taking the next step. Hannah was gorgeous, we had a healthy sex life, and she'd been comfortable from the start about taking it slow (though that hadn't stopped her joking that it went against lesbian law not to be living together already).

I liked her. A lot. We'd connected from the moment we'd met. Hannah was energetic, ambitious, with a sharp mind and a penchant for art and history. When we'd first started dating, we could lose hours in each other (fucking or talking), just enjoying each other's company.

Yes, it wasn't always easy to make it work (between my

nights tending bar and her day job, our hours didn't always line up), and Hannah could occasionally be unintentionally selfish, but she respected my independence, and there was more good than bad.

Still, something was holding me back.

Audrey had given me the same advice I'd given her barely a year ago when she had similar concerns about her "situationship" with Jackson ("It's a leap of faith, Tiff"), but recklessly throwing myself into things had never been my issue (just ask my mama).

"Hey," I said, changing the subject, "have you seen Riley yet?"

Indicating no with a shake of his head, Devon pointed to the bar. "I'm going to restock the speed rack. Is there anything else you need me to do?"

The ice would need to be replenished, but I'd rather wait until opening to do that. "Nothing that can't wait until tonight."

As I watched the others enter and exit the back office for their chats with Sam, I shot off a text to Riley to remind her of the meeting this morning. She'd become increasingly unreliable of late, constantly swapping shifts behind my back or showing up late. I was close to firing her.

Shit. Would I still be able to if it came to that? Smug Sam (and didn't that have a nice ring to it) had made it obvious that he was in charge now (but maybe he'd like to whip it out and piss on everything just to make it really clear), so I could only imagine he wouldn't love the idea of me giving anyone the boot, no matter how deserving they were.

Great.

Although … It might be nice not to have to deal with the fiddly admin stuff for a change. Let his royal smugness fight with everyone over penalty rates and tip allocation and getting nights off for their cousin's dog's birthday or whatever.

And … Ok. If I was going to be totally honest, I was

starting to feel that itch. The one that prickled under my skin anytime I'd been in a routine for too long. And the last four and half years? That was a new record for me. Lately, I'd started to wonder, what next? I felt the familiar buzz of adrenaline when I pictured leaving to throw myself into something new.

And secretly (extremely secretly), I had hoped I could use the change in ownership as an excuse. Maybe it was the perfect time to move on.

Yeah, well, after meeting "sir asshole," there was a fat fucking chance of that happening. Even if it was time, there was no way in frozen hell I was going to leave my bar, my friends, in the hands of this douche.

By the time it was down to Devon and me, I had decided on a few things. One, we needed a coffee machine in this godforsaken bar (was lack of caffeine a medical problem?). Two, Riley's continued ignorance of both my text and this meeting had broken my last straw. And three, if Sir Smuggington the Third wanted to try my patience, he had absolutely achieved his goal.

Devon left with a short wave, leaving just me and the asshole. Like I was waiting to be summoned into the principal's office. Which was ridiculous. I knew my worth to this bar. He would have to be out of his mind to get rid of me. But I couldn't stop the flare of panic that lapped at my brain. My short nails began to tap rhythmically on the bar top.

What was he waiting for? An invitation?

Actually, what was I waiting for?

I walked across the empty space to his office, rapping a quick one-two on his open door (my mama gave me manners) but not waiting for a response before I entered and sat down (manners only went so far when you were dealing with a smug son of a bitch).

2

————

SAM

Very few things surprised me these days, and Tiffany Young could not be counted as one of them. While I usually tried to refrain from presuming anything based on second-hand accounts, I was willing to make the exception when it came to the spitfire of a woman who marched into my office.

Because within the short period of time that I'd had the misfortune of knowing her, she had all but confirmed every single thing Harry had told me. Though, I hadn't yet had the opportunity to witness her professional talents. But since my older brother was not one for over-exaggeration, I had a nagging suspicion she at least had earned her reputation through credible means. It was with reluctance that I admired that quality.

However, no amount of talent excused rudeness. And yes, she was beautiful, but she was also brash and volatile.

On first look, it would have been easy to pass her off as all bark, her loud appearance not enough to distract from the fragility of her slimness. But she was anything but fragile. That impression could only pass for a moment because everything else about her screamed control, power, and energy. This was not a person to trifle with.

So, I shouldn't be blamed for letting a bit of snark seep into my voice. I felt so much older than my thirty-six years. "Miss Young. Take a seat."

She folded herself into the chair with ease, one leg tucked underneath her in a way that I thought must be constricting in her skintight jeans. The position highlighted the curve of her waist and the sharp angle of her hips. I pressed my lips together. As casual as the pose looked, there was nothing casual about the way her eyes bore into me. "It's Tiff."

"Okay. Tiffany." Her eyes narrowed, but her smile didn't waver. It was mildly terrifying, although impressive.

"I wanted to thank you for coming in this morning and for waiting." I might be biased when it came to the most decorated employee here, but I could at least appreciate that she'd shown up. I had noted not everyone had.

"You're welcome." She had manners. Surprising.

"As I mentioned before, I will be making some substantial changes around here, some which will take place immediately, others that will be more gradual."

"What sort of changes?"

Put bluntly, the bar needed an overhaul. For years, Harry had kept this place open every day from 2 p.m. to midnight. After reviewing the figures, I couldn't see anything to warrant it. And from the number of staff employed, there was hardly enough people to appropriately cover those shifts.

I'd worked the twenty-four-hour lifestyle, and it was deadly. As soon as I'd met them today, I could see how rundown the staff and the bar were from being stretched thin.

"I'm changing the opening hours. Starting next week, we'll only operate Wednesday to Saturday. I also will be reviewing the cocktail list, replacing some of the obscure choices with more popular drinks."

"Don't you think, as head bartender, I should make the decisions about the drinks?"

"You are, of course, welcome to provide suggestions, but no. As the owner, I will have the final say."

"And if I disagree?"

"Then you might need to reconsider if you're comfortable working here."

She laughed at that, humorless and dry. "So, you're demoting me *and* castrating me in the same day? Classy."

My muscles tensed, although I kept my expression clear. I'd always had a great poker face, but I knew immediately that Tiffany would test the limits of it. Of me.

"You'll still be in charge of the drinks. I might not approve of the way you handled my brother, but I am aware of your reputation, and your skills should be considered an asset to this bar."

I moved a pen perpendicular to the paperwork in front of me before affecting my own "casual" recline in my chair. If she wanted to play power games, then I'd be happy to return the favor. "However, if you decide that you cannot accept this new arrangement, I won't stop you from leaving. I suspect you won't have an issue finding work elsewhere. I would only ask that you give appropriate notice so that we can replace you."

"I don't know what you think you know about me, Mr. Cooper," There was venom beneath that sultry voice, and I did not enjoy the way it made my blood sing. "But I'm not a quitter. You got one thing right, though. I'm a hell of an asset to this bar."

The Basement had a good rep, and the last thing I wanted to do was risk that, but I wasn't here simply to keep the lights on. If I was going to run this place, I wanted to put my stamp on it.

And in my experience, there was always room for improvement. No matter how talented the head bartender was.

"Are you claiming the success of the bar is entirely your doing?"

"Never." The conviction in her voice caught me off guard. I quickly quelled the flicker of curiosity that sparked within me. There were layers hidden beneath her staunch exterior, and I had an unfortunate affliction for uncovering mysteries.

I could not afford to let this be one of those times. Strong women were my weakness, but there was no way I was letting this one get too close.

Tiffany was clearly trouble with a capital T, and I was still dealing with the aftermath of the last woman who had ripped my heart out.

"I'm not demoting you. I appreciate that while my brother was here, you accepted additional responsibilities, but I don't run my businesses like that. I prefer to work at least as hard as the people who work for me. Yourself included.

"Now, I'm going to review the sales figures for the last two months and make some decisions. In the meantime, the bar will operate largely as normal, but I will require you to honor the managerial changes and redirect any staff queries to me."

"Ok," she said quickly. Too quickly.

"Ok?"

Then came a smile, too calculated to be cheerful. "Sure. Take the bar management stuff. Have fun. But if you really want to know how things work around here, you could just ask me. I've been running this place for years. I know every single person who has taken a sick day, every bottle we need restocked, the name of every wholesaler we deal with."

"So, tell me."

She snorted. "Didn't your mama ever tell you to say please?"

"Tiffany."

Her grin sharpened, but I had the distinct impression it was forced. She really hated her full name. I locked away that piece of information. "Riley. I want to fire her. She's been either late or skipping out on shifts, and she didn't turn up today."

I thought it over. "I'll consider it. Is that all?"

"We need a coffee machine."

"I hardly think that's a requirement for a bar."

"I think it's a crucial requirement if you're going to want me awake before noon. Besides, aren't espresso martinis a popular drink?"

I flexed my fingers against my thigh, grounding myself so that I wouldn't do something irrational like laugh. She was gunpowder, kerosene, and oxygen to my system.

Definitely. Trouble.

It was going to be crucial for me to put some distance between us. Be professional. For one thing, I was her boss. And that was absolutely not something I wanted to take advantage of. The fact that I had to sit here and remind myself of that did not bode well.

"I have work to do. I'd appreciate it if you locked up on your way out."

With a smirk, she left.

Once I'd heard the tell-tale click of the lock, I allowed some of the tension in my shoulders to bleed out, finally relaxing back into my chair and contemplating the enormity of the job ahead of me.

There was no denying it. I felt tired. Drained and battered if I wanted to be honest about it. And yet underneath it, there was a small thrill in starting over. With the benefit of distance, I was able to face that I had been running on autopilot these last few years.

Not since opening my first bar had I had the option of being bold. After that, I'd been a brand. I'd needed to be consistent.

Now, I had the chance to do something fresh. Re-evaluate my brand. Re-evaluate myself. I groaned. Great. My therapist would be thrilled.

Drumming one hand on the desk, I mentally started splitting up the tasks ahead of me, the first of which had to be cleaning up Harry's office.

My office. Right.

Then I'd finalize the order for the new POS we needed.

I couldn't help replaying the conversation with Tiffany. Her statement about the bar almost failing was news to me. In the many years since I'd left, I'd tried to keep in touch with Harry, but my work had always been my priority. Of course, I'd known he was out of his depth, but I had my own businesses to run, and I'd accepted it whenever he'd told me things were going well. Even though I knew I should have questioned it. Guilt that had always plagued me about leaving him behind now stirred worryingly from Tiffany's accusation, even though there was no chance she'd meant it to. But my mind filled the gaps anyway.

The bar had been floundering, and she'd been the one to step in. Because I hadn't.

He never asked me to, but I knew he hoped. I should have been here. Perhaps if I had, I wouldn't feel the weight of my guilt so heavily now.

Over the years, I'd listen to my brother's stories about Tiffany, although he'd been careful to be diplomatic. But I'd read between the lines. I'd seen how she had railroaded Harry into their current working situation, and I'd grown angry on his behalf. It was easy to recognize Tiffany as similar to my ex —someone who would take advantage when the opportunity arose.

There was no doubt in my mind that she wouldn't be getting her way with me.

Dialing my brother, I toed off my shoes under the desk and undid the top button of my shirt, flexing my back against the hard back of the chair.

There were distant sounds of a baby crying when he

answered. "Hey, Sam. How'd the first meeting with the staff go?"

Mostly well. With one exception. "Acceptable."

"Acceptable?" He didn't believe me and sounded happy about it.

"For the most part. Tiffany will be a handful." Instinctively, I looked over at the empty chair, still seeing the ghost of her. Unique and bold. She was as magnetic as she was frustrating.

"She always is."

"Only because you let her walk all over you."

"Brother, you'll soon find that you don't *let* Tiffany do anything."

It was easy to believe that. Already she'd shown how quickly she was provoked, telegraphing her every feeling. How emotionally driven she was. It wasn't necessarily a bad thing, but passion did not make for good business decisions. It was exactly why I prided myself on my planning and strategy.

I liked things that made sense. And Tiffany was illogical. "Actually, I think you'll both find I can be quite immovable when I want to be."

"That, I can believe."

"How are Imogen and the baby?"

"Good. We're still working on night feeds, but it's easier now that I'm home more. Thanks again for taking the bar off my hands so I could do this."

"It was an easy decision. You and Imogen have been through so much with the IVF. I know how much it meant for you both to finally have a family." We both knew it had more to do with my circumstances than his, but he was kind enough not to say anything.

"Thank you. It means a lot. You should come over and meet your niece now that you're back."

"I will. I'm still waiting on a few boxes to arrive from over west, not to mention all this paperwork I need to work through. You know, for an accountant, you have a hell of a way of being disorganized, Harry."

His throaty laugh was all too familiar and something I hadn't heard in a long time. It twisted the guilt and nostalgia that had been building in my gut since I'd stepped off the plane two days ago, reminding me of how long it had been since I felt close to him. The last decade of my life had been lived on the other side of the country, focused entirely on work and very little else. Due to my lackluster efforts, we'd barely seen each other outside of special occasions and, unfortunately, our parents' funerals.

"Can't do much about it from here, I'm afraid. Besides, anything outside of the money was Tiffany's realm. You'll need to work with her to wrap your head around it."

I grimaced. "I was afraid you'd say that."

"Don't be like that. It was a good thing. I didn't know what I was doing, and the bar wouldn't have made it without her."

Harry confirming her statement was not what I wanted to hear. No wonder she was so insufferable. She'd been right.

Not that I would ever tell her that.

As I let out an unimpressed hum, Harry chuckled. "Welcome back, baby brother. A lot has changed since you were here, but it can't be worse than what you left behind." He didn't need to remind me twice.

Nine years. It had been nine years since I'd packed a bag for the other side of the country and taken a chance on my future. I'd left my family behind and gone as far as I could go, convinced I could make something of myself.

And I had.

It had been a long shot, but over time, I'd learned that I quite liked disproving other people's expectations. Of putting in the work to move beyond the "shoulds" that everyone else had thrown at me.

Years of hard work, long hours, double shifts, and pushing

myself beyond what I was getting paid for, all in service of my goal.

Until I'd finally had my own bar. Then two. Then three.

And now I was back at square one.

"Has Piper signed the dissolution papers yet?" Harry asked.

"No. She's dragging her feet."

I sincerely hoped it wouldn't take much longer. Considering that the benefits were heavily weighted in her favor, it made no sense why she was delaying it, and I knew that she knew that. This was purely a power play.

So, it was with bitter amusement that I now found myself back in a city I had long left behind, starting over and facing off against another maddening, intriguing woman.

When I'd first met Piper, it had felt like the universe aligning itself. She'd arrived just when I'd needed it, promising to help find the funding for my first bar. Like destiny, it had felt perfect. Love and work colliding. She'd brought in the money, I'd built the brand, and it worked.

It seemed like the perfect partnership.

I'd had no idea that she would rip my world out from under me.

"Need me to take a look over the figures? Make sure she isn't reneging on your deal?"

"No, the lawyers are taking care of everything."

"You should have fought for more."

Removing my glasses, I pinched the bridge of my nose. I was completely sick of this conversation. The faster the papers were signed, the faster I could move on. "There are a lot of things I should have done, Harry. But I have my name and the settlement, and I will just have to accept it as a lesson learned."

"It's still disgusting that she's profiting off of your hard work."

An understatement if ever I'd heard one.

There was no doubt that I was angry—at myself most of all. All that work, undone by a single document I'd signed years ago. Before anything had even existed.

My own feelings of outrage were stirring, making it clear this conversation needed to move on before I got worked up. "Right. Well, there's a lot to do, and I'm sure you're busy with the baby, so I'll let you get back to it."

"Don't be a stranger, Sam. And good luck."

I sighed, staring at the phone.

How did I end up back here? Starting over after a decade.

At least half of the blame rested on me. Piper and I had hurt each other deeply, but if I hadn't let love blind me, I wouldn't have made the decisions I had. Taken the risks that had ultimately resulted in my downfall. Her actions since the breakup were fueled by a pain I understood, and for that, I was fully to blame.

I'd left Chicago convinced I'd return a success. I'd left behind family, friends, my life to achieve it. I'd moved as far away as I'd been able to, to chase it.

And in the end, it hadn't mattered. I'd still failed.

Home had been a backup. The last resort if all else didn't work. I just never thought I'd actually need it.

So, ok. I'd fallen. But I could get back up. I would make this work. I just had to stay the course. Be smart. Not do anything reckless.

3

———

TIFF

I was still thinking about the meeting as I waited for Audrey to rock up at my place. Stupid smug Sam and his floppy hair and arrogant attitude and little hoop earrings (what was he? A freaking pirate?).

And that outfit? So polished and primped. He probably wore shorts on the weekend and played tennis, the bastard. I bet he'd never worked a day in his life.

Telling me I'd overstepped with Harry and that if I didn't like it, I could quit.

The fucking gall he had to act all nice in front of the others when he was really a sadistic asshole. And what the hell had Harry told him about me?

I measured out an extra shot of espresso tequila and added it to the espresso martini I was mixing. Ever since the conversation with Sam, I'd been craving one. I couldn't help but make it a little interesting, adding a cold brew from my favorite artisan coffee place and a splash of Irish cream.

It tasted like tiramisu, and my first thought was that I would love to add it to the menu.

Then, I remembered.

Fucking. Sam.

At the sound of my phone ringing across the room, I put the cocktail shaker down and ran over to answer it, smiling at the sight of my girlfriend's ID.

"Hi, sexy."

"Hey. How did the meeting go?"

I groaned. "Terrible. He's a pompous, pretentious ass."

"Please tell me you didn't say that to his face."

My spine bristled at the implication. It wasn't far off, but her tone, that implicit judgment, made me defensive. "Not in so many words."

"Geez, Tiff. I'm surprised he didn't fire you." Guess I won't mention that he'd threatened to. "You need to learn to be nicer when you dislike people. It's not a crime, you know. It's actually the normal thing." She chuckled, but all I felt was cold.

"Maybe I like not being normal." Whatever that was.

"One day, it's going to bite you in the ass."

I swallowed my irritation, glad she couldn't see me. We'd had this same conversation too many times. *Why couldn't I be more like other people? Why did I always have to say what I was thinking?* I was starting to wonder whether I'd ever measure up to the image Hannah had in her head. If I even wanted to.

"Did you at least manage to get the night off next weekend as you promised?"

Shit. Fuck. Damn. "Shit, no. I forgot, but I'll make it happen."

"Tiff, you know how important this is to me. My parents are only in town for two days, and I've already booked dinner. I told them you'd be there."

"It'll be fine. I'll be there," I promised before turning on a sultry tone. "I'm not working tonight. Did you want to come over after Audrey leaves? I miss you."

"And deal with your tipsy ass? No, thank you. I know how you two get."

"You like my ass."

She giggled. "It's alright. Besides, I'm heading over to KC's to hate-watch MAFS. It'll be too late to come back across town by the time we're finished."

Ah, KC. Hannah's best friend. She was … I wanted to say nice, but honestly, I couldn't remember ever hearing her say anything nice. Ever. About anyone.

They both majored in art history, and when Hannah had started an internship at the Art Institute, KC had followed. When Hannah had finished the internship and taken a job at the Museum of Contemporary Art, so had KC. They loved hate-watching dating shows, judging all things art (and people), and I knew getting into KC's good books was a major stepping stone to making my relationship with Hannah last.

The problem was that KC seemed not to like me very much.

It wasn't for lack of trying, though. KC wasn't subtle about the veiled jokes she had given Hannah about our relationship. It reminded me of the way Audrey's ex-husband had been.

And yes, he was a douche canoe of epic proportions (the size of which I'm sure would even impress Smug Sam), but at this rate, I had to wonder if I wasn't the common denominator. No matter how much I'd love to call everyone assholes and move on, I knew that wasn't fair.

I was a lot to take. I knew that. And I had no intentions of changing myself to fit in with how other people thought I "should" be.

But that didn't lessen the sting.

"You know, KC thinks you're putting this dinner off on purpose because you're scared to meet my parents."

Yeah, well, KC is a jerk (was what I absolutely didn't say).

"Absolutely not. I'm looking forward to meeting them." And I was. Hannah wanted this, and I wanted to make her happy.

"It's just … I know you haven't taken that step before

because you've been afraid of a commitment," I bit my lip and said nothing (although I wanted nothing more than to tell her the million reasons that wasn't true), "but that's why it's so important to do this. Then, maybe you'll see that it's not that big of a deal."

It sounded to me like she was trying to convince herself, but I knew now wasn't the time to question it. If we were talking in person it would be better; I could read her expression clearer. And the last thing I wanted was to give KC any further ammunition. I couldn't tell if it was platonic jealousy or something more, but that woman apparently knew all the right ways to dig her nose into our relationship, so it was best if I put a pin in my concerns for now.

"I know," I said finally, and maybe I should have felt worse about misrepresenting myself, but sometimes you just have to pick your moments, you know? Plus, I was brain tired after that morning's run-in. "I promise you I'll be there. I better go. Audrey should be here soon. Have fun with KC."

There was always a beat as we said goodbye, a hanging silence. Neither of us had said the "L" word yet, and I was fairly sure I wasn't the only one who wasn't feeling it yet. Despite Hannah's insistence to meet her parents, she was just as content to maintain the status quo in our relationship.

To be honest, I was caught most days between being glad to keep things as they were and wondering whether I shouldn't be feeling something more by now. I liked Hannah; she was beautiful, smart, artistic, strong-willed. She always smelled of rose and cherry and trembled so fucking delicately when she came.

But it wasn't love.

And I was starting to wonder if it ever would be.

And if it wasn't, then how much longer would we last?

We hadn't really discussed the future beyond our short term plans. I knew she was working hard to get a curator job, and while I was settled into my life at the bar, I hadn't really considered what would come next. Long-term was not really my jam unless you counted my rainy day fund. Hannah had questioned me on it a few times, wondering, "Why save all that money and not have a plan for it?"

My answer, "because I don't know what I want to do with it yet," hadn't really satisfied her.

Our phone call had unsettled me, and it was still sitting badly with me when Audrey's knock came.

I raced to open the door, relieved to see a friendly face, and I smiled for the first time in hours. "Thank god, I need a drink."

"Like you've ever needed me to do that."

"It's called growth, Auds."

Her bright laughter reverberated throughout the room as she shucked her jacket and arranged herself comfortably on the couch. I brought our drinks over and watched the appreciation on her face when she took her first sip.

"Mmm, this is amazing, Tiff. New menu item?"

"I wish. Our new dictator will probably have something to say about it, though. No, just something I was thinking about today."

"He was really that bad, huh?"

"I can't even describe it, Auds. It's like, on the surface, he's so smooth and smiley and 'oh I didn't get your name' like he's come right out of a fucking campaign tour, and then he's calling me Miss Young and telling me to get in line."

Audrey's lips formed a tight line, and her shoulders shook with restrained laughter.

"Oh, fuck you," I playfully retorted, causing her to openly laugh at me.

"He's awful, Auds. Got this chip on his shoulder like he knows something everyone else doesn't, but he plays it so nice, so you can't actually say anything bad about him. The rest of the staff is practically smitten."

"Ooh, I'll have to come around and meet him."

"Don't say that like you're excited. He's an ass."

"Noticed, have you?"

"Don't even start. I have not noticed, and I'm happily taken, thank you."

"So, things are going well with Hannah, then?" Dammit, I knew she was going to jump on that.

"Yeah, I think so." Unfortunately, I hadn't quite managed to disguise my hesitation.

"Everything alright between you two?"

"She's at KC's tonight."

"Oh." Yes, oh. And here was why I was so glad to have Audrey in my life.

"I'm trying not to worry about it, but every time she spends time with KC, I end up having to apologize for something." I didn't typically like airing my problems like this because Hannah and I were adults, and if either of us was having issues in this relationship, we needed to be talking to each other.

But Audrey was my best friend, and now that the can was opened, the worms spilled themselves. "Ok, so. We have mostly been good, and I told you that I'm meeting her parents next weekend," Audrey nodded, "which I'm excited about. I mean, how could you not love me?" I joked. "Lately, though, Hannah seems to be getting annoyed more often. Things that never got in the way before are suddenly a debate. Maybe it's just work stress. She's been putting in lots of hours, and it's gotten really hard to spend any time together."

"Maybe. Are you ok?"

"Yeah. Fine. I mean, I'm exhausted, and I have no idea how I'm going to work with this new guy, but yeah."

"What's his name anyway?"

"Sam."

Her eyes sparkled. That couldn't be good. "Last name Cooper, right?"

Oh, no. No, no, no. "Yeah, why?"

She whipped out her phone, typing quickly, her growing smile making me wonder what shit I was about to wade into. "Oh my god, it is him. I always wondered if there was a relation there."

"Who."

"TIFF, Sam Cooper is like a restauranteur wunderkind." She cracked out a laugh. "I can't believe you didn't know that!"

"I can't believe you do. This? This is who you know? One year ago, your superstar boyfriend—"

"Fiancé," Audrey corrected.

"Right, fiancé, walks into my bar and nothing. But this guy. This asshole, you know."

"Tiff, I work with alcohol on a daily basis; it's my job to know people like this. Shit, how did you not know Sam Cooper was Harry's brother?"

"We didn't really talk about stuff like that."

"I mean, I hadn't considered it before because his reputation is huge, you know? He's been on the west coast for the last nine years, even Vegas, but it makes sense that they're related. Both of them being in the bar business and all."

"Ok, I think it's a bit of a stretch to say that Harry was in the bar business." I considered the other information she provided. "Vegas, huh? Explains the attitude." Like a snake charmer in the desert.

"There have been some pretty high-profile pieces done on him. I wonder what made him want to come back?"

"Maybe his ego didn't fit in the great state anymore."

"Wow, you really hate this guy."

"He's just so …" I grunted in frustration. "Anyway, can we not talk about him anymore? We're meant to be wedding planning."

"Oh, god. Between you and Sarah, I swear." Sarah was

Audrey's sister-in-law-to-be. "I don't want this wedding to be a big deal. It's not like I haven't been married before."

"Yeah, but at least this time, it's to the right guy."

Her smile suddenly got a dreamy quality to it, the way it always did when Jackson was mentioned. "That's true."

"Ok. If you're sick of wedding talk, can we at least start planning your bachelorette? I already know exactly which stripper to get."

She turned serious. "Tiff."

"What? It's a perfectly respectable job, Auds. And Marcus can move. His hips are downright dangerous."

"I'm not having your ex-lover strip at my bachelorette."

"You know we're cool. He's got a boyfriend now anyway. Or an on-off thing from what he tells me."

"Still. No exes."

"Fine. But if we try to avoid all the people I've slept with, that isn't going to leave us with many options."

"I was thinking of something a little less," she searched for the word, "raunchy. And a little more relaxed."

"Ix-nay on the dick straws, then."

"That was never in question. Also, why do I get the feeling you have those lying around?"

"They're in case of emergencies."

The couch practically shook with the force of Audrey's laughter, and a little of her drink spilled onto the coffee table as she struggled to put her glass down.

I grabbed a Kleenex and cleaned up, then topped up our drinks. "So, something relaxed, ok. I can work with that. Drinks are a must, though."

"As if I'd want anything else. But I don't want you working all night. As my maid of honor, I want you to enjoy yourself."

Taking in her bright, happy demeanor, I couldn't help but reflect on the shift in her from this time last year. So much had changed for her since meeting Jackson, and here we were talking about her wedding. After her divorce, I hadn't expected her to want to take that leap again, and certainly not so soon, but I was so glad she had.

And what had really changed for me in that same time?

Barely anything. Would I still be here in another year, life unchanged, while the world revolved around me?

And why did it bother me in a way it never had before?

4

SAM

P assive observation lasted a week until I couldn't sit by any longer. Considering I'd already been approached by a few local media sites for comments on my return and my subsequent plans for the bar, it was time for me to stop watching and start making changes.

Most importantly, I'd updated the lagging point of sale system. With expedited delivery, the installation wasn't an issue. The issue was training.

And other words starting with "T."

It didn't thrill me to pigeonhole Tiffany as a problem. I liked to believe that people were fundamentally good at their core.

But.

That fact never stopped them from being capable of some incredibly bad things. And Tiffany might be able to get under my skin, but I'd been doing this a hell of a lot longer. I had stamina. Patience. Time.

I could outlast her.

Hell, I'd spent the last nine years dealing with larger-than-life egos. And I had always loved a challenge.

As expected, not everyone had been pleased to come in

early to learn the new system. Interestingly, Tiffany and Devon had picked it up quickly and had taken point on getting the others across the line.

Devon was a natural, which I could already see. Harry's comments about his reliability hadn't been exaggerated. As he sat across from me in the office, I was pleased with his confident, respectful air.

"I've poured over the last two months of sales, and I see an issue."

"Okay," Devon said slowly.

"It's obvious that Tiffany's one-offs sell well—not a surprise since that appears to be the main draw for customers. How long would you say it takes to make one on any given night?"

He thought for a moment, then offered a half-shrug in response. "For Tiff, a minute or two. For the rest of us, on average, probably five to ten minutes."

That's what I expected. And I appreciated that he included himself in that and didn't call anyone out. He'd definitely make a good manager someday.

I nodded. "As of tonight, I'd like to reduce the more complicated cocktails. Take it down to a single special for the night, and we'll rotate it each day."

That much time per drink was fine if you were running a small bar with limited capacity. But my goal was to boost numbers and sales. And you couldn't do that if you were slowing down serving for a single drink.

"Sure. If that's what you think is best."

"Also, explain the ice sculpting to me." Yesterday, I'd watched in horror as Devon had spent time personally shaping a cube of ice into a smaller cube of ice.

Completely ridiculous.

"Ah. Yeah, that's a real pain in the ass. It's just for the look, really."

Blinking slowly, I let my internal rage subside. Snobs and

their aesthetics. It wasn't Devon's fault. I could pinpoint very quickly whose idea that must have been.

"In that case, let's cut it. If we need to, I'll buy new molds. But in the meantime, I don't want the team wasting time on chipping ice."

"Got it, boss." Devon stood, then paused. "Have you told Tiff about this?"

"I have." Saying that it hadn't gone over well was the understatement of understatements.

A sharp laugh escaped him before he quickly turned it into a cough. "That explains some things."

Watching Tiffany training the team was not a sight I was prepared for. She was both in her element and almost a completely different person. Gone was the competitive opponent, and in her stead was a patient, supportive guide.

I followed Devon out into the bar and stood to the side, observing Tiff. It made sense now why the staff looked up to her beyond just her accolades in the field. She was a natural leader, confident and assured.

It was frustrating in more ways than one because it made it infinitely harder to consider firing her.

It also made it more difficult to stay clear-headed when she went back to treating me with disdain.

When she noticed my observations from the side of the room, she left the two barbacks she'd been supervising and stalked over. "What the hell are you doing?"

And so it began. "Excuse me?"

"You've put Riley and Nathan on tonight."

She stood with her hands on her hips. It had the unfortunate side effect of highlighting her sharp collarbones and the elegant line of her neck.

Neither of which I should be noticing.

I kept my eyes level to hers. "Is there a problem?"

"No. No problem. Just thought it might be weird since

they can't stand each other." I wasn't aware that much sarcasm could be expressed in one sentence.

"I'm sure they know better than to let that get in the way of their work."

She snorted. "Oh, yeah, twenty-year-olds are known for their professionalism in the workplace."

"I'll have a word."

"You do that."

Finding Nathan first, I asked him to follow me into the office. No need to have this conversation within earshot of the others, though I knew it would likely make the rounds afterward anyway.

"What's up, boss?"

"I wanted to check that everything is going well?"

"Yeah, of course. New system's great."

"Good. I'm glad to hear it."

There was another moment when I wondered whether to push or leave it be.

"Was there anything else?"

"Hmm. I understand there might be an issue with the schedule tonight."

"Uh, no."

"There's nothing I need to know?"

"Nah, boss. It's all good."

"Ok, thank you."

I decided to trust his answer for the time being. It wouldn't be the first interpersonal conflict I'd had to navigate, but he hadn't given me any indication that it was going to be a problem, so I'd give them both the benefit of the doubt and wait to see how that night went.

It wasn't that I didn't believe Tiffany's assessment of the situation, but I was also aware that these types of disagreements could be resolved over time. I was also painfully aware that we were not flush with excess staff, so petty squabbles could not always be accommodated.

As opening crept closer, it appeared I'd made the right decision since nothing untoward occurred.

Unfortunately, as all best-laid plans did, it fell apart at the exact moment it was inconvenient.

The night had officially moved past after office hours to the evening crowd, and the bar was full. The sound of a glass breaking was not a welcome one but also not uncommon, especially in a crowd of this size. The second and third glass were, however.

As I stepped out of my office, the problem was immediately apparent; Riley and Nathan were arguing behind the bar. I watched as Tiffany smoothly stepped between them and, with a few words, sent them to separate ends of the bar.

When she caught my eye, I could feel the weight of her stare. One brow arched.

She couldn't have telegraphed, "I told you so," better if she'd said it.

Riley was serving closest to me, so I decided to start there, quietly asking her to step into my office. She was on the back foot before she even walked through the door. "I don't know what the hell Nathan told you, but he started it."

I pointedly shut the door. "I haven't been told anything. Would you care to explain what that was about?"

"He's poaching customers off me. He knew I was about to serve that rich suit, and he swooped in when I had my back turned. Now, he's saying he won't split his tip with me."

"I hardly think that's an excuse to argue in front of the customers."

"But he's a lying prick! Ever since I turned his ugly ass down, he's had it in for me."

"I'd appreciate it if you lowered your voice." There was no way I could send her back onto the floor like this.

"Aren't you going to do something about it?"

"I'll talk to Nathan. In the meantime, I think it would be best if you went home. I'll make sure you still get paid for a full shift."

"This is bullshit. I have to go home?" Riley ripped her apron off, throwing it onto the desk. "Fine, whatever." With that, she stalked out.

Tiffany's head snapped to me as I stepped in beside her behind the bar, tying an apron around my waist. After that first meeting, I'd moved from wearing my old uniform of a suit to the more comfortable all-black ensemble that the rest of the staff wore. Not since my years of actually working the bar had I worn a t-shirt with slacks. I hadn't quite made the jump to jeans, however, and while I was tempted, I hadn't put a pair on in years. I'd have to work my way up to that.

"What the hell are you doing?"

"That's twice you've asked me that. Can I expect this to be a regular occurrence?"

"Only if you continue to be an ass."

"I'm still your boss, Tiffany."

"Oh, I remember. You still haven't answered me."

"I sent Riley home, and it left us one short, so I'm stepping in."

I shouldn't ask. It was my bar, and it would only invite her to volley back, but the question escaped anyway. "Do you have a problem with that?"

"Only if you don't know how to mix drinks."

"I'd wager that I've been mixing drinks for longer than you have."

Tiffany rolled her eyes. "Ok, hotshot. But as head bartender, I hope you'll respect the hierarchy of authority." She was baiting me on purpose. I shouldn't have liked it as much as I did.

There was definitely something wrong with me.

Never in my life had I said or even remotely thought of

using the words "yes, ma'am," but I would be damned if they weren't sitting at the tip of my tongue at that very moment.

Not trusting myself, I cleared my throat and turned to take a customer's order, thankful that I had already familiarized myself with the bar as soon as I'd gotten the keys from Harry. I was also endlessly thankful that the team who'd installed the POS system had trained me on it before they'd left.

To be honest, it had been years since I'd worked behind the bar. Not since I'd opened my own because my time had been overrun with other duties. But this was where I'd started.

I was a little surprised that I still knew what I was doing, but it came flooding back like muscle memory.

Tiffany threw me a few quizzical looks during the first hour, keeping a close watch, but other than that, said nothing. Which surprised me most of all. I kept waiting for the other shoe to drop.

Instead, we were able to work around each other seamlessly, weaving within each other's space like a dance.

It made me wonder what it might be like if we actually got along.

5

———

TIFF

The early afternoon crowd on Saturday was sizeable, although not unusual for this time of year. The beginning of August always brought more people in, hoping to escape the humidity. Still, it was hardly enough to warrant Sam working behind the bar.

I really hoped it wasn't going to be a regular thing. That week had been a test of my patience in every way, and the only thing that had gotten me through was the fact that we always retreated to our separate corners. Me, the bar; him, the office.

Then, last night, he completely surprised me. (He actually knew what the hell he was doing. Who knew?). I was almost, and I couldn't fucking believe I even thought this, impressed. After what Audrey had told me about him, I'd done my own googling (although seeing his annoying smile plastered across the internet kept me from spending too long on it), and so I knew he owned at least three different bars. But every focus piece on the guy was about his inspiration (ugh) and his thoughts on the social contracts within the service industry (don't even get me started).

In interviews, he was that same smooth, charming bastard

he seemed to be with everyone (except me), and it was clear that the interviewers fell for it, just like every single customer he served.

They didn't see what I did, though.

Case in point.

Christine was a regular on Saturdays, a retiree slash true crime novelist who liked to spend an hour a week sitting at the bar swapping stories with strangers. We'd seen her come in for the last two years, so, of course, she loved the fact that there was a fresh face.

From the corner of my eye, I watched him move smoothly through mixing the drink, short shaking the ingredients before topping it up with tonic. He moved with ease, only ever tensing up when we crossed paths. Without fail, if there was even the slightest chance we might come into contact, he stiffened.

I'd never met anyone so determined not to touch me, even though there was little to no room to avoid anyone else behind the bar. And yet, he managed it.

I watched as she reached over to pat his arm. "You are a good man, Sam."

"It's easy to be when I have such wonderful customers." Sam's bright smile brought a blush to Christine's face. He could probably ask her to donate her firstborn, and she'd say yes.

The effort it took not to roll my eyes could have fueled one of those old-timey blimps they used in the war.

I knew this was an act. It had to be; no one was this nice. I could see in real-time the way men and women reacted to him, endeared from the get-go. I assumed that was the whole point of his little act. Get people on side early and then get whatever he wanted.

Everything about him was carefully crafted for this purpose. From the slightly too tight slacks that hugged his toned ass and thighs to the shaggy haircut he was always combing his fingers through. He was perfectly casual.

Just scruffy enough that you were disarmed. Just charming enough that you were drawn to him.

He was the worst kind of slime ball, the one no one suspected.

Of course, he was careful about it. It was only with me that he was even remotely antagonistic, and even then, never in front of the other staff or customers. I appreciated that, at least.

He might be a smug son of a bitch who liked to make my life endlessly miserable, but he was professional about it.

————

AUDREY'S WORK schedule had increased tenfold in the last year, and she now had multiple successful launches under her belt. Still, between her workload as a senior liquor distributer and her loved-up home life, it meant we'd gotten less time to see each other. (Story of my life lately).

So I was more than happy to see her walking into the bar that afternoon, her lovestruck fiancé in tow.

"Hello again, pretty boy," I said.

Jackson smirked as he pulled out a chair for Audrey at the bar, then took the seat next to her. I wasted no time in passing them their usual drink order.

"It's good to see you, Tiffany," he said.

"To what do I owe the pleasure?"

Audrey linked their hands together. "We were in the neighborhood, and I wanted to say hi. Since I missed our usual Saturday morning get-together."

"First round's on me, then." I snuck a look over to Sam, who was thankfully in conversation with Christine and hadn't noticed.

Audrey visibly perked up. "Oh! Before I forget, I'm going to come by this week so you can sign the contract renewal."

I smiled back. "Sure thing."

The bane of my current existence materialized suddenly. "Excuse me?" Of fucking course, Sam had heard that. He stood stiffly at my side. "I believe what Miss Young meant to say was that as the new owner, I'll be signing any contracts."

No, what I meant to say was, I hate you.

I plastered on a smile, wishing my best friend didn't look so gleeful. "Auds, meet Sam Cooper, Harry's brother. Sam, Audrey Adams, the rep from Bespoke Beverages."

Sam's smile was warm and inviting. My jaw clenched tighter. "Lovely to meet you, Audrey."

"You, too, Sam." She mouthed "Miss Young?" to me while Jackson introduced himself. If Sam recognised him from the wildly popular tv show he starred in, it didn't show. I rolled my eyes, and Audrey hid her smile behind her glass.

Sam returned his attention to Audrey. "I apologize if that came across a little insistent, but considering that there appears to be a personal relationship here, I would argue it is a conflict of interest for Tiffany to be involved in approving any contractual obligations on behalf of my bar."

I could practically hear the grinding of my teeth. Made all the worse by the way even Jackson looked to be holding back his laughter.

Just you wait, pretty boy.

"Of course," Audrey replied sweetly because she was ten times the person I was. "Would you prefer to make an official appointment? I can call you from the office on Monday."

"I'd appreciate that, thank you." He shook her hand. "Nice to meet you again. Enjoy the rest of your evening." He turned to me. "Tiffany," he said before stepping away.

I'd never met anyone who could weld a name like a challenge before, but Sam fucking Cooper managed it.

Keeping a straight face, I attempted to exhale the

frustration. My eyes narrowed at the two amused people I dared call my friends. "Not a fucking word."

Jackson's smirk increased. "Seems you've met your match."

"One more thing out of you, and I'm going to elope with your fiancée before you get the chance to marry her."

He simply laughed. I missed the days when I still intimidated him. Those were good times.

"Maybe it's best if we leave you to it, Tiff. I don't want to cause any more issues between you and your boss." Audrey worried her lip.

"Great, now he's running off my best friend! I really, really hate him."

"Take it easy on him. You know how you are." Audrey stretched up as far as she could from her seat to give me a half hug and kiss on the cheek. I caught Sam's raised eyebrow from where he stood before saying goodbye to her and Jackson.

———

There was no shortage of rich douchebags in the city. Possibly less than in New York or LA. But like. No shortage.

And I had a very short fuse when it came to rich douchebags.

Especially ones who drank past their limit and started verbally abusing the staff. When he reached over the bar and roughly grabbed my elbow, the last straw broke. "Out. Now." The crowd around him parted as he yelled profanities on his way out.

Sam was hovering behind the bar when I moved to serve another customer, and I waited for the inevitable comment, letting our eyes meet as I dumped the beer bottle in the trash.

His quietly commented, "Nicely handled," which wasn't what I was expecting, but I shook it off and continued to work.

Sam shocked me again as I was clocking out for the night. "I'm surprised you held out for so long. I was about to kick him out myself for his attitude." It took me a moment to realize he was referencing the douche in a suit from earlier.

What was his play here? Was he trying to butter me up for something? Oh, god, was he about to tell me I had to keep working? Hannah would kill me.

Still rattled from the drunk, and now off-kilter from Sam's compliment, I hid my confusion under a joke. "He kept calling me doll. If I didn't throw him out, there would have been bloodshed."

Something resembling a huff, but may have actually been a laugh, escaped him. "You really hate pet names, don't you? Tiffany."

"When they are that belittling. Yes, I do. Samuel."

As his eyes darkened, I felt a rush of adrenaline. Good. Let him know I could give it just as well as I could take it.

When he took a step towards me, my pulse rose. Sam didn't get close. Sam kept a respectable distance. So, why was I suddenly aware that this was the closest we'd ever been to each other? And was it just the blood rushing to my ears, or was his voice rougher than usual? "I believe that's sir."

My mouth gaped open. "If you think I'm going to call you —" But he'd already walked off. Asshole.

Every time I thought maybe we could work together, that maybe he was ok, he'd pull something like that.

I checked the time. Dammit, I needed to get out of there to meet Hannah and her parents on time. At least dinner would take my mind off of work.

6

———

SAM

Devon was clocked in and managing the crowd seconds after Tiffany had left. I would have preferred to have her working tonight, but she'd done a commendable job ensuring that the staff knew the menu well enough, and she'd been working grueling hours herself.

Come to think of it, Harry may have mentioned her work ethic before, but it had always been lost when compared with his throw-away comments about how she had added new liquor to the shelf or made new arrangements with their distributors.

Worryingly, Tiffany wasn't my biggest issue right now. Since coming home, I'd been contacted for interviews and requests to comment on local events—my reputation proceeding me all the way from the West Coast.

A notification sat ignored on the screen of my laptop, taunting me. Since returning, I'd refreshed my news alerts to include any reference to The Basement, as well as ones for my name.

It had been a mixed bag so far. One piece with the headline "Out With The Old, In With The new" had been favorable, commending me on replacing the overly fancy menu we'd had in favor of simpler staples and an expanded craft beer and local wine selection. They were changes I was proud of, and thankfully, our customers were responding well to them.

The only downside of this was that the journalist had all but declared a war between myself and another local owner, Stephen Pierce, whose bars represented a very boutique, exclusive style of service; going so far as saying that "it's refreshing to see a bar embrace its customers and not treat them like peasants who could only hope to afford the lifestyle it promises."

On the other hand—because there was always an opposing opinion—another article had commented that the bar was losing its touch, calling me out for removing the more creative drinks from the menu and "completely negating it's one redeeming quality, creative mixologist Tiffany Young."

It had been posted that morning, marking one week since I'd taken over, and had irked me all day. The sentiment was misguided, not to mention a little premature. Despite what the post said, the changes had actually boosted our business. Which was the point.

However, it would be foolish of me to ignore the reviews completely. All information helped, and if these were the first of many comments like it, I'd need to prepare myself.

Forcibly loosening my jaw, I sighed. If this was the start of a trend, I'd be disappointed. Tiffany had already taken the chance to preen over their praise, using it as an example of why I was wrong. In return, I'd explained that the success of a business could not rest on the shoulders of a single employee, but she'd simply pointed out that the last four years only proved that wrong.

As a direct result of Tiffany having the night off, I'd made sure we were fully staffed for the night, although it had been a stretch to arrange everyone's schedules. Apparently, they'd all gotten a little too used to Tiffany always being there and taking on their shifts when they had other plans. A habit I'd be correcting as soon as possible.

"Everything under control?" I asked Devon. He was busy building a round of three drinks and kept his focus on that while he responded.

"All good, boss. Got a few regulars who are asking about the old menu, but we're handling it."

The customer Devon was serving spoke up. "I was just saying it's a shame the menu changed. Tiff's drinks were the only thing keeping me coming back."

"Hopefully, we can impress you enough to keep your business."

This was precisely why I didn't want the bar to rely on a single person. If Tiffany left, the bar would lose its supposed "redeeming quality," and then what? We needed to be able to run smoothly and successfully with or without her.

So far tonight, we were managing it.

The only complication, as far as I could see, was Riley. Or, more specifically, the lack of Riley. After her clash with Nathan the night before, I hoped she wasn't acting out. I was willing to accommodate certain things, but that was the sort of behavior I wouldn't allow to continue.

When Devon confirmed that she hadn't swapped shifts or called in sick, I decided I would grant her the grace of another half hour before I called her and told her not to bother showing up tonight.

When she did finally saunter in, forty-five minutes late for her shift, I'd already decided that it was time for a formal warning. I didn't want to leave any room for misinterpretation. If this behavior continued, she could start looking for a new job.

Since it was busy, I decided to wait until the end of her shift to speak with her.

Action became necessary at around 11 p.m. when I overheard a customer ask her for a recommendation, and her response was a terse, "How about you pretend you've been to a bar before and just tell me what you want."

Devon was quick to cut in and ask her to get some clean glasses so that he could take over, and I knew I'd have to find some room in the budget to start paying him more.

Once Riley had returned, I ushered her into the office. She followed and took a seat in the small room. I shut the door to drown out at least some of the noise, even though it was futile at this hour.

Sitting down, I considered her. Arms crossed, back straight, prepared for a fight. "Can I ask you a question?"

"Sure."

"How long have you worked here?" I knew the answer already but wanted to lead into this gently.

"A year."

"And before The Basement, did you bar back anywhere else?"

Her brow furrowed, clearly trying to pre-empt where I was headed. "Yeah, a bunch of places. Why?"

"At any of those establishments, was it ever appropriate to be rude to a customer?"

A huff of breath that sounded suspiciously close to a scoff escaped her, but she still said a petulant, "No."

"So, you can understand why I wanted to speak with you."

She threw her hands up. "Look, I'm sorry, okay? I fought with my boyfriend last night, and now he's not texting me back, and I didn't mean to be rude or whatever, but, like, it won't happen again."

I doubted that. "I know that it can be difficult to separate work and home life." And I certainly knew from personal experience how badly it could blow up in your face if you didn't. "But I would ask that you leave your personal problems at home when you come to work."

She gaped. "So, I should just not care that my life is falling apart?"

"Does that explain why you were late to your shift today?"

"I was barely fifteen minutes late. Getting through Lower Wacker was a nightmare." Huh. Not a local, then.

"It was forty-five minutes, actually. And it wasn't the first occasion. If you aren't able to get to work on time, Riley, then I'm the one who's sorry because this isn't going to work out. Consider this your only warning."

Her face broke out in disgust as she angrily stood up. "This is her, isn't it? She's totally gaslit you into this." I was insulted that she thought I couldn't come to this decision myself, but that thought was immediately forgotten when I heard Riley spit out, "Fucking bitch."

A torrent of rage washed over me. "Get out."

"Finally."

I heard the deep rasp in my voice, the only outward sign of the extreme prejudice I was feeling about her. "No, I don't think you understand me. You're fired. I don't want to see you here again."

"What the fuck?"

"You're fired. Hand your key to Devon and get out of my bar."

She mumbled as she turned to leave. "Probably slept with you, too."

I slammed the door behind her.

It didn't escape me that I was now in a position where I couldn't return behind the bar for the exact reasons I'd just admonished Riley for. Unfortunately, I would also drive myself to distraction if I spent any longer in this tiny office. Instead, I found Devon and asked him to call me if there were any issues, and I walked the short distance home.

Once I was inside the apartment—*my* apartment, I had to remind myself—the vice around my ribs eased.

At the sound of my keys hitting the kitchen counter, a wary Siamese slinked around the corner, loudly complaining even as I filled her bowl with dinner.

"Yes, Luna, I can hear you," I said fondly, scratching her neck. She let out another loud meow before digging in, and I left her to eat.

Pouring myself two fingers of whiskey, I sagged back into the leather couch, a purchase that was only days old, and looked out the floor-to-ceiling windows at the sparkling lights of the city.

Home.

It still didn't feel one hundred percent real.

A month ago, I'd been in a suite overlooking the strip, finalizing notes for an interview with Eater. In the span of four weeks, I'd been dumped, kicked out of my own company, and forced home.

How had Tiffany phrased it the other day? Demoted and castrated.

I snorted into the silence of the apartment. It felt oddly fitting.

Soon, even the whiskey wasn't doing enough to soothe, so I called the one person I knew would be awake at midnight.

Jordan and I had worked together when I'd first started bartending, and even though he was a good decade older than me, we'd hit it off. He opened his first bar a year later, and I was happy to take the offer to work for him. He taught me a lot in those years and was one of my biggest supporters when I opened my own place.

It rang a few times before he picked up, but I could hear the distant sounds of conversation in the background, so I knew I hadn't woken him.

"Buddy!"

"Hi, Jordan. Not interrupting, am I?"

"Wouldn't matter if you were. How are you? I heard about Piper."

"Good news travels fast."

"Need me to send you the name of a good lawyer? I've got a few that specialize in contract law."

"No, thank you. I appreciate the offer, but I'd rather not drag this out any longer than it has been. I'd like to focus on what comes next."

"Yeah, understood. Well, offer's there if you need it. Still, can't believe she pulled that. It's not right."

Would there be a time when I wasn't doomed to have this conversation with every person in my life?

"Few things in business are. Anyway, it's done now, and it's a lesson I won't soon forget." Not to mention a memory best left in the past. "How about you? What are you working on right now?" Jordan was always working on something.

"Funny you should ask. I'm in Brooklyn right now, looking at a new project. I can't share much yet, but I think you'll like it. If you weren't running your own place there, I would have asked you to join me. Would be like the good old days."

"You'll have to drop by here sometime and tell me about it."

"You know I will." There's a break. "Are you looking after yourself?"

"I'm fine."

"Not what I asked. Is the shoulder still giving you issues?"

I rolled it on instinct. The ache never went away, but the movement helped. "Nothing worse than usual. Though, I might need to get back to a physio soon. I forgot how much work it was behind the bar. I'm growing soft in my old age."

"Careful who you're calling old."

"I'd never insult you like that. Besides, you pull it off better than I do."

"Just don't push yourself too hard. I know how stubborn you can be."

"Who, me?" We shared a laugh.

"I'd like to meet the person more stubborn than you, buddy."

I couldn't help it; I barked out a laugh, surprising both of us. "Well, then, you'd have a field day with my head bartender."

"Handful?"

"And then some."

Something about my tone must have conveyed more than I meant it to because he made a suggestive sound, and I rushed to cut him off before he could insinuate anything. "Not like that. I'm not about to mix business and pleasure."

"Says the man who dated his business partner for four years."

"It's a new rule. I don't plan on making the same mistake twice."

"But you've thought about it."

And that was the problem, really. I had thought about it. I needed to stop thinking about it.

"Goodnight, Jordan. Make sure you drop by when you're in town."

"Like I'd miss up the opportunity to support you. Good luck, Sam. I've heard the crowd over there is a bit of a tough club to get into."

7
___
TIFF

If I slept at all last night, it didn't feel like it.

I'd tossed and turned next to Hannah for hours until eventually giving up and wandering out to the couch. I hadn't even bothered to turn a light on; I just sat on the couch in the dark, trying to get my head clear.

All night my thoughts had been a running loop of yesterday's uncomfortable dinner and the unavoidable conversation Hannah and I needed to have this morning.

Fuck.

It had been going well, if a bit awkward. Hannah's parents were polite, and we'd discussed their trip to the city. I'd recommended a few restaurants that I knew had great food but without the extortionate prices.

THEN, Hannah's dad, Clinton, had asked about work, how long I'd been doing it, and what had gotten me started in bartending. I'd told him the truth; that I'd started mixing drinks for my college boyfriend and had quickly learned as many recipes as I began trying to make up my own. That's where I'd discovered how much I loved coming up with new combinations and surprising people with twists on their favorites.

Her parents had shared a pointed look during my story, and that's when I'd realized Hannah had stiffened. She interrupted with a laugh and told her parents, "Tiff is joking. She's never had a boyfriend."

I'd been too confused at the time to say anything (and the last thing I'd ever do is embarrass someone in front of their parents), but it had killed my appetite. I'd choked down some food along with my complete and utter rage at Hannah's lie and somehow managed to make it through the rest of dinner with a forced smile.

I knew Hannah wasn't exactly enthusiastic about my bisexuality, but I'd never thought she would outright deny it to anyone. Especially after she'd made such a big deal about how important this dinner with her parents was to the future of our relationship.

By the time we'd gotten home, I'd been silently seething for so long, I didn't trust myself to talk to her without blowing up in her face, and we were both too tired to start fighting so late at night. So, without talking about it, we'd both silently ignored it, knowing that we'd have to face it in the morning.

And now it was morning.

The bedroom door creaked open, and Hannah stood in the doorway, watching with an unreadable look. "You didn't need to sit out here. I'm already awake."

Hannah moved to the bathroom, quietly shutting the door behind her. My head immediately fell back against the couch.

Fuck.

If I had any hope of getting through this conversation, I was going to need coffee. A lot of coffee. I was half a cup in by the time Hannah made her way into the kitchen.

It was awkward, to say the least.

But if there was one thing I'd never learned, it was to leave anything the hell alone.

I faced her head on, jumping straight in. "You lied, Hannah. To your parents. About something that isn't even your goddamn business. Do you know how hurtful that was? You know I don't lie about my sexuality. I'm not about to hide who I am. Not to you, not to your parents. You didn't even warn me."

"Because you would never have gone along with it."

Which was correct. "Why? Why would they even care that I'm bi?"

Her arms crossed tightly across her chest. "Do you know how hard it's been trying to get them to accept my sexuality? For them to understand that this isn't just a phase? You don't get it. My mom is Japanese. Gay marriage still isn't legal there. Getting her to understand that this is who I am and I'm not able to flick a switch and turn it off has been hard. We didn't talk for a year after I came out."

I felt for her; I did. But that didn't explain her actions. "What does that have to do with me?"

Her shoulders sagged. "Because it gives them hope. If they heard about you talking about dating men, they'd start asking me why I don't. They don't understand the difference."

I could see how badly she felt, and it chipped away at my anger. It didn't make it right, but she had her reasons, and she sounded pained. Family meant a lot to both of us, and it was obvious that her parent's approval was important to her. I just wished it hadn't required her to erase a part of my identity. "You made me feel like there's something wrong with me. Which is bullshit."

Her face crumpled, eyes glassy with unshed tears. "I know, I'm sorry, I really am. But can you at least understand why I did it?"

I sighed, sagging against the counter. I still wasn't a hundred percent okay with what had happened, and there was a nagging worry that Hannah wasn't as accepting of me as I'd assumed, but I could (frustratingly) understand why she'd said what she had.

"I don't like it, but I think I can."

"Are we ok?" She whispered.

The last of my fight left me, and I stepped closer, pulling her into a hug. "I won't lie about who I am," I said, soft and firm, into her hair.

She sniffled into my shoulder. "It's not even lying. It's just … selective sharing. I don't know why you'd need to bring it up to my parents anyway. Why you'd bring it up at all. Unless you miss it."

I pulled back, needing to see her expression. "Miss what? Being with men?"

"Do you?"

The embers of my anger flared at the question, which was ignorant and rude and the kind of complete nonsense partners had asked me in the past.

I cupped her face with both hands, letting my words leave no room for doubt. "No. I don't miss it. I'm with you. I'm dating you. I don't want anything else."

Hannah leaned up to kiss me, relieved, and I forced myself to move past the lingering disappointment I felt to meet her lips, accepting her murmured apologies as she pressed against me.

When she exited the bedroom a second time, much later, we settled into a semi-comfortable routine. I quickly devoured another cup of coffee while Hannah fixed herself a juice and spoke at length about her work.

I wanted to pay attention, but it was difficult. Even if I wasn't coming off of two hours of restless sleep, my mind kept returning to what she'd said and how I felt last night.

As I sat curled up on the couch, staring into my coffee, Hannah's words blurring into white noise beside me. I wished I was alone. Some quiet would really be nice right about now.

"Tiffany?"

I snapped my head over to Hannah. "Sorry, zoned out a little."

"I was telling you about the new curator. She's a very interesting person."

"That's sweet," I said, distracted.

She frowned. "What's wrong? Is this still about last night?"

"No. I'm just …" tired, "thinking about work."

"If you hate it so much, just quit." There was disdain in her tone as if this job wasn't worth keeping anyway. As if it hadn't been the last four years of my life. As if she didn't know exactly how much it meant to me. "It's not like there's much of a future in it anyway. You could be earning twice as much if you got a desk job. And we'd get to see each other more."

"I don't want a desk job. I love what I do."

"Then why do you complain so much about it?"

Even though we weren't moving, she was backing me into a corner. I hated it. "I'm supposed to like every part of my job?" My irritation bled through, and I took a calming breath, urging myself to be reasonable. Hannah had been listening to me complain; that was true. And she wasn't wrong about our mismatched schedules. My job meant working multiple nights a week and most weekends. It was hard to date around that. And I might still have a nagging urge to move on, but that didn't mean I wanted to completely change who I was. I adored bartending. If she couldn't accept that …

Hannah sighed. "Yeah, but what about the future?"

"This is my future. Bartending might not be glamorous, but I wouldn't want to do anything else."

"I don't understand why you won't leave. You've said yourself the new owner is an ass."

"He's …" And I was surprised to find myself on the cusp of defending him. Bastard. He'd started to get to me. "I've worked with people like that before. He's just declaring his territory. It's only been a week." I didn't really think Sam would change in the future, but I was about as willing to have this conversation with Hannah as I was to rehash our earlier one.

My mind, my body, and my spirit were drained. Everything in the last week had culminated in a bone-deep exhaustion. All I wanted was for things to keep working smoothly. Was that so hard to ask?

What had felt right a month ago (steady girlfriend, a job I liked and was good at) now left me questioning … Was I doing the right thing? Was I still happy?

———

Finally alone, I weighed my feelings from last night. I knew I'd forgive Hannah (some part of me had already). Yes, it sucked, and I wasn't going to discount my hurt, but I got it. Not everyone's parents were onboard or enthusiastic. My dad still had issues with it. Sure, he was supportive, but he never could understand that I was still bi, no matter which gender I was dating.

Eventually, I just accepted his support ("You do whatever you want, sweetheart. As long as you're happy.") and let the rest slide.

So, yeah. I got that it wasn't easy. I'd just hoped that maybe being someone's girlfriend would have extended to, oh, I don't know, not being blindsided by bi-erasure at the dinner table? But, hey, this was my first relationship rodeo, so what did I know?

Before I knew it, I was pulling butter and eggs out of my fridge. This called for cookies. The good kind.

Placing my phone on speaker, I started mixing the ingredients. I'd made this recipe so many times that I could do it blindfolded with my hands tied.

Mama picked up after the third ring, sounding flustered. "Hi, honey, give me a second. I've got to put a roast in the oven. Here, talk to your brother."

There was a rustling on the other end of the line, and I wondered which of my three brothers I'd be talking to. I hoped it was my baby brother, Theo.

My two older brothers, Tom and Tyler, were … fine, I guess. But they'd gone all serious as they'd gotten older, their silly competitive nature driving them to constantly one-up each other. Thomas had gotten into real estate ("growing his portfolio" by flipping houses), and so Tyler went and made partner at a law firm. Total pissing contest. Whatever. At least they seemed to enjoy what they did. Although, I felt for Thomas' wife. Story was, even on their wedding day, he'd interrupted the photoshoot so he could take a business call. I had been lucky enough to catch the tail end of mama chewing him out (fuck reality tv, that was the most entertaining thing I'd ever witnessed).

Anyway, we got along just fine. They'd been as supportive as they knew how to be when I came out, but we were just never that close. Theo, on the other hand. Well, he'd been my first real friend.

"Hey, what are you making?" Theo asked, and I looked over to see that he'd changed it to a video call. Smiling, I leaned my phone against the splash back so he could see me better.

"Mimi's choc chip cookies," I said, referring to our grandmother's treasured recipe.

He looked jealous. "With the brown butter?"

"Is that even a question?" I spooned out the mixture onto a baking sheet before stuffing it in the preheated oven. "I needed a pick-me-up."

"Everything ok? How's the bar?"

"Fine. Got an issue with the new owner," I refused to call Sam my boss. "But I'm figuring it out."

"You always do."

"How's the ICU?" Theo worked as an RN.

"The same." He sounded tired. He always sounded tired.

"Are you getting enough sleep?"

He scoffed. "You sound like mom." Which meant no, he absolutely wasn't.

"That's not an insult, loser."

"Mom! Tiff just called me a fucking loser."

"Language!" Mama called out.

I gave him the finger while he laughed. Little shit. I loved him.

"Sure you're ok?" he asked, growing serious. "How's Hannah?"

No one in my family had met Hannah yet, but I'd sent Theo a photo of the two of us together a few months ago when he'd been pestering me about finally getting a girlfriend.

"It's …" As quickly as I'd prepared a lie, I realized I wanted to tell the truth. This week had really taken its toll on me. "Rough. We just had a fight, and I'm not sure where we go from here."

"Shit, sorry, Tiff. Want to talk about it?"

"Not right now. Maybe if you get some free time soon, you could drop by the bar? I know your hours are awful."

"I'll make time. But, yeah, work is wild right now, so I can't promise it'll be soon."

"That's ok. It'll just be good to see you."

So, yeah. I loved Theo. He was the closest of my brothers to me in age (only ten months apart, go mama) and temperament. He was my baby brother. I would burn buildings down for that dork. But growing up, he'd been invited into the "boys club" while I'd been told to stay with mama and do what good girls should.

It really hadn't taken very long for me to stop giving a single shit what people said I "should" do.

Of course, I quickly learned a secret. Time with mama and my Mimi was by far more entertaining than anything my brothers got up to. I had, up to that point, known that my mama came from a long line of strong Southern women, but damn.

I learned three important lessons in that time; learn the recipe but always cook from the heart; always say fuck you with a smile, and there was nothing more impressive than someone with a kind soul. I wanted nothing more than to be like them when I grew up. I was in awe. Still was.

"Theo, baby, help lay the table while I talk with your sister." The image rustled around as the phone changed hands until I was looking at my mama's beautiful beaming smile.

Seeing her reminded me how badly I wanted to reach through the phone and wrap her in a fierce hug. "I missed you," I said, feeling a little overwhelmed.

"Oh, sweetie, I missed you more. Gosh, you look thin. Are you eating enough? You know if you don't get enough sleep that can wreak havoc on your digestion. I saw a show about it last night."

Goddammit, I loved this woman. "Yes, mama, I'm eating enough. And I sleep just fine." Most days. I wasn't going to count last night.

"I don't know how, working all hours of the day and night."

"Theo works longer shifts than me. Why aren't you worried about him?"

"Oh, I am. But Theo is on a journey," Lord, give me strength. Here we go. "I don't want to be eighty and still see you behind that bar slinging drinks for the rest of your life. Especially since you keep telling me I won't get grandchildren."

Wow, not even five minutes. That had to be a new record. I couldn't help smiling at her. "Ok, that's it. Where's dad?"

"Oh, your father? He's watching a property brothers marathon. Did you want to talk to him?"

"Nah, that's ok. I just called to check in, see how you were doing. Chat."

"I'm wonderful, darlin. It's you I'm worried about. Are you sure you're ok? I'm going to send you a new scarf. I know how much you hate the cold." She was right; I did hate the cold. But it was still July. It wouldn't get cold for months.

"Thanks, mama. And yes. I'm ok. I just wanted to hear your voice." The timer went off, and I pulled the cookie sheet out as fast as I could. The smell was amazing, full of vanilla and memories, and I barely missed scarring the inside of my mouth by tearing into one immediately.

"Alright, well, you make sure you're looking after yourself. You deserve to be happy, baby."

I swallowed the lump of emotion that rose up. Mama always had a way of making it sound so simple. Just be happy, as if it were that easy.

8

———

SAM

With Riley gone, the team settled into a stable routine in our second week. I still saw some areas that needed tweaking, but the priority for me right now was the big three:

- the décor—and honestly, Harry, what were you thinking?
- the name—I'd learned a long time ago that a rebrand was always a good idea,
- and the one that I knew I'd have the biggest fight on, the menu.

I could see how the bar had survived thus far. Despite the clashing menu and décor, the drinks were always well made and Tiffany was a highlight. She was, in more ways than one, a stand-out. An exceptionally talented mixologist who deserved to be headlining at a far more upscale establishment than this. In fact, she should have been poached from here years ago. I wondered if the lure of having the run of this place kept her here.

However, exceptional cocktails were great, but smoke machines and custom-made ice weren't the direction I wanted to go in. I'd seen the locals come but also saw the younger millennial set, who didn't want trash but didn't want pomp either. They wanted affordable, well-made drinks that served as a backdrop to a good night. They'd come in groups, talk and celebrate. It didn't have to be a party. It was a vibe.

Having a list was only half the battle, though. Before I could even think of my next steps, I needed to know what I was up against.

Before I'd even landed at O'Hare, I'd reached out to a few contacts, who passed on the details of a few names. Some I'd heard of, and they'd had varying levels of enthusiasm, but more often than not, they always had a cutting remark about Tiffany to add to the conversation, as if badmouthing her would get them into my good books.

It was strange to get protective over someone I could barely tolerate.

It also gave me a rather underwhelming impression of my "peers," if I could call them that. Jordan hadn't been misleading; there was an established order here, it seemed, and while they were happy to play nice due to my reputation, they weren't opening their arms in welcome.

Well, no matter. Jordan had been right about another thing, too.

I was nothing if not persistent.

Stephen Pierce was my highest priority. After the initial article, which had unfortunately compared our reputations against each other, others had followed. Pierce had responded with a series of interviews and comments, where he disputed the idea that high-end bars were losing traction and managed to call me out specifically, saying that "this imagined competition would only have legs if Sam Cooper was close to being on the same level."

So, that's how it was going to be, then.

His name had already come up enough that I knew he would be a good ally to have, and now that he'd called me out,

I knew it was more important than ever to get on his good side. It was never good business to start with enemies.

But after finally getting him on the phone, it was obvious that Stephen Pierce had an ego that rivaled some of my acquaintances back home.

Hmm.

It would take some time to stop thinking of it as home.

"I wondered how long it would take for you to call me," Pierce said as soon as I introduced myself. "Heard you'd gotten some criticism recently. Unfortunate, but the sheep always complain about the lions, don't they? Although, can't say I completely disagreed, either."

An ache formed over my left eye, and I shifted the phone to my other ear so I could rub at it. Working in the business I did, you could never forget that there were people like this, but it never got any easier to deal with them. "Oh? Can I ask what in particular you agreed with?"

"Hmm. Well, I don't usually like to tell others how to run their business," he said. A baldfaced lie. "But I honestly can't see how you expect to succeed when you're stripping your menu of any creativity. Unless it's a ploy to rid yourself of that bartender of yours." One guess who he was referring to. "But you really should reconsider the lowest common denominator approach you've taken up if you want to be taken seriously."

My gut instinct was to disregard everything he said. It struck me as a lot of enthusiastic generalities that, combined, sounded like the words of a wise, successful man. The reality likely was that his success came at the benefit of money and connections and was sustained due to the hard work of others.

One thing that stopped me from dismissing his point completely, however, was the echo of a growing sentiment that said, to succeed, I would need to project an air of "luxury" and "exclusivity" with the type of drinks that took a highly skilled person five minutes to make.

Now, there was nothing wrong with that direction. But

that wasn't what I wanted the bar to be. One of the insights I'd gained from my time away had been that quantity didn't have to negate quality, but it almost always resulted in more profit.

Pierce had it wrong. I wasn't chasing the "lowest common denominator," and honestly, he could shove that term up his ass. What I was considering were the customers. And they'd proven, both before I'd arrived and since, that they preferred the more accessible options.

I didn't like my options here. It was becoming clearer that I would either have to "join the club" or follow my gut. I wasn't used to going against industry players, and I didn't enjoy being outwardly antagonistic—despite my actions with Tiffany—especially publicly. But the fact was, I had a business to run. I was aiming for success that would last. And now that I was back in Chicago, I was here to stay.

I wanted to make this work.

Failure wasn't an option.

Then, I was treated to another nugget of his wisdom.

"See, Samuel," Pierce said, and I was glad he couldn't see my reaction because Sam wasn't short for anything, and his assumption of that, and the false casualness of him using it, said a lot about him. "The thing you need to understand about working here is that we're leading innovation for small bars across the country. It's about more than just popularism here. You've got to have an edge. Now, don't get me wrong, I know you have a reputation, but you need more than just some good press in this city. You've got to have substance."

I very much doubted Stephen Pierce knew anything about substance, but I let him continue.

"You'll find we're not very welcoming to charlatans here. You might think you can coast on your reputation, but in Chicago, we demand a bit more than some song and dance. Just keep that in mind. Now, if you ever want to see what the best of the best looks like, you've got an open invitation to come by my bar, and I'll show you what we do best."

"I appreciate the offer, Stephen."

"Steve, please. We're all friends here." I wanted nothing more than to disagree, but I'd played this game long enough now to swallow that instinct.

"Steve. Thank you for your insight. It's been enlightening."

"Of course. It's a tough market out here. I thought I should warn you before you get your hopes up."

It was a close call to not curse a blue streak after hanging up. Guys like Stephen Pierce were part and parcel of working in this industry, but that didn't make it any easier to deal with them.

A slow grin spread as I tried to imagine Tiffany dealing with them. Now, that would be a sight to see.

Unfortunately, Stephen had had a point. While I was used to meeting the showy expectations of my old stomping ground, the research I'd done so far had shown that wouldn't play in this market. And if I was going to have any chance of making this work—really making it work—then I needed to understand what would. And for that, I always preferred an insider's perspective.

Harry answered my call quickly, and today the background was quiet. "I can't remember the last time you called me this often. I'm going to get a complex."

Warmth bloomed in my chest. I'd missed this. "I can hang up if you'd prefer."

He laughed, a reminder of how relaxed he sounded these days. It was good to hear. "How are you? Can I assume this isn't a personal call?"

"Yes and no. And I'm well. How much have you dealt with Stephen Pierce?"

His scoff told me that my initial perception had been correct. "Very little and yet enough for a lifetime."

"That sounds about right. How much should I worry about him?"

"I couldn't say. He's a pompous ass, but I wasn't the one lucky enough to deal with him."

The implication was clear. "Tiffany."

"Exactly. Why do you ask?"

"Research. From the few people I've spoken to, he's the one the beat. Since I'm trying to understand the ins and outs of the market here, it was easier to go directly to the source. I'd hoped he be amenable to a supportive arrangement. But if the conversation I just had with him is any indication, he's the last person I should be talking to."

"I'm sorry to say I won't be much help there."

"Good thing I wasn't asking you."

"Yeah, ok, rub it in. You're the successful one." There wasn't any malice in his tone, but I knew he had felt overshadowed in the past.

"Sorry. That's not what I meant."

"Sam, it's ok. I was joking. Wow, you sound more wound up than I used to be."

"Ok, now you're just being cruel."

"So, you can throw it but not take it, huh?"

"I see becoming a father has made you more mature."

He laughed again, and I was interrupted from making any further comments by a sharp knock on the office door, seconds before a very familiar nest of thick blonde hair and bright green eyes appeared.

"Why am I just now finding out you fired one of my staff?" Her eyebrow was raised in question, and she clearly didn't care that I was in the middle of a phone call.

"Need me to call back later?" Harry asked, amused.

"No." I told him, then to Tiffany, "I seem to remember you telling me that you wanted to fire Riley. Am I supposed to believe that you now have a problem with it?"

She didn't back down. "Are you always this difficult?"

"Are you?" I countered.

"Are you sure you don't need me to give you two some space? A room, maybe?" Harry cooed in my ear.

"Shut up," I told him.

"Excuse me?" Tiffany had fire in her eyes. It should have angered me. It absolutely shouldn't have my skin tingling.

"If you don't mind, Tiffany, I'm in the middle of something. We can discuss this later." My tone was terse, but it felt like a dangerous tease, a ploy to get under her skin, revenge for the way she'd so quickly and easily gotten under mine.

She rolled her eyes, then left, shutting the door behind her.

"You know, if you really want to talk to someone who understands the local bar trade, I know who you could talk to," Harry said.

I closed my eyes. "Please don't say it."

"Tiffany." He sounded far too happy with himself.

I released a long sigh.

"Did you hear me?" Harry asked when the silence dragged out.

"I heard you."

"It's not the worst idea."

"Define worst."

Harry laughed. "You said it yourself; she's smart, capable—"

"Incorrigible, sarcastic, confrontational."

"Look. If it's really going to be that bad, you can do this on your own. You have before."

"Yes, but back then, I was the one with insider knowledge, while Piper …"

"Hmm."

"At least she won't put you in the same position Piper did." I could imagine all too many positions I'd like to be in with Tiffany, none of which were professional. I got back to the matter at hand.

"I'm still not sure it's a good idea."

"You could be right. But you should think about it. I know you're not her biggest fan, but she knows what she's doing. I could see that, and I barely even know what I was doing. Considering what you're like, I thought you'd pounce on her."

His phrasing was unfortunate. "I'm not denying she's a skilled worker. And I," I paused, "can admit that I may have judged her unfairly before I came here. I should have given you more credit than to assume you could be walked over like that."

"Yes, you should have. But I appreciate you saying that. And you know," I already hated what was coming, "you should give her a second chance. She works harder than anyone else at that bar." A fact I'd already observed. "Except maybe you."

"We're nothing alike," I said, beating him to whatever conclusion he was about to get to next.

"Sure." He sounded unconvinced. I banished the possibility from my mind. It would only complicate matters that were already complicated enough.

But dammit, he was right. I needed someone who knew what we were up against and who I wouldn't have to worry about undermining the bar's interests. I might dread working in proximity with Tiffany, but as long as I maintained a professional distance, perhaps it wouldn't end in complete disaster.

9

___

TIFF

I was back in Sam's office before the end of the night, half expecting another comment about how he was "in the middle of something," but instead, he motioned to the chair on the other side of his desk, removing his glasses with a (somewhat worryingly) serious look on his face.

"Tiffany, thank you for coming." Like he'd summoned me. Seriously, what was with this guy?

"Ok, what is going on? You're acting weirder than normal."

I watched him blink. Geez, not even a smile? Tough crowd.

"Firstly, I wanted to apologize for not taking your advice about Riley."

Had I accidentally entered an alternate reality? "Alright, what did you smoke, and do I need to call a hospital?"

His eyes narrowed in exasperation (which was so much more normal that I actually felt relieved), but did I spy a hint of a smile? Granted, it was gone before it really appeared, but damn, that felt like a win in a way I wasn't expecting.

If I ever made him actually smile, I might pass out with surprise.

"Alright. You might as well get it out of your system now because I have a serious matter to discuss."

Oh, right. I forgot that Sam didn't have a sense of humor.

"My apologies," I said, sarcasm in full force. "Is this an official staff briefing? Should I be taking minutes? First order of business." I mimed flipping a notebook open. "Regarding the matter of the firing of Miss Riley Williams, the head bartender states, and I quote, I told you so."

There was that flicker again. Damn, almost got him.

Sure, I could try not to be so antagonizing to him, and I wasn't about to consider why I even enjoyed doing it in the first place, but I couldn't help myself.

"Yes, thank you, Tiffany."

I chuckled at his dry tone, although dammit, no. This wasn't meant to be fun. He was an ass.

Fixing my face into something more neutral, I said, "Fine. What was it you wanted to talk about?"

"Can I take it that you're familiar with the bar trade here?"

Did he seriously just ask me that? Without words, I expressed my best form of "what do you think?" and from his nod, I could tell he understood.

He drummed his fingers against the desk. He had nice hands with broad palms and long fingers. They were constantly reaching out, I'd noticed. Raking through his hair, scratching his beard, running along the seam of his lips when he was deep in thought. Considering the very careful distance he maintained between us, he appeared incredibly tactile. What the hell was I doing even noticing, though?

Jesus, I needed my head checked.

"I am man enough to admit that, despite my experience, I'm a little out of the loop when it comes to the local culture and expectations here. If I have any hope of rejuvenating this bar successfully, then I need to understand what will and won't play in this market, and that will require the expertise of someone familiar with it."

I had a bad fucking feeling about this.

And yet …

He wasn't wrong. I didn't have any experience with what he was used to over in Vegas, but I could imagine what the bars there were like, and nothing would play worse in Chicago than dollar shots and hurricanes.

There was a deep sense of pride where alcohol was concerned and a hell of a lot of egos.

It didn't surprise me that he'd recognized that, but I was (regretfully) surprised that he'd admitted he needed help. Guilt was not a feeling I enjoyed.

I was aware that he was waiting for me to comment. "That's probably a good idea. People here are …" how to say this nicely? "a bit picky about these sorts of things."

"Glad you agree. Now, I know we haven't exactly gotten off on the best foot, but I think when it comes to what is best for the bar, we're both capable of acting like adults in order to make this work."

"Woah, woah, woah. Hold up there. What makes you think I want to help?"

"You don't?"

I'd definitely slipped into an alternate reality. "Why do you even want my opinion?"

"Because you know what I'm dealing with. What we're dealing with. I have to believe, Tiffany, that you want this bar to be as much of a success as I do. If we have any hope of doing that, we'll need to put aside our differences."

"I'm not going to be your yes man."

How was it that he could make a simple head tilt look so annoyed?

"And you're going to have to, you know, actually listen to me," I added.

"I understand that."

"Because I know what I'm talking about."

"Yes, I believe I already mentioned that earlier."

"And I've been doing this a long time."

"Tiffany." The exasperation in his voice triggered my urge to smile, but I held back, still unsure of whether I even wanted to agree to help.

I took a deep breath, considering. My instincts were all over the place. On the one hand, it made sense, and what did I even have to lose (apart from all the time I would have to spend with him. Just because he could admit to needing help, it didn't change all the other times he'd irritated me. Working together would likely be a nightmare.) On the other hand, the idea that the bar would change into something so unrecognizable that it became a flop broke my heart.

Without meaning to, I'd dedicated the last four years of my life to this bar, and I'd come to care about it deeply.

"I'd like to think it over."

"Of course." Ugh. He really needed to start being less accommodating. I might go and do something ridiculous such as start liking him.

"Just for the record, this doesn't mean I like you." There. That should stop me from getting any dumb ideas.

Unfortunately, the bastard actually smirked. Fucking smirked.

"The feeling is mutual."

10

TIFF

I was on my third cup of coffee by the time Audrey knocked on my door. I'd finally convinced her to start wedding planning. Despite my own reservations about the institution, it was easy to find the excitement for my best friend.

After all that she'd been through in her last marriage and the rollercoaster that had been the start of her relationship with Jackson, she deserved nothing less than unicorns and glitter.

She was, without a doubt, my favorite person in the world and the exact thing I needed to forget the buzzing thoughts that had been keeping me up lately.

As usual, she was bright and cheerful, although when I saw who was standing behind her, I had a better idea of why.

"I didn't realize this had become a group activity," I said, eyeing her fiancé.

Audrey, god bless her, actually looked worried. "Is this ok?"

"Just don't start inviting me to your little double date brunches," I said, adding a wink, and her smile returned.

"Come in, pretty boy, before your groupies start swarming my apartment."

Jackson wrapped me in a hug before I could protest. "Thanks for letting me crash your morning. Filming kicks off next week, so I'm trying to get as much time with Audrey as possible."

They were cute. Too cute, honestly. It made me simultaneously yearn and groan. "Ugh, fine. As long as you keep the PDA to a minimum. There's not enough coffee in the world to help me through that." It didn't come out anywhere near like the threat it should have since I'm smiling too widely.

"Yeah, yeah. You love me, really."

I only scoffed in response. He was right, but I'd never tell him that.

"Did we miss Hannah? I brought her the bottle of MacMillan's she was asking about." Audrey placed the bottle of rum on my kitchen counter.

"Ah, no. She's at her place this weekend." I'd been aiming for casual, but judging from the awkward silence that filtered through the apartment, I'd missed the mark.

We made ourselves comfortable on the couch, and I could tell they wanted to ask me about it. Jackson tapped a finger on the armrest, his back so straight I was getting an ache just looking at him. Audrey, fitting perfectly into the space beside him, reached a hand out towards me. "Everything ok with you two? We can talk about it if you want. The wedding stuff can wait."

It was a sweet gesture. And although I wasn't in the mood to rehash the entire thing, there was comfort in having them here. It wasn't as if Hannah and I weren't trying to work it out on our own anyway. Bringing it up wouldn't solve anything.

"Everything's fine. And don't think I don't see what you're doing, trying to avoid this." I motioned to the stack of wedding magazines she'd brought with her.

She grumbled. "Fine. But no favors."

"Yes, I remember from the three thousand times you've told me."

We each take a magazine, flipping through them and calling out when something caught our eye. Most of what I was looking at was a little too staged for my taste, and I could tell Audrey felt the same from the way she was working her bottom lip and sighing into Jackson's shoulder.

Eventually, I got tired of wading through pages of models in wedding dresses, and I threw the magazine onto the coffee table. "There has to be a better way to do this. How much do you really need to figure out anyway?"

"You'd be surprised." Audrey closed the magazine in her lap with a sigh. "I'd forgotten how many decisions you needed to make for these things. Photographers, hair, makeup—"

"One of the crew might be able to help with that," Jackson interjected. "Or I can find out who Sarah used."

She passed him a quick smile in thanks before continuing, already sounding stressed. "Then there's the venue, whether we want to sit down or stand up, how many guests we'll have, what speeches we want, the music, the cake …"

"Why are you doing this again?" I joked.

"Don't worry," Jackson said, pressing a kiss to her forehead, "We have plenty of time to figure it all out." Audrey twisted on the couch to cuddle deeper into the embrace, and my eyes slipped down to the floor.

After another beat, Jackson asked, "Do you and Hannah ever talk about this stuff? I know you aren't the biggest fan of the 'M' word." There was no judgment in the statement, which I appreciated.

Nodding, I said, "We have. She knows how I feel about it, and I know that she wants to be married someday."

"Who knows, maybe you'll change your mind." He stroked a wayward hair behind Audrey's ear, watching her lovingly. "Sometimes it just takes meeting the right person."

"Maybe for everyone else, but I'm not going to change my mind on this."

"How does Hannah feel about that?"

I took a deep breath, taking a long look at the ceiling as I rolled the question around in my head. Hannah and I were in a weird holding pattern at the moment, one where I wasn't sure what the future looked like. The last time we'd talked about it, she'd made the same comment Jackson had, potentially hoping I'd change my mind if we ever made it that far.

Now, I was beginning to wonder if our opposing views weren't another sign that we'd never get far enough for her to find out.

"She'd prefer it if I felt differently," I said, working my way around how I wanted to say it. Ripping the bandaid off had rarely failed in me in the past. "Honestly, even if I wanted to, I don't know that I can see it with Hannah. I thought I'd feel more by now. And if it isn't love, what are we doing?"

"You're having fun, seeing where things go. It doesn't have to be forever right now. Just take it at your own pace." Audrey picked up her mug only to find it empty, and Jackson immediately stood, offering to replace it. He ducked down to steal a kiss from Audrey, and their easy intimacy caused a spike of jealousy within me.

As a highly capable, secure, functioning adult, I enjoyed being alone. But that didn't mean I couldn't also enjoy the fantasy of a "someone" in my life who felt as integral to my existence as these two so obviously did about each other.

"No relationship works from the start," Jackson said, pouring another cup. My apartment was small enough that there really wasn't any delineation between the couch and the kitchen (everything was probably five steps away at all times and the whole place was about ten in total). But it had character, and I could live alone on my salary and still save, and that's all I cared about. Jackson wiped a spot on the counter (such a polite boy). "Maybe it's good that you're going through a rough patch now."

"Exactly," Audrey continued, following his lead. "If you

can work this out, then you know you two can make it work long term."

Is that all I needed to do? Push through this? I didn't have enough experience to judge what was worth accepting and what I should stand firm on.

"You know me, Auds. I know I'm not built for the same type of happily ever after most people go for. But forever—or commitment," I correct, "still matters. And it should be something I'm certain about. Someone I'm certain about."

Jackson returned to Audrey's side. "So, you do want something serious? I just assumed …"

I knew what he assumed. What everyone assumed. "Hell, yes. Eventually. And with the right person. Who doesn't want to wake up next to someone who's sweet when you're sad, values your mind, and looks at you like they can't believe they got so lucky?"

Audrey smiled at her fiancé. "Sounds perfect."

Ugh, they were so cute I couldn't even be mad at the blatant lovefest. I should have known this was bound to happen as soon as I let Jackson inside. But it gave me the opportunity to slip into the kitchen and get another coffee. My blood levels were roughly seventy percent caffeine at this point.

"Alright, enough of this," I said as I dropped back onto the couch. "That's twice now you've changed the subject so that you could avoid planning this wedding. I swear, the two of you are impossible. Maybe we should start with something simple. Like the date."

Jackson hummed, considering. "I'd prefer not to be working, so that kind of rules out the rest of this year."

Beside him, Audrey sat up, surprised. "Even if it didn't, I would. What happened to not rushing the engagement?"

He pulled her back in with an arm around her waist. "It's not rushing when I already know I'm going to spend the rest of my life with you." They came together for a long, sweet kiss.

"What did I say about PDA!" I protected my mug while I playfully nudged Audrey's leg with my foot. She pulled out of the kiss with a laugh.

"How's Sam?"

I should have been happy about a change in subject. And I would have, had the subject not been that.

"Still an ass, thanks for asking." My foot started nervously tapping on the floor, and I stilled it. "He uh, asked me if I wanted to work with him on fixing up the bar. Said he needed someone with experience with the local market." God, he was such a snob. "I told him I'd think about it."

"What's stopping you?"

"You mean, apart from the fact that he's a smug son of a bitch and I hate him?"

Audrey threw her head back. "You don't hate him."

"Like hell, I don't."

"Tiff, I've known you long enough now to know when you really hate someone."

I counted on my fingers. "He's arrogant, smug, cocky—"

"I'm pretty sure those are all the same," Jackson cut in.

I kept going, "---stubborn, opinionated, acts like he knows everything."

Audrey thought it was hilarious, of course. "You two are like peas in a pod, no wonder you don't get along."

I groaned. "Don't say that. I'm nothing like him."

"Sure."

Jackson shrugged. "It is his bar. Maybe you should work with him."

"I should just quit, then he'd be sorry."

"Why don't you?"

That stopped me in my tracks. Despite Audrey being my best friend, I'd been keeping my recent inklings to myself. The whole time I'd known her, I'd worked at The Basement. And while I knew she would be supportive, she was also the most planned and put-together person I knew. Would she understand it if I told her that I was starting to get fidgety just because I'd been in one place for too long?

That I was close to making a ridiculous, completely left-field decision with no planning and no direction because of a feeling?

When I was quiet for an uncharacteristic amount of time, Audrey asked, "If you did quit, what would you do? Go work somewhere else?"

"Ever thought of opening your own place?" Jackson asked.

"God, no. I mean, yes, I've thought about it, and it's the last thing I want to do. I'd rather be behind the bar than stuffed in that office all day and night. Paperwork is my nightmare."

"There's lots of other things you could do. Start a Youtube channel, write a recipe book ..." Audrey suggested.

"I don't know ... The book's not a bad idea. But the YouTube thing ... Can you imagine me in front of a camera?"

They shared a look. "I can, actually," Jackson said. "Might need to tone down the swearing, though."

"Oh, am I offending your virgin ears, pretty boy?"

"What did you do before you worked at The Basement?" he asked, ignoring my comment.

I looked between them. Fuck it. "Worked around. I actually hopped from bar to bar for a while, doing a year or so at each. I actually worked for an event planner for a while, running cocktail lessons for corporate events. Never again."

"You really should look into the Youtube angle. You could film in your own time, work from home, make it all your own thing," Jackson said.

A telltale tingle went down my spine. The good kind. The one that always came before an idea got its hooks in me. "And people actually make money from that?"

He nodded. "You'd be surprised."

"I'll think about it," I said, my nonchalant tone disguising the fact that my mind was currently somersaulting through potential ideas like an Olympic gymnast. "For now, my problem is how to deal with Sam."

"What's so bad about working with him?' Audrey asked. "You've said yourself you wanted to change the decor at the bar, and this way, you'd be involved in whatever he plans on doing. You might even be able to make some of the decisions."

"I miss the days when you were the one freaking out, and I was the sensible one giving advice."

"Turnabout is fair play. Besides, I owe you after what you did for us."

"Oh, that's right. I guess I am completely responsible for this, aren't I?" I joked, like any of us had forgotten that I'd set them up a year ago.

"No changing the subject," Audrey warned. "Now, the Tiff I know doesn't a) care what anyone thinks, and b) goes down fighting. So, I think you should give this a go. We both know you want to," she put a hand up to stop me from interrupting, "no matter how you feel about Sam. And we both know you'll kill it. I've never seen you try your hand at anything and not be amazing."

And, well … fuck. How could I not at least consider it after that rousing speech?

The Basement had done well in the last four years, but it could do better. The thing was, the only way any bar did anything in this town was by playing by the arbitrary rules of what the greying mammals in their gilded clubhouse had decided was "in." Okay, strictly, that wasn't the entire truth.

Customers were savvy, and while some enjoyed the relaxed comfort of a sports bar or cozy restaurant, they held their bars to higher standards. Craft breweries, wine bars with extensive imported wine lists, historic locations with prohibition pasts, and in one case (and one of the ones I favored) a hidden little twelve seater with some of the best (if not *the* best) rare liquors in town.

And despite my efforts, there was only so much good booze could do for a place like The Basement.

Something I'd mentioned to Audrey a few times in the past.

Oh, Jesus, I was actually going to do this, wasn't I?

"Fuck." I said, eloquent as I knew how to be. "If we end up killing each other, I'm blaming you both. And haunting you. You'll never get to have sex again, you hear me?"

Audrey squealed a little "Yay," that I pointedly ignored, while Jackson chuckled. "This ought to be good. You, working with someone."

"Hey," I said, indignant at the suggestion that I was unwilling to compromise. "I'm open to suggestions."

Jackson barked a laugh. "Good one."

"Shut it, pretty boy. You're here on a probationary period." I took a deep breath, feeling a lot better now that I'd made at least one decision.

———

AFTER THEY LEFT, I jumped on my laptop and brought up Youtube, flagging a long list of videos to watch. Maybe if I watched a few, understood the effort involved, it would stop my (currently overenthusiastic) brain from racing ahead of me.

While I searched, I dialed the number for the bar phone, hoping I wasn't about to regret the other decision I'd made.

It didn't surprise me that Sam was there. He had workaholic written all over him (among other things). Did he ever leave the bar? Before he could say anything, I spoke. "Fine. I'm in. When do we start?"

"Okay," he said slowly, but he didn't question who'd

called, so either he recognized my voice or had put the pieces together. "Right. Good. Glad you made the right decision."

I should never have agreed to this.

Whatever goodwill Sam might have earned from me disappeared quicker than sunshine behind storm clouds after our call. He made us swap phone numbers (I'd labeled him "Sir Smuggington" just to make myself laugh) and emails, then waited approximately five seconds before sending me a lengthy request along with a stack of articles to read. It was probably the first email I'd received in years that wasn't marketing spam.

Apparently, Sam's style was obsessively reading about what was happening instead of experiencing it, which I told him in my reply. He responded that it was a waste of time to visit every place without doing the proper research first and that he expected me to give the requisite time to craft a response by filling in any details I knew about each bar. I wanted to crush my phone in my hands but decided to blatantly ignore replying while binge-watching TV for two hours until I'd gotten sick of his smug voice nagging the back of my brain and went through the list he sent.

A handful were links to economics articles on Gen Z vs. Millennial spending, some general discourse on the fall of the neighborhood bar, and (more surprisingly) a rather in-depth piece on personal branding and the creator economy. He'd marked that last one with a question, "The new competition?" I skipped past all of that for the time being to focus on the first half of the email, which was a list of the currently ranked bars on the North Side. He'd even separated them by area and made notes about the estimated target audience and pricing.

Honestly, if I hadn't already seen him make a drink with my own eyes, I would seriously doubt he'd ever left the office before.

It was a hundred percent clear why he needed a second person on this. Within seconds of seeing the names, I knew exactly which ones were more hype than substance, which were popular because they'd made deals with local tour guides, and which were worth our time. I began listing out some names he hadn't included that I knew were hidden gems—outliers who were small enough not to make top ten lists but were where anyone who worked in the scene actually went when they wanted a drink. I also marked a few of the new ones that I'd heard nothing about yet. The city was a big place, and there was always *something* going on, and it hadn't been my job (until now) to really notice it.

Time had passed quickly while I'd typed it up on my phone, and I shot it off to him as I watched the coffee pot brew for a second time, feeling oddly productive. It had been a long time (ok, maybe ever) since I'd been asked for my opinion on other bars outside of quick recommendations for afterparties, and I hadn't realized just how much I knew until that moment.

Still, I hoped this wasn't going to be a regular thing. I certainly didn't want to be spending my spare time reading and writing emails. If I'd wanted that in my life, I wouldn't be tending bar.

Clearing out the dozen new junk emails I'd received, I audibly groaned when Sam's response came through. It was a Saturday; didn't he have a life? (Says the person still wearing their pajamas at 11 a.m.). Curiosity drove me to open his email, which I realized was a mistake as soon as I'd read the first sentence:

`While I appreciate the effort, commentary on which establishments "have hotter bartenders" or where "the owner's a real dick" were not valid critiques.`

This guy. I swear.

Without reading any further, I wrote back:

`News flash—hot bartenders bring in girls, which bring in guys, and any place where the` owner is a dick is also where the drinks are overpriced water and the staff is treated like shit. Kind of thought both those things were worth noting. But what do I know.

His response was quick:

Noted.

I swallowed a scream. Quitting was suddenly looking a hell of a lot more appealing. The next three hours were spent down the Youtube rabbit hole.

11

———

SAM

Her acceptance of my offer had been, like all things with Tiff, thrown at me with a vehemence that rivaled forced political alliances.

With anyone else, I might have been surprised at the quick turnabout of events, suspicious even, but with Tiffany, I was becoming used to her unique brand of hotheaded fortitude. She dazzled like a solar flare, but once her mind was made up, she was practically immovable.

She was also, rather unfortunately, determined to disagree with me at every turn.

"I'm going to restyle the bar. Make it sleeker, more upmarket."

"You don't think the whole 'everything and the kitchen sink' look is upmarket?" she joked.

"Current market trends," I ignored her groan, "show that dark and moody spaces are equated with exclusivity, especially in the service industry."

She was once again draped over the chair opposite my desk, although today, she'd chosen to lay sideways, letting one leg hang over the arm while the other was tucked underneath.

I couldn't see how it was comfortable, but she was admiring her nails and looked positively bored. "That's ridiculous."

I pointed to the article in question. "It's what the research says."

Her head fell back. "So, we get to turn into another wanky cookie-cutter bar? Great."

"And what would you propose?"

She swiveled, straightening in the chair, more engaged now. "I don't have anything in mind, but damn, we should have our own voice. Make a statement. Say. Something."

"With décor."

"Yes." Like it was obvious.

"Why do I get the sense you're arguing with me for the sake of it?"

Instead of the smirk I'd been expecting, she looked hurt. "Wow, you really think a lot of me, huh?"

"Sorry. That was rude."

She chewed her lip, looking hesitant. I wondered if I'd finally pushed her too far. I never spoke to staff this way, but then, I'd never worked with anyone like Tiffany before. And she'd never backed down from pushing me right back, always with a smirk or a wink or a smart comment.

Before I could say anything else, she seemed to return to herself, her tone back to its usual prickliness. "I'll give you this. I'm not exactly married to the grandma chic we currently have going on, but that doesn't mean I want to become a clone of every other hyped-up place that's all about glitter and show."

"You mean like the ones I've owned before."

"If the shoe fits."

I bit down a flare of indignation. I shouldn't have to prove anything to her. "And I suppose it doesn't matter to you that those 'hyped up' bars were extremely successful?"

She rolled her eyes. "Yes, I've heard all about your

reputation, hot shot. I thought we'd already established it means jack shit out here."

Yes, I'd been made aware of that already. Yesterday, a reporter had pushed me to respond to Pierce in print. But there was no way I was going to be baited into personal attacks.

This was getting nowhere fast. Why had I thought this was a good idea again? If she was just going to argue with me on every point, we weren't going to achieve anything. If she could just give some ground … Well, I might die of shock first, but something certainly had to give if we were going to work together. It rankled me that it was likely going to have to be me, which was a first. With anyone else, collaboration was something I fostered, focused on. It drove innovation, and I enjoyed challenging pre-conceived notions with data-driven insights and a fresh perspective.

So, why was the idea of giving in to Tiffany such an issue for me?

And why did it fill me with as much of a thrill as it did fear?

Calling a truce, I turned my attention to the magazine in front of me. I slid it across the desk, tapping the image of the latest "bar to watch." It was called Agenda and was highlighted as an example of "fresh, romantic, & modern" that "encouraged lively conversations and a return to personal interactions that was sorely lacking in today's digital age."

I didn't have the faintest clue how any of that differed from any other bar, but it was apparently revolutionary, and they had made several references to the outfitting of the space. I knew it would be a good idea to visit and find out what the fuss was about.

"They open tomorrow night, but I've reached out to the owner, and she's agreed to let us in to have an early look. I planned on going and asking her some questions."

She skimmed over the article, and I had to hide a smile

when she made a face of revulsion. I suspected she'd just read the part about "personal interactions."

Finally, she looked up. "Looks pretentious. You'll love it."

"You're determined to hate everything, aren't you?" I asked, shaking my head.

"Not everything." Her eyes dropped back down to the article, avoidant. I'd hit a nerve. "So, when do we go?"

"Now, if you're available."

"Well, considering you asked me to get here hours before my shift started, I guess I'm free."

———

Fortunately, the owner hadn't been lying when she'd said she was happy for me to come by before the launch.

Unfortunately, Agenda had the worst decor I've ever seen.

Actually, "decor" was a very loose term for what was, essentially, a handful of high tables and a long bar. The walls were painted in a tan that faded to off-white from one side of the room to the other. From the ceiling hung drop lights with frosted glass; every detail so minimally added as to be invisible to the eye.

And that was it.

No artwork. No extras.

No chairs.

Perhaps coming before opening wasn't the best idea, considering they clearly hadn't finished fitting the room out. Because if it was on purpose? *Save me.*

"Is this it?" Tiffany murmured to me when we entered.

It couldn't be. This couldn't be the finished product. I hoped against hope it wasn't.

Georgia, the owner, greeted me readily with a handshake, although I noted her smile became clipped when she turned to Tiffany.

"So, what do you think? It's different, isn't it?" She waved to the extremely bare room.

"It is," I said because I had nothing else nice to say.

"We really wanted to just go for it, you know? Bars have become so stale, all these unnecessary details."

"Like chairs," Tiffany chimed in.

"Exactly!" Georgia clearly hadn't heard the sarcasm in Tiffany's voice. "It ruins the flow of the room. We wanted something that agitated. Energized. This way, there aren't any barriers between people. The limited table space will mean we can fit more people in, or when there are fewer people, give them the opportunity to fill the space with their own energy rather than conform to what some designer thinks. And since people will have to hold on to their drinks, they can't be on their phones all night. It's about forcing people to own themselves and interact with each other."

"How very …" I struggled to finish my sentence. Every description I wanted to use was hardly polite.

Tiffany was the last person I expected to assist me. "Imaginative."

Georgia looked pleased. "Thank you. We're proud of it. And I'm really looking forward to seeing how the public reacts tomorrow, but it helps to know we have industry support." A voice came from behind us, getting Georgia's attention. "Sorry, I better take care of this," she said, motioning to the back of the room.

Left in the middle of the—apparently on purpose—empty room, I inwardly groaned. If this was what customers in Chicago wanted, I was regretting coming home. There was no way come hell or high water that I would let my bar become a philosophical embodiment of a new age, self-help con artistry.

And I had spent the last few years living in sin city.

Tiffany turned her back on the bar to give me a death stare. "Just so you know, I'd rather quit than have the bar turn into this place."

I choked on an unexpected laugh, watching her face jump in surprise. "I'll keep that in mind," I said, schooling my expression into something flatter.

ONCE WE'D RETURNED to the bar, Tiffany propped herself up on a stool, eating a sizeable bag of gummy worms. She hadn't been carrying anything with her earlier, and we didn't serve them at the bar, so I had no idea where they'd come from.

I was immensely aware of her presence in the empty bar. I was incapable of ignoring it lately. Somehow she always smelled like nutmeg and sugar. It was alluring. Maddening. We worked in a sweaty, boozy environment, but sweetness always lingered around her.

At first, I was convinced it was the syrups behind the bar, but no one else ever registered that way to me. Only Tiffany.

Now, I was being tormented by her sigh of pleasure as she dug into the stash of sweets. "You don't like doing anything by the norm, do you?" I asked.

"Define normal," she retorted. Touché.

Her lips curled into a smile when I didn't answer.

"So, that was a bust," she said.

Indeed. It certainly hadn't been what I was hoping for. I'd need to take another look at my research. Make some notes.

"I'm surprised you wanted to see it," she added.

"It's important to know what the competition is doing." At her eye roll, I said, "What surprises me is that you didn't like it."

This definitely got a reaction. "All that self posturing wank? Fuck no." Despite myself, a huff of laughter bubbled out of me.

"That's a little hypocritical, considering your snobbery."

"You? Are you calling *me* a snob?" I watched as her body

shifted, straightened, coiled like a wild cat preparing to strike. *Dangerous.*

"Would you prefer the word connoisseur?" I'd meant it as a joke, but she only looked confused, like she wasn't sure what I was doing. I wasn't sure I knew for myself.

Damn, she fascinated me.

Despite her elitist attitude towards the drinks she served, it didn't seem to extend to the competition. In fact, her comments led me to believe that she favored more relaxed environments, as did the way she carried herself. It intrigued me that she was so particular about her cocktails.

I wanted to ask her about it. Despite everything, including my own sense of self-preservation, I wanted to get to know her better.

Clearing my throat, I said, "Getting back to the subject at hand, what would you do if you had to change the décor here?"

She paused, mid chew, looking at me like she was trying to decipher how serious I was being. Mind made, she swallowed and said, "It's your bar."

Surprise showed on my face before I could stop it. It was the first time I'd heard her acknowledge that. Which was my only explanation as to why I then offered, "I'd still like your opinion."

She pulled her hand free of the gummy bag and wiped her hands on her jeans. She really did act like a grown child. Normally, I would have found it distasteful, but on Tiffany, it was oddly endearing.

"Well, obviously, we have to take all this down," she said, waving to the ceiling. "I'm not sure if you want to box it up and store it or decide with Harry who keeps what."

I eyed the collection, confused. "I'm sorry?"

"I know it meant a lot to him," she said as if that made any more sense to me. Why would Harry want a box of random items he'd collected at a garage sale?

Maybe this was something I'd missed while I'd been away.

I nodded, my only recourse when I had no clue what was going on.

"And while the booths are nice, I think it's probably time for an upgrade. Maybe some couches instead? Velvet or a leather Chesterfield. Something textural."

Interesting. I'd had the same thought. It would open the room up, allow seating for more customers, and couches would be a good alternative.

Maybe working together wasn't going to be a disaster.

"Of course, we'll need somewhere for the frozen margarita machine and the roulette wheel."

I blinked slowly and counted to ten.

"And we'll probably have to reinforce the bar if we want people doing body shots off of it."

"Tiffany," I warned.

"Geez, it was a joke. Lighten up, Sam." She chewed on another handful of crisps. "I'd like to hear your 'alternatives'."

I took another look at the room. The walls were nondescript; the light gray paint faded to a muted color that only added to the hollow nothingness that the place exuded.

Warmth was needed. Woods, metallics, stone. Natural materials. Something earthy, elemental. A far cry from anything I'd designed over west.

And maybe that was why I was suddenly reluctant to share my ideas with her.

This was the first time in a long time that my reputation was on the line, that I was putting myself into something that could fail and would have consequences for me if it did.

There were no safety nets this time. No backup plans. No business partners to weather the storm with.

It was just me. And for the first time in a long time, I was nervous. Determined but nervous. And Tiffany was the last person I was comfortable sharing that with.

Firmly locking away those feelings, I ran a hand along the

bar, feigning deep concentration. "I think perhaps you're right."

A spark ran through my veins as she visibly startled. It was nice knowing I could affect her composure as readily as she did mine. "Come again?"

"We'll definitely have to reinforce the bar."

For a moment, I worried her eyes would roll out of her head.

12
——

SAM

The ache in my shoulder had intensified. I intended to get it seen to, but I hadn't yet made the time. I'd been hoping that the thirty minutes of yoga I started every day with would be enough to keep the pain at a minimum.

That strategy had worked before, but I'd been working a lot harder in the last few weeks than I had in a long time.

I dug my fingers into the crook of my neck and massaged at the tightest spot, wincing at the pressure.

I'd have to see someone if I wanted to keep working behind the bar.

A smarter man would take it as a sign to stop messing about and get back into the office where I belonged, but I genuinely enjoyed getting my hands dirty again. It reminded me of my earliest days behind the bar and all the reasons that I'd wanted to own my own place.

It also meant more time getting to know the staff.

Now that it had been a few weeks, I'd gotten to know each of them, and I was glad to say that we now felt like a cohesive team. They'd gotten used to me helping out behind the bar and were, with one exception, warm and open. Devon was a godsend. He absolutely deserved the raise I'd given him.

And while no one specifically made a comment to my face, I'd heard them fondly teasing Tiffany about our disagreements. While I could have done without the gossip, I'd missed this sense of family. I'd forgotten what it felt like.

Gossip, of course, also had its benefits.

For example, there didn't seem to be a member of the staff, minus the new additions, that Tiffany hadn't helped in some shape or form. For Devon, it was helping him move; Nathan said she was always the first to take on extra shifts, and Hallie had mentioned a princess costume situation at her kid's birthday.

My first instinct, sadly, was to believe that her favors were intentional. A ploy to get the staff on her side. It was a trick I'd seen used in the past. But the more likely, and more difficult to accept, reason appeared to be that Tiffany was a kind and generous person. It added another dimension to her that I couldn't unsee.

The only saving grace was that, while my own feelings were distressing, Tiffany clearly couldn't stand me. I was glad one of us was smart.

As the coffee pot brewed for the second time this morning, I eyed the large manila envelope on the counter. It had arrived yesterday, but I hadn't had the energy to deal with it.

Ripping open the envelope—and the bandaid—I supposed, I skimmed the paperwork inside, confirming that all the required signatures were there, waiting for my own to join them. Piper had obviously gotten sick of delaying the inevitable.

So, this was it.

The last nine years of my life diluted down to a thumbs breadth of paper.

My bars, my work, my damned name. All signed away to my ex.

For a minute, I stood still in my kitchen, contracts in hand, waiting for the familiar burst of anger to erupt in my gut, seep into my bones.

But it never happened.

On a deep breath, I realized I might have reached the end of my resentment for this whole mess.

The hurt remained, but the hurt I could deal with. Live with.

Although, that would be easier to do if I no longer had to deal with Piper. As her name popped up on my cell screen, I briefly cursed. "Hello?"

"Hi, Sam."

Her voice was molasses, thickly sweet. I hated the memories that surfaced at the sound, late nights of her curled around me in bed; mornings spent discussing ideas for marketing campaigns or promotions. Not that long ago, I'd had everything I wanted. Now, I had next to nothing. "Piper."

"You could at least pretend to be happy to hear from me." Why? I wanted to ask. I would have, a month ago. I would have used the excuse to fight with her. Now, I was too tired to bother.

"What is this about?"

"I wanted to make sure you got the papers. I sent them days ago." Of course, that was why she'd called. She'd taken weeks to get them to me and then barely waited twenty-four hours before needling me to have them signed.

"Okay. Was there anything else?"

"Jesus, Sam, we dated for years. That's all you have to say to me?"

"What do you want, Piper? I'm not the one who's been stalling. If you'd signed the papers before I'd left like I had asked you to—"

"I told you, I needed the lawyers to look over it, make sure both of us got what we wanted."

What *we* wanted? "What you wanted, you mean."

"Sam, we've been through this. I—"

"No. I don't want to hear it. Thank you for finally sending the papers. I'll get them back to you as soon as possible. In the meantime, don't call me."

"Sam."

I hung up.

My day didn't improve from there.

"You want to add what to a drink?" Confused, I placed my glasses beside the now cold coffee on my desk. The cup was still full. It was the second cup I'd forgotten about today.

"Saffron," Tiffany repeated, her hip popped to the side.

"Saffron."

"Yes."

"You want to add saffron to a drink."

"Yes."

"You want to add that to a drink. On my menu. In my bar."

"Yes! Jesus."

"No."

"It was the Jesus, wasn't it?"

I put my glasses back on, eager to end this conversation. "It wasn't."

"Come on, Sam. It could be really good. Think of it as an experiment."

"I'm not letting you experiment on my customers."

She stared me down, challenging.

"It won't work," I repeated to make it clear.

"You don't know that."

"It's saffron. I can quite positively say it will not work in a cocktail."

A guttural groan. "Where's your creative spirit?"

"The answer is no."

———

Later, when I hoped Tiffany had calmed, I steeled myself for what I knew would be an uphill battle.

"The menu needs to change. Research shows that bars in this area do better when they attract a younger target demographic. And—" I caught Tiffany rolling her eyes. "Yes, Tiffany?"

"Well, Samuel." Her inflection of my first name was thick.

"Don't call me that."

"I don't know what you think you know about bars in this area, but we didn't get a name for ourselves by aiming for tik-tokers and," she shivered, "zennials."

"And why is that?"

"What?"

"Why shouldn't I be aiming for them? Research shows—"

"For fuck's sake," she interrupted.

"That they are the fastest-growing market in the US, and their spend rate has doubled since last year."

"Do you know why?"

"Not yet, but I'm sure you're about to enlighten me."

"Because they go out to get wasted. And yeah, they might end up spending a bit of money in a single night, but only after downing drink after drink of cheap watered-down swill. Most of them aren't coming in for a cocktail unless it has a dirty name. We're about craftsmanship. Flavour. Inventiveness."

"No. That's what you are about. This bar is about making money."

"I'm not going to let you change my menu."

"You don't have to 'let' me. I'm the owner."

"And I'm the bartender. Best one around."

"Need you remind me." This wasn't the first time she'd referenced her awards, but it had also happened far less than I'd been expecting, and she'd only ever mentioned it when I pulled the "owner" card. Less like a brag and more a shield. A proof of worth. I put that thought away for later.

Sighing, I changed tack. "What do you know about sours?"

"I know no one makes them anymore." Her pout was distracting.

We locked eyes, then understanding dawned. She blinked slowly, heaving out a deep sigh. "I'm going to hate this idea, aren't I?"

A small smile spread before I could stop it. "In my short experience, I'll wager yes." I shouldn't be enjoying myself as much as I was. "But you don't have a choice."

"Yes, sir." It was delivered in a petulant tone, but I'd be damned if hearing the term from her lips didn't stir up some undeniable urge within me. Something that was immediately buried because Tiffany was both an employee and, if bar gossip was to be believed, already in a serious relationship. It wouldn't do me any good to harbor any sort of attraction to her.

"Don't tell me," she said, interrupting my thoughts. "You actually like sours."

"I think they're understated."

"God, that just explains so much about you."

"Regardless. My point is that there might be drinks we personally believe would be better served, but that won't do us any good if people aren't buying them. We need to appeal to the right people, and right now, that includes college students and new adults."

"God help us all. Two dollar shots and Jägerbombs for everyone."

And while I shuddered at the thought, I didn't let it show. Tiffany would likely never let me live it down. For all her bluster, she couldn't convince me that this was a bad decision. The Basement had previously survived by the talent at her fingertips, but considering how frequently she came up with new ideas and how unfazed she was by mistakes, I had to wonder if it hadn't been a mix of talent and luck that had gotten her this far in life.

This bar would continue to be successful, but it would not be one because I made decisions in the heat of the moment. That was no way to run a business. Trends, analytics, data. That's how it worked. Smart, planned business decisions.

"I'm going to be making the changes anyway, and you can be involved or not. It's your choice."

None of her fight left her, her entire body taut like a stretched elastic, but she relented. "Fine," she finally said through gritted teeth. "It's your bar."

"So glad we agree."

13

———

TIFF

"**A**nd then he turns it around like I'm the one who doesn't know what they're talking about. He's just so …" I growled around the bite of honey chicken I'd stuffed in my mouth.

Hannah and I were having Chinese take-out at mine because it had been a long week for both of us, and cooking was more than we had the energy for.

Somehow, I still had the energy to complain about Sam.

"Tiff, can we not tonight? I'm tired."

"Sorry. I don't mean to make it worse, but … I just don't understand what his deal is! One minute he seems like he might be alright, and then the next, he's got the biggest chip on his shoulder and talking to me like I'm a child."

"Sam, Sam, Sam. It's all I've heard from you for the last five weeks."

"Because he's such a pain in my ass!"

"KC thinks you're weirdly obsessed with hating him." Fucking KC. I had a sneaking suspicion she was in love with Hannah, but I kept that to myself. For her part, Hannah had started phrasing things she wanted to say but didn't want to face the consequences for as "KC thinks." She thought I hadn't noticed. But I had.

"What's that supposed to mean?"

"Just that you seem to care a hell of a lot about someone you don't like."

"That makes no sense. Of course, I'd care if I didn't like him. Am I just supposed to not care that he's a raging asshole?"

Hannah huffed, her shoulders hunched as she pushes the bowl away from her. "Right. He's the problem here. It wouldn't have a single thing to do with the fact that you hate change."

"Excuse me?"

"You. Hate. Change. It's why you've never been in a serious relationship," Wrong. "Why you didn't want to meet my parents," Also wrong. "And why you hate that someone else is reminding you that you aren't in charge." I could write an ode to all the ways this was wrong.

"My issues with Sam—"

"I'm so sick to death of hearing his name," she cut in.

"Whatever is going on with my work," I restarted, "has nothing to do with what is between us."

"Sure doesn't seem like it."

My own appetite disappeared. "What is really going on here? I know I've been complaining a lot lately, but this feels like something bigger than just my bad day."

"Why aren't we living together yet?"

Well, that came from left field. We'd never even talked about moving in together. "I didn't know you wanted to. Is that why you're upset?"

"I don't think you'll ever be ready," she said, and I tried to catch up to whatever conversation she was having in her head because it was clearly not the same conversation I was having with her.

I opened my mouth to argue, but she halted me. "Actually, you know what I really think? I think you like being with women, so you can call yourself queer, but you don't actually want to be with a woman. Maybe you just like fucking everything that moves, I don't know. Or maybe you just like being bi because it makes you different from everyone else. You sure do love waving that banner around."

On instinct, I slapped my hand so hard against the coffee table that my glass tumbled over, shattering against the floor.

Fuck.

What in the world was happening right now?

I took a long, steadying breath.

Hannah had pushed up from the couch, arms crossed against her chest, and I abandoned my urge to clean up the glass to face her. Her glare was cutting. "You need to figure yourself out, or else you're going to end up alone. You might think you're so much better than the rest of us, but the rest of us live in the real world. Not everyone has the privilege of free speech, Tiff. Some of us can't take the risks you do. Some of us have to face the consequences."

"I live in the real world. But sometimes the rules are illogical, prejudiced, and damaging, and I'm not going to be quiet about it."

"Yes, we all know that, ok! You're not some fucking enlightened being far beyond the rest of us. We get that the rules are unreasonable, but sometimes we need to actually follow them unless we want to hurt ourselves or other people."

"I'm not trying to hurt you."

"But you're not putting me first either. Why can't you just let people be assholes without commenting on it? Or pretend every once in a while?"

"Because then they win. They get to have the world be exactly how they want it, knowing that we'll just slink into the shadows to please them. I don't know what you want from me. I'm not going to wake up tomorrow as someone else. You either like me like this, or you don't."

"That's it? I have to accept you one hundred percent or not at all? You know how conceited that sounds?"

My breath came hot and heavy through my nose as I tried to calm myself. My pulse beat fast in my throat, our arguing echoing in the otherwise quiet room. "I'm not asking for blind acceptance, but, Hannah, come on." I wanted to take a step forward, close the gap between us, but I didn't trust my legs to hold me. "Ever since we started seeing each other, it's been something. I should work less, I should get a desk job, I should have my future planned out, I should lie about my sexuality. I can't commit to someone who constantly wants to change me."

Her disgusted laugh stung. "How could you commit to one person when you can't even commit to a sexuality?"

"That's enough." My voice boomed throughout my apartment. I stood, my blood boiling. If I didn't move, I would scream.

The air was rife with tension, and I couldn't tell what Hannah was thinking, but I knew that I couldn't look at her. That bubbly, insightful woman I'd been interested in when we first met had been replaced by the callous, ignorant person before me.

I tried to keep my voice even. I mostly failed. "Look, I'm not perfect," I said. Hannah's eye roll lodged itself in my gut, adding to my conviction that we were over. "I never claimed to be, no matter what you think. But I'm not going to change myself just because you think I should. And I might not know much about commitment, but I know I'm not your plaything to script and puppet around."

"Tiffany, that's not fair."

Fair, she said. Fair. On her.

I said nothing. There was nothing left to say. Hannah had

made it clear that she couldn't accept me, and that wasn't something I could see us working through.

"Oh, fuck you, Tiffany. You know what? Fine. I've had enough of this shit anyway. Go back to sleeping with whoever will take you. Wouldn't want you to have to choose a side or anything."

"Get. Out." She was already walking away. "Find whatever it is you've left here and never contact me again."

"Gladly."

The door slammed behind her as she left, and I was shellshocked, frozen in the middle of my apartment. The broken glass was laid out on the floor next to the couch, and the food sat untouched. I should start cleaning up, but I didn't want to spend another minute here.

My chest was too tight, my stomach clenched in anger. The fucking nerve! I couldn't believe it.

I needed to get out. To breathe. To think.

The tears had started to fall by the time I'd made it to the sidewalk.

14

———

SAM

On the days the bar was closed, I'd taken to working from home. There was hardly much of a difference, but even that small variance in my surroundings meant I could at least pretend that I was keeping better hours than I was.

By the early evening, I'd managed to finally finish what I was doing, only to realize that I'd missed August's numbers completely, and they were sitting in the office at the bar. Five weeks since starting this new life, and I still felt like I hadn't completely adjusted.

Considering the bar was closed, I was more than a little surprised to find Tiffany there when I arrived. And even more so to find her sitting on a bar stool, nursing a drink.

"Do you often make it a habit of drinking my alcohol on your days off?"

If she was surprised to see me, she didn't show it. In fact, she didn't move at all, not even to turn her head to look at me.

Her posture was all wrong. Slumped where she normally lounged. When I rounded the bar to stand in front of her, she avoided my gaze, but I noticed, with a flash of concern, that her eyes were glassy and red-rimmed.

I actually felt bad for asking, but I wasn't sure what else to say. "Bad day?"

She gave a pained laugh, sounding wrecked. "Yeah."

And just like that, I put aside all the arguments we'd had this week and saw the person underneath all that bravado. It felt sacred, as though I was witnessing a side of her not many saw.

"I've never seen you like this."

"Huh?"

I cleared my throat. "I mean, I've never seen you drink here before. Have I finally driven you to it?"

That earned a weak smile. One that didn't make it to her eyes. It felt wrong.

"Unless you're celebrating?" I ventured, hoping the ill attempt at humor would conjure something. She was really worrying me.

"It's not that kind of drink."

Oh.

I took a step toward my office then turned back. "Can I join you?"

"Free country."

"That's debatable." This earned me a smirk. I'd take it. I'd never seen her so deflated. I didn't like it. "Can I make you something?"

She looked surprised. "A Sam Cooper special? Sure." She watched me. "Are you going to try to impress me?"

Turning back to the bar, I thought about what to make her. Whatever it was that was bothering her went deep. I didn't know much about her life outside of the bar, but I could at least tell that much.

Whenever I felt like that, I'd console myself with a glass of whiskey, but if we were going to do that, then …

I made a decision. I hoped I wouldn't regret it.

"Get up."

"You're kicking me out already?"

"I'm not kicking you out. We're going upstairs."

"Upstairs? There's no upstairs."

I said nothing as I checked the lock on the bar door and then led her towards the fire exit. Next to it was a nondescript door that I knew led to the apartment upstairs. It had sat empty while Harry ran the bar because he already had a house out in Buffalo Grove. But I'd needed somewhere to live when I moved back, and it made the most sense since I would be spending all my time at the bar anyway.

I heard her quiet little breath of surprise when I unlocked the stairway door. As she followed me upstairs, she said, "I didn't even realize this was here."

Once we were inside, I made quick work of getting us both a drink. When I turned back, she was standing in the middle of the room, taking in the black painted brick walls and polished floorboards. It wasn't much, not yet, a stack of boxes in the corner making it obvious that I hadn't quite moved in. I'd gotten as far as unpacking my books, mostly non-fiction or biographies, which were scattered around the apartment, strewn across surfaces and a lone bookcase. A large philodendron cascaded down the bookcase, and there was a bird of paradise sitting by the window.

It wasn't yet home, but it felt like mine, and I liked that.

I waited as Tiffany curiously observed the organized chaos. With a quick glance, I checked for Luna, not surprised that she hadn't shown herself. She was notoriously suspicious of strangers and still settling in from the cross-country move. Her bowl was empty, though, so I could only imagine that she was curled up under my bed, her second favorite spot to occupy in the apartment.

Directing Tiffany towards the couch, I purposefully sat in an armchair that faced her but kept me at a respectable distance.

From her interactions with the rest of the team, I'd seen that Tiffany was comfortable letting people into her personal space, whether it was through a warm hug hello, the ease with which she splayed herself on any piece of furniture, or the way she never seemed bothered by the confined conditions behind the bar on a busy night.

But I'd never seen her vulnerable like this. And something told me to be cautious about how I approached it.

She accepted the drink with a tight nod, still not making eye contact.

Gently, I asked, "Are you ok?"

"I'm fine."

"You don't look fine."

"What do you care?" She said it so quietly, I felt my resolve cracking. She honestly believed I didn't care about her?

"Despite what you think, Tiffany, I care. I would rather not have my employees drinking themselves to an early grave, especially with my inventory." Another terrible attempt at a joke.

I expected a retort. Something. Her usual barbed sneer and flippant air. But instead, she remained quiet. Worse than that, she was … deflated. Despondent. I'd never seen her like this before.

I had no idea how to approach it.

Talking wasn't working, but we weren't close enough for me to offer much else except the drink and the company. Suddenly, I felt guilty that I'd let our … rivalry distract me from getting to know her. It was a failure on my part.

The apartment was too quiet. Muted sounds of street life could be heard from below, but the lack of anything else was stifling, so I pulled out my phone and used the Bluetooth speaker that sat in the corner to play a mix of smooth blues.

Acoustic guitar rang out, the first few bars soft and melodic. I let myself relax deeper into the armchair, taking another sip of whiskey and letting the warm amber seep calm into my blood.

"This is good." Tiffany's soft voice was rough with emotion. At first, I thought she was referring to the music, but when I peered over at her, she was appreciating the whiskey in her glass, swirling it again before taking a sip. "Japanese?"

I give her a gentle smile, even though it didn't surprise me that she recognized it. "You know your whiskey."

"I wouldn't be a very good bartender if I didn't."

"And I have it on good authority you're the best in town." Again I hoped for a smile, but she looked pained instead.

I felt completely out of my depth.

"You know that doesn't mean anything, right?" she said, finally meeting my eye. "Those awards. It's just their way of showing they can be inclusive. It's not why I do this."

"Why do you?"

"Because I like it. And I'm good at it. Why do you do it?"

There were so many answers, many I wasn't yet comfortable sharing. "I like providing people with something they want. And I'm good at it."

Finally, the corner of her lips curled into a smile, and I felt the tightness in my chest shift. Ease.

"You, a people pleaser," she said, a hint of her usual humor threading itself through the words. "I hadn't noticed."

"Normally, my work isn't cut out for me. You've been a difficult one to please," I dryly joked.

It was the wrong thing to say. Whatever lightness was there before fell flat, and I couldn't take seeing her like that for another minute. I needed to know.

"What's wrong?"

I wasn't entirely sure she was going to answer. Instead, I was half-convinced she was going to put her glass down and walk out without another word. But I hoped she didn't. I avoided acknowledging why.

She finished the last of her whiskey in one long gulp, setting the tumbler down on the oak coffee table. "Are you sure you want to know?"

"Yes." It was an answer that felt too telling.

"My girlfriend and I broke up. It wasn't pretty."

"I'm sorry to hear that." So, what I'd heard was correct. She'd been in a relationship. I'd been such an asshole.

"It's fine. Or it will be. Once I finish wallowing."

Even considering my own recent relationship disaster, I hardly felt like an expert, and I couldn't imagine any advice worthy of giving her. How could I offer anything when I had nothing but romantic failure in my past?

"Were you together long?"

"Four months, give or take. Which is nothing as far as most relationships go, but it's the longest one I've had in a while."

"Were you in love?" I shouldn't have asked that. I didn't know why I was asking, and from the widening of her eyes, it was clear she didn't know either.

"No." A self-deprecating laugh sprung forth. "I know. I look like someone who's had their heartbroken, but that's not really the reason I'm taking it badly."

"Then, why?"

Before answering, she picked up her glass and reached over for mine, "Another?" It was a distraction technique, but considering how strained her smiles still were, I didn't call it out.

I nodded, watching as she walked over to where the bottle sat, nestled in a curated collection on my bar trolley. There was no hesitation to her actions, moving comfortably among my belongings as if this was something we did often.

The music changed to something somber, a rich timbre voice and a lone piano.

She only spoke again once our drinks were in hand and she'd sunk back into the couch. There was a deliberateness to her expression, but she'd tucked her legs underneath her in her usual style, and I took that as a good sign. "I'm beginning to wonder whether I'm better off being single."

"I'm sure that's just the breakup talking."

She shook her head. "That's experience talking." She sighed heavily and leaned forward, elbows resting on her arms. I realized, belatedly, that there was a tattoo hiding on the inside of her bicep, something typically hidden under the shirt she wore for work. I saw fine lines connected by something I couldn't quite make out. I wanted, more than anything, to be able to ask.

"I'm sure you've heard by now that I date both men and women."

"I don't make it a habit of digging into my employees' lives." It was an obvious non-answer.

"Cut the crap. I know what working at a bar is like. We gossip more than a 10 a.m. talk show."

"I may have overheard that piece of information, yes." I then made an assumption that I hoped I wasn't wrong about. "I take it your girlfriend had an issue with that?"

She let out a cold, harsh bark of a laugh. "Among other things. For someone who dated me for four months, she sure didn't like me much."

"That's bullshit. If that's true, you're better off without her."

Her lips curled into a smile. Then, her entire expression shifted into confusion. "For someone who hates me, you're being awfully nice."

"I don't hate you." I could tell she didn't believe me, which seemed reasonable based on our interactions to date. Unfortunately, the truth was more dangerous than that. I'd been curious about Tiffany from the moment I'd met her—probably before that—and it had only gotten worse the more I got to know her. Seeing her like this, placid and vulnerable, made me want to know every side of her.

Clearing my throat, I shoved those thoughts aside. They wouldn't do either of us any good. "Do you want to talk about it?"

A pair of guitars danced around a chord progression in the background, building in a playful staccato. My pulse matched the pace as I waited for Tiffany's answer.

"She said I hated change. That I think I'm better than everyone else."

"Do you?"

"No," she said sharply.

Shit. I was making this worse. "Sorry, that came out completely wrong. I meant," I paused, wanting to word this the right way. "I know we haven't seen eye to eye on the bar," her expression contorted into the strongest physical embodiment of "no, shit" I'd ever seen, and I stifled a smile, "but it is obvious to me that your ... arguments are always backed up by your experience. Not because you dislike change. I would expect someone who was sleeping with you to know that."

Tiffany shifted on the couch, folding her lean legs underneath her in the same way I'd seen her do in my office many times. A muscle in my neck unclenched. But she stayed silent, staring out the window and bringing a hand up to chew on a nail.

There was a long silence, where I debated whether it was wise to open my mouth again, having done a horrible job of cheering her up so far. In my defense, I hadn't had much practice. Outside of mediating the occasional work dispute, the last person I consoled was my ex-girlfriend, and I knew none of my usual tricks—sex, dessert, or a holiday—would work here.

On the other hand, the idea that Tiffany's girlfriend had had a problem with her sexuality bothered me too much to keep quiet. "Also, I don't, and forgive me, but I can't understand how she could possibly have a problem with you being bisexual."

This got a reaction. "Really? You don't think it's slutty of me to pander to all genders?" Judging by the venom in her words, this was a specific quote. A vile, inconsiderate quote.

"Absolutely not. I happen to be more attracted to women with," I stalled, knowing my next words were "blonde hair," and decided to sidestep that minefield, "certain attributes. That doesn't mean I'm automatically attracted to everyone with those attributes. I suspect it's the same for you."

She let out a playful snort into her glass. "You know, outside of the fact that you just sounded like an AI learning how words work, that was surprisingly insightful."

"Thank you," I said, returning her teasing with my own. "And just so you know, as a hard-working cyborg who is very proficient with how words work, we really don't like being referred to as 'AI'. It's a misnomer."

She laughed, incredulous. "Excuse me, where the hell have you been hiding this?"

"What?"

"This sense of humor. You've been a puckered-up a-hole since I met you, and now you become a human?"

If the sight of her brightly smiling at me wasn't making my insides flip, I would probably be more put out by the a-hole comment. But instead, I was almost giddy.

I cocked an eyebrow at her. "Because you've been absolutely pleasant this whole time."

She dropped her head onto her forearms, groaning, but when her head tipped back up, she was smiling with that familiar spark in her eyes, and I felt immeasurably better. And comfortable enough to add, "For what it's worth, I'm sorry for acting like an ass."

I heard her suck in a surprised breath. "Wow. Ok." A flush graced her cheeks again, which she tried to cover by draining her glass. "I guess I should apologize for being a little difficult, then."

"A little?"

"Don't push it." She grimaced. "I may have referred to you as Sir Smugington the Third."

I choked on a laugh, surprising even myself with the force of it. Damn, I really liked her. This was definitely not going to end well for me.

I'd have to be more careful around her. Returning her playful banter was a terrible idea. I should stop it. She clearly felt better. I could say goodnight, send her home, and berate myself in the morning.

I should have. But I didn't. "At least you got the title right."

This earned me another hearty laugh. I felt my toes curl in my shoes and the edges of my own smile lifting. "How about we call it even and try to work from a fresh slate?" I said.

"I think I can do that." Her piercing green eyes snapped up to meet mine, and I was stunned to realize the pupils were ringed in gold, like an eclipse. I was so taken by them that I almost missed her words. "This doesn't mean I'm just going to agree with you on everything, though."

I mentally shook myself. Distance, remember? "I wouldn't expect it to."

She held her glass out, an olive branch if ever I saw one. "Then, to fresh slates."

I clinked her glass with my own, knowing this was exactly the opposite of keeping my distance.

I didn't care.

15

TIFF

Despite the whiskeys last night, I slept like utter crap with Hannah's words playing on repeat in my dreams.

When your own girlfriend couldn't accept you, where did you turn?

Above all else, I hated bullies, and since I had about zero interest in changing who I was or questioning myself because of someone else's misguided beliefs, I just stayed away and lived my life.

If you asked me what a perfect world look liked, it would be everyone minding their own goddamn business and letting the world be happy.

I was sick of having guys treat my bisexuality like a free pass for a threesome and girls treating it like a red flag. Some personal slight against their own choice because I was able to "pass" as straight if I was with a man, or like I was just "playing around" at being gay.

This. This was why I hadn't chased relationships in the past.

Because if I was going to commit to someone, then I wanted that commitment back, two hundred percent.

I wasn't about to give my heart and soul to someone who couldn't accept me. All of me.

So, if that meant being single, then hell, yeah, I could do that.

———

THERE WAS a new energy humming under my skin as I made my way to work today, remembering the bizarreness of my conversation with Sam last night (and hello, how long had there been an apartment upstairs?!) and our truce.

He still was the same occasionally charming, oddly stilted, consistently maddening man he was before. But.

Last night he'd been thoughtful. And … ugh. Sweet.

What a bastard.

How dare he make me like him after all the shit he'd given me. He'd even apologized!

He was insufferable.

Except he, of course, wasn't. Which was worse.

Last night, he'd surprised me, and now, I saw him through new eyes. Details I'd ignored before had become unavoidable. The sparkle in his eye if he told a joke, his face giving nothing away. How that stirred something playful in me, like we were sharing a secret.

He'd started dressing differently, too, more appropriate for working behind the bar. When he first started, it was all tailored pants and dress shirts. The occasional vest. Now, well, the pants hadn't changed, but he'd adopted the uniform the rest of us wore. It's better, I thought. Not that I couldn't appreciate a crisp button-down, and he certainly didn't look out of place in one. In fact, I could picture him looking pretty ok, actually. Sleeves rolled up. Collar undone. Glasses …

He didn't look entirely hideous, that was all. And the black t-shirt he had started to don did show off some surprisingly muscular biceps. Lean without an ounce of fat.

What had I been thinking about again?

Right. Last night.

It had been a long time since someone else had looked after me. I was so used to handling everything on my own or being the shoulder other people cried on. And having gone to the bar when it was closed on purpose, I hadn't expected to talk to anyone about what happened with Hannah. Sam wasn't supposed to be there.

He wasn't supposed to listen, offer advice. Make me feel better.

Fuck.

Whatever. I'd have to freak out about it another day. Hours of restless sleep had not prepared me enough to deal with whoever the hell Sam was.

Except. That fucker always seemed to have something new up his sleeve.

My attempt to start a normal shift was halted immediately once I spied the industrial coffee machine being installed at the end of the bar.

A beautiful, bold, black and brass coffee machine.

It was heaven itself.

Oh, I could already feel my mind racing to think of how we could start to use it. Namely for double espressos pre-shift, but there were a hundred work-related uses as well. I'd been thinking recently about a possible drink with cold brew (chilled espresso wasn't the same thing, but I'd make do), triple sec, and tonic. Any orange liqueur would work, but I'd need to test a few recipes before I settled on a style, and here was the perfect opportunity.

Installation complete, the two laborers packed up their tools, and one went into the office. I sidled up to the other, eager to learn what I needed to operate the machine.

"Any tips for me?" I asked.

The young guy was fit, his t-shirt a size too small and stretched across his prominent pectorals. He crossed his arms across his chest in a clear move to accentuate his muscles. I wasn't unappreciative.

"A few," he said suggestively.

"How about we start with the coffee, then we can see."

Movement near Sam's office caught my eye, and I was suddenly all too aware of Sam watching us. Me. His arms crossed, leaning against the door frame, stoic as ever.

Tim, the coffee guy, walked me through the machine, flirting the entire time. "You know you're lucky," he said.

Not the best line, but he was young. "Oh? Why's that?"

"We weren't meant to deliver this for a few weeks. But apparently, your boss called us first thing this morning and paid a lot of money to make sure this was installed today."

"Oh." *Oh*, Sam did that? I resisted the urge to look over at him.

Shit.

I was going to have to be nice to him now, wasn't I?

Thirty minutes and two double espressos later, I felt more human. Devon arrived for his shift while I was practicing on the machine, and I spent the next twenty minutes teaching him everything (as little as it was) that I knew about it. He then schooled me in milk art, the talented little shit.

Soon, he moved on to prep work for tonight while I switched gears and checked out inventory, ensuring we had enough stock on hand so that we wouldn't need to venture to the storeroom for anything later.

"Everything working out?"

Turning, I realized Sam was beside me. Feeling unnaturally nervous, I nodded. "Great job on the coffee machine."

He sighed tiredly. "Are you going to now tell me you don't think the bar needed it?"

"What? No, I mean it. Thank you. It was really sweet of you."

He stared at me, face pinched, blinking. It was really

rather disconcerting, and I could feel the hairs pick up on my neck under his unwavering gaze.

"Hello? Sam?"

"Yes?" He asked, tentative. I didn't know what the hell his problem was.

"I said thank you."

"I heard you." He was still eyeing me suspiciously.

"Ok. Well, I'll just get back to work now, unless you needed anything?"

He pinched his nose, confused. "What are you doing? Stop."

I threw my hands up. "I can't be nice?"

"No. It's not normal."

"Fuck you, too."

"Much better." When his smile appeared, it took me a moment to realize what was happening. It felt momentous. A firm shift, more so than last night, from the cold antagonism we had to whatever this was.

The sight of his grin was unique for me. I was so used to seeing it directed at others that I only just realized he had dimples.

They were gorgeous.

Oh, no.

A spark of excitement rippled through me. Those damn smiles of his were a weapon, softening my insides like warm cocoa. How dare he. He was becoming so irritatingly hard to hate.

And increasingly difficult to ignore. Fuck.

16

TIFF

At the end of the night, the staff split into two groups: those who left quickly and those who didn't.

As a self-proclaimed overachiever, I was in the latter category. I wasn't surprised that Sam fell into it, too, although it had annoyed me when he first started.

Now?

Now, I was almost glad for the company.

After Devon had finished cleaning up, I sent him home with a wave until it was only Sam and I loitering in the bar.

I busied myself reviewing the next week's schedule while I spied Sam studying a selection of paperwork in one of the booths. It was odd to see him there. He usually preferred to be in his office or working behind the bar.

Something I'd noticed he'd spent less time doing lately, and I remembered how he'd almost dropped a box the other night. Normally, I would have made a crack about not having what it took to do what he bossed us around to do, but I've worked with him for multiple shifts now, and he'd never shown any weakness before.

I hated to admit it (and you'd have to torture me before I

told him), but I could at least acknowledge that he was an objectively handsome man. Lean, fit, good-looking. He wasn't built like Jackson, but he clearly looked after himself.

Considering his slender build, I'd been surprised by the strength in his body and even more by the muscular thighs and ass (one thing I'd always loved on a person). He'd surprised me today by forfeiting his usual black dress pants in favor of a slim cut jean.

And wow, that ass.

That tight, tight ass.

Dammit, that was not something I should be noticing about my boss.

I was already spending too much energy ignoring the way his smug smile accentuated the cupid's bow of his lips or the way his glasses softened the intensity of his eyes. I did not need to add this to the list of things I needed to ignore about him.

"Can I get you anything?" I asked from behind the bar.

His head turned towards me, but his eyes stayed glued to whatever he was reading. It was not adorable. "Hmm?"

Goddammit (it was *not* adorable). "Do you want a drink or anything?"

Finally, he looked at me. "Oh. No, I was about to make myself a coffee."

I nodded. When ten minutes had passed and he still hadn't made a move, I made him a cup (it was the least I could do since he was the reason we even had a machine) and walked it over to him.

"So," I said as I took a seat across from him in the booth, a packet of chips in hand. It was the first meal I'd eaten in hours, and my stomach was turning on itself. "How are the plans coming?"

At his quizzical look, I added, "for the bar?"

Realization hit, and then he did a double-take at the cup

of coffee sitting before him, the corner of his lips curling into a half-smile. "Ah, yes. Well, I'm still having some issues pinpointing a theme." He gestured to the litany of papers in front of him, which I now realized were samples, vision boards, and news clips of assorted bars. It was like an interior decorator's wet dream.

"Well, what is it you're trying to say?" From the little I knew about this sort of thing, there was always an angle.

"I want the bar to be somewhere everyone feels welcome. Somewhere they can come to connect. The way I see it, not everyone can relate with lofty, expensive drinks." His gaze shifted to mine, worried. "No offense."

When I smiled, he relaxed and continued. "There's a disconnect. Yes, they look great. Yes, they taste great." I preened under the compliments. "I recognize that they have been a big deal for the bar up to now, but I think we can do more than that. Bars like that are 'somewhere to be seen', not 'somewhere to be'. Everyone that comes here should feel welcomed, no matter who they are."

"Wow," I said, breathless from the passion he exuded. Who knew that was under his stiff, stubborn exterior? "How do you plan on saying that with furniture?"

He lifted the coffee to his lips, and I tried not to pay too much attention. "That would be the issue."

"Ah," I said. "May I?"

"Of course." I flipped a few of the pages around to face me, skimming over sconce options (eh, maybe) and wallpaper designs (surprisingly chic, actually) and some schematics for replacing the back shelving, when he spoke again. "I meant what I said earlier; I don't expect you to act any differently towards me this morning just because we had an actual conversation last night. Our first, it would seem."

This guy. Seriously.

A smirk was itching to spread, and I gave in to the urge,

throwing an arm across the back of the booth. "Despite what you think about me, I'm not a bitch all the time. I am actually quite nice. To people I like."

"Is that your way of saying that you like me?"

I expected a denial or a change of subject. What I didn't expect was for Sam to meet my eyes across the table or for the rolling wave of goosebumps that erupted across my skin.

Sweet heaven, his eyes were mesmerizing. So soft and caring. For all his sharp edges and defensive tactics, there was a gentleness to Sam I hadn't noticed before. Dammit. Didn't he know that was my kryptonite?

"Could be."

The fluttering in my chest increased. "Don't hurt yourself there. You almost gave me a compliment."

"Tiffany," he said, and there was that look again. *Sam. Always so serious.* I giggled, and pleasure rippled through me when he smiled in return. *Oh.* Oh, that was nice.

Suddenly, keeping his gaze was too much. Shifting in my seat, I dropped my attention back to the table.

There were several good options here. He seemed to favor warm tones and natural materials, which I appreciated. In particular, I was drawn to a mockup of the back bar that mimicked industrial shelving and what appeared to be pocket alcoves within a mammoth copper and concrete structure, inlaid with alternating grating or mirrors and a Tetris design that would really show off the alcohol.

It looked fucking cool.

"This is amazing." It came out easily, the awe apparent in my voice. "Did you design this?"

"I did." Holy shit. "It's been something I've had on the back burner for a while now. I just haven't had the right space to try it in."

I couldn't believe it. It was beautiful. "I thought you said you were having issues." I met his gaze. "This doesn't look like an issue. It looks like my dream bar come to life."

Long eyelashes fluttered against his cheeks (could I just stop noticing his face now, please?) as he took the compliment.

I moved to hand back the sketch as Sam reached forward to take it, and. Our hands brushed. Minimally. So softly, I wanted to cry. Just the lightest glide of his fingers against mine and everything stopped.

My brain shut down and rebooted itself. I pulled my hand back, wanting to hold it to my chest but dropping it awkwardly to my lap instead.

Strained, he said, "Thank you. But it's too much of a risk for now, so I'll reconsider it maybe in a year."

Sam looked flushed. My ears felt hot. Was Sam blushing right now? Electricity buzzed along my spine.

This really was starting to get weird. I prayed for him to shut down or insult me so we could get back to normal.

"Then, you're a bigger ass than I thought because this is incredible." Ok, that was better. Half insult, half compliment.

Sam nodded, a small smile still playing on his lips. Lips that I definitely did not need to be paying any goddamn attention to. When his tongue snuck out to wet his bottom lip, I realized I was still staring. Fuck. Get back on track. "In my experience, it's worth taking a risk every once in a while. No risk, no reward, right?"

Seafoam eyes stared back at me, charged with … what? What was he thinking about right now?

"Ok."

My skin tingled. "Ok?"

"Yes. I'll call contractors in the morning."

"Wow." I fought the urge to squirm under his open gaze. "I don't know what's made you so pliant all of a sudden, but keep it up. Maybe now you'll actually start listening to me."

"Tiffany." It was a familiar scolding, although now flooded with fondness and a growing familiarity. When had that even happened? And dammit, the way he said my name did things to me. How had I not noticed it before? I dug my clipped nails into the soft pad of my palm, but it did nothing to calm the growing need in between my thighs.

Fucking hell, body.

GET A GRIP.

TIFF

Sam was doing this on purpose.

He was practically making it his job to get under my skin. And more annoyingly, it was working.

Sam was behind the bar again tonight, doing his best to bother me. Our stations were beside each other, which served as a constant distraction. Every inch between us. Every brush of skin or clothing as we worked. If he reached over to pick something up, I would zero in on his hands, watching his dexterous fingers as he stirred a bar spoon.

There was little relief when he turned to the back bar, especially if he was getting any of the top-shelf stuff because then I would be met by his broad shoulders, the implication of taut back muscles burning themselves into my brain.

It was like a dam had burst, and I was being flooded by all things Sam. A pillowy lip. That damn lopsided smile. His melodic voice as he greeted customers. How confidently he could switch between charm and authority, dealing with difficult customers or unforeseen problems with calm. How a soft command from him made my thighs clench.

Sometimes, I caught him watching me. Observing. Our eyes met, tangled, and he'd look away. Sometimes the light would add a flush to his skin, and I'd feel my own cheeks heating in response.

Of course, Sam was (as always) very careful to maintain distance. Always stepping out of my way like he was afraid to touch me. If he knew me at all, he would have realized that was the worst possible choice. Because it only made me want to reach out to him more.

While I took an order for three French martini's, Sam sidled in beside me to serve another customer. A quick flick of my gaze told me that she was gorgeous. And clearly giving him the eye.

I hated her. For completely unselfish, non-jealous reasons.

Because this was Sam. Annoying, calculating, surprisingly toned, cynically funny, with dimples I wanted to lick, Sam.

"What do you recommend?" I overheard her ask him, and I waited to see his reaction. It wasn't an extremely busy night, so we had the time to mix up something special, but typically this question was a sort of make or break for a bartender. Any time we spent trying to guess what you wanted was time we lost making tips.

It was usually a death knell.

So, of course, Sam responded with a winning smile and genuinely tried to help her decide on something, recommending a few things off the menu and explaining their flavors to her while she stared dreamily at him.

What a bitch.

I couldn't recognize the cocktail from the ingredients he pulled out, which meant he was making something of his own creation. Knock me over. Was there anything he couldn't do?

Reaching for the Chambord, only to grab air, I cursed when I spotted it on the other side of him.

Over my shoulder, I asked, "Can you pass me the—"

Without missing a beat, he reached over and placed the bottle in my waiting hand. I paused, blinking at it. "Oh. Thanks."

"You're welcome." He continued working.

Shaking the martini, I had to ask. "Where did you learn to bartend? I thought you just ran places?"

"I have a long and varied career."

Neither of us had bothered to look at each other, focusing instead on our drinks, but at this, I had to turn. "Oh, come on. Give me something."

Something odd happened to his mouth that I couldn't discern (I was tempted to imagine he was annoyed with me because it was an expression I'd grown used to seeing on him), but he still answered my question. "When I was seventeen, I tended bar for a local place. Completely kitsch, screens everywhere, lots of jerseys on the wall."

"Sounds like the kind of place my dad loves."

"It was a great place. The decor was horrible, but it was busy every night. For years, I wondered why, considering how run down it was. The drinks weren't that good, the food was even worse. But the locals still loved it."

I could picture it exactly. I'd worked in my fair share of those places. "It was home."

He nodded. "Yes."

When the martinis were done, I took the card payment, surprised when Sam turned to the woman I'd served. "Enjoy your night. I take it Tiffany treated you well?"

She practically beamed at him. Charming bastard. "Yes. Very well."

He chuckled. Fucking. Chuckled. "Good. She can stay employed for another week then."

Oh, very funny, asshole.

His voice was low when he turned to twist the knife. "Wasn't that nice? People can be lovely."

Smug bastard. "I hate you."

The corner of his mouth lifted. "Now, Tiffany, why would you say something like that?"

It turned out it was very hard to scowl while fake smiling. But I still managed it.

———

THE NEXT DAY, I found myself unpacking a box of Elderflower liqueur, eyeing the bottles, and enjoying the quiet of the storeroom before opening. Such a pretty color, even under this horrendous fluorescent lighting. Glassy and not-quite-gray. More like sea glass, maybe, with a barely-there blue/green tone that reminded me how long it had been since I'd visited the museum with Hannah.

It was beautiful.

There was something familiar about it that I didn't realize until I was back upstairs and saw Sam passing by the bar.

Surely I had noticed before this, but damn. Those eyes.

They were ethereal sea foam.

Clear like shallow water, but endless as a deep well.

Fuck. I definitely shouldn't be waxing poetic over Sam fucking Cooper's eyes. No matter how haunting they were.

But they were. Haunting. Always standing out against the dark brown of his hair and beard.

Except, the beard was gone. I shifted to take another look at him, disguising my movements by pretending to rearrange bottles on the back bar. He was clean-shaven. Gone was the soft fuzz that had been keeping the lower half of his face covered (I'd say warm, but considering how threadbare it was, it wouldn't have been doing much in that department).

But not all of it had gone. No. He'd kept this silly little mustache. And it was anything but silly because, for some annoying fucking reason, it actually made him more attractive. Brought the focus to his prominent cupid's bow and the little beauty mark on his right cheek and the crooked way he smiled and no, no no no no.

I could not, would not, absolutely fucking refused to

acknowledge the fact that he was good-looking. Even objectively.

———

WHILE I WAS IMMEDIATELY thankful when the mustache disappeared a day later (had he kept it on a dare? Why did nothing he did make any sense?), the smile was still all I could see. Blinding me when I least expected it until I had to turn away.

It was frustration, was all. The fact that this … show, this act, wasn't the real him.

Because with me, it disappeared. His face was like stone when we talked (ok, argued), but I'd see him with other people, his face loose and open, smiling like he knew exactly the reaction it caused and acting like he was perfectly friendly.

But with me, he shut down.

The change wasn't lost on me. And I was caught between anger and disappointment.

We almost got along. Almost. It would probably help if I wasn't snipping at him or giving in to the urge to snark back all the time. But he made it so easy. He set himself up for those fights, with his "Tiffany" in that husky, reprimanding tone and his constant dismissal of my ideas and his fucking refusal to smile around me.

I'd arrived early again today because Sam wanted to talk more about these changes he wanted to make. The office was open when I arrived, so I made myself comfortable in one of the chairs, a takeaway black coffee cooling in my hands.

"I'm going to change the name," Sam said as he swept into the office.

I sat up straight, surprised. "Wait. Really?"

"You have to admit. It doesn't make much sense. The Basement? We're on the ground floor."

"It is pretty ridiculous."

He blinked at me for a moment until I started to think his brain had stalled and gone offline. "What?"

"No, I'm just … Did you just agree with me about something?"

I rolled my eyes. "Don't get used to it. I still hate you."

"Noted." But there was a crease in the corner of his eye that I decided to absolutely not make anything out of.

"What are you going to change it to?"

"I haven't decided yet."

"'Cooper's Place' too ostentatious?"

His lips flatlined. There, that was more familiar. "I suppose you would prefer 'Tiffany's'?"

"I would, but I'm pretty sure that name's taken."

He said nothing. It was obvious he'd lied about not having a name in mind, but he didn't want to tell me. It angered me. I thought we'd worked past this, but clearly not.

"If there's nothing else, boss, I've got actual work to do." Slamming the door on my way out wasn't nearly as satisfying as I'd hoped it would be.

One step forward, ten steps back.

18

———

SAM

"Of course," the older man shook my hand, "we love Tiff and The Basement. We'd be happy to support you guys."

"Thank you. I appreciate that," I returned the handshake. "I'll come back tomorrow with the paperwork drawn up. We can make things official."

"Good to be doing business with you. 'Bout time the community started supporting each other."

Walking the few feet back to the bar, I tried not to feel disheartened. I'd spent the day canvassing every to-go food place in a two-block radius of the bar. The proposal was this: I'd stock their menus if they agreed to deliver to the bar. It was a win-win: people who ate drank more, and vice versa. The Basement didn't offer food, but we did have to compete with restaurants nearby, and this would allow us to cater to a wider customer base.

The problem was, none of the businesses I'd spoken to wanted to do it. Until now. I'd hoped for more, but I'd take it. It was a start.

Tiffany, of course, hated the idea. "This is meant to be a

serious bar, not a fucking backpackers serving nachos and beer."

I eyed her over the rim of my glasses before returning to my notes. I wanted to prepare the contract today so that I could take it to my lawyer in the morning. "It's good business."

She made a scoffing noise. "We should do something with the ceiling," she said, with seemingly no segue.

With her attention on the ceiling, I stole glances of her across the booth, a habit of mine lately. A knit jumper hung asymmetrical across her chest, exposing one shoulder and most of her collarbone. Shadows dipped into the hollow of her throat. My fingers itched to reach out.

She was sporting a fresh shave, and I idly rubbed at my jaw, wondering how her hair might feel against my skin. How Tiffany might react.

Surreptitiously, I re-adjusted my posture, hoping to relieve the pressure against my dick. "I will be. Now that everything is removed, it will be repainted, and the lights will be replaced with pendants."

The redesign of the back bar was already costing enough since it had to be custom-made pre-installation. Blessedly, the contractor I'd decided on had promised he would handle the city approval for the structural changes. Adding any further alterations to the bar was beyond my current budget.

"Or," and I already disliked where this was headed, "we could keep the downlights and instead commission a mural. How old is this building anyway? We could make it subtle, too, like a trick of the light, where it looks like vintage molding."

There it was again. We. A single word that concocted images of the two of us together.

"Thank you for the suggestion, but considering I am the only one who has successfully launched a bar before, I'll stick to my original plan." In my head, it had been meant as a friendly jibe. Dry. Sarcastic. Unfortunately, my ability to regulate my composure around Tiffany screwed with all normal human functions, so I sounded angry and pedantic.

"Sorry," she said, in a tone that was far from it. "I thought you'd asked me to help. But if you want to make terrible decisions, go ahead." Her stare was intense, lighting my blood on fire.

There was no escaping my growing attraction to her, which worried me. I was here to focus. To get my life back on track. Not sidetrack myself with impetuous decisions.

I had to end this conversation. If she had any idea of my completely unprofessional feelings, she'd probably punch me. And I'd deserve it.

"Is there anything you think that you don't say? Sometimes, you could choose to keep your opinions to yourself."

"Excuse me, did you lose your mind? I was only making a suggestion about the ceiling."

"An unsolicited one."

"Oh, so I guess you don't need my help anymore? Or am I just forgetting the whole 'Tiffany, I need you' conversation we had last week?"

I flushed. *If you only knew.* "I most certainly never said I needed you."

She threw her hands up. "Oh, my God, I don't know why you ever thought we could work together on this. You ask for my help but don't ever want to hear any of my suggestions."

"I hear them. And if they were any good, I'd consider them."

She groaned. "You're impossible!"

"You're quick-tempered and judgmental."

She pushed angrily out of the booth, storming off towards the staff room. "And you're self-important and uptight."

After she'd left, I slumped back in my chair and let the anger go with a long exhale. Instead of any kind of relief, I felt guilt and regret.

The right thing to do would be to apologize. And I wanted to, but Tiffany could likely use some time to cool off, so I focused instead on reviewing the liquor contracts that were up for renewal.

Except, I found myself reading the same paragraph a few times over before understanding that I wasn't getting anywhere. If only she didn't push my buttons so effortlessly, I wouldn't be in this position. If she understood the stakes, would she back off?

Tiffany might be able to treat the consequences flippantly, but I couldn't. This meant too much to me. If it didn't work out, she could get another job, but what would I be left with? A ruined reputation and a lifetime of guilt for choosing work over everything else.

No. I had to make this work.

Being around Tiffany made me feel alive. Wildly present. Daring. The exact opposite of what I needed to be to save my career.

My shoulder twinged painfully a few hours later as I was lifting a box onto a shelf before opening.

The box lurched in my hands, but I regained my hold and pushed through the pain to put it on the shelf. Tiffany unfortunately noticed. "You ok?"

"Yes." It was the curtest I'd been with her, even when we'd been fighting.

She immediately backed off, a hurt look in her eyes.

I felt awful, but I didn't want to explain why it happened.

"I have to finalize next week's schedule," I lied.

"Ok."

I turned and walked back to my office so that I didn't have to see her expression, but the sad turn of her gaze was already burned into my mind.

The last thing I heard before closing the office door was Tiffany asking Devon to finish unpacking the boxes I'd left behind.

Damn. I hated letting the pain get to me. It honestly wasn't even that bad, a dull ache that I'd grown accustomed to.

Pride was the problem.

I needed a distraction. From my shoulder, from Tiffany. From the bar.

Harry picked up just as I was preparing to leave a voicemail. "Sorry! Gracie hasn't eaten in four hours, and Imogen is beside herself." He sounded harried, and I couldn't blame him.

"Do you want me to call back later?"

"No. She's just gone down for a nap, and we're going to try a bottle soon. How are you?"

"Fine." Liar.

"How are you really?"

"Awful. I have half a mind to give up and retire to the countryside."

He barked out a laugh. "You'd hate it before the first day was over."

"True. But at least I wouldn't have to spend another minute thinking about the benefits of matte vs. low sheen paint."

"Riveting." He chuckled.

"Come to think of it; I have a question for you that's been bothering me all week. Is there a reason you would want to keep the inane rubbish that's decorating the ceiling?"

"What?" He asked, then burst out laughing. "Oh, damn, I'd forgotten," more laughter, "about that."

When he finally collected himself, he explained. "I may have told a little white lie. I'd originally put it up on a whim, saw how ridiculous it looked, and went to take it down, but a certain headstrong bartender—"

"How did I know she was going to feature in this?"

"I don't know, dear brother, but you do seem rather attached to her."

"Finish the story."

"Anyway, she told me she was going to take it down and redecorate, so I may have told her that it had sentimental value." I waited for the other shoe to drop. "She might be under the impression that it was mom and dad's old things."

"Harry!"

He only responded by laughing. He really was a shit under that unassuming exterior. "I know I shouldn't have. They would turn in their graves if they knew, but it didn't hurt anyone, and as much of an eyesore as it is, I liked having one part of the place be mine."

I could relate, but it still surprised me. "Damn, Harry. You know she'll kill you if she ever finds out."

"Aww. Is that concern for her or me?"

"No comment." But I couldn't hold out, it seemed. I needed someone to talk about this with. "I know you warned me that she was unrelenting, but I never expected her to get under my skin so badly. I can't decide if I want to scream or …" I couldn't finish that sentence.

"Or?"

"Nothing. Anyway, I'm her boss. All the options available to me are inappropriate."

"Not all of them. You could fire her."

"I'm not going to fire her. She's the biggest asset we have. I know a dozen bartenders out west who would kill to have her mixology skills. Whatever little crush I have," and damn me for using that word, "will just have to be put aside."

He hummed sympathetically. "You sure do have a strange affinity for putting yourself into difficult situations."

"Trust me, I know." I paused. Deciding to change topics to another uncomfortable conversation I needed to have with my brother. "I spoke with Maria Ortega this morning."

"From middle school? She still works there?"

"She's the principal now. I, uh ..." my sentence stalled. This was ridiculous. Harry wouldn't be upset. Would he? "I talked to her about the possibility of sponsoring a literacy program. In mom and dad's names."

"Sam, that's ..." My heart fell when he stopped. He hated the idea. Damn, I should have asked him first. When he spoke again, he sounded as raw as I felt. "I think that's a wonderful idea. They would have loved that."

Suddenly aware that I'd been holding my breath, I breathed deeply, the relief almost palpable. "It's the least I can do."

———

TIFFANY HAD a knack for finding every one of my buttons and charging at them. It was surely the only explanation. Walking out of my office, I found her refilling the cheater bottles.

Placing the menu, newly printed without my knowledge, on the bar before her, I asked, "What is this?"

Sparing a single glance, she continued re-inserting a speed pourer on a bottle of sugar syrup. "A menu."

Outwardly, my expression doesn't change. Inside, I was fuming. "And why is this," I pointed to a new cocktail, one I knew to be a Tiffany original, "listed?"

"Because I made at least a hundred of them last night, and our customers are tired of ordering off menu."

The altered menu stared up at me from the bar. What she'd said was correct. The receipts from last night proved her point, but that didn't mean I had wanted to make the change immediately.

"It's one drink, Sam, not the end of the world. If they stop ordering it, you can take it off the menu again."

My customers, it seemed, were as stubborn as Tiffany. Yes, they had embraced a smaller and less complicated menu overall, but that didn't stop them from always petitioning her for something special.

Since I'd taken to working behind the bar, I'd had a front-row seat.

Most tended to avoid the sickly sweet or overly bitter flavors of traditional drinks. They liked the smooth, the smokey, twists on the classics. I shouldn't have been surprised. Tiffany was talented and passionate. Who wouldn't want to taste what she had to offer?

But giving Tiffany an inch was a risk. Soon, she'd be taking far more than a mile. And likely taking me with her.

Abandoning the bottles in front of her, Tiffany crossed her arms, looking like a warrior preparing for battle. "Since the minute you started, you've not listened to a single one of my suggestions. What does that say about you as a manager? Or do you really think so little of me?"

"That couldn't be further from the truth."

"Then what is it?"

"I …" I was caught. Well, shit. Compromise had to go both ways, and I'd been pushing back on Tiffany since the beginning. Heavy was the ghost of Piper's memory. While I could ostensibly differentiate this as a different situation, letting Tiffany in on business decisions, giving her the opportunity to derail my efforts, made me uneasy.

I was the only one taking a risk here. If the bar failed, it would land solely on my shoulders. Controlling the outcome was easier when I was the only one involved, but by shutting her out, I was wasting a valuable resource. Just like that article had said.

"Next time, ask first," I said, already retreating to my office.

"A simple thank you would be nice."

Her laughter was muted by the closing of my office door.

19

TIFF

Sam had asked me to open the bar that afternoon, saying a meeting had run late. It was … odd, not having him here. I'd expected to enjoy it more since it was the first time since he'd started that he wasn't holed up in his office or hovering behind the bar while Devon and I prepped.

Instead, I felt … unsettled. Like something was missing. Which was ridiculous. Clearly, I was going through some sort of early midlife crisis.

Nathan was busy wiping down stools and tabletops while the rest of the team filled in the ice trays, restocked the glassware, mixed syrups, and jotted down what we needed to restock. Devon took receipt of a delivery, and I felt oddly … bored.

Without Sam here to argue with me, what was there to do?

Pulling out my phone, I restarted a video I found that morning. For weeks, I'd been devouring Youtube's best attempts at cocktail advice. Some were better than others. More often than not, I was cataloging what I'd do differently, and a long list of video ideas had started to bank up.

Maybe I should do this. I definitely could (at least, I knew I had the experience and knowledge). The filming part would be harder, but that couldn't be that hard, right? Surely Jackson would have some tips.

Devon reappeared at my shoulder as the video closed out. "I've seen that one. Have you tried Mr. BarFly? He's funny."

"Not yet, but I'll add it to the list. You ever watch that channel 'ThisCocktailRocks'? Someone made a huge Long Island Iced Tea in a toilet yesterday. Total clickbait."

"That's disgusting."

"I almost puked."

Devon chuckled, and I decided that it wouldn't hurt to know what he thought of my plans. "What would you do if you had something like that?"

"What? A Youtube channel?"

"Yeah. I've been toying with the idea."

"You should do it. If anyone could make it work, it'd be you."

Pure dopamine filled my brain. This was how it always started for me. An idea turned into an itch, which wouldn't be satiated until I acted on it.

But acting on it would mean quitting and leaving all of this behind. Leaving my friends. Ever since I acknowledged that I wanted to move on, this had been the hurdle I'd yet to accept. Leaving would mean adventure and excitement, but I was conflicted. I loved the team here (and dammit, that actually included Sam now). I hadn't ever planned to stay here forever, but that didn't mean I hated every second of it.

Once upon a time, this had been a part-time gig that I'd agreed to because Harry had been so hard up for employees and I'd seen the opportunity to have more autonomy. I'd seen it as a stepping stone, a layover that would connect me to whatever was going to come next as soon as I figured out what that was.

Now, over four years later, I still had no clue. But had I ever really stopped to think about it? I felt torn. I loved this place, the staff, the familiarity, the routine. I liked bartending, and yes, selfishly, I liked the reputation I'd built for myself. I didn't want to start from scratch, but that itch that I'd been feeling wasn't going away. Change had been looming for a while now, and it was not going to let me hold it off any longer. I wasn't really built for settling in. I never had been.

So, what did I do? I'd never wanted to walk away before because I was so fearful that everything would fall apart without me. Which was disgustingly arrogant, I could see. Yes, maybe Harry would have had problems, but Devon and the rest of the team were amazing. They'd figure it out. And now they wouldn't have to. Sam was many things (so many damn things), but the one thing he wasn't was incompetent. He was practically the epitome of a competence kink. If he ever felt out of control, he never showed it, and that wasn't something I could ever claim. Hannah, if she ever had met him, would probably have taken one look and then told me, "see? This is how you are supposed to act."

Devon jolted me out of my thoughts. "Does that mean you'll be leaving us?"

My hands had settled on the familiar wood of the bar top. Nathan could be heard singing along to the latest Jonas Brothers song playing on the overhead speakers.

"Honestly, D. I don't know. Maybe."

Devon had the grace not to look too surprised, but his sad expression punched me right in the heart. "Well, if you do, we'll all miss you."

"You, too, D."

The decision solidified itself within me, clicking into place in the way all the right decisions do.

Now that the *what* was in place, I only had to decide the *when*. Shit was definitely about to get real.

20

SAM

Tiffany took a sip of wine, and a kaleidoscope of emotions, all of some form of disgust, played across her face. "What, and I mean this nicely, in the fuck is that?"

We were seated at Stephen Pierce's wine bar in River North, at his behest. It was unsightly, with supposedly French décor that was a frustrating mix of various European styles (and decades) and waitstaff who were apparently trained in the fine art of snobbery.

It took an immense amount of energy not to roll my eyes at every bit of it. A habit I suspected I was learning from Tiffany.

"A Grenache." *Apparently.*

She placed it as far from her as she could. "It's an abomination, is what it is. That's the most disgusting thing I've put in my mouth, and that's a low fucking bar."

I swallowed a snort, fixing my features into nonchalance. I wouldn't quite have put it in those terms, but I couldn't disagree with the assessment. The wine here was terrible.

So far, all we'd gathered from this visit only served to confirm my suspicions of Stephen Pierce. Clearly, he valued pretension over flavor, so the wine list was littered with organic and exotic styles that he thought would give them a modern edge.

Unfortunately, he didn't have the palette to discern great wine from blended swill, although his customers didn't seem to mind.

Which …

Worried me.

Because these were now potentially my customers.

And while I reluctantly agreed to expand the cocktail list —nothing fancy, despite Tiffany's protests—I didn't want to become the kind of bar where you had to earn six figures to drink there.

"Did you want to try this?" she asked, edging it towards me.

"I'd rather not."

"No? Would you prefer something else? I saw a Pét Nat on the list."

I would rather drink prison wine. "No, thank you, Tiffany."

Slowly, her grin spread, brightening her features into near blinding proportions. It would take a stronger man than me to turn away. Not that I wanted to. Since I'd known her, I'd been drawn in.

"Anytime, Samuel."

"Stop calling me that."

"Would you prefer Sammy?"

I grimaced. "Absolutely not."

"Pity. I can see you as a Sammy."

"I can see you as unemployed."

Her boisterous laugh was out of place among the antique paintings and Gustavia chairs, but it was sunshine for my mood. I was becoming disgustingly addicted to drawing it out of her.

"Come on." I stood, ready to get out of there. "If we leave now, we won't have to speak with him." Stephen Pierce, it seemed, grew more insufferable with every added experience.

"Finally, something we agree on." She quickly followed me out, shrugging her suede jacket back on and pulling her hair out with one hand. It glittered like golden thread in the afternoon light, making her even more beautiful.

I shook off the image before she could catch me staring.

"So, I guess I'll see you at this thing tonight?" she asked.

The "thing" in question was an industry dinner thrown by the local restauranteurs' guide. It was purely a networking event, where owners, promoters, bloggers, marketers, you name it could spruce themselves and make contacts.

In my case, it was my first real opportunity to mingle with the competition and ensure that everyone knew I meant business.

"Sam?" Tiffany was looking at me expectantly. The ring around her eyes flared amber in the light, highlighting the way her pupils dilated.

I really had to get myself sorted out if pupils had started to do it for me.

Clearing my throat, I nodded; short, shaky jerks that felt like an obvious sign of how off-balance I felt. There were at least two hours before dinner. I'd need to pull myself together by then.

———

IN A SHOW OF NON-FAVORITISM, they had crammed all 150 of us into a function room that was semi-connected to one of the oldest restaurants in the city. Of course, said restaurant was owned by one of the attendees, but I decided that commenting on that would be a non-starter.

We made the rounds, greeting as many as we could. I was introduced to far more due to Tiffany's connections, an added bonus of her joining me. Most of the people in the room maintained a certain level of distance, which I determined to be either competitive jealousy or outright dismissal. But a few stood out as welcoming and friendly.

One, in particular, greeted Tiffany joyfully, with a friendly hug and big smile. "Has he accosted you yet?" the statuesque brunette asked, her cut and dry tone the first sign that she was both a close friend and seemingly as enthused to be there as we were.

She stood taller than Tiffany, who had shocked me by not wearing jeans. Not that I had expected her to, but I hadn't realized until tonight that I'd never seen her in anything else. Her hair fell across an exposed shoulder, her delicate frame otherwise draped in a loose, deep rust-colored knitted dress that moved gracefully around her. She was, I noted amusingly, still in her usual pair of flat black boots, looking comfortable and effortlessly beautiful.

My black velvet suit jacket and charcoal shirt now felt like I was trying too hard.

"No, thank God," Tiff replied. "But he's slinking around here somewhere. You know what Pierce is like."

Her friend made an unimpressed face. I was immediately a fan. "Unfortunately." She brightened, turning to face me. "I take it this is the new boss I've been hearing all about?"

I shook her hand. "Sam Cooper."

"Quinn Fisher, nice to meet you."

"The pleasure's all mine. Are you having a good night?"

"As much as I can at these things. Tiff'll tell you; I'm not really great at all this crap. I'd rather be home. Or working."

"Well, I'm glad you decided to join us tonight, at least so I could have the pleasure of meeting you."

"Alright. Looker and a charmer, huh? As long as you aren't a prick, we should get on fine."

"Trust me, he's not like the rest," Tiffany said, her tone unreadable. I couldn't determine whether that was a compliment or not, but it appeared the best I would get from Tiffany, and her friend seemed pleased, so I let it be.

"It was good to meet you, Sam. I better finish doing the rounds so I can get out of here. Good luck with this lot." Quinn waved her hand at the room.

I watched her continue through the crowd and asked Tiffany, "Old friend?"

A waiter passed with an empty tray, and she scowled before answering. "Quinn? Oh, yeah. Does it surprise you to know that I have friends?" she teased.

She chuckled at the flat look I gave her in lieu of a response.

"Oh, come on. Not even a smile? You're always such a tough crowd, Cooper." Her attention wavered when another waiter passed by without stopping. "You should know that not everyone is like Pierce and his buddies. Quinn's one of the good ones."

"Do they really hold that much sway here?"

"They don't have their fingers in every pie, but they do make it pretty much impossible to go up against them without them swinging their influence around, which usually ends up just hurting everyone. Pissing them off isn't a good business idea, no matter how good it feels."

"Hmm."

"What?" She abandoned her search for a waiter, now focusing intently on me. "That's your, I'm silently judging you 'hmm'."

"I have a judging 'hmm'?"

"Honey, you have many." Honey was new. I didn't hate it.

I felt a grin peek through, and she looked pleased with herself. "So, what is it?" she asked.

I returned my attention to the room, taking in the very white, very male crowd. And feeling my own contribution acutely. "There is an unfortunately disproportionate demographic here."

She barked out a laugh. "Oh, yeah. Total Mr. Banks situation."

My mind sifted through the possibilities, merging what I knew to be Tiffany's unique brand of audacious humor with the people in the room. Then it occurred to me. "Are you really referencing Mary Poppins to describe ... this?"

"You can't tell me those old dudes that run the bank aren't an exact replica of this room."

I wasn't quite quick enough to stifle my laugh before it escaped, and the surprise that showed across Tiffany's features was immediate. And then, she smiled. Soft. Genuine. Like I'd given her a gift.

A hint of blush graced her cheeks, a dusty rose color that could be seen touching the high planes of her cheekbones, sharply curved to fit perfectly in a palm. My own face heated.

I was about to retort with an unprecedented quip of agreement when the very man we'd managed to avoid earlier made his way over to us, his navy suit having just enough weight to be expensive if cut a little too closely for a proper fit.

"Mr. Cooper! I thought that was you." He shook my hand, ignoring Tiffany at my side. I couldn't see her expression, but I felt her silently seething.

Pierce dropped a heavy hand to my shoulder, and I tightened my smile so that I wouldn't grimace. "It seems I missed you this afternoon. How did you like my place?" For someone who'd spent a lot of time calling me out in public, he was awfully friendly. *Pretentious dick.*

I brushed imaginary dust off of my lapel, hoping the movement would encourage him to remove his hand, and was grateful when it did. "Yes, my apologies. We needed to make a quick exit to make it here on time." I was stalling, wanting to be polite about my opinion of his bar, but not lie outright. "I was impressed. It's very richly appointed." Impressed was a stretch, but it had the desired effect on Pierce. "It's clear that you had a very specific vision for it and must have had a hand in every detail. It's no wonder you're considered so highly." I knew that boosting his ego would defer from the fact that I hadn't technically praised any part of the business in any way.

"Absolutely. It was a passion project. I adore France, even if I could do without the French. Fantastic wines, though. I'm glad you had the chance to see a booming business. Quite a bit different than what you're used to, I'm sure."

He wasn't wrong there, but I suspected he meant it in a wholly different way. "Yes, very."

He leaned in then, either ignorant that Tiffany was still there or not caring. "I wouldn't normally do this," I could imagine that wasn't true at all, "but I have a lot of contacts in this town, and if you're in the market for a new head bartender, I can send you some names. Good ones."

In my periphery, I saw Tiffany's jaw drop, a mirror image of my own reaction, if I had allowed myself to react physically to his completely disgusting suggestion. I spoke before she could. No doubt she could take of herself—and in a far more entertaining way than I would--but I wasn't in a position to burn bridges here, so my absolute hatred of Stephen Pierce and everything he stood for would have to wait.

"That won't be necessary, Mr. Pierce. I'm sure you're aware that I currently have the most awarded bar staff in the city working for me."

Pierce only grinned wider, his snide expression in keeping with his personality. "How about you think about it. Give me a call when you're sick of playing babysitter to the misfits."

My blood boiled. I didn't need to burn this bridge to let him know I wasn't going to tolerate his attitude. "I think you'd be better off if you spent more time worrying about your own business than mine, Stephen. Didn't you recently have to close one of your restaurants because of low sales? Or maybe it was the accusations of abuse from your staff. I forget."

"I can see she added another notch to her bedpost, then. You two suit each other."

"How about you go fuck yourself, Steve." Tiffany spat from beside me, and I had to shove my hands into my suit pockets to stop myself from punching him. I couldn't even remember the last fight I'd been in. Middle school, probably.

"Delightful as always, Tiffany." Pierce sneered, then nodded to me. "Cooper. Think about what I said." He thankfully walked away.

I wanted to congratulate Tiffany for so quickly disposing of him, or at the very least for saying what I wished I could, but I wasn't sure how either would be received, so I simply settled for a mumbled, "What an ass."

Her snort turned into a groan. "I'm not drunk enough to deal with this."

I flagged down a waiter as he passed, took two glasses, and, with a hefty tip slid into his palm, instructed him to bring us the bottle as soon as he could.

Tiffany wasn't the only one too sober right now.

It was only when the bottle was half-drunk that I asked the question I'd wondered all evening.

"Why haven't you ever learned to play nice with them?"

She carded a hand through her hair, the satin strands gliding softly through her fingers. "I think you'll find I don't give a shit. But I'm surprised they aren't kissing your boots."

I frowned. "It seems my reputation proceeds me."

"Which is exactly why they should be more fucking respectful."

"I imagine they're hoping I'll go back to where I came from."

"Aren't you originally from here, though?"

I was surprised she knew that, not that it was a secret. It was easy information to come by, but that would mean that she'd done her research on me. It pleased me to imagine it.

"Anyway, fuck 'em," she said, delightfully succinct, as

always. "They should be glad that you're the one who has to deal with me. God knows most of them wouldn't hire me if I was a free agent."

What a disgusting thought. That someone of Tiffany's talent and caliber would have a hard time getting work elsewhere for no other reason than the idiocy of the Pierce and the apparent cowardice of everyone else there.

"They would be lucky to have you, and they know it. You're worth more than all of them put together."

She blinked, speechless, and I was all too aware of the short distance between us. This was dangerous territory I was treading, but oh, it was the most alive I'd felt since I'd come home.

____

21

TIFF

Now that the bar was closed for half the week, I had more opportunities to see my best friend, which was good because there was a very pressing matter I absolutely needed to tell someone before I imploded.

"I think I want to fuck Sam."

Audrey spluttered on her coffee, taking a minute to cough and right herself on my couch as she placed her mug down and wiped at her skirt before setting her shocked gaze on me. "Want to try that again when I don't have a lung full of caffeine?"

I nodded. "Oh, and I'm quitting. But it's the other thing that's got me hot and bothered."

"Okay. Those are two very different topics. How about we start with the job first."

"I'm quitting."

"Yes, you said that. When did you decide?"

"For certain? A few days ago. But I've pretty much been thinking about it for weeks now."

"Are you sure?"

"Without a shadow of a doubt. Honestly, I should have done it a while ago, but I got comfortable."

"That's not a bad thing."

"No, I know. But I haven't been challenged in a while, and now that Sam's taken all the experimental drinks off the menu, I'm getting bored. Well, bored by the drinks, anyway." Being around Sam had become anything but boring.

"Okay. This is where you explain to me the other thing."

"Wanting to fuck Sam," I said, watching Audrey nod with wide eyes and a shocked grin.

I groaned, "He's just so … and then, like … Ugh! And he'll look at me with those beautiful eyes and smile in that sweet crooked way of his, and it's like fireworks and warm laundry and my mama's best cooking all at once."

"Damn."

"I know." My head thunked against the back of the couch. What I needed right now was pie. "Hold that thought. I made dessert earlier. Come on."

"I wondered what smelled so good."

Skipping over plates in favor of two forks, Audrey and I dug into my Mimi's family pecan pie recipe (she always made it with an extra shot of bourbon). It was my ultimate comfort food. Even though it was only mama's side of the family that came from Texas, and I'd been born and raised right here in Illinois, it tasted like memories, family, and home; and I made it as often as I could justify (and sometimes when I couldn't).

"Are you going to miss the bar?"

"Absolutely, are you kidding? But the idea's there now, and you know how I get with an idea."

"Relentless."

"Exactly." I groaned in pleasure as the sweet nuttiness of the pie filled my mouth. Cinnamon was the second best thing in my life, next to coffee.

"I wish I could make decisions as easy as you do. Do you ever second guess anything?"

"Not often. How would I know if something was a bad decision if I didn't take the chance?"

Audrey shook her head, amused. "So, what's next?"

"Tell Sam, obviously. Then … I've been thinking about that video idea Jackson mentioned."

"Really? Wow. I don't know much about it, but will you be okay for money in the meantime?"

"Oh, yeah, I'm not too worried about that. There's some savings, and if I need to, I'll get a side gig. No matter what that dickhead Steve thinks, there are bars here that would kill to have me. Even Sam said—" and I stop, remembering how firm he'd been last night about my worth.

My worth.

I hadn't heard anyone talk about me in those terms since I was five years old.

"Oh? What did Sam say?" Audrey asked, eyes sparkling and an undisguised emphasis on Sam's name in that tone that reminded me of high school all over again.

"That they would be lucky to have me."

She hummed, smile wide. "Maybe they aren't the only ones thinking they'd be lucky to *have* you?"

And yes, that thought had occurred to me, too.

"You used to be so innocent."

"What do you expect? After years of listening to your exploits," she said before taking a bite, humming around the taste. "You really like him." It was a statement.

"I'm not sure I'm going to be able to work with him like this. It's distracting." Which was a massive understatement at best. He had this way of inflecting his tone in ways that buried the words themselves under my skin until my thoughts became a running commentary of *SamSamSam*.

"I bet," she chuckled. "I thought you hated him."

"Fuck, it would be so much easier if I did."

This was all Sam's fault.

· · ·

SAM and his irritating kindness the night he found me drinking by myself at the bar.

Sam and his defense of me last night at the dinner and to King Asshole himself, Stephen Pierce, no less.

Sam and his unfairly lovely eyes and kissable mouth that fought with me and said nice things and teased smiles and … Goddammit. I felt my body responding to the thought of those lips. Of shutting him up with my own.

"So, what changed?" Audrey asked.

Where did I start? We still fought, but somewhere along the line, it had become charged with something electric. Something physical.

And maybe it had always been there, simmering beneath all my frustration, or maybe it was a recent thing, but did it really matter? I knew what I wanted now, and I was going to have a tough time either way.

"I've seen a different side of him recently. He's not as terrible as I first thought."

Indecision had never been my thing. Ever. Mama had always said I talked quick and acted quicker. I'd rather deal with the consequences of a bad decision than wallow in the misery of not choosing.

"Do you think he's interested?" Audrey asked.

"Who knows. He's coiled tighter than a spring. I just wanna …"

"What?" she asked, curious.

"Make him fall apart. Give in to him. I can't decide."

"You've given this some thought then."

"I have. It's ridiculous. I know it is. And if it were anyone else, I would just tell myself to deal with it and move the hell on. But he's …" I waved my hands in the air, coming up short. "I don't even know what he is, but it's intense and distracting. And sometimes I get the feeling that he wants it, too? I couldn't sleep last night because all I kept thinking about was the way he looked at me at dinner and how he said I was worth more than everyone else put together."

"He said that?" There's awe in her voice.

"Exactly! What kind of an asshole says something like that after weeks of constantly disagreeing with me and telling me how wrong I am about the bar? This," I point to nothing in particular, "is why us working together is a terrible idea."

"One nice comment can't erase that. No matter how nice his ass is." She said.

"It is a really great ass, though." What I wouldn't give to get my hands on it, so pert, so perfect.

"It's a good thing you're quitting. The way you're talking about him, I'd be worried about a harassment claim." She squawked when I swatted her arm with my fork. "When will you hand in your notice?"

"No time like the present."

———

EVERY STEP towards the bar steeled my resolve. The facts were simple: even if this was just a weird horny crush, it was time to move on from the bar and start the next chapter of my life.

No doubt he'd be glad to see me go. Sam and I had never worked particularly well together, and whatever changes he made to the bar were just that—his changes. To his bar.

To stay would mean giving up my creative freedom to fit his vision of the bar and stifling my instincts just to be what someone else wanted me to be, which went against my every molecule.

And if he really still needed help understanding the scene here (which I honestly doubted, I mean, I'd seen him be polite to Stephen jackoff Pierce. If he wanted to, he could charm the panties off every person in town. He hardly needed my help there).

So, if he still wanted my help, then I would stand by my word and help him.

I just couldn't work under him anymore.

If he wanted me under him in any other capacity. Well …

That could easily be arranged.

So, yes. By the time I was at the bar, up the stairs, knocking on his apartment door, I was resolved. Resolute. Convinced.

I would quit.

Whether he liked it or not.

He opened the door, looking like he was about to step out, wrapped up to shield himself from the strong wind chill that had swept through town this morning.

"Tiffany. This is a surprise."

Damn those ethereal silver eyes and plush cupid's bow and clipped beard. Damn him in that thick woolen coat and scarf, looking like he stepped out of a damn catalog. I bet he even smelled amazing, the bastard.

He didn't even have the guts to look smug anymore. These days when he smiled, it was too genuine. Jesus, I wanted to hate him for making me feel this way.

I never thought I'd want Harry back, but fuck. At least I never wanted to screw Harry.

Pushing past him, I walked into his apartment, unable to bear the weight of his gaze any longer. "We need to talk."

I would have laughed if I wasn't so keyed up. The first time in my life that I utter that phrase, and it's to a boss who made me so mad I couldn't decide whether I wanted to throw a drink in his face or tie him down and ride him until he forgot his own damn name.

Both. Either. All of the above.

Fuck.

"Ok. Please come inside." I could hear the dry humor in his voice. That uniquely Sam way of telling a joke that I'd always taken as cold disdain.

Hell, it could still be. I was so hopped up on horniness I wasn't thinking straight.

A loud meow startled me, and within seconds, I saw a black and white cat slink around the corner to sit at Sam's feet. Another loud meow was aimed at him.

Sam leaned down to scratch behind her ears. "Hello, Luna." I'm too stunned to think much of anything. Sam had a cat?

When he straightened, there was another loud meow, the cat clearly unsatisfied.

Sam used the same tone I often found directed at me. "Luna, you've already been fed."

Then, I found her attentions redirected towards me, as if only now noticing my presence. After a sweep past my legs, she came to a stop by my feet.

I leaned down to scratch at the soft fur of her neck, surprised at her pliant nature. Sam wasn't saying anything (which, ok, wasn't unusual for him), but he was oddly still. Without pausing in my attention to the cat, I looked up. There was an odd look on his face.

"What? I can't pet your cat?"

A small shake of his head seemed to free his strange expression. "Sorry. She's just not usually friendly."

I snorted. "Gets that from you, I 'spose."

This earned me an uptick in his mouth. I was getting better at coaxing humor out of him.

Just as he corralled her out of the room, I could have sworn I heard him whisper "traitor" in the cat's direction.

He then turned back to me, his coat and scarf removed and neatly tucked over the back of a chair. "So, care to tell me what this is about?"

22

SAM

She stood in my kitchen, as real and imposing as ever. Her cheeks were flushed from the chill outside, and I imagined a heat beneath the skin, that ever-present fire that I'd come to associate with all things Tiffany.

I barely knew what to expect from her words or her sudden appearance at my door.

There was a sense of purpose, not uncommon for her, but one tinged with something heated, something …

I stopped myself. Best to see what this was before I ran off half-cocked.

"Drink?" I asked, aware of the spark in the air between us. It was different tonight. Intoxicating. I'd been avoiding it for weeks now, although not very well. My only consolation was that she hadn't appeared to have noticed my struggle or shown any returned interest—something I was now beginning to question.

Hell.

I crossed over to the bar and poured us both a measure of whiskey.

I'd barely finished pouring when she spoke. "Sam."

Turning, I discovered she'd moved closer, now only an arm's length away. Much closer than I had been expecting.

When she licked her lips, I fought to maintain eye contact. Her arms crossed over her chest. "I can't work for you anymore."

I abandoned the drinks, facing her. "What? Why?"

"It's just time for me to move on. Does it matter?"

"Yes, it matters."

"I thought you'd be happy. It's not like we get along."

Yes. For a very valid, very inappropriate reason that was entirely my own fault. "I'm your boss. We're not meant to get along."

"Well, that's just bullshit."

"You know what I mean." If she did, I'd be surprised. Because I was talking out of my ass, trying futilely to salvage this without having to disclose the exact reason I'd been keeping my distance from her.

"No. I don't. Why are you fighting me on this? It's not really your decision, anyway. I don't want to work for you anymore."

"Is this because I didn't like your ideas about the menu?"

"No, it's not." She stood firm, her hands on her hips. Immovable. No. More like a predator in wait, an undeniable tension present. Or maybe I was hoping. I kept expecting her to lash out, get angry, but as I watched her, all I could see was indecision. As the seconds ticked by, her focus never swayed, making me itchy with anticipation.

And then, it ended. Whatever she observed in me eventually made her shake her head, and the previous tension I felt slipped away. "You know what? Sure. That's exactly what it is. I can't deal with you taking over the bar—"

"My bar,"

"—and I need to leave before I," she stopped abruptly. Her eyes slipped down to my lips, and my breath caught in my throat.

"Before you what?" It came out rougher than I'd intended, and I realized, rather belatedly, that we had inched closer together.

I couldn't let this happen. No matter how much I thought about it.

Clearing my throat, I turned back to the bar cart, eager to put some distance between us.

I gulped down a large amount of whiskey and was glad when my voice returned somewhat to normal. "Last night, you told me that no one would hire you if you quit."

"Actually, I believe I said none of those assholes would hire me, but I have a lot of friends. I'll be able to find something."

"I thought we'd moved past this."

A firm hold on my elbow spun me around until I faced her. "Jesus, Sam. Why are you trying so hard to change my mind? When we first met, you hated me."

"I didn't hate you."

That earned me a stern eyebrow raise.

"Fine. I may have harbored some unsavory feelings towards you."

"Oh, my god." She groaned. "Would it help if I said I hated you?"

"Do you?"

"I ..." She huffed. "No. Don't distract me. You haven't answered my question. Why do you care so much that I want to leave?"

"I ..." Oh, god, it was catching. I tried to think about it. Despite her professional expertise, which I would be justified in not wanting to lose, there were a hundred ways that life would be made easier if she wasn't working for me anymore.

And yet, the idea of her leaving bothered me.

After months of a slow decline, she was a rush of adrenaline to my life.

"Sam?" she asked when I still hadn't answered her.

She stepped closer. My gaze caught on her mouth, and I

shivered when she licked her lips before they curled into a knowing smile.

Damn, she knew what she was doing to me.

"Sam." Another step. Body heat rolled off of her, warming up the parts of me she was nearest to.

I stepped back. Felt the rustle of the bar cart as I brushed against it. I couldn't go any farther. "We can't."

I really needed to get myself together.

With a steadying breath, I began to walk away, putting some distance between us. Distance was good. Necessary.

She followed me into the living room, hot on my heels.

"That's it? Jesus, do you even hear yourself?"

I stopped mid-stride. She had a point. If I could get my head out of this haze for one minute, I would be able to see this from her perspective.

"Sam! Are you just going to ignore me now?"

I turned to face her, enamored by how radiant she was, despite, or maybe in spite of, her anger. Lust coiled around my spine, growing deep in my gut, and for once, I felt dangerously close to giving in.

I'd been holding back before, unwilling to cross that boundary, and unsure of her reaction. But from the way she was holding my gaze now, I was almost certain she wanted the same thing I did.

And dammit, it made it impossible not to give it to her.

I've been drawn to her since the moment we met. It's a terrible idea, but … what was the risk here? Tiffany had quit. In short time, she'd leave the bar, and me, behind, and this would be forgotten.

Her features twisted in frustration, hands now clenched at her sides. "Fuck, you're so frustrating! With your calm. And your reason. And your gorgeous eyes. I mean, what's up with them anyhow? Are they gray, are they green, are they blue? Who fucking knows?"

Fire erupted through me. One I'd grown accustomed to

whenever she was around. This time I took a step forward, getting in her face.

"I'm frustrating? Do you know how completely and utterly infuriating you can be? You're smart, talented, easily the most beautiful woman I've ever met … You could be doing anything. But you seem to get a kick out of making me want to tear my hair out at every possible turn."

Our eyes were locked on each other. Then, a slow smirk warmed her face. "You're kind of hot when you're angry." She stepped forward to meet me.

"Tiffany." A warning. For her or me, I couldn't be sure.

And then, I reached up, my hand neatly fitting in the curve of her elegant neck, just as I knew it would. Or maybe I was finally following her natural gravity, pulling me in until our lips collided.

It was glorious.

She kissed the way she talked. Fast, hot, passionate. We grappled with each other, teeth bumping, tongues clashing, hands gripping. She smelled like cinnamon and tasted like dessert. Felt like fire under my skin.

My senses caught up to me, and just as quickly as it began, I ended it, pulling back. Our breaths mingled between us, short and sharp. My heart was racing. "Wait. We can't do this. Not while you work for me."

"Good. Because I quit." She dived in for another kiss, but I stopped her.

"That's not funny."

"I'm not trying to be funny."

"I'm not going to let you quit."

She was unimpressed. "You're not going to let me?"

I dropped my hands from her body. "No, wait. That's … that came out wrong. I don't want you to quit." I sighed. "I won't deny that you're a very attractive woman, Tiffany, and maybe in different circumstances, we could explore whatever this is."

"We should just get it out of our system, you know? We barely even like each other, so you don't have to worry about me catching feelings."

I said nothing, torn.

"Look, I'm quitting whether you sleep with me or not. I'm just asking you if you want to."

My body was already reacting to the idea, my dick half hard in my pants, and I was desperately trying not to let it call the shots here. Apart from her quitting, this was everything I'd been trying not to think about. Trying not to want.

And it was being offered to me.

I needed to think logically about this while I still had the northward blood flow to do so. "You can't just leave. I'll need time to replace you. You'll need to train someone new."

"Ok. I'll stay as long as it takes to find a suitable replacement."

"And, where I can, I'll help you find work."

"Thanks, oh gracious one, but I don't believe I asked you for help. I'm perfectly capable of getting work."

"Ok. Good."

She curled one hand into my shirt. "Are you done?"

I was already chasing her lips. "Yes."

Her hand curled into my hair, her nails scratching my scalp with just a hint of pressure. It sent a lightning burst of pleasure down my spine. My hands gravitated to her waist, gripping, holding her body against mine, her pert breasts crushed between us. She felt amazing. I desperately wanted to slowly map out every inch of her skin with my mouth and hands, but this was only going to be a one-time thing, and right now, slow was not possible. I needed her now. Wrapping my hands around her back, I finally got to bury my fingers into that thick blonde hair that had been taunting me and cradled her head as I deepened the kiss.

Our breaths tangled in the small space between us.

Every kiss was a jostle for control, a relay race of desire.

"Don't think this means I'll change my mind on the menu," she said as I pressed hot kisses along her jaw.

"Doesn't matter. You don't work for me anymore, remember?"

"And this doesn't mean I like you."

I pulled back. "We don't have to do this, you know."

The hunger in her eyes was undeniable. "Shut up and kiss me, Cooper."

Damn, she was bossy. I loved it.

Knowing that this powerful woman wanted me as much as I wanted her fueled my arousal, making my entire body buzz with anticipation.

23

———

TIFF

Sam kissed down my neck, one hand curled into my hair. My hands finally got a hold of his ass, and good lord, it was just as fucking fantastic as I'd thought it would be. Fucking him might be a really bad idea, but it was also the best bad idea I'd ever had.

With a firm grip on his chin, I pulled him back to lick into his mouth, and I was thrilled at the moan he let out. Oh, shit. He liked that. I moaned back, gripping him tighter. Every single response he gave was driving me wild. Who the hell was this guy? Had this been hiding underneath that tight, controlled exterior this whole time?

Fuck, I wanted to ruin him.

Pleasure throbbed between my thighs when his fingers wrapped around my wrist, pulling it free of his chin with a surprising amount of strength. *Yes.* God, he was pushing every single one of my buttons right now, and I could feel myself getting wetter.

And when he held my wrist at my side, then squeezed like a command … like he wanted to test the boundaries of power and play between us. *Fuck.* I almost climbed him like a tree and finished myself off right then and there.

His hands were strong around my waist and quick to slip under my shirt to grip underneath. They worked their way up and around, touching my ribs and back, pushing my top upwards as a side effect of his hurried exploration of my skin.

Tearing one hand away from him, I reached down and pulled my top the rest of the way off. He barely paused, making quick work of removing my bra, his hands eagerly exploring as our mouths met again. I was already unbuttoning my jeans when he started on his shirt. Before he lifted it, I reached out to still his hand, wanting to take control. Wanting to see how he would react.

Once he let go of his shirt, I spied the couch behind him and started moving us towards it with a sly grin. He let me walk him backward, a smile playing on his lips, which I leaned in to taste. Damn, his lips were addicting. I would never again be able to look at them without wanting to nibble on them.

When his knees hit the couch, I gave a playful shove and watched as he fell back, still clothed, lips parted, pupils blown wide.

I made quick work of removing my pants until I stood bare before him.

Now naked, I shivered, a mix of the cool air against my skin and the rush of desire coursing through me. It only heightened as Sam's gaze raked over me slowly, hungrily, and my body reacted as if he was touching me, my nipples coming to attention. I knew the exact moment he noticed, too, as a low moan emanated from him while his fingers gripped his thighs. And *oh*, I spied a very hard cock straining those pants. Even confined, it looked long and thick, and I licked my lips at the image.

Fuck, this was so much hotter than I'd imagined.

"Are you sure?" he asked, as exasperating as ever.

One hand on my hip, I gestured to my state of undress with the other. "What about this isn't clear to you, Sam?"

His signature smirk curled into place. "You don't have to be rude about it." *That smug son a …*

"Sam!"

I growled low in frustration at his responding chuckle, but it turned into a strangled moan when he reached for me, pulling me into his lap and pushing his tongue into my mouth with a surety that left no question about what he wanted.

Any question that he wasn't interested was blown away between the conviction with which he's assaulting my lips and the hard line of his cock pressed up against me. Needy, I ground harder against him, both of us groaning in pleasure as the material roughly teased the sensitive parts of my pussy, delicious in its promise of what was to come.

Every nerve ending was on fire, from my nipples to my clit, and I was drunk on his reactions. Every hot breath, every moan, every aborted thrust fed my own, making me want him more. And we'd barely even started.

Although I'd hoped (and suspected) that he wanted me as much as I wanted him, feeling him hot and hard and frenzied beneath me was a relief. No part of him was passive in his assault—all of him as hungry for me as I was for him.

God, his fucking jeans were not making things easy. Maybe we should be naked. Why had I stopped him from getting naked? Goddammit I just needed it a little bit harder.

Even grinding down onto him, it was impossible to get what I needed, but it was so damn hard to pull away. Every sound that spilled from his lips, every desperate touch of his hands, kept me magnetized to him.

We clawed at each other, lips and teeth and bodies colliding over and over. It felt like every fight we'd had, each of us unwilling to back down and neither of us willing to give ground, and it was hotter than anything I'd experienced before.

Fuck.

Sam's hands were everywhere, my face, my breasts, my

thighs, my ass. Feeling and searching and kneading in this dizzying pattern that made me feel like a fucking teenager again. If this was all that happened tonight, if he put a stop to this now and I got dressed and went home, it would still be the most incredible connection I'd had with someone in … maybe ever.

With a firm grip on my ass, Sam lurched forward and up, and I immediately wondered if he was gonna call it. That his right mind had reappeared (I had no idea *how* since I was barely more than a bundle of shot nerves and adrenaline at this point), and he was going to hand me my clothes and send me on my way.

And, fuck, that would be disappointing, but I wouldn't push him, even if I already knew there was no way I was going to forget the taste of him.

But no.

I stepped out of his lap as he stood, but he didn't let me get far, his hands cupping my face as he devoured the sounds I made. Then, he tilted my chin and dipped to nip at my neck (Goddammit, his lips should be illegal). I was too distracted to realize that he was walking me backward, pressing his advantage and taking control.

I moaned, loud and indecent, when I realized.

A fine sweat had broken out over me, doing nothing to cool the fire that was raging underneath, so when the cold glass of his window met the line of my back, I jumped.

He laughed (laughed!) into my mouth, capturing my surprised gasp with his lips and pressing against me.

I could barely believe this was the same man I'd been fighting with for weeks. That stoic façade was hiding some seriously hot primal energy, and fuck, I couldn't get enough.

At the same time, we both zeroed in on his clothes, our hands tangling as we rushed to get them off. It would probably be easier if we stopped kissing, but neither of us seemed willing to do that.

His lips were as maddening as they'd ever been, and I devoured his groan when I bit down on his plush bottom lip.

"Wait," he breathed between kisses, "I need ..."

Cold air assaulted me when he stepped back. "Protection." He seemed only capable of single words.

"In my jeans," I said, nodding towards them. It had seemed presumptuous when I'd left my apartment, but all I could think now was—*Thank fuck for presumptuousness.*

When he returned, sans clothes and condom in hand, he surprised me by spinning me around until I faced the street. The lack of streetlights and the late hour meant little chance of being caught, but the thrill of it still sent a shudder through me.

I could imagine the view we would paint if anyone were to look, and although I was no stranger to exhibitionism, it was a damn surprise that Sam was into it. He was just *full* of surprises.

"Okay?" he rasped in my ear, and I arched into him as he softly stroked my straining nipples.

"Yes," I breathed in response.

He nuzzled into my neck, sucking a mark into the sensitive spot just under my ear and humming his enjoyment as I showed him how much I wanted him by grinding my ass against his cock.

I leaned my forehead against the glass and watched our breath crash against the window. Sweat was beading on my forehead and under my palms, and I felt an errant drop making a path down my back.

He caught it with his thumb, rubbing it into my heated skin before pulling my hips back, making me take a half step backward and rest my head on my hands as I rebalanced myself.

That same hand traced a path around my waist, following the curve of my hip until it was between my legs. I knew he could feel how wet I was, how willing.

"Sam." I sounded wrecked.

"I know." There was humor in his voice, and I hated that I couldn't see his face in the reflection of the glass, too foggy from my ragged breaths to make anything out behind me.

His feet nudged my legs wider, and I eagerly complied, rocking my pelvis back and trying to beckon him closer (Seriously! Just fuck me already).

"Sam," I pleaded, insistent.

His answer was wordless, simply lining his dick up and slowly pushing in, not stopping until he was buried to the hilt.

Fuck. Yes.

I'd always been more of a switch in bed, happily sharing control depending on the scene or what my partner needed at the time. And although most of my partners had sided one way or the other (leaning more towards dominant or submissive, even if they didn't use those terms to describe it); it was rare (as in never) that I'd had a partner who enjoyed both the way I did. And with Sam's hands searing a brand on my hips as his thick cock stretched and filled me, just moments after he'd been a desperate mess beneath me on the couch … I realized I wanted that.

I wanted an equal, someone to give when I took, to take when I gave.

Demanding. Relenting. Balanced.

"Fuck."

"Agreed," he said, and if I weren't so turned on, I would have rolled my eyes at him.

"I hope you plan on moving sometime soon." The window was hot and slick under my forehead now, and I wondered how much pressure it would take to break it. *Hopefully more than it's about to take.*

"So bossy," came his low, rough reply.

Any response I had was lost as he started to thrust, steady and deep.

It was good, so fucking good, but I needed more.

With a whine, I used the leverage I had, pushing against the glass and back into him, to meet his every thrust, taking pride in every grunt it pulled from him.

One hand reached around to cup my breast, gently squeezing before moving upwards. For a split second, I worried he was about to reach for my throat, and I kicked myself for not having had the whole "what gets you off" chat, which I usually tried to make time for before fucking someone for the first time. But instead, he pressed against my collarbone, guiding me upright, changing the angle deliciously, and pulling a wanton moan from deep within me.

Now that he was plastered along my back, I twisted my head towards him, angling for a kiss, our mouths meeting in a clash of teeth. Keeping one hand on the glass, I reached back, curling my hand into his short hair and gripping it, holding his lips to mine as I arched into his next thrust.

My back was on fire where his skin met mine, and all I could think was more, please, *yes, more.*

There wasn't much leverage to move, but that didn't stop him, and he held me steady against himself as he picked up the pace, his other hand dipping between my thighs to tease my clit, and damn, I was floating. Nothing had felt better than this.

Stars burst behind my eyes, and I fell forward against the glass, my forehead smearing sweat against the cool surface. I was about to vibrate right out of my damn skin. "Do it, Sam. Take what you need." Reaching for him, I guided one of his hands into my hair. "You can pull if you want."

I felt his fingers separate as he combed along the base of my scalp, caressing the roots before closing his grip. "Yes," I moaned, immediately impressed. He'd done this before.

"Yes. Just like that. Fuck." I was rewarded with a moan, his hips pumping into me faster now. "Harder, Sam. Please."

Bracing myself against the glass, I reached down to rub my clit, and fuck, I was so close already, on edge from Sam's lips and Sam's hands and Sam's fucking incredible ability to use his dick like it was his fucking job.

All I could hear was Sam's punched-out little "Oh's" and the harsh slap of his skin against mine. His fingers gripped my hips so tightly I was sure there would be bruising there tomorrow, and I couldn't wait to run my fingers over them as I remembered tonight.

My body shook when my orgasm finally crashed through me, and Sam let out a raw moan as I clenched around him, slamming into me hot and hard before I felt him jolt and come inside me.

As the sounds of our panting breaths filled the air, his hand slipped out of my hair to stroke down my side, making me sigh. Those damn hands were magical. There was no way I would be able to look at them without remembering how good they felt on me. Without wanting them to worship me.

I had no idea what was holding either of us up since my legs felt like jelly and the glass was slick with sweat under my palm. When he pulled out, I stayed a moment against the glass, eyes closed as my heart beat wildly in my chest.

I was grateful when he helped me stand with a strong hand. Finally getting a better look at his naked body, I was impressed. He was lean, firm, and sexy as all hell.

"Well," I said as he discarded the condom. His face had gone back to his usual collected expression, but his fringe was matted against his forehead, and there was a flush cascading down his neck and chest, so I knew he was affected. I smirked. "You weren't half bad."

And finally (finally!) I got to see that damn chuckle in full effect. It was like a double shot of electricity, straight to my system. "Same to you."

And, for a second, I could see him question what had just happened, and no. Just no. Before he could start getting into his head about it, I stepped up and kissed him slow and deeply before slipping back into my clothes. "Glad you finally accepted my resignation. See you tomorrow, boss."

"That's not funny." Yep. There was that tone I knew and loved.

My laughter reverberated in the stairwell as I made my way out.

24

———

SAM

Well. That was certainly unexpected.

And maybe a little bit of her impetuousness was catching because I knew I shouldn't be thinking of sleeping with Tiffany again, but I honestly couldn't stop. The dam had broken, and I felt my self-preservation fading against the memory of last night and the possibility of more.

And, well. It was hardly going to turn into anything more, was it?

Which was for the best. After Piper, I'd like to believe I'd learned my lesson about falling before thinking.

There'd be little chance of that here. As alluring as Tiffany was, it didn't distract from how utterly incompatible we were. We could barely get through a conversation without disagreeing.

No. As Tiffany had said herself, there was no chance of "catching feelings." Prior to last night, I had wondered whether all I would need to rid myself of my preoccupation with her was to satisfy that urge, allowing sense to return.

The opposite had been true.

Now that I'd had a taste, I most definitely found myself more occupied than ever.

But first things first. It seemed I had a head bartender to replace.

Utilizing the new coffee machine in the bar, a fine addition, I had to admit, I was on my second espresso before moving to the office to start making calls.

Whatever time zone Jordan was currently in didn't stop him from answering, and it reminded me of a time, long ago, when we had the opportunity to talk more regularly. But between his business ventures and my own, conversations were few and far between. It was a shame.

"Bit early for you, isn't it?" he said as he answered.

"Since when have we had regular hours?"

"True, true. What's going on? Is this a friendly chat?"

"Yes and no. My head bartender quit last night, and I was hoping you'd have some names to pass on. I have some people to call on the West Coast but wanted to see who you knew over here that might be a good fit."

"Of course. I'll send you some options. Sorry to hear that, though. From what I've heard, she was quite the talent." Ah, seemed he'd been checking up. "It's always hard to lose the good ones. What were her reasons? Do you think the rest of the staff will follow?" Damn. I hoped not.

"Ah, no. No." Get it together. "She was clear that she needed to make a move." In more ways than one. "The staff definitely respects her, but I don't think they'll walk out once she's left."

"Once?"

"I've asked her to stay on until I can find a replacement."

"Good idea. Makes for a smoother transition." There was something there. Something in his voice. "And how do you feel about her leaving?" There it was.

"It's not the most convenient timing, but I'm happy." Dammit.

"Happy?" He chuckled.

"I meant, I'm ..." Think.

Even though I couldn't see him, there was no mistaking his smile now. "I think I might need to move up my plans to see you. I can't remember the last time I heard you tongue-tied."

"Don't read into it."

"Oh, I will, my friend. I've known you for too long."

"Yes, well."

My next step was to call Devon and Tiffany into the bar early. After Jordan's comments, I was determined to head off any staff discord early.

The fact that it also meant seeing Tiffany again was not a factor.

It wasn't.

When they arrived, I had to bite back a laugh. Tiffany had her hair in a rather complicated top bun braid style that completely exposed her neck, as well as the dark mark I'd left on her from last night.

Of course.

Any concerns I'd had that she might regret last night were obliterated, and honestly, I should have known better than to even contemplate it. This was Tiffany Young, resident firecracker, heavyweight bickering champion. She hadn't done anything less than completely project herself in every interaction we'd had, so why should this be any different.

Devon handled the news well, and I was extremely pleased when he said he had no plans to go anywhere. Thank god. He might not have the same flair as Tiffany, but he was an incredibly hard worker. I held him back, ignoring Tiffany's sly wink as she left the office to start bar prep.

While Devon and I spoke, the sound system came to life beyond the door. It was always clearer to hear in the hour before opening when the bar was empty. As the lyrics filtered through, I made out the words, "Take me from behind" and "Make the glasses shake." I was glad that I was out of view, heat rippling through my body. No chance of Tiffany being subtle about this, then.

I refocused on the conversation at hand. "If you're interested in a promotion, now is the time to let me know."

"While I appreciate the offer, Mr. Cooper, mixing isn't something I'm planning on pursuing."

His phrasing interested me. "How about the bar manager position?"

"Isn't that something you're currently doing?"

"It is. But it was never going to be a long-term arrangement, and I'd like to focus more on the refurbishment and expansion." Among other things. "You're more than capable, and from what I've witnessed, already doing the work. If you want it, it's yours."

"I'd like the think it over."

"Of course."

"I also know someone perfect for the bar, too."

"Oh?"

"Yeah, my sister Jade. She's maybe not gotten as many awards as Tiffany—"

"Few have."

"But she's incredible. Has a real mind for flavors and combinations, and she can mix anything you ask her to."

"And you're not a little biased?"

"I am. But that doesn't mean what I've said isn't true."

"Ok. Have her send me her resume, and I'll take a look."

"Thanks, boss."

———

AFTER CLOSING, I made a concerted effort not to be in a rush for everyone to leave. I wasn't so much hiding in my office. I was reviewing paperwork. I was handling important business things.

I re-read the same paragraph four times before I gave up.

The office door closed with a click. The bar was quiet

beyond it, and from the way Tiffany very openly leered at me, I assumed everyone had finally gone home.

"We should probably talk first."

"Really? That's what you want to do right now?"

My expression still, I raised an eyebrow, daring her to disagree.

"Fine. You might be." She trailed the last word into a mumble.

"Sorry, what was that?"

"You might be right."

"I wasn't even aware you knew that word."

"Don't push it."

I allowed myself a laugh then, glad that last night hadn't resulted in Tiffany acting any different around me. "You should probably sit."

She eyed the chair on the other side of the desk. "I think you're right." What she didn't do was sit in said chair. Instead, she walked around and sat on the desk before me. I shifted my chair back in the minimal amount of space available to me.

"So, what did you want to talk about?" She looked far too pleased with herself.

Talking. Right. I'd wanted that.

Why had I wanted that?

"We need to establish some boundaries."

"Ok." I'd expected her to fight me. Huh.

"No sex during work hours. We maintain a professional relationship around the rest of the staff."

"Ok. What else?" When I paused, not entirely sure, she elaborated. "Likes? Dislikes? I should have asked last night, but, uh, I wasn't really expecting to be pounced on."

My skin flushed. "I hardly pounced."

Her smile grew lascivious. "Oh, no. I liked it. A lot. I just didn't know you had it in you."

It was growing harder to have this conversation without touching her.

Harder still when she toed off her shoes and placed a foot on my chair in the space between my legs. Not yet touching, but there. Waiting.

"I'll go first," she said. "I don't mind it rough, hair pulling, biting, but no choking. Spanking's good. Any markings, really." She touched the spot behind her ear. "I should probably warn you that I get pretty loud when I'm enjoying myself. Talk a lot, sometimes. Though, that shouldn't be surprising."

When had these pants gotten so tight? I adjusted in the chair, but the friction only made it harder to ignore.

It wasn't that I was unadventurous when it came to sex, but to have it laid out, so openly, so plainly, like we were discussing the weather. Well.

I tried to ignore my growing interest in favor of actually talking.

"I, uh, like talking. From other people." Damn, why was this so hard? I'd had this talk with exes before. I cleared my throat. "I like it a little rough, too, but I won't hurt you. Or degrade. Praise is good, and uh," I rubbed my palms on my thighs, "bondage. That's, um, I'd be into that."

Her bottom lip was caught between her teeth as she nodded slowly, her eyes raking over my body, pausing for a lengthy moment at my crotch, which absolutely preened under the attention.

"Interesting," she said, sliding her foot the last few inches until it brushed against me. "There's a lot I think we agree on. We'll have to swap lists sometime."

I held back a moan. Coherent thought was getting more difficult.

"Are you familiar with traffic lights?" she asked.

"I am."

"Good. How do you feel about submission?"

"Yours or mine?"

"That," she said, her smile widening, "is the right

question." She pulled her foot back, letting it hang over the desk with a swing. "I enjoy both, but I don't expect you to do anything you're uncomfortable with."

My blood was singing in my veins now. This woman was a gift. "Both is good."

I stood, the strain against my dick intensifying, and stepped forward. Tiffany's legs spread wider to accommodate me between them, and she leaned back onto her elbows, smiling like she'd won something.

"Take your shirt off." There was no mistaking her command.

"Are you asking or telling me?"

"Asking." She trailed her eyes over my body, and I felt it as surely as any physical touch. "Firmly."

I pulled my shirt over my head, tossing it back onto the chair behind me.

"Pants, now."

One button undone, I stopped. "What about you?"

"I'm enjoying the show." She then proved this by shifting her weight onto one arm and snaking a hand into her jeans, maintaining eye contact the whole time.

It might have been the hottest image I'd ever seen.

But that didn't mean I wasn't going to have some fun with it.

I fished a condom out of my wallet and placed it on the desk beside her, then reached for the zip of her jeans. "Let me help with that."

She chuckled, pulling her hand out slowly and licking her fingers. She hummed to herself at the taste before resettling to watch me. I groaned, my eyes fluttering closed, and I dropped a hand to palm my erection. She knew exactly how to drive me out of my mind.

After removing her pants and underwear, I got to work on

my own but was barely out of them when Tiffany sprung forward, gripping my hips and driving me forward with force. I managed to catch myself on the desk, her legs wrapping around my waist, her hands sliding up my back as she arched into me.

Taking advantage of the proximity, I assaulted her mouth with mine, nipping and licking while she moaned beneath me. It had barely been twenty-four hours since the last time I'd tasted her, and I couldn't get enough.

When we separated to breathe, I quickly found the condom and took care of that before diving back in to kiss her. She used her mouth like a goddamn weapon, as creative with her tongue as with her words. I wanted her so badly. It was quickly overriding every other thought I had.

Likely erasing something while it was at it.

Goodbye, middle school geometry. Replaced by the hot, sweet taste of Tiffany.

Her heels dug into my back, pulling me forward, and I followed eagerly, reaching down to line myself up before easing into her with a rough breath. Then I needed a moment to take it all in. This—she—felt incredible.

So much more than the tight heat around me was the image of her laid out on my desk, eyes blazing with the same fire I'd seen many times in this office. Dammit, what a sight.

She moaned. "Fuck. You feel so good." Then, with a wink, she rolled her hips and squeezed, and all the blood left my brain. I leaned down, hungrily sucking a bruise into the hollow of her neck, a spot I'd wanted to get my mouth on for weeks now.

"Fuck, Sam. I've been thinking about you all damn day."

Smiling against her skin, I continued to mouth along her neck as my hands snuck under her shirt, breathing a laugh against her skin as she writhed beneath me. "Sam. Move." I didn't, enjoying the thrill of having her at my mercy, dragging my hands up her body at a maddeningly slow pace.

"Sam." Her feet locked around me tighter, her heat clenching around me until I needed to close my eyes and count to ten just to pull myself together.

"Patience."

I continued to explore her body. Finally getting to appreciate her body the way I'd wanted to last night. She was a goddess. Beautiful, powerful, passionate. And here she was, pleading me to move. Wanting me. It was enough to do me in.

I was aching and desperate for more, and I was *already inside her.*

Danger had nothing on this woman. She was a menace on every conceivable level.

Slowly, I continued to guide her shirt off, taking a moment to brush a thumb over the tattoo on her bicep, the fine lines of the constellation delicate against her pale skin. Beautiful. When the material bunched around her wrists, I held it in place like a cuff, meeting her eyes. "Color?"

"Definitely green." Tiffany licked her lips, smiling wickedly. "That what you want, Sam?" she breathed. "Do you want my hands bound? Do you like that?" She twisted her wrists, wrapping the shirt tighter around her hands. She held her arms above her head, her fingers laced together in an approximation of being bound.

My dick throbbed at the sight. "Yes."

"Good."

Suddenly, the dynamic shifted, and I felt more like the prey, even as I stood over her, buried inside her.

"You look so good like this." Her feet caressed the backs of my thighs, teasing. "Are you going to give me what I want, Sam? Are you going to fuck me into this desk until I come? Can you do that for me?"

As if on cue, I bucked into her, and any thought of going slow was obliterated by her command. It'd be a miracle if I lasted at this rate.

She continued, goading me. This was the Tiffany I was

used to. The one who had stormed into my office, my home, my … pants. Shit. "I bet you've pictured this before. I bet you've gotten yourself off to this. Haven't you?"

I nodded, completely under her spell, my sole purpose narrowed down to the push of my hips to hers.

"Yes, Sam. That's good. Keep fucking me."

And I wasn't about to disappoint her. Hooking my hands underneath her hips, I altered the angle, getting a reaction immediately.

"Yes, yes, yes. Right there, Sam. Fuck. Harder." She managed between gasps.

My pulse was jumping in my throat, pulsing hard and strong. Keeping my hands on her hips, I started to move, faster and deeper, watching as she gripped the edge of the desk and cried out.

Suddenly, her knee jerked, a quick, startled movement as she called out, "Ah! Yellow." Immediately, I slowed down, releasing my grip on her hip to stroke the muscles. She chuckled, the intensity of the previous moment distilled while she stretched her leg out. "Cramp," she explained, still smiling up at me. "Either that or you hit something you shouldn't have."

She surprised a laugh out of me, loosening the tightness of my chest and spreading a different kind of joy through me. Only Tiffany. Jesus. What a revelation.

Not able to help myself, I leaned down to steal a kiss, swiping my tongue across her lips and deepening the kiss when they parted so easily for me. It would be so easy to get lost in those lips, in the terrifying way she set my entire body alight.

So easy to lose myself in her completely.

Pulling back, I softly kneaded her thigh. "Better?" I asked, happy when she nodded.

"Now, if you wouldn't mind." Once again, she rolled her

hips, pushing a groan out of me. "I believe I asked you to fuck me into this desk."

A huff of a laugh escaped me, the side effect of the giddiness I was feeling. Has sex ever been this all-encompassing before? Stupid question. *Definitely not.*

"Sam." Her gaze was laser-focused. Powerful. "Fuck me."

Damn, that about did me in. It wasn't only the act of her commanding me that I was getting off to, but the power of her and this explicit expression of it. There was no doubt in my mind who was fucking who right now.

The slap of our bodies colliding intensified as I redoubled my efforts, hooking my arms under her legs to change the angle, make it sharper, deeper.

"Fuck, Sam. Yes!" Then, she was coming, clenching, tightening around me as she screamed my name.

It was all I needed to throw myself over the edge, coming inside of her, while her hand released her shirt, throwing it aside to caress my chest, where I felt my heart thrashing loudly.

I barely had enough energy to throw away the condom and pull my pants back on before I slumped back into my chair, trying to catch my breath. Out of habit, I rolled my shoulder, but there was only the same dull ache there always was.

Tiffany sat up on the desk, pulling her shirt back on. It was creased beyond recognition and did nothing to conceal the new marks blooming on her throat, but she didn't seem to mind. "You, Sam Cooper, really are a surprise."

"Is that praise I hear?" I asked.

"Don't get used to it."

"I would never." I located my shirt on the floor and pulled it back on. "What do you think you'll do next?"

She shrugged. "I haven't decided yet. I've been approached by a few people, even a couple of bars in New

York, but I'd need to know it was worth the move. I did get asked to write a book."

"You're a writer?" What couldn't she do?

"Like a cocktail recipe book."

"Because there's not enough of those."

Tiffany playfully kicked my shin. "Fuck you."

"I think you just did."

She arched a brow with playful surprise. "Wow, another joke. I'm starting to think I don't know you at all." She stood, pulling her jeans on before running her fingers along the design cut into her shave. "It's late. I better get home. This was fun."

"Goodnight, Tiffany."

"Night, Sam."

25

———

TIFF

It was a fairly innocuous Thursday night when Jackson's friend and co-star Wesley showed up at the bar. He'd been dropping by for months now, whenever he felt like it, occasionally flirting with strangers, but mostly just there to drink and annoy me.

He was harmless, though, and I could tell from the way his expression turned blank sometimes that he was holding back some pain, covering it up with that aloof bad boy attitude.

Too bad my bullshit meter was finely tuned.

"Oh, look, it's you," I said wryly, placing his usual beer in front of him.

"Hey! It's my favorite bartender."

"How's it going, Wes?"

"How do you think?" He smirked, holding the beer to his lips, trying (and failing) to be seductive. I'm sure it worked for some women (ok, I'd seen it work on plenty of women), but cocky little shits just weren't my type.

Not to mention, he had an almost permanent case of sad puppy eyes, and I'd learned a long time ago I didn't want to "save" anyone.

"You really want to know what I think?"

He gave me a noncommittal shrug, but there was a hesitation in his eyes. I decided to take it a little easy on him. "I think you come here so you can forget about someone, but no matter how much you drink or joke or flirt, you're only delaying the hurt."

The façade drained away from his face, and he drowned half of his beer in one move, dropping it back onto the bar with a thud. "Well, fuck, Tiff."

"Everything alright here?" Sam asked, suddenly appearing at my side. Obviously, he'd overheard Wes' comment, but I couldn't pick if it was Wes or me who he'd come over to check on.

Wes' usual smile sprang back so fast that I got whiplash. Guess it paid to be an actor. "Oh, yeah, just having fun with my best gal."

Sam looked between us. "You two know each other?"

"Unfortunately," I deadpanned.

"Ok. Sorry. I'll leave you to it then." Sam took another customer's order farther down the bar, leaving us alone again.

Wes nodded towards him. "He's cute."

I kept myself from looking over at Sam. "He's a pain in my ass. Just like you."

Wes' canines showed when he smiled knowingly. "You don't look like you mind it that much."

"We're …" How to phrase it? We were technically non-friends with benefits (ex-coworkers with benefits?), but we had agreed to keep things professional when working, and I didn't need any of the barbacks overhearing me. "None of your goddamn business."

He winked, the little shit. "Mum's the word."

I huffed a laugh, despite myself. "Shut up and drink your beer, mopey. Now, did you want to talk about it, or are you just here to get on my nerves?"

"Nah, it'll just bore you."

I dropped the sarcasm and placed a reassuring hand on his forearm. "Try me."

I watched him chew on this for a moment, probably deciding how honest to be with me. He reminded me a lot of my brothers. It was probably why I could see through the fake bravado so well.

Avoiding my eye, he picked at a corner of the beer label. "Have you ever had someone get you in a way that no one else does? But not even just that, it's like …" he took another swig of beer, "like they accept you, even though they see how fucked up you are? Like, the real you, even the parts you don't like about yourself?"

Wow. Color me surprised. Puppy dog here had some depth. "Goddamn, Wes. Way to lay it on me."

He gave another half-hearted shrug, looking like he regretted saying anything. God, from the look of him, I was probably the first person he'd ever said this to.

Fucking dammit. I was starting to like the little shit. I decided to repay his honesty with my own. "I'll tell you a little secret. If we're talking romantic shit, I've never once had what you're talking about. That unconditional acceptance?" I shook my head. "But if I did? I'd do whatever I could to keep it. As should you."

He was silent as he finished his beer, but there was a small nod of appreciation. Later, when he left, I realized he hadn't flirted with a single person all night.

"Wait, I thought they were family heirlooms?" I asked Sam when we were upstairs in his apartment for a post-closing drink. Luna was purring quietly beside me on the couch while Sam sat on my other side.

"Is that what Harry told you?"

Sam's smirk taunted me, and the realization hit. "That

little shit." My gut clenched at the warm sound of Sam's laughter. I ignored it. "Well, score one for Harry."

"He needed some way to stop you from taking over completely."

Ouch. Guess I deserved that.

"He picked it all up from a garage sale in his neighborhood."

"I never thought he had it in him. I might actually like him now."

"High praise. I'll have to let him know." He leaned in for a kiss, and I turned my head, letting his lips hit my cheek instead.

"I can't believe he got one over on me. I mean it, I'm impressed."

Sam ignored me, guiding my chin back with a strong hand and slipping his tongue into my mouth. I fell into the kiss, enjoying the way his (now regrowing) beard brushed against my skin; the bristle contrasted with the soft, plush pressure of his mouth.

I pulled back. "You know you can't just kiss me to shut me up."

"Can't I?" His voice was a soft, low a rumble. Like he was sharing a secret with you. I'd seen the way people would lean in close, pulled by gravity to him. I was (to my horror) not as immune as I'd like to be.

It was only afterward, when we were lying tangled in his bed (and thank god we were upstairs this time because my back was getting sick of hard flat surfaces) that I brought up the scar on his left shoulder.

I'd noticed it the last time we'd fucked but hadn't said anything, and I'd seen the way he rolled it occasionally or massaged the joint when he thought no one was paying attention.

"What's with the shoulder?" Because tact was not

something I had mastered. And frankly, tact was hard to come by when I was post-orgasmic.

To be fair, he'd hidden it well enough. When I'd started, I hadn't noticed it at all. But lately, I'd become all too aware of him. And now that I had a decent sample size to go off, I'd realized that when we had sex, he always preferred positions that didn't put pressure on it, which had lent itself to creativity (something I've always been a fan of).

If he could have moved it out of view, I was sure he would have. Tonight must be the night I accidentally asked invasive questions. I was going two for two. Eventually, he took my hand, turning my palm inward so he could kiss it. I wondered if he didn't like to talk about it, and I was about to change the subject when he answered.

"It's an unfortunate side effect from a car accident I was in a year ago."

"Shit. What happened?"

"It was a minor thing. No one's fault. A woman swerved to miss hitting a child that wandered into the street and hit me instead. There was minimal damage to the cars, and no one got hurt, thankfully, but the impact messed up my shoulder enough that I'll feel it for the rest of my life. At the end of the day, it was the best case scenario."

"Best case would have been no accident." I relented at his judging look. "But, yes, considering the circumstances, it's the least that could have happened. How much does it hurt?"

"It's manageable."

I groaned because if I knew anything about Sam by now (and it was a short list, to be fair), it was that he would always defer his own needs or concerns when asked.

He was stubborn like that. It reminded me of me.

I stroked the healed streak of raised scarring above his pec, white skin cutting through the otherwise clean chest. "Is this from the accident?"

"No." I was surprised when he laughed. "That was a

renovation gone wrong. A box fell from a rack, and a wayward nail scraped me on the way down. It's not very sexy."

"Hmm." I ran my finger over it, then leaned down and followed it with my tongue, kissing it reverently, noticing how his fingers buried themselves into my hair, holding me to him. My lips curled against his skin as I lowered myself to his perfectly prim nipple. "I think it's very sexy."

26

———

TIFF

I wasn't one to play by the rules most of the time. Rules were usually just arbitrary lines people drew to play it safe or whatever, and I just didn't want to waste any of my life acting for the sake of pleasing people.

Sam, I'd thought, would be a stickler for the rules (and he certainly had a hard-on for setting them). Especially ones he'd specifically set. The same rules I was abiding by (and that alone deserved a gold star, frankly).

So color me surprised when he asked me into his office one afternoon before opening and said, with utter hunger in his eyes, "Lock the door."

We had a full team on shift, meaning there were people outside. People he had expressly told me he didn't want to know about this little tête-à-tête we had going on.

But, fuck me, if I wasn't immediately turned on by this turn of events. That didn't mean I was going to fight fair, though. I leaned against the closed door, crossing my arms. "And if I don't?"

• • •

"THEN YOU'LL JUST HAVE to stop anyone from coming in. And make sure they don't hear you." He stalked over to me and sank to his knees.

Fuck.

Yes.

My hands instinctively slid into his hair, the dark strands fine silk between my fingers, before he reached up and removed them, placing them against the cool surface of the door, with a silent command to leave them there.

It was going to be like that, then. A wave of anticipation flowed through me.

Each button of my jeans was undone slowly, neither of us speaking. My hands flexed against the wood, itching to reach for him.

Patience was not a virtue I'd ever been comfortable with.

Competition, however. Competition could make me very patient indeed.

I just needed to hold out longer than he did.

Which wasn't easy. Especially when he dragged my jeans and underwear only as far as he needed to get what he wanted, slowly taking me apart with long confident swipes of his tongue.

There wasn't enough room for him to get too deep, but that didn't stop him. My jeans dug into my thighs; the material taut as I rocked into his mouth.

My breathing was ragged, my whole body shaking with the strain to keep still, keep quiet. My mouth was clapped shut, even if I was screaming inside my mind.

All I could hear was the indecent sounds of his lips, slick against my skin. Wetness coated the inside of my thighs, and I imagined his face was a mess.

When he snuck a couple of fingers into me, my eyes snapped down to meet his. He looked fucking smug, but, goddamn, had he earned it. My control was hanging on by a thread, and he knew it.

The wood felt rough against my fingers as they scraped against the door, and as I felt myself nearing my peak, my hand reached out for him. When I remembered not to touch, I rushed to slam it back against the door, too far gone to care about the sound. He pushed me over the edge, and I bucked against him, my blood pounding in my ears as I climaxed.

It took a few shaky moments before I came back to my senses, my heart beating high in my chest, rapping solidly against my collarbone.

Soon, my knees buckled, but I didn't sink down, held in place by my jeans and Sam. I was weak all over, completely wrecked by the mind-blowing orgasm I'd just had.

There was a sheen of sweat along my brow, cooling in the afterglow. My head sagged back against the door, and I turned to find a cool purchase on the wood.

Sam rocked back on his heels and tugged my pants back up. I could see the hard line of his cock straining against his pants, felt it press against me when he stood and kissed me with the same slow strokes of his tongue that he had used to great effect before. Tasting myself on him, I finally succumbed to the need to moan into his mouth, the first sound I'd made in minutes.

Finally recovering the ability to move, I traced the shape of him, but he reached for me, taking my wrist lightly in hand, a gleam in his eyes. "Break's over," he said before opening the door.

That. Absolute. Bastard.

The memory of what we'd done played in my mind for the rest of the night, reshaping my image of Sam as the stick in the mud, repressive suit into something compelling. Had I been too quick to judge him in the beginning?

The idea that there was more there called out to me like a moth to a flame. It was probably a good idea to not dig too deep, keep it casual and not get too close.

Too bad I never really liked doing what I "should."

27

———

SAM

It should have been a one-time thing. Two, at most. Three, at a maximum.

The problem was, we couldn't keep our hands off each other.

It had become increasingly difficult to stop noticing little things about her. The way she would hum to the music playing, a sway in her hips, her foot tapping out of time to the beat.

How she would set herself away from the others when she needed to think, creating a quiet little bubble around herself, but would never scowl if she was interrupted, always lighting up any time she talked to the staff.

Tiffany had begun to pop into my head at inconvenient times. I'd find myself staging pre-emptive arguments in the shower, imagining the fire in her eyes as she'd bicker back, those perfectly pink lips and sharp tongue teasing me in more ways than one.

I'd retort verbally or physically, and she'd respond in kind.

Considering the number of times I'd conducted this little routine in the last week, I wouldn't be surprised if I got a repetitive strain injury in my wrist.

Despite my growing distractions, the plans for the refurbishment were moving ahead nicely. Tiffany's previous comments about the liquor display had resolved me to go ahead with that plan, although I'd revised the copper to brass, which would match the warm beige that was planned for the remaining walls.

It wasn't going to be the easiest job. I didn't want to touch the front and under bar areas, mostly because I'd learned that the building was slab on grade, so any changes to the utilities would be costly (and largely impossible without major reconstruction).

But the back bar was simple enough. The shelving design needed to be pre-fabbed, then installed, but thankfully I'd been given the name of one of the top contractors in the city, and they'd promised me to meet my tight deadline.

Changes to the main room were easier. Removing the booths was a cosmetic job, so if the fabrication of the back bar needed to be delayed, I'd be able to manage that part separately, and the bar would only need to close temporarily for a few days to paint everything.

"Sounds good, Sam," Harry said from his perch on a barstool. It was mid-morning, long before anyone else was due to arrive, and he'd surprised me with a visit. "I thought it was about time I checked in on my little brother."

"So far, so good. I still plan on replacing the bar tables, probably something in a dark stain, and there's a few other plans I have going. But enough about the bar, how are you? How are Imogen and Gracie?"

"They're both amazing. It's incredible watching Imogen with her. She's a natural at all this parenting stuff, whereas I feel like a bumbling moron half the time."

"I'm sure it's more than that." I ducked when he swatted at me.

"I can't remember the last time I slept for more than four hours. But I can't describe how rewarding it is." He proceeded to show me a few hundred photos of Gracie, from sleeping to laughing to playing. I'd never seen him as tired or as happy. It was a good look for him.

"I meant to ask you if you've smoothed things over with Pierce yet. Those comments he made about you being kicked out of Vegas were a real fantasy."

I groaned. Pierce was the perpetual thorn in my side. "It's clear he's trying to make it me versus him, but I'm not going to play that game."

"Good."

"He came out the other day saying that 'businesses live and die because of the fortitude of their directors, not because of sensationalism and gimmicks', which is the most hypocritical thing I've ever heard." I ran a hand through my hair. "But other than that, the press we're getting is much more positive, especially since business has picked up, and everyone's really liked the changes." I smirked, "Mostly."

"How are things with Tiffany?" Harry asked while I was still smiling at a photo of Gracie in an "I love my mommy" onesie. He was trying for casual, but he failed. Miserably.

"Fine."

His laugh told me he knew otherwise. I'd never been able to get anything by him. "Tell me you didn't."

I felt the need to play innocent when I was anything but. "I don't know what you're talking about."

"You did! You slept with her." I prepared myself for the inevitable lecture. "I thought you said it wasn't going to be a concern."

"I know what I said."

"So, you were lying to yourself? Or just me?" He sat back in the chair, arms crossed, but I could tell he was more amused than upset.

"It's not anywhere near the same as with Piper."

"Yes, because this time you're her boss."

"Not technically. She quit." It was a poor excuse. I wasn't proud of myself for using it.

He laughed, disbelieving. "Oh, in that case, everything's fine."

I ran a hand over my beard. He was right, as much as I hated to admit it. This was a bad idea, and yet even hearing Harry echo that fact didn't change how much I wanted her. That alone should have stopped me from pursuing it further.

"Are you sure you want to be doing this? You and Piper only just broke up a few months ago. I know you're hurting, but—"

"I am. I was. I loved Piper. Am I sad that it worked out the way it did? Yes. Do I want to repeat that? Definitely not. But it's not the same."

"Just be careful, Sam."

"I am being careful. I know what I'm doing, and I promise you, even if I were about to settle down again, Tiffany would be the last person I'd do it with." I'd meant to say it, but as I heard the words back, they felt cruel. I didn't see much of a future with Tiffany—hadn't ever considered it, to be honest, and who knew how she felt about it—but the truth was, we barely knew each other outside of work and sex. We were only having fun.

And after the last six months, hadn't I earned a little bit of that?

"Of course, you have," Harry said when I asked him the same. "Just don't expect me to stop worrying about you."

"I know you far too well ever to expect that," I joked.

The front door opened. "Hey, are we still—" Tiffany paused, smiling when she saw who I was talking to. "Harry. Long time, no see."

He stood when she reached him, and they shared a half hug before she took up the seat next to him. "It's good to see you, Tiffany. I hope you haven't been too hard on my brother here."

I cleared my throat in warning, but of course, neither of them paid me any attention. Apparently, now that they had something in common—namely, me—they were content to get along better than they had previously.

Her eyes flickered to mine briefly. "I'm only as hard as I need to be."

He coughed out a startled laugh, which only caused her smile to widen. "That might be too much information for me."

"What brings you into the city? Are you checking up on him?"

I might as well have been invisible.

"Something like that. Imogen has taken Gracie to a mother's group, so I had some time on my hands."

"Can I see?" she asked, expecting him to have the requisite thousand proud father photos on his phone, which he proceeded to show her.

"She's gorgeous," she said, handing the phone back before joking, "Pity she has your nose."

"God, I know. I'm hoping she grows out of it. Or into it."

Tiffany appraised him. "You look good. Happier. Fatherhood agrees with you."

"Thank you. It was a long time coming, so we're happy. Even if we're constantly worried that we'll screw it up somehow."

"I'm sorry that I didn't know sooner."

"I don't know why. There isn't anything you could have done. Unless you're secretly an IVF specialist? Not that that would surprise me."

She chuckled, then relaxed. "What is it about you two," she gestured between Harry and me, "secretly hoarding your senses of humor? All this time, I thought you were a grump."

"I guess I didn't feel all that funny when I worked here."

She looked chastised. "It probably helps not to be dealing with me all the time either."

"I think Sam is handling you enough for the two of us."

I delighted in the blush that graced her cheeks.

"Did he show you his plans for the back wall? It's amazing."

Something about hearing her praise always surprised me. Not because I didn't believe her capable of it, but having it directed at me was unexpected.

"He did, although I'm used to him impressing me."

"I'm sure. It's no surprise he was named the one to watch by Timeout last year."

She knew about that? Pride flooded me. Harry shot me a look that I promptly ignored.

"Yes, it'll be good to see him freshen this place up and not have to share the accolades this time around."

Damn it, Harry.

Tiffany threw me a confused look. "I think I'm missing something."

"Nothing important." I cut in before Harry could open his big mouth again.

However, my effort was in vain. "Ask him about Piper sometime." I loved my brother, and I didn't throw this word around lightly, but fucking hell, Harry.

Tiffany looked shrewdly between us, weighing up her options. Then, after a beat, she said, "I think I'm going to leave that one alone. If Sam wanted to tell me, he would have."

And I knew my brother enough to see that he was impressed by that. As was I.

He pocketed his phone, standing. "I better get back home, but it's good to see you both again."

The air was thick after he'd left, and I could tell that Tiffany wanted to ask, but she didn't, and it was appreciated. Piper was a mistake that I had difficulty discussing even with my brother, and though I trusted her not to judge me—and when the hell had that happened?—now was neither the time nor the place.

"You know I was thinking," Tiffany started, interrupting the silence that had gone on a little too long, "about your sours idea. With some interesting pre-made infusions, you could turn something simple into something more exciting."

It wasn't that it was a bad idea. If I'd thought about it, I would have realized that there was something there.

But Harry's comment had left me on edge. Piper was still haunting my mind, memories of her helping me plan my first bar a ghost over the conversations I'd had with Tiffany. Was I doomed to keep making the same mistakes with different women?

His insinuation that I could be walking the same path now nagged at the back of my mind. It might be one thing to indulge in a physical relationship, but I couldn't let Tiffany get too close. It would never lead to anything good.

"I'm not planning any further changes to the menu."

I ignored it when I felt her eyes on me and heard the softness in her tone like she was treating me with kid gloves. "Sure, I mean, it's your bar."

"Exactly," I said, feeling like an ass.

Her words imprinted on my mind. *Your bar.* It was a sentiment I'd pushed many times before, and yet it was starting to sound less like a good thing and more like a dictatorship.

Just because I wanted to protect myself didn't mean I needed to be an ass about it.

When Tiffany turned to leave, I reached out, my fingers grazing her forearm. "Wait. I'm sorry."

"No, I am." There was genuine concern there, and I recognized the same regret she'd shown when she spoke to Harry. "You can just let me know when I'm overstepping, you know. I know I have a loud opinion, but I don't expect that you'll always like it or agree with me. You can just tell me."

Immediately, the guilt clawing at me grew, making me feel even worse. She wasn't even wrong about the damn sours, and now I found myself stuck having to choose between my pride and what I knew to be the better choice.

If I weren't plagued by the same errors in judgment that had brought me back here, I would have explained myself, but Piper was a sore subject. Tiffany didn't need to know the extent of my stupidity. Let her keep the small sliver of respect I'd manage to earn from her in recent weeks.

Not trusting my words, I smiled, but it felt false.

"Guess I'll get to work on prep unless there was something else you wanted to do?" Tiffany asked, a glimmer in her eyes.

I considered it, but my past felt too close to the surface. It wouldn't take much to uncover it, and Tiffany was all too talented at getting under my skin. Allowing her to see me like that was a step too far. A boundary I wasn't ready to cross.

"Maybe later."

I closed the office door behind me as I entered, wondering why it felt cold and all too quiet.

28

TIFF

"Ok. Who are you and what have you done with my friend?" Audrey said with a yawn as soon as she opened her door. We had been spending Saturday mornings together for the last few years, but usually, it was Audrey standing at my door with two coffees in hand, and not (to our mutual surprise) the other way around.

Until today.

What could I say? That I'd been having such incredible sex lately that I found myself waking up excited to start every day?

Yeah, even I thought it was ridiculous.

"It's too early in the morning for jokes. Now, is pretty boy decent, or do I need to walk in blindfolded?"

"Jackson has a shoot this weekend, so he's already gone." She ushered me inside with another long yawn. It didn't take a genius to guess what had kept her up last night. Strange, I was sleeping better than ever lately.

"Damn. Remind me never to become an actor."

"What are you doing here anyway? I thought I was coming to yours? Not that you're not welcome, but ..." She took a sip of the coffee I offered her. "You're right; it's too early."

"Late night with the fiancé?"

As expected, she blushed. "Something like that."

"Yeah, okay, let's get going before I fall asleep."

———

I ALREADY REGRETTED THIS.

By our third florist, I was so over hearing the words "floral journey" and "special day" that I was about ready to scream, but I wasn't here for me (thank fuck), and Auds really did deserve the best, so I bit my tongue and didn't throw the very perky girl speaking to us into her display of peonies, even if I really, really, wanted to.

"Please tell me that was our last stop," I asked Audrey as we walked out.

"You're lucky. I have at least three more to see this afternoon, but Sarah's going to meet me there."

I said a silent thank you. Sarah, Audrey's future sister-in-law, just got bumped up to lifesaver status in my eyes. I'd met her a handful of times in the last year and a bit that Audrey and Jackson had been together, and I was glad we got along, seeing as we were Audrey's two bridesmaids.

Luckily for me, Sarah also loved weddings and had gladly wanted to share planning duties with me.

"Sorry, Auds. I just don't know how you do it." Just because I didn't get over-excited about this stuff didn't mean I wanted to ruin the experience for my best friend.

She made a face at me. "Are you kidding? I love having you at these appointments. Just because I'm getting married again doesn't mean I love all things wedding all of a sudden." She let out a laugh. "Oh, God, the look on your face when she said 'authentically organic'! I almost laughed in her face."

"Fuck, don't remind me. I mean, what's the alternative?

Falsely organic? I wanted to stuff those damn ranunculus' down her throat."

It had been a long morning, and we were now hungry and (in my case) a little hangry, so we treated ourselves and ordered pizza while we settled back at my apartment.

"So, now that you've quit, have you started looking for another job, or are you too busy getting busy?"

"Getting busy, Auds? You sound like my mama." I chuckled before taking a bite. "Actually," I swallowed, "I was thinking of contacting my friend at The Tribune."

"Diego, your ex?" Ex was probably a strong term for someone I'd slept with a handful of times a year ago. He was a great guy, and we'd stayed in touch, mostly texting each other gifs and memes every once in a while.

"One and the same. He's mentioned before that they could use a guest writer for insider tips on where to drink, the industry, at-home recipes, all that. Said I should capitalize on the whole 'four time bartender of the year' thing. Figured I could at least do that while I worked out what was next."

"Do you think he'd still be able to help?"

I devoured another piece, wondering why we hadn't gotten more than one. I adored leftover pizza, probably more than the fresh stuff. Maybe Sam did have a point about my eating habits. "I can't see why not. It's not like we ended badly, and he's always been a sweetheart."

"That's great news, Tiff. And how's the bar going?"

My eyes narrowed. "You're not as sly as you think you are, Auds."

She laughed. "Ok, fine. How's Sam?"

"Virile," I said, just to get a reaction.

"Oh, my god, don't tell me that! I have a meeting with him next week."

I bent over, laughing at the full-faced flush she was sporting. "You asked." Not to mention it was true.

Her face was buried in her hands, trying to shake out what

I guessed was a mental image of Sam and me. "Right, ok. I guess I set myself up for that one."

She tried again a few minutes later once her blush had faded. "So, is it just hate sex?"

"I thought it would be, but …"

"But?"

I sprawled back in the chair, sorting through my thoughts. "He's surprising. Don't get me wrong, he's still frustrating as fuck, but he's also smart, and he's got this wicked sense of humor, like evil." Audrey looked overly pleased. "Ok, don't go getting that look, Auds. It's not like that. I just don't hate him, is all I was trying to say."

Then, it hit me. "Fuck."

"What?"

"I think we might be … friends?" That smug son of a bitch. Probably planned this. With his compliments and his clever observations and weird way of being able to charm anybody.

"Mmm-hmm."

Immediately, I pointed a finger at her. "Nuh-uh. None of that."

Her hands raised in surrender. "So, what happens when you leave?" Audrey asked.

"It ends, I guess." What else could happen, really? We weren't anything to each other. There wasn't any talk of the future, we only saw each other at the bar (or his apartment), we didn't talk about our feelings or our past. We worked. We fucked. That was it.

"Are you ok with that?"

The wall was suddenly very interesting. "When have I ever cared before?"

Audrey's voice was gentle. "There's always a first time."

29

SAM

"You're good at this." I watched Tiffany as she poured us both another cocktail of her design. Campari, vermouth, coffee, chocolate bitters. Delicious.

"I've done it before." She threw a wink over her shoulder.

We'd taken to testing out recipes on each other. Creating was a habit I was out of practice in, and Tiffany was a good sounding board, blunt to a fault and enthusiastic when she tried something she enjoyed.

"No, I meant, watching you work. It's clear you enjoy it, and it's fascinating to see what you choose and how you bring it together. Like I'm watching a show."

A soft mewl sounded from the corner, where Luna had curled up in an empty cardboard box. The new bed I'd gotten her sat pristine and unused beside it. Tiffany detoured to scratch her behind her ears, and Luna ate up the attention, stretching and purring within her confines.

Suitably pleased with Luna's response, Tiffany passed me a drink, then fell back against my sofa with her own in hand. "It's funny you should say that. I've been thinking of starting something like a show. All about cocktails."

"I'd watch it. You'd be a good teacher. Hell, you should be running your own place."

"Maybe I should buy you out."

"In another life, we could have been partners."

"Fuck, can you imagine the two of us running a place together?"

I could. "You're right. Forget I said anything."

It was late, or early, depending on how you saw it, and we were more than halfway through at least one bottle of liquor. Which was to say, we were past tipsy, and I was more relaxed than I remembered feeling in a long time.

"Why bartending?" I asked her, curious.

"I kind of fell into it. Got really good at making my ex's favorites in college. Found I loved it enough to teach myself as much as I could."

"And how did you learn to make drinks like this?" I raised my glass.

"Lots of trial and error," she laughed.

"It's more than that. You have an incredible mind for flavors, and you're not afraid to try, even if it doesn't work. It's not something everyone knows how to do."

"Thanks." She hummed pleasantly around a sip of her cocktail, and I liked that she was comfortable acknowledging her skills without being cocky. For someone so accomplished, she certainly had a habit of waving off praise more often than she accepted it. I'd misjudged that about her. What I'd initially seen as arrogance was now rearranging to something more akin to defiance and defensiveness.

She was playing absently with her hair, and I couldn't help but smile at the picture of her, bare feet tucked underneath her, her back resting against the arm of the sofa as she faced me. She looked cozy. Comfortable.

It might be my favorite view of her yet.

"Actually, if you want to praise anyone, you should be thanking my Mimi. Cooking was serious business in my family, and she ruled her kitchen. Every time she visited, I'd spend hours just watching her bake and listening to her stories. Never saw her use a recipe. Had it all up here." She tapped her temple.

After another long sip, I heard a soft little sigh, and Tiffany continued. "Being around her was where I felt safest. I used to be scared of storms—thunder, specifically—and Mimi would bribe me from my blankets with a cookie. She always made me want to be stronger. Braver."

Clearly, these were fond memories for Tiffany. Her smile was deep and warm, and it gave her a glow. I wanted to soak in it. "Is she still around?"

"Not for a long time."

"She'd be proud of you."

"Don't I know it." Her inquisitive eyes meet mine. "What about you?"

"It's going to sound silly, but I didn't ever question myself when I was a kid. My parents had a wonderful ability to make us feel capable of anything. If anything, I was too sure of myself."

"You? No," she said, overdoing the sarcasm.

"But I do remember being jealous of having to share my mom. She was a teacher, and she cared about all these other kids all the time, so I would make up reasons to steal her away from it. Have her all to myself. Eventually, she figured it out, and we made a deal—I would pick an activity, and she'd make the time for us to do it together, as often as we could. Just the two of us. They're my favorite memories of her."

"That's really sweet. She meant a lot to you."

I nodded, then held out what was left of my drink in a toast. "To formidable women."

Tiffany clinked our glasses together with a chuckle. "Jesus, only you would use four-syllable words when you're drunk."

"I'm not drunk."

"Tipsy, then. And she was. A fucking amazing woman. Same as my mama."

"I can see where you get it from."

"Careful, honey, or I'll start to think you like me." She winked. Surely, the warmth in my chest had everything to do with the whiskey we were drinking and nothing at all to do with the term of endearment she'd used.

Although, I wasn't about to tell her to stop.

"So, tell me," Tiffany started, and I steeled myself for whatever was going to come next, "what brought you back here?"

I'd later blame the alcohol for what I said next. "A broken heart."

There was a long silence as I drained what was left of my glass before walking over to make a new one.

If my admission surprised me, it was nothing compared to what Tiffany admitted. "I don't think I've ever been in love."

Abandoning my original plan of mixing another cocktail, I walked back to the sofa with the bottle, filling both our glasses. "Never?"

"Most people only want me for sex."

"I doubt that's true."

She reached a foot out to poke me in the thigh. "Do you want to tell this story?"

"Carry on." I caught her ankle before she could retract her limb, tracing the soft skin as she spoke.

"I think the closest I ever came was in high school. I'd already realized I liked guys and girls, and I had the biggest crush on this chick. I've forgotten her name now … Wow, that's terrible. I really should remember that."

"What happened?"

She blew out a breath. "We kissed a couple of times until she told me she wasn't 'like that' and that she was just experimenting. That hurt. Then, she outed me to half the school, and the bullying got bad enough that I had to transfer to another school. Mama was pissed."

I swallowed, knowing I was teetering on the precipice of another dangerous decision. But Tiffany had opened up, and at that moment, with the soft glow of the streetlights extending through the window and the delicate feel of her under my fingertips, I felt the truth slipping past my defenses. "Her name was Piper. We met at a young entrepreneurs event,"

"Of course you fucking did," Tiff groaned, making me smile. It eased the ache in my chest and made the memory easier to bear.

"I fell straight away. She was incredible. Larger than life. My first bar was already a success, and I was looking for investors to start a second. Piper was the one who rallied for capital. It felt like kismet."

"Destiny, Sam? Really?" Tiff stretched out her other foot, brushing my thigh. "What happened?"

"I was blinded by love. After the second bar was a success and I was planning for the third, I asked her to be my business partner. We'd been dating for a few years at that point, and we were in love. I thought it was forever. We decided that I'd continue to run the business, and she'd handle the investors. We made a great team. So, I signed over half of everything over to her. It was my way of committing to her since I never wanted to get married or have kids. Only, when we broke up, she had better lawyers. She told me I could go quietly and keep benefiting off of the company's reputation, or she would tie me up in court until I had nothing. So, I took the payout and came home."

"Fuck."

And that one word, empty of pity and full of everything I'd been unable to say about the situation myself, was probably the most perfect thing she could have said.

Laughter bubbled out of me, unexpected but freeing, until

I was doubled over with it. Like a dam broken, the release left me light-headed. Or maybe that was just the alcohol.

Tiffany eyed me like I had lost my mind, and maybe I had, but honestly, it felt good to let it go like this. Months of pain, first the heartbreak of losing the person, the partner, I'd spent the better part of nine years with, then the loss of my business. My hard work.

Every single hour of pushing and learning and growing. Every sleepless night. Every time I pimped myself and my work out just to get seen, get heard in a sea of voices vying for the same.

All because it would boost the business.

And in the end, I was relegated to being the glorified spokesman.

As quickly as it had come, my laughter died, and with one long, deep breath, I came back to myself, finishing my drink with one large swallow.

"For what it's worth, you didn't deserve that, Sam. I know we don't really know each other, but no one who spends any time around you could miss the fact that you're a good person."

As her words, her conviction, settled under my skin, my breath caught in my throat. I pushed the next words out. "It's worth a lot."

"Can I ask why you broke up?"

In for a penny. What was another truth added to what I'd already shared? "She wanted to have children, and I didn't."

Tiffany shuffled closer, her hand landing on my shoulder, her face clouded in concern. "I'm sorry."

"What for?"

"That would have been difficult. You cared for her, and not being on the same page sucks. Not to mention how she's acted since."

"Thank you."

"You're welcome."

"Do you? Want children?" I tried not to think about why I wanted to know.

"No. I knew early on that marriage and kids weren't for me. I like kids, but I've never been inclined to being a parent. I'm happy being a kickass Aunty."

I thought of Gracie and how happy Harry was now. "I know how you feel."

It seemed Tiffany had the same thought. "I still can't believe I didn't know Harry had a kid. I'm glad he's happy. He always seemed so solitary."

"To be fair, he didn't like owning this place."

"Why did he start it anyway? I've never asked him."

"When our parents died, he took it really hard. After I'd left, he'd been the one to keep an eye on them. He saw more than I did of their decline. He said it made him think about his future and why he'd always played it safe when life was so short. He bought this place because he hoped we could run it together, but I'd just received funding for my third bar, and I couldn't get back home. I've always felt bad that I wasn't able to help him run it. But then it turned out I didn't need to."

"Because a hotheaded bartender went and took over."

"Tiffany, that's not what I meant. I'm glad you were here to help. I'm sorry I never told you that earlier. I guess I felt guilty. You were a reminder that I'd let my brother down. And if I'm honest, I was jealous."

"Really?"

"Yes. You managed to do what I couldn't. And you were able to help my brother when I'd abandoned him."

"You didn't abandon him."

"He didn't even mention me to you."

"Sam, no. Ok, he didn't talk about you, but we never talked about anything personal. I was too busy taking over the bar, and he was busy trying to have a baby. But it's obvious he cares about you."

"Do you have brothers?" It sounded like she spoke from experience.

"Three. They're ..." She chewed on the inside of her cheek. "Ok, if you ever tell them I said this, I'll kill you, but I love those jerks more than anything. I don't always get along with them, but I wouldn't want anyone else in my corner."

"I know we don't really know each other," I said, mirroring her own words, "but I imagine they feel the same. You're a force, Tiffany, and I mean that in the best way possible. For what it's worth, I'm glad I have you in my corner."

Her expression was thick with vulnerability. Our eyes met and locked, and I felt far too raw for what we had established was a purely physical arrangement.

In wordless agreement, we both downed the rest of our drinks and scrambled to refill. Anything to break the tension. To reestablish the status quo.

Because there was one thing I wasn't able to give to anyone right now, or maybe ever again, and that was my heart.

30

TIFF

Those were good drinks.

Wait.

I cracked an eye open. Where was I again?

Shit. Loft. Sam. Alcohol.

Fuck.

Ugh, my mouth tasted like shit. Where was the bathroom again?

Gathering what little energy I had, I rolled out of his bed and stumbled to the bathroom. Using the old college method of finger and toothpaste, I scrubbed what I could of my mouth, willing my stomach to settle.

So thirsty. Need water.

I walked to the kitchen and grabbed a bottle from the fridge (because, of course, Sam was the type to be prepared in these situations), chugging half before I dragged myself over to the couch. With a heavy thud, I flopped on it, face down, my brain pulsating a beat against my skull.

Ugh, why?

"Morning." Sam's voice carried across the room.

I groaned into the cushion, not bothering to open my eyes. How did he sound so chipper?

"This is your fault," I grumbled.

"I don't see how that's true." Was he smiling right now?

It took an enormous amount of effort to sit up. "You were the one who wanted to test those recipes."

"And you were the one making them."

"I don't see how that's relevant. Also, aren't you meant to be the responsible one?"

"You think I'm responsible?"

My eyes narrowed so much they practically closed. I didn't handle hangovers well, ok? "I hate you."

He smiled. "You know, you say that a lot."

"It's true a lot. When it stops being true, I'll stop saying it. Until then, go fuck yourself." I laid back down.

"Come on." He tapped my shoulder.

I cracked one eye open. "What are you doing?"

"We," he emphasized, "are walking."

"And why would we do that?"

"For many reasons, but right now, to burn off the hangover."

"God, you don't even hangover like a regular person. Who are you? Who made you this way?"

"If that is a dig at my parents, I'd rather you didn't."

"I'd rather you didn't exist right now."

We were still inside, but I didn't care. I threw my sunglasses on anyway, sighing at the relief of sweet, sweet darkness on my eyes. Sam looked far too smug this early in the morning, and I gave him a dirty look, not caring if he couldn't see it.

It didn't matter. He could still tell, smiling as he said, "I know. You hate me." Smug bastard.

At the bottom of the stairs, he pulled me in for a kiss, then chuckled against my mouth at my semi-indignant grunt. I might be hungover, but I still had Sam's lips on mine, and their tenderness was almost enough to make me feel better. *Almost.*

"That's right," I argued, but I didn't hide my smile.

We walked to Millennium Park (stopping blessedly for strong, large coffees), and I followed him as we crossed through into Lurie Garden. There was a chill in the air, the weather finally turning towards lower temps now that we'd officially entered fall, and I was glad for my jacket. But, even through the haze of fatigue (and smattering of early tourists), the garden was beautiful.

I didn't think I'd actually visited before.

Sam looked personally affronted when I told him this. "That's really a shame. There are over 126 native species of plants here, and they wanted it to be a wild meadow that lasted through all four seasons. It's actually incredible the way they—"

"I swear to God, if you don't stop talking right now, I'm going to throw you off this track."

He went quiet, but I spied a smile in my periphery.

"Why do you like this so much anyway?"

He said nothing.

"Are you ignoring me now?"

"You said to stop talking." He chuckled at my low growl. "And, by this, I'm assuming you are referring to my enjoyment of the outdoors?"

I dropped my sunglasses to glare at him.

"Is there something offensive about fresh air and trees?"

"You used to live in Vegas, and you're going to lecture me about the joys of fresh air and trees?"

"My parents loved gardening. I spent a lot of time growing up outside, learning about herbs and the virtues of a green thumb."

"I had no idea. You spend so much time in the bar."

Pointing to himself, he said, "Workaholic, remember? I enjoy pushing myself. But it doesn't leave much time for a life."

Another round of the garden and (I fucking hated to

admit it) my head actually felt clearer. Damn fresh air. Damn Sam and his smartness.

"Herbs, huh? Guess you're a whiz in the kitchen, too?"

"You'd be mistaken, I'm afraid."

I stopped in my tracks. "Wait. Really?"

He nodded.

"The great Sam Cooper has a flaw? I must notify the news."

He chuckled, rough and low. It was the one he let out when he was truly amused. I didn't have the brainpower to even tell myself off for cataloging them. Instead, I had a brilliant idea. "Ok. Since you can't cook, and we've established last night was your fault—" I said.

"Oh, we did, did we?"

"—you need to take me to breakfast." Shit, that sounded like a date. "Since I figure we're friends now." Not better. Jesus, hungover me sucked at this.

"Are we?" And goddamn it, why did he have to sound so earnest?

"Sure." Abort. Abort.

I grabbed his arm and started walking us towards a great brunch spot nearby. "Come on. I have a craving for French toast."

"Oh, my favorite."

Damn he was cute. I made sure to walk with some distance between us. Not too much, but, like, a friendly amount. Whatever the fuck that was.

———

AFTERWARD, I should have gone home. Really, what were we doing? We never hung out outside of work. But we were friends now (no thanks to my alcohol-addled brain for letting that term slip), and friends spent time together outside of work, right?

Even if they also happened to be fucking.

And look. It wasn't that I hadn't had friends before. I've had many. Of varying genders and situations.

So, why did whatever this was with Sam feel so different?

It felt like a secret to admit that I kind of understood him. I recognized that stubborn streak and need to prove yourself. To cut your own path, regardless of what stood in your way.

He cared about people, about what they needed, how they should be treated. That was easy to see in how he approached his work, his customers, his brother, hell, even me (now).

Sure, there were times that he was quiet or overly serious or a little stuffy; but could I really judge him all that harshly when I was at the other end of that spectrum?

He'd judged me too fast in the beginning, but I was guilty of the same to him. And, if the tables had been turned and I was about to face off with someone who had done one of my brothers dirty for years (and ok, I didn't think Sam or Harry would say that about me, but come on, I had overstepped on occasion. I wasn't completely blind to that), I would have acted the same way as Sam. Actually, I probably would have been worse.

So, yeah. We were friends. Who fucked.

And who apparently went on garden walks and brunched and then visited a museum.

It was honestly the city's fault. The Art Institute was. Right. There. And it was amazing. You live here and not visit. I dare you.

And ok, maybe it was a little more touristy than, say, the Museum of Contemporary Art, but (and forgive me, this was just my personal preference) I liked the classics. I know. Me. A lover of the classics over modern.

I got the hypocrisy.

Sam, it happened, was a fan of them as well, but that was far less surprising. So, we walked over and enjoyed the peace of a mid-Monday crowd.

As much as I loved it there, it had honestly been a while since I'd visited because Hannah never enjoyed it. She acknowledged its place but cared more about local artists and the traveling exhibits that showed at the MCA (which I one hundred percent supported).

But still. The classics.

I don't know what I expected from Sam. See, the way I saw it, creativity was a personal journey. It's your way of expressing yourself. What you liked in art and what you created artistically was unique.

So, I was curious to see how Sam approached it.

The way I liked to experience museums usually annoyed people (see: Hannah). I wandered aimlessly, sometimes doubling back on myself, letting my eyes roam until something caught my eye, and I'd have to get closer. Take it in. On and on until I'd had my fill or my time was up.

I didn't want to wax poetic about the influences and why this piece worked and why that didn't, what the style was, or what was so revolutionary about the time period or what the artist intended to say.

I just liked what I liked. Simple as that.

Mimi would probably joke that that should be the slogan of my life. She probably had, and I'd taken it as a personal mantra.

Sam, I was pleased to discover, was as studious and attentive as always, quietly taking in each piece, occasionally pausing but never overstaying his welcome. The time passed quickly as we quietly wandered from room to room, Sam not hovering but never too far from me. It was nice.

I'd checked in with him once, only to be told, "I'll be quite alright here without you, you know." At that, a breath had escaped me, larger than the one I'd remembered taking. It was like relaxing a muscle I'd held tight for a long time.

And if we did stop at the same piece, he always had something insightful to say. It was comfortable to continue like that for an hour or two, periodically noticing him nearby, always close.

The quiet was nice. I'd forgotten just how refreshing it could be.

I liked that Sam was a silent observer.

I liked even more becoming his silent observer.

The Art Institute was always beautiful. Warm and comforting, like one of Mimi's desserts. I knew these rooms as well as my parent's house.

Between pieces, I found myself taking as many moments to admire Sam as I did the artwork. It wasn't difficult to see the beauty there, either.

Did I want to kiss the soft, contemplative look off his face every time I saw it? Hell yes. (Sometimes the light would shine off of the small hoop in his ear and I was tempted to walk over and pull it between my teeth). But it was more than that, and fuck, wasn't I in the perfect place for that realisation? More than the strong nose and hypnotic eyes and broad curve of his shoulder; he was gorgeous in his focus. His care. His passion.

Soon, I was watching him more than the art. Over the last (what had it been now?) four weeks, my understanding of him had evolved. The still, controlled way he held himself had gone from cold to composed. Sterile to pensive. I'd been mistaken, in the beginning, to think that he didn't express anything. He did; you just had to know what you were looking for.

The way his fingers would drag under his lower lip when he was turning a decision over. The slightest twitch in his right brow when he was surprised but trying to hide it. How a slow blink and tight smile would signal that he didn't like the person he was talking to, despite the polite words. The way he spoke in short, sharp sentences (sometimes only a single word in a low, gruff mumble) whenever he was burning with anger.

The way he said my name. Conveying so much in three syllables.

Huh. What do you know? I might actually like him.

The water was a steady stream of warmth on my back, Tiffany's skin hotter against my own as we kissed roughly under the shower spray. Her grip tightened on my ass as I pressed her against the tiles, and she broke our kiss with a gasp as I trailed my lips along her jaw, teasing the extremely sensitive skin below her ear with the scrape of my teeth.

With a growl, Tiffany spun us around, and I had barely enough time to brace myself for the cold before the tiles hit my back.

"You have a seriously great ass. Been driving me wild," she said, sinking to her knees and palming the tight muscles with her hands.

Thinking quickly, I reached above my head and redirected the showerhead until the spray hit me on the chest, sparing her the force of the water. Like this, the rivets tickled my stomach like fingertips, warm and insistent, like her hands were everywhere on me.

She teased a single finger down the cleft of my ass, humming a pleased little sound when I bucked and clenched. I'd not had a woman do that before, but it was definitely something I'd thought about, and I was hard within seconds. "Fuck. You like that, don't you?"

Then, with her fingers teasing me from behind, she engulfed my dick in the hot wetness of her mouth, tongue laving along my shaft as she bobbed. Damn, she was incredibly good at that.

When she swirled her tongue around the tip and moaned, I could have sworn the vibrations reverberated all the way through my spine.

I knew what I wanted, but I hesitated to ask for it. It meant sharing something with Tiffany that I'd kept to myself, letting her know me in a way no one else did. And that was where I paused. Because who else knew me the way she already did? What was one step further than where we were already?

When she pulled off with an obscene pop to lick down past my balls, teasing the tender skin, I felt white hot lust rip through me until I was convinced I had briefly passed out.

She pulled off, a question in her eyes as she stroked, and, to answer her, I pulled at the hand that had been gripping my hip, dipping my head down to suck at two of her fingers, delighting in the way her eyes widened with lust. Her smile grew lascivious when I removed them and lowered her hand back to my ass where I wanted it. "Would you finger me?" I asked, my voice raw and needy.

She dropped her forehead to my hip. "Fuck, Sam. You don't know how hot that is."

I rocked against her, sliding my dick against her cheek and moaning when she sucked a deep bruise on the sensitive skin beside it. "Is that a yes?"

"Fuck, you're so sexy. Yes." She pulled back from the spray to look up at me, her hair darkened from the assault of the water and eyes glazed with lust, like a wet dream come to life. I gently brushed her drenched hair away from her face, stunned at her beauty. "Have you done this before?" she asked.

I felt giddy and breathless, my skin aflame. "By myself. Have you?"

"A few times. Do you have lube?"

My skin flushed from cheeks to chest. I reached over to a small alcove in the wall, grabbed it, and passed it down to her. It normally stayed in my bedside table, but I was extremely glad that I'd forgotten to return it there yesterday.

She took the bottle from me, eyes fluttering around a moan before staring up at me as though I'd just handed her a winning lottery ticket. "You're somethin' else, honey." My dick twitched as she poured lube onto her fingers, and the sight alone pushed me closer to the edge. I took a few long, steadying breaths.

If I was something else, she was beyond comprehension. Even in my wildest experiences, I'd never felt brave enough to express my fantasies. With Tiffany, I wanted to explore all of them. Wanted to know what turned her on and be the one to give it to her.

"You look so fucking good; just the thought of it is getting you off, isn't it? I don't even need to touch you." She bent forward, licking a hot stripe from root to tip as her fingers massaged the tight ring of muscle.

She dropped her smile back around my dick, sucking in earnest while she began to ease a finger into me gently.

My head roughly thudded back against the shower wall. This was the hottest thing to happen to me, and I was torn between watching her and letting my arousal burn me into cinders.

She held me firm in her grasp, my body at her complete whim. Every choked sound ripped from me as I pulsed with broken, needy little thrusts into her. My hands fell limply to her shoulders, content to let her set the pace, have the control.

When a second finger joined the first, I was sure I would combust. I could feel everything tightening, peaking, and at the curve of her fingers against that perfect spot, the one I could barely reach myself. I was undone, pulsing hot and heavy into her mouth. My shrieked orgasm was loud in my ears, and every fiber of my being was now completely lost and spent.

I didn't know how I continued standing. Didn't know how I'd get out of my shower, even to walk the few feet to crash on my mattress. Barely knew how I was processing thoughts right now. As my brain rebooted, I became aware of Tiffany still kneeling on the floor of the shower, nuzzled into my hip, while I tenderly stroked her hair.

"You're incredible." The words were barely above a whisper, and as soon as they left my lips, I panicked. It was the closest to an endearment as we'd gotten, and I wasn't sure I hadn't crossed a line.

"Honey, I could say the same thing about you." The sugar-sweet drawl that crept into her voice on occasion caused me to open my eyes to gaze at her. She'd collapsed back so that she was sitting on the floor of the shower, eyes glazed as if she'd been the one to have the mind-bending orgasm. "Damn, Sam."

Damn, indeed.

After stumbling our way out of the shower, we dried ourselves as best we could in our current states and made the half dozen steps to crash next to each other on my bed.

"That was fucking hot. Was it ... what you expected?" It was the first time I'd heard her as anything other than confident.

"I think the results speak for themselves," I said with a lighthearted laugh. "Really makes you wonder why sodomy isn't more popular."

The mattress shook with the rhythm of her laughter, and the still relaxed state of my mind had me reaching over to pull her closer until she was draped over my side.

I breathed in the soft, floral scent of her hair, running my fingers along the shaved side, the feel of it fine like fur, and heard her sigh softly. Her warm breath ghosted along my damp skin as she spoke, "Religion ruining it for the rest of us."

"That's a rather pointed statement. Bad memories?"

She hummed. "You could say that. I spent years going to Sunday school."

"That explains so much about you. And now you don't believe?"

"Oh, I believe there's something out there, but they're probably an asshole."

"Why do you say that?"

"They created this incredible thing, the planets, the universe, mountains, animals, people, and then what? They got bored and fucked off, or even worse, are just up there watching all this fucked up shit happening and not doing a damn thing to stop it."

"What if it's a lesson in humility? In human redemption?"

"Catholic?" she asked.

"On my mother's side."

"Funny," she chuckled. "Does that mean I have to call you Saint Sam now?"

"Absolutely not."

There was a teasing scoff. "Where's your sense of fun?"

"I'm fairly sure you swallowed it in the shower."

Watching her gape at me in shock was almost as satisfying as the raucous laughter that followed.

Our stomachs rumbled, and I joined in her laughter. "Not a word," I said as I reluctantly swung my legs off the bed and pulled a pair of loose sweatpants on. I hadn't eaten in hours and could only imagine Tiffany was in the same position. Padding softly into the kitchen, I mentally checked off our options. I was far too tired to cook and was sure we'd both fall asleep before any form of take-out arrived.

Blinking against the bright light of the fridge, I cataloged a handful of items that would work—dates, strawberries, prosciutto, a few cheeses. After piling a generous amount on a plate, I added a handful of cashews and crackers and walked it back to the bedroom, where Tiffany sat propped against the headboard, the bedside lamp casting ethereal shadows across her sharp features.

"Eating in bed, Sam? You rebel."

Climbing in beside her, I leaned over to place a teasing kiss on her lips, careful not to jolt the plate in my hands. "Maybe you bring it out in me."

Her lips chased mine, and we kissed once, then twice more before parting. Tiffany passed a wry glance at the assortment. "Nice spread."

I moved to stand. "Should I whip up a lasagna, then?"

Her grip around my wrist halted any further movement. "Don't you dare. Get back here."

We ate, passing stories of our childhoods, our families, our first experiences in bartending. Tiffany had a wonderful way of crafting a story, embellishing with a natural flair that would make a comedian jealous. I'd known a number of entrepreneurs take courses on public speaking to learn the ease with which she spoke.

"Then, there was the time Audrey caught me in the storeroom with the Don Julio delivery woman."

"Please tell me you're joking."

"What? I cleaned up afterward."

"I'm going to pretend you didn't say that."

She playfully poked my side. "Excuse me, but how many times have we fucked in your office? Mr. 'you better be quiet, someone will hear you'." I felt her body tremble with soft laughter. "Besides, haven't you worked in Vegas? Surely, you've seen some strange shit."

That was an understatement. I chuckled. "There might be a few stories."

When I added nothing further, she rolled her eyes jovially.

"Fine, don't tell me." The food was long gone, and we'd settled in beside each other, a small distance between us. I wondered if she might leave. I hoped she wouldn't.

It was easier to forget like this, that we weren't coworkers, that I didn't have to separate the bar from us. Here, we were just two people sharing space. I could leave all that behind.

"I hope you're proud of yourself," she said, apropos of nothing. At first, I assumed it was a tease, but her tone was soft and tender. "No matter how it ended, you still did all that work, started those bars, and made a name for yourself. You might not have them now, but you'll always know what you're capable of. And you've been able to carve out a second chance for yourself. Not a lot of people get that." Her body, so close to mine, and her words, so intimately whispered in the dark, hit me with unexpected force.

Suddenly, it was very important to keep my composure.

Even prior to the fiasco that led me here, I'd prided myself on not chasing other people's approval. It mattered, of course, it did, but I wouldn't chase it. I would earn it.

I wasn't sure what I'd done to earn this, but it meant more than I could say. More than I'd been expecting.

Tiffany placed a gentle kiss at the corner of my mouth. "You should be proud, Sam. I know I am."

Long after her breathing evened out, I stared at the ceiling and wished that things were different. That there was a way to stave off the inevitable.

32

———

TIFF

The office chair had become increasingly uncomfortable as Sam and I poured over more "research" (or what I referred to as Sam's complete inability to be chill, which he did not find as funny as I did).

"What's this?" I asked, picking through the pile of papers on the desk to find an agreement for an ongoing donation and sponsorship of a local children's literacy program. A very generous sponsorship, from the looks of it. Fuck, he really was a saint.

"That? It's ..." He plucked the paper out of my hands, holding it close as the tips of his ears tinged pink. "Nothing. I don't even know how this got in here." He stuffed it under his laptop, avoiding my eyes.

I continued to watch him squirm for a moment until he cleared his throat and pointedly gestured towards the pile of articles on his desk that I'd promised to help him read. Picking one up at random, I sank back into the chair, a warm smile clinging to my lips.

Sam looked up as I stretched again, trying to ease the ache in my back. "Coffee?"

"Please." I smiled when he didn't immediately move. No

doubt he'd get lost in what he was reading and completely forget. Again. No matter. Once I'd finished this article, I'd go and make one for both of us.

Unfortunately, finishing it was proving difficult. "Ugh, this article is complete BS. Millennials don't want a neighborhood bar? What kind of uninformed ass wrote this?"

"I hardly think the city's longest-serving paper would employ someone that meets that criteria."

"Oh, really?"

He adjusted his glasses before rolling his shoulder; for the third time in the last hour. I was tempted to massage it but wasn't sure he'd agree (according to Sam, we needed to maintain professional distance or something). As a consolation, I admired how handsome the thick frames made him. Very sexy professor. I dug it big time.

"Regardless, it's worth knowing if this is the pervasive perception, even if it isn't true." That would explain the notes Sam had made in the margins. Which. Was fucking adorable. Not that I was going to tell him that.

"Which this isn't. Jesus, they realize that the problem with these places that have shut down isn't the location, right? Firstly, 'millennials' isn't the term they should be using. It completely excludes people born after '96. Secondly, have they seen these places? They're stuffy and utterly rude to anyone under the age of forty-five. Of course crowds are avoiding them!"

I threw the article onto the desk. "Ugh. This is exhausting. Why did I agree to help you do this again?"

"Frankly, I have no idea." Amusement curled around his words, his eyes never leaving his laptop screen. I watched, transfixed as his eyes darted over some text, seeing in real time the way his eyes narrowed and his brow furrowed in response to whatever he was reading. "Dammit," he whispered.

"What?" He rarely swore aloud, so I could only take this as extremely serious.

One hand scrubbed the rough shadow on his chin as he continued to read. When he was done, he shook his head, disappointed. "The contractor has informed me they are unable to start construction on the back wall for another month. Which will delay the re-opening."

"Fuck. Did they say why?"

"No, but I'm going to find out." He was already dialing the number.

If he wanted me to clear out, he didn't make any gesture to do so, and I was far too curious not to want to hear, so I leaned back in the chair, crossed my arms, and waited.

Polite as always, I could still hear the terseness in Sam's voice and see the downturn of his mouth. Whatever they were telling him was not good.

"Well, I'm disappointed to hear that. Please have him call me so that we can work this out," he said before hanging up.

"What's the verdict?"

"He confirmed the delay. Said another job has taken precedence."

"That's ridiculous. Weren't they set to start next week? For them to bump you, someone must be paying them a lot of money."

There was a pause while Sam massaged his temples, and oh. I realized, belatedly, there could be only one person with enough contacts to persuade a delay like this.

Someone I'd just so happened to tell to go fuck themselves recently.

God. Motherfucking. Dammit.

Anger and guilt had already formed a substantial lump of coal in my gut when Sam confirmed it. "It appears Pierce is quite close to the construction manager. He spun some story about there being a scheduling conflict, but it's obviously a lie."

That slimy piece of chauvinistic, pretentious, land waste.

This asshole didn't have anything better to do? He wasn't

busy enough? He needed to find time to fuck things up for other people?

Without a word, I stalked out of Sam's office and shoved on my coat and scarf, blood rushing in my ears. If Pierce had something to say, he could damn well say it to my face.

The bitter cold did nothing to cool my anger as I stalked the six blocks to Pierce's wine bar. Damn October chill. At least it wasn't raining. Yet.

It wasn't difficult to find the man of the hour. Tucked behind a sleek desk, in a room fresh out of "executives monthly," Pierce looked grotesquely pleased with himself. My eyes fell on the large Dali hanging behind him, and I barely stopped myself from rolling them. *Yeah, okay, Pierce. You're very cultured. We get it.*

"Miss Young, I wasn't expecting you."

Liar.

I skipped the pleasantries. "Mind telling me what the f—" I caught myself. I was here for Sam. *Be nice.* A visible shudder rolled over my shoulders. "—hell is going on? Our contractor just delayed by four weeks. You wouldn't happen to know anything about that, would you?"

"No. And I'm not sure I like what you're implying."

Lying liar asshole. My fists were balled by my side, and it was taking all my effort not to scream in his splotchy face right now. *Breathe.* Flexing my fingers, I counted another long breath before I trusted myself to speak. "I don't believe you. I think you know exactly what I'm implying. Everyone knows you and Mike are tight. I want to know why you did it."

"If I spoke with him, I don't see how that's any of your business. And if my close personal friend decided to make a call based on some information I shared with him, then that's his prerogative. Perhaps he felt it wasn't in his best interest to partner with a business whose staff are so openly hostile."

The pressure in my jaw tightened, and I forced myself to release it. There was nothing I wanted more than to tell Pierce precisely what I thought of him. In detail. Preferably with some sort of physical instrument in hand. And if I were only here to defend myself, maybe I would. But this was bigger than me.

I tried to remember what Sam had said about diplomacy.

"What is your problem with me?"

"You've disrespected me from the beginning."

"You haven't earned my respect, Steve."

"Is that right? And this visit, what were you hoping to gain?"

"I was hoping you'd realize that you're punishing a good man for no reason."

"I hardly think a small delay is a punishment. Sam's a businessman. He understands that these things happen. And you're wrong. I have a very good reason. Your boss doesn't appear to understand one fundamental principle: don't fuck with me."

"You have some nerve."

Silence ensued. Somewhere in the room, a clock clicked loudly as the seconds passed, driving my blood pressure higher with each tick. My skin itched under Pierce's soulless stare. If I gave one inch of a shit about what Stephen Pierce thought of me, I might have gotten uncomfortable. Instead, I dug my heels in, ready for a fight.

"You know, all these years I knew you were callous, cruel even, but this? This is beneath even you. What do you even get out of fucking with Sam like this?"

Finally, his expression changed. Immediately, I wished it hadn't as a slimy smile spread over his reddened cheeks. "Maybe this will teach you some manners. It's been frustrating to be in your orbit these last few years. Every chance you've had, you've managed to insult me. If I'd had any other opportunities, I would have taken them and kept this between us. Sam isn't worth petty inconveniences. Given his current choices, the bar will close itself by the end of the year."

"The fuck you talking about? Sam's ten times the businessman you are."

"He's fine," Pierce shrugged. "Although, it does surprise me that he's kept you on. I wouldn't have expected the two of you to work well together."

Little did he know.

Pierce continued. "Maybe now he'll see what a liability you are."

Oh, what I would do to smash something in this room. Probably that damn clock. After another slow breath, I said, "This doesn't have anything to do with Sam or the bar, so I'd appreciate it if you would leave them out of it."

"You'd appreciate it, would you?" Pierce bared his teeth in a condescending grin. "How about this, Miss Young. You get the hell out of my office, or I'll have you thrown out and charged with trespassing."

"You fucking piece of—" The door slammed satisfyingly loud behind me as I stormed out.

33

SAM

My phone screen flashed beside me. There was an email notification and an alert for an appointment. I ignored them both.

An hour ago, I'd read the email regarding the delay and been frustrated. Five minutes ago, I'd received a phone call from the contractor canceling the contract, and frustrated didn't begin to describe what I was feeling.

As quickly as she'd stormed out, Tiff barrelled back into my office. "That no good, piece of sh—"

"What happened?" I had a fair idea based on the phone call, but I needed to hear it from her.

"Pierce happened. I couldn't stand the idea that he was messing with you to get back at me, so I went over there to straighten him out." She dropped into the chair opposite me, fingers gripping the armrests. "Fuck, Sam. I think I just made things worse."

"You shouldn't have done that. I can fight my own battles."

"And just stand by while that fossilized jerkoff slanders your name and messes with the bar? Yeah, ok. You clearly don't know me very well."

"This is about more than just you, Tiffany. This is the bar. My bar. My business. Did you think about that at all when you were over there, yelling at him?"

"Of course, I did! Why do you think I went there in the first place?"

"Because for some reason, you couldn't sit this one out when I needed you to."

"Excuse me?"

"What did you think was going to happen? That Pierce would apologize and everything would fall into place? Were you even thinking at all? Or did you just react?"

"At least I stood up for you. What were you going to do? Sit back and take it? If Pierce thinks he has you in his pocket, he'll never let you forget it."

"There's a way to do things. There are rules. They might be unfair, but that doesn't change the fact that I have to play by them if I want to stay in business." My fingers rubbed over the growing ache in my temple. "Do I want to tell him to back off? Yes. But there are better ways to handle it. Ways that don't result in me losing thousands of dollars."

"Like a nicely worded … Wait, what?"

"The contractor called back. Unfortunately, due to threats made by staff, they no longer feel comfortable fulfilling the contract here. They aren't going to seek damages, but they are going to keep my deposit."

"That's bullshit!"

It was.

"Fuck, what do we do?"

"There's nothing we can do. I've been over the fine print twice already. They're within their right to withdraw their commitment if the working conditions put their staff at risk, and the deposit was non-refundable."

"But I didn't even threaten them. We should sue."

It was an option. But one that would cost considerable time and money that I didn't have.

"I really wish you hadn't gone to see him. You need to be able to hold your tongue occasionally. Not all of us can afford to say what we want when we want. There are consequences."

"You think I don't understand that? That's why I went over to Pierce's in the first place. I didn't mean to fuck things up further."

Tiffany's head hung low; her hands clutched in her lap. All at once, my anger seeped away.

"How did it feel?"

Slowly, her gaze lifted, questioning.

"Telling Pierce off. How did it feel?"

Though she smiled, it didn't reach her eyes, and I hated Pierce for putting us both in this position. "Not as good as I thought it would."

Rounding the desk, I pulled her out of the seat into a hug, feeling grounded once she was in my arms. Her breath was warm against my neck, where she'd buried her head. "So, what's the plan?"

That was a great question. Technically, this meant there was less to do to prepare the bar for the re-opening. It wasn't a relief.

"We move on. Keep going."

Disappointment filled me. It would be easy to blame Tiffany, but I should have known better. If I'd stuck with my first instinct, I wouldn't be in this position. I'd taken the risk. And once again, I was facing the consequences.

34

————

TIFF

Sam had more integrity in his little finger than Pierce could ever even hope to have. He didn't deserve this.

If only I'd punched him.

If only I'd quit sooner.

If only I'd kept my mouth shut at that damn dinner.

Fuck. It was one thing to run my mouth when it only affected me, but this was Sam's chance to start over, and I'd just gone and messed it up because I couldn't handle a little worm like Stephen Pierce for five minutes.

"Sam. I'm so sorry."

"You have nothing to apologize for."

But that was a big, fat lie, and we both knew it.

I'd have to make this right. I wasn't sure how exactly (the thought of apologizing to Pierce was the equivalent of ripping off my fingernails), but there had to be something. Some way to help Sam kiss the collective asses of the bar elite and get them back onside.

I excused myself and started thinking. I was fucking capable woman. I had to know a way to fix this.

Two phone calls and one favor later, I had a solution.

"Thanks, Diego. This means a lot."

"Hey, I'm the one who owed you, so no skin off my nose. It's just, are you sure this is how you wanna call this even? I know we talked about getting you a column here, but that's off the table if we go ahead with the interview. Is this worth more to you than that?"

It was disappointing to lose out on a job opportunity, but there'd be more, right? Sam deserved a strong shot at making this work and not having Stephen fucking Pierce punishing him for my carelessness.

"Yeah, Diego. It is."

"Ok, if you're sure. But you're still my number one go-to for recommendations. You know, if you wanted to, you could just start tweeting this stuff, and you'd find a following."

My eyes found the ceiling. Even Diego was getting in on this now? "You know I'm an acquired taste. Not sure my special brand of sweet and salty can come through in text."

"Then film it. Come on. Tiff. Media is changing. There's a million different platforms you could use to share this stuff. Make TikToks, get on Twitch, whatever you want. But trust me, you've got a voice people would listen to."

Everyone but Pierce. "I've got a voice that makes a lot of people angry."

He laughed. "Sometimes that's even better."

35

———

SAM

Despite the fact that the back bar changes were now dead in the water, I'd at least been able to make progress with the rest of the bar.

Removing the booths required only some heavy hands and a destination for the materials, and after reaching out to a few contacts I'd made in the area, I'd been put in touch with a local group who reclaimed the wood, and they'd worked quickly. They were in and out in two days.

After that had been done, I'd had the walls repainted, and the new tables were due to arrive tomorrow.

I still needed to decide on a name.

Tiffany strode into my office, unexpected but looking beautiful in her determination. I fought the urge to kiss her breathless or lock the doors and keep her in my bed for hours.

She stood, arms crossed. "Right. I hope your calendar is clear this morning because a reporter from The Tribune is going to be here in ten minutes for an interview."

"What? How?"

"I know a guy. Now, I figure if you kiss Pierce's ass a little and mention that you're about to replace the head bartender before you reopen, you should be able to fix this shit show with the contractor and get things back on track."

"If I say it like that, it'll sound as if I'm firing you because of what happened with Pierce."

"Exactly. He'll love it."

"That's hardly fair on you."

"Please," she said, dismissive. "I can handle whatever backlash there is on me. You need to look after yourself." She cleared her throat. "After the bar, I mean. This is the perfect way to amp up the re-branding as well. You can't lose."

I stared back at Tiffany in disbelief. But before I could say anything further, there was a knock on the front door. Tiffany turned on her heel and opened it to let in an attractive man dressed in jeans and a button-down. His wide smile tucked into Tiffany's shoulder as they hugged, an obvious familiarity between them.

Putting aside my reluctance, I straightened my clothes and walked over, offering my hand out to the man, who quickly took it in a firm hold. His eyes were bright. "Mr. Cooper, it's an honor. Diego Garcia, from the Tribune."

"Pleasure is all mine. Please, come in. We can use my office."

"Great."

Diego followed me into the office and spent the next few minutes arranging his things. "I appreciate you being free on short notice," he said, placing a handheld recorder on the desk between us.

"Of course. I'm pleased that Tiffany was able to arrange this."

"She's a good friend to have." His tone seemed to be reaching for something, but it wasn't my place to dig, so I left it alone. Diego, however, did not. "I owed her big time after she helped host my sister's birthday a few years back. I've actually been hoping to finally get her to agree to start a column at the paper."

"That sounds more like a favor to you than to her."

"You know Tiff. She either has everything she wants or is halfway to getting it. Anyway, she said this was more important."

My mind screeches to a halt. "Excuse me?"

"The interview." He motions between us. "Tiff called in her favor so that we could set this up. She didn't mention it?"

"No."

He shrugged. "It's a damn shame. Not that I'm not excited for this," he corrected himself. "And it clearly means a lot to Tiff if she's passing up a job for it." He pressed a button on the recorder. "Ready to start?"

I blinked.

"Mr. Cooper?"

Shaking off my shock, I nodded, feeling my professional mask slide back into place.

When the inevitable question came up regarding my return and finding my place among the established bar owners in town, I was reminded of Tiffany's sentiment earlier, and anger curdled in my stomach.

It never occurred to me that she would throw herself under the bus like that. And all because that overinflated pompous douche Pierce had decided he had a bone to pick with the both of us.

When I arrived in town, I'd understood that my reputation would result in some ruffled feathers that I would need to smooth if I wanted to make this work.

What I hadn't expected was for none of that to matter because I was dealing with a group of toddlers who were angry that a woman had stood up for herself and called them out.

Frankly, Tiffany had been right. Stephen Pierce could go fuck himself.

It shouldn't have taken this to happen to show me that I wasn't doing enough to protect my bar.

I should have been the one to set Pierce in his place.

It seemed I'd acted passively for long enough.

And Tiffany. Going out of her way to arrange an interview where I could kiss the shoes of that … that ass.

In the past, I would have questioned the motives behind it. Not because it was Tiffany, although perhaps I would have initially, but because I was far too used to every person acting in their own interest.

For her to apologize and ask me to give Pierce exactly what he wanted …

I knew there was not a chance in hell I was going to say what she'd told me to.

———

I HAD no idea how things would turn out after my comments to Diego made their way to Pierce, but I was done caring what that man thought. Of course, I could guess that he wouldn't be pleased, and that wouldn't result in any change with the contractor.

But that was a lesson I'd have to move on from.

On the plus side, Devon had come through yet again, his sister's resumé was rather impressive for her age. I saw a lot of ambition in between the lines of her experience, and I'd agreed to a probationary period, hoping to see how she worked under Tiffany's guidance while Tiffany was still around.

Which wouldn't be for much longer. And when she left, this fanciful blip in my behavior would be over, and I could focus.

Jade was ready and willing to start that night. It was easy to see the resemblance to her brother. Same kind eyes, same steely determination. And when she got behind the bar, she was impressive. Smart as a whip. Picked things up quickly, asked questions, practiced until she felt confident, and then moved on.

I could already tell she was going to be a good addition. Not quite a replacement for Tiffany, but that was always going to be an impossible task.

After Devon had taken her through the basics, Tiffany took over, testing her knowledge on recipes and selecting a few for Jade to prepare so that she could judge. There was no reason for me not to be in my office, except for a flimsy excuse to keep an eye on the proceedings, but no one questioned my presence, perched on a stool at the bar instead of my usual seat in the back corner.

Almost no one.

Tiffany's fond glances at me between directions washed over me. This was nice. The camaraderie was light, teasing. It reminded me of friends I'd had when I was growing up, big families who got along. Harry and I were close, but we'd never had this. I might not be a part of this, but I was glad to be near it.

After a while of watching them work, two things became glaringly obvious. Tiffany was pleased with Jade's skills; and Jade was very interested in Tiffany.

I honestly couldn't tell if Tiffany had picked up on this second fact because she wasn't acting any different than she did with the rest of the staff, and, I realized with a start, I hadn't ever witnessed Tiffany flirt with anyone apart from myself.

"This is good," Tiffany said, pleased with Jade's replication of one of her recipes.

"It's easy when you have such a good teacher." Jade tucked a tuft of tight curls behind her ear, head cocked, smile warm and inviting.

Tiffany let out a delighted laugh, then caught my eye again. "I like this one. You did good, Sam."

I couldn't help the curl of my lips as Jade preened under Tiffany's compliment, and I wondered again if Tiffany had any idea that Jade was putty in her hands. Wondered if this was just how Tiffany rendered everyone she interacted with.

She was a force. A magnet. A revelation.

What had begun as a teasing amusement at the interaction twisted into something darker when I began to wonder whether it was time to step aside; end things with Tiffany now before it became too difficult for me to do so. If it wasn't already. She deserved someone who could give her a future. Give her all of themself.

Whether it was Jade or not, it wasn't for me to say. Still, the truth was that I had always known where my limits were, and even though I had been selfish enough to indulge this attraction, I couldn't let my selfishness ruin any possibility of her finding someone who would treasure her and be what she wanted in a partner.

When one of the kegs needed replacing, Tiffany put her hand up and walked downstairs with a passing wink that I hoped no one else noticed.

Devon and Jade were working side by side, simultaneously cleaning and managing prep work, when Jade asked him, "Hey, Dev, you know if Tiffany is seeing anyone?"

So, I hadn't been imagining it, then. I began reading more intensely, even if the words were blurred in front of me.

"You don't waste any time," Devon joked.

"What? She's hot as fuck. Funny, too."

I couldn't argue with either sentiment.

He shrugged. "All I know is that she broke up with her girlfriend a couple of months ago, no idea if she's seeing anyone now."

Jade's smile widened. "Can't hurt to ask."

Devon shook his head. "I've told you before; I'm not getting involved in your love life. If you want to know, ask her yourself."

"Oh, I will."
I swallowed the lump in my throat.

36

———

TIFF

When the scruffy head of my baby brother walked into the bar midweek, I squealed, surprising Sam and a number of patrons who were at the bar. Without waiting a beat, I threw my apron at Sam, shouted, "Taking my break!" and then rushed around the bar to wrap Theo in a hug.

"You just keep getting taller every time I see you." I patted his head like I would a golden retriever, laughing when he smacked my hand away.

"Fuck off, Tuff Stuff." He chuckled.

"Language," I said, mimicking mama's tone perfectly.

Taking in his tired appearance, I couldn't help but be elated at seeing him again. I took the opportunity to squeeze in another hug. "You made it! It's so good to see you."

"You, too. What's it been? Three months?"

"Almost nine, you asshole." God, had it really been that long? He looked so much the same and yet older, wearier. "But I'm glad you're here now. Can you stay long?"

A seat opened up at the edge of the bar, and I ushered him over to it, keeping us out of the way of paying customers. He looked relieved to be off his feet. "I can't stay late, but I've got some time. So, hey, I know we already talked about this when it happened, but I'm sorry about Hannah."

I nodded solemnly, not wanting to rehash the past. Only getting to see my brother every once in a while meant relaying life events via text and then cramming in our congratulations or consolations in person, long after it had passed. "Thanks."

It was at this point that Sam wandered over because, of course, it was. What better timing to have my current fling arrive than at the moment my brother brings up my ex?

Which was how I would explain the sudden butterflies I felt if anyone asked. Nothing at all to do with the fact that this was the first time someone I was sleeping with met my family.

Fuck.

My mouth turned dry.

Without asking, Sam passed me a glass of water, then turned to Theo. "Can I get you anything?"

"Just a light beer."

"This is my baby brother," I said, hoping the non-sequitur would be put down to my usual brashness and not because I was irrationally fearful they'd hate each other (though, really, how irrational could that be? I hated Sam in the beginning. That said, Theo was an angel compared to me).

"Good to meet you. Theo, right? Tiffany's told me lots of good things. I'm Sam, the owner." He put the beer on the bar, then held out his hand.

Theo shook it before giving me a sly grin. "Really? Because I've heard only terrible things about you."

Nurses don't need their external limbs, right?

I was relieved when Sam laughed. "Now, that doesn't surprise me."

When Theo went to hand over a bill for the beer, Sam pushed it back. "On the house."

It was busy enough tonight that Sam couldn't stay to chat, and I was as disappointed as I was relieved.

"He seems like a good guy."

Instinctively, I looked over in Sam's direction. He was cleaning glasses while taking an order, his easy charm pulling a smile from the burly guy he was talking to. I didn't blame him. Sam was like a slow-burning flame, warm and comforting. "He is."

Theo was immediately interested. "Oh, is he now? Just how good are we talking?"

I smacked him. "Not a word."

"Is it serious?"

"No." But it sounded like a question.

I looked away but couldn't help being drawn back like a magnet to Sam, who was making one of our Saturday night regulars laugh. I felt my lips curl up in response like I could hear what he'd said.

"Does he know how you feel?"

I tore my eyes away, running a finger over a groove in the bar, just feeling the indentation over and over, the grain soft and worn. "I don't even know how I feel."

"I think we both know that's a lie."

Ugh, Theo was the worst. "It's complicated."

"What isn't."

"Wow, you're really helpful. Why aren't you getting paid to give love advice, Miss Bradshaw?"

"Oh, fuck off, you know I'm probably the only one with a worse track record than you. Alls I know is, the only other time I've seen you with that dreamy look on your face was when you watched *The Mummy* for the first time and couldn't decide between Rachel Weisz and Brendan Fraser."

I took a moment to just bask in the loveliness of that memory. Total bi awakening. "Ok, fine. I'm not saying I know what this is yet, but yeah, it's special. Different. He's ... he's so calm and thoughtful and planned. And funny, but in this totally devious way that you wouldn't think he was capable of. Like sweet as sugar on the outside and a devil underneath."

"Sounds perfect for you."

I swatted him on the arm. "You know I don't believe in perfection. That's too much. It's more like he's ok with me as myself. Likes me like that, but also makes me want to be better, you know?" I swallowed harshly against the weight of feeling in my throat, aware suddenly of how fast my heart was beating. Fluttering, so close to the surface.

It was too much. Forcing a self-deprecating smile, I feebly tried to push it down. Now was not the time to get my hopes up. "Clearly, he's a fool."

Unconvinced, Theo eyed me carefully. "You always do that. Anytime you find something good, you minimize it. You've always said you're happier with short term, but I think it's easier to be with people you know aren't serious prospects because then you never have to give anyone the ability to hurt you. It's ok to let someone in you know. Hurts like hell, but the only way you'll know it's worth it is to try."

Theo knew better than anybody (maybe even better than Audrey) how fast I usually ran. It was funny, now that I thought about it, how similarly different Sam and I were. He was meticulous, measured but always up early and ready to get started. I slept in late, took ages to come online, but ran at breakneck speeds once I was there. Maybe we could balance each other out. We already made a good team.

But that ... was short-lived. Now that Jade was there, I wouldn't be needed anymore. And what did that mean for us? Was there an us?

I eyed Theo's beer, envious. I could really use a drink right now. He seemed to understand, holding his beer out to me, which I waved away. "Enough about my love life. What's going on with yours?"

He sighed and scratched the back of his neck, a resigned droop affecting his posture. "Ugh, nothing interesting."

"Seriously? Whatever happened to cute coffee guy?"

"He must've switched shifts or moved or somethin'. I never

see him working there anymore. I was gonna text him, but it's hard with work, and it's just …"

"Complicated," I finished for him. God, what a pair we were. "Damn, sorry."

"It'll be fine." He reached over, clicking his beer bottle to my glass of water. "To complicated."

———

JADE WAS WORKING OUT GREAT, and while I was impressed to see that she fit right in, working with the rest of the team and barely slipping once all night, the first turn of realization occurred in my mind.

This was it. The beginning of the end.

In the time (fuck, had it really been a few months now?) since I'd quit, I always knew it was coming, but I hadn't given much thought to when. I'd assumed I'd feel a little sad (it had been over four years of my life after all) and somewhat relieved, but this? There was a storm of … something mixed in there, churning in my chest like murder hornets, electric and dangerous.

Foreboding.

Sam and I hadn't spoken yet about how long I'd be needed. From the looks of it, it wouldn't be long. At least where Jade was concerned. Maybe another week of teaching her some recipes, testing her on the ins and outs of the bar … After that, there'd be no reason to have me around, no reason to see Sam at all, unless …

Unless we kept seeing each other.

I liked the idea; I couldn't deny it. Even without the sex (which was, admittedly, some of the best I'd ever had), I liked Sam. Liked being around him. Talking to him. Hearing his opinions, even when they were wrong (although he was rarely wrong, which was all the more frustrating).

So, seeing him outside of this place? Outside of the

bubble we'd created between work and life? It was easy to admit that I wanted to.

But would Sam?

He'd been adamant from the beginning about the boundaries of this … fling. And as much as my first instinct was to say something, push those boundaries, ask him outright … Well, I'd seen first hand the consequences of my impulsiveness where Sam was concerned.

In fact, ever since Sam had arrived, I'd had to face the realities of my actions. Hearing both him and Harry say to my face how I'd overstepped had definitely dented my ego, but they'd been right. And mama had taught me that kindness always started with humility.

Maybe it was time to be patient? (I hated the thought already).

I was just about to start packing the bar down and shooing Devon and Jade home so that Sam and I could get some time together when I was the one given the signal to leave.

Devon took the rag out of my hands, "Go on. You've earned an early night for once."

"Early is right. It's 2 a.m."

"All the more reason for you to get."

My eyes darted to Sam, where he was leaning on the door frame of his office, arms crossed over his chest, looking tired but happy. It was a good look on him. Our gaze met across the room, but Jade stepped into my line of sight before I could do anything.

"So, how did I do?"

I smiled. "Good. You're a natural."

"Thanks. Hey, if you're not doing anything, we could go for a drink to celebrate? I'd love to pick your brain on a few things."

And with a little half step towards me, it clicked. Oh. *Oh.*

A bubble of wild laughter threatened to emerge, but I kept it down. "That's really flattering, but,"

"You're seeing someone," Jade said.

And fuck. Was I? "It's complicated." Word of the day, it seemed. Thanks, Theo.

Jade retracted the half step, now standing at a more casual distance, but was still smiling brightly, so I guessed she wasn't too offended. "I get it. Maybe another time."

This time the laugh did bubble out of me, causing Jade to ask, "What?"

"For a hot minute there, I thought you were interested in Sam."

Her face scrunched up, but even so, there was a joy to it. She was, frankly, beautiful. In another life, I would absolutely have taken her up on her offer. "Cooper? No. I mean, I guess I can see it. He's sweet, but not really my thing, you know?"

"Yeah." Why did I sound so breathless all of a sudden? Thankfully, Jade just said goodnight and got to work packing up while Devon continued to push me out of the bar.

"Okay, okay. I'm going." I hadn't had a chance to talk to Sam, and it bothered me now that I couldn't do so without needing to explain it to Jade and Devon. It was the first night in a long time that we weren't going to see each other after, and it left me disappointed.

A smarter me would have gone home and let it be.

A smarter me wouldn't have quit because she wanted to sleep with her boss in the first place.

But life was too short to always be smart.

So, I grabbed my things, said a final goodnight, and texted Sam my home address, telling him to come by when he finished.

I'd done some unexpected things in my life. Rushing ahead and facing the consequences later was just something I preferred to do.

They didn't always work out badly, but they never worried me like this.

I'd never cared much about speaking my mind

(understatement of the century) or about the consequences. Now, I cared. And I wasn't willing to risk the consequences this time.

Because this time?

This time, I was *feeling* things.

And that was bound to be trouble.

37

———

TIFF

Should it have been strange that Sam hadn't been at my place before? Probably. But it was always so damn convenient to end up in his apartment. I hadn't even realized until tonight.

It was just another way we'd separated reality from … whatever this was. Everything that had happened with Sam had only ever existed between the walls of that building, and now I was extending that boundary. Pushing. As always.

I caught my toes scrunching the rug and ceased their incessant movement and huffed an incredulous laugh at myself. I didn't get nervous! I'd had lots of lovers in my apartment before; this one was no different.

No. Different.

Except he really was. And if I knew him at all, he'd probably have a million ordered and rational reasons why it was a better idea for us to stop seeing each other (probably in some pros and cons list, I was sure). I shouldn't find that so cute, but I was beyond help at this point, apparently.

So, what to do?

Normally (if this was in any way normal or something I'd considered before), I would bulldoze my way through it. But I wasn't sure I wanted to do that this time. Theo had said that I preferred casual so no one could hurt me, and … My knee began bouncing quickly in place. I stilled it, but the restless energy beneath it pulsed under my skin.

The fluttering in my ribcage started again.

Sam's sharp knock startled me, and I laughed out loud at myself. I was being ridiculous. This was Sam. Pain in the ass, hot as sin, sweet, caring …

Okay. I needed to get myself together. Right this second.

Jesus.

I yanked open the door with more effort than was necessary, adrenaline driving me. "Hey, you're here."

"I am," he said, amused. It set off a firework of goosebumps throughout my body. Damn him for looking so good. "Are you going to invite me in, or should we continue this in the hallway?"

He was infuriating. And irresistible. I rolled my eyes, grabbing a fistful of his shirt, and pulled him into a fierce kiss. "Get in here already."

"So," he said, between kisses, "this is your place."

"Mm-hmm." I pushed him back against the now-closed door. "Want a tour?"

Sam's fingers dipped under the waistband of my jeans, not pushing but lingering as we parted. His eyes darted behind me, taking in the rest of the apartment with a soft grin. "Sure."

His hands drew out from where they rested but never strayed from me as I showed him around the small space. Eventually, we settled on the couch, and I lost time to long, slow kisses and the comfort of Sam's body against mine.

When he sucked a bruise onto *that* spot below my ear, I wanted to tattoo an X there.

When the bulldog that lived upstairs barked so loudly it startled us both into giggles mid-thrust, I wanted to bottle my happiness for rainy days.

And, when I was close to the edge, Sam's whispered, "Always so good. Needed this. Needed you," pushed me into a full-body orgasm. I wanted to crack open my ribs and bind him to my soul.

Afterward, I wasn't about to make him trek back across the city, so it made more sense for him to stay (purely a logistical decision). Leaving our clothes where they'd been discarded, I slipped naked into my bed while Sam used the bathroom.

The bed dipped down behind me, his warm flesh a welcome presence along my back, ass, and thighs. Everything except … "Fuck! Your feet are freezing!"

His chuckle wormed its way into my gut, spreading warmth everywhere it wasn't already. He tugged at my arm. "You're the one who's cold. Turn around, let me warm you up."

I did. I shouldn't.

Facing him, I tangled our legs together, and his arms returned around me. He hummed a low, pleased sound. "Better?"

I made a non-committal hum. Didn't want him thinking anything special. "Just don't let me fall asleep on you." Wouldn't want to make him uncomfortable.

Only I couldn't fool myself that my reasons were purely selfless. Theo's damn words were now plastered across my brain. Let someone in. Just … let them in. Right. Because it was that easy.

Sam smelled of soap, clean and fresh, something a little grounded, like grass or earth or eucalyptus; I didn't know (he was the gardener, not me).

The rhythm of his breath was nice.

Steady. Soft.

"Can I ask you something?"

"Could I stop you?"

I raised my head off his chest and whatever retort I had in

mind stuck in my throat at the way the light hit his cheekbones just so. His pale eyes, sparkling with amusement, waiting for me to (no doubt) banter back. Because he knew me. Because he liked it.

Blinking myself out of my reverie, I ducked my head, propping myself on an elbow beside him. "What do you think I should do next?"

"You're not sure?"

"I have my own thoughts. I'd like to know what you think." My eyes flickered to his face. "I respect your opinion."

Something complicated crossed his face before he leaned in to press a chaste kiss to my lips. "Thank you," he whispered, and I hoped the darkness hid the blush I felt spreading across my cheeks. Hoped that from this distance, he wouldn't feel how my heartbeat skittered and jumped.

He contemplated for another moment, and I enjoyed the wait. Unusual for me, but with Sam, it was always worth it.

"Hmm. I think you have an opportunity to take any direction you'd like," he said, ever the magnanimous. It was as adorable a trait as it was frustrating.

"Want to be more specific?"

"I would never presume to tell you what to do, Tiffany."

"I know, and I appreciate that. I'm not about to promise you that I'll take whatever advice you give me. But I want to know what you think."

"Okay." Again, he took a moment to collect his thoughts. "You have a talent for what you do. And I've seen how much you enjoy it. I think it would be a shame for you to stop. I don't know if you've ever thought of having your own bar, but I could definitely see you succeeding if you did."

"Honestly, I've never thought about it. I ..." and I paused because I wanted to be honest, but I knew that this was delicate territory, "before you came back, I felt like The Basement was mine, in a way, and I liked it. Liked building something of my own. Seeing all my hard work become something. You know?"

A hand rose to cup my cheek, and he tenderly stroked the skin as he spoke. "I do. You shouldn't feel bad about that. I'm sorry I reacted so poorly in the beginning."

"No. You were right to. I'd overstepped. But I am glad I got to have that for a while. It's something I want again. Do you really think I could do it?"

"Absolutely. I have no doubt you'll land on your feet. You're very self-motivated."

"Takes one to know one," I joked. "Have you always been that way?"

He nodded. "To the mutual concern and appreciation of my parents."

"That the nice way of saying they didn't always know what to do with you? I can relate."

"Your brother seems nice. I heard him call you Tuff Stuff? Is that a joke between the two of you?"

"Not really," I said. While they weren't the best memories, thinking of my baby brother always made me smile. "I was super protective of him when we were growing up. He was a little bit shorter than some of the other kids before he hit a growth spurt in high school, and one day I clocked a kid for pushing him around. My older brothers came up with it. They all think it's hilarious."

"So, you've always been a fighter."

"Oh, absolutely. Mama always joked that they needed a new word to describe me because I was always arguing that everyone should just get along, but then I never backed down from a fight."

"You must have been a handful."

"I used to get in trouble for talking too much in class." I joined him when he chuckled at that. "What were you like growing up?"

"Quiet. Curious." His smile deepened, and he added, "I

would occasionally get in trouble from correcting the teacher's notes."

Of course, he had. I kissed the crease where his smile was deepest, playfully knocking my nose against his. "So, the same, then."

"I was lucky. My parents had steady jobs; they were both teachers, did I tell you that?"

I shook my head. "You told me about your mom. I didn't realise your dad was one as well."

He nodded. "My childhood was nice. Uncomplicated."

"What made you want to move and make a name for yourself?"

"I wanted to. There's no great story there, I'm afraid. But I saw in my parents the value of giving back, of making people happy by understanding their needs and being in a position to provide them."

Fuck. Respect, gratitude, fucking *love* flooded over me, and I was (a rarity for me) without words.

"I know it's not exactly the same, what I do compared to my parents, but I enjoy it."

"It doesn't have to be the same. You're still doing good, in your own way. You think you're sneaky but I saw the email about the literacy program."

"Don't be too impressed. It was the least I could do for mom and dad." *This beautiful, selfless man.* My heart skipped in my chest. "I should be doing more."

I scoffed. "Should is a dirty word. Everyone *could* do more, and if you have the opportunity to, and want to, then do it. But don't live by the 'shoulds'. Your life won't be your own if you do that."

His calloused thumb rubbed tenderly at my cheek. "Is that how you've lived your life?"

I nuzzled into the cradle of his palm. "I never wanted to have regrets. Never wanted to look back and wish I'd done something I hadn't. But," I looked down, "sometimes I wonder if it's a trade-off. If one day, I'll wish that I hadn't done some of the things I have. Or," I said, once again thinking about what happened with Pierce, "what would be different if I'd just played by the rules."

Sam was unimpressed. "Then you wouldn't be you."

My smile felt weak. It was a nice sentiment, but I never wanted to be blind to the effects of my actions. "Sometimes that isn't a bad thing."

"I'm sorry, and excuse my language here, but fuck that."

A surprised laugh escaped me. "You're starting to sound like me."

"That isn't a bad thing, Tiffany. More people could use your courage."

And what could I do but kiss him at that point? If only to silence the confession that was on the tip of my tongue.

But good God, it was difficult to stop myself. This whole "patience" thing was hard.

Of course, that didn't mean I couldn't at least edge around the subject. Test the waters. (There was only so much holding back a girl could do).

"What about you?" I asked. "What's next? After the bar opens to astounding success, I mean."

And if I weren't so practiced in the art of Sam's expressions, I wouldn't have noticed him clamming up. The quick retreat of his gaze, the harsh bobble as he swallowed. The tightness of his smile when he finally said, "Hopefully, a toast to your next success. If you haven't forgotten me, that is."

With a playfulness that I didn't really feel, I halfheartedly slapped his chest before settling back down against him and tucking my head under his chin to hide my expression. "I don't think I'd be able to forget you if I tried."

I wondered what a relationship with Sam would be like. Probably a lot like working together. Two independent bodies in mutual orbit. We'd talk, tease, fuck. I'd bake, he'd read.

We'd walk. Visit the museum. On nights off, we'd sit side by side; I would catch up on whatever show I'd found to binge; he'd catch up on whatever book he was behind on.

It felt natural, like an extension of who we'd always been. Nothing scary about it. I knew him. He knew me. We liked each other anyway. We'd already fought and made up or moved on a hundred times, so I didn't have to worry about that. I'd never held back from him, and I had to believe he'd mostly done the same. The idea of more, of (fuck) forever, was more like never saying no to what we had, not saying yes to anything new.

Nothing would change between us if we made it official. I wouldn't wake up one day to a new person or expectations that hadn't existed before. It would be this, wrapped up together, working side by side, as a couple.

I'd never quite been able to imagine giving my heart away. I'd held too tightly onto it to imagine it any less like giving something up. In the end, it felt as natural as breathing.

I bit back a smile.

No, not breathing.

With Sam, it was a shot of liquor, a burst of flavor that at first burned, then soothed, then swarmed. Until you were loose and relaxed and feeling the best you've ever felt.

Silently, I flattened my palm against his chest, above his breast bone, feeling for his heartbeat. Did it harbor the same sense of belonging that mine did? The same recognition of a kindred, an equal?

I wanted it to.

38

TIFF

I woke to the soft sounds of music (odd) and the smell of coffee (sweet Jesus, what a wonderful invention). The coffee I found still steaming on my side table, within reach. With greedy hands, I sat up in bed and grabbed it, thankful that it had cooled enough to drink, and I gulped down at least half of it before I threw on shorts and a tank and shuffled out of my bedroom in search of the music.

What I found was … unexpected.

Sam was in the kitchen, his back to me as he cracked a few eggs into a bowl. Music was playing softly from his phone, and …

He was humming.

Delight bubbled up through me, sparkling, waking me quicker than the coffee had. With the cup still cradled in my hands, I walked over, silently basking in the beauty of the moment. Like the most vivid dream or a memory I would replay.

Since neither of us had planned this impromptu sleepover, he had stuck simply to his boxers and t-shirt. I'd seen him lots of different ways, but something about this; the softness of him, the music, (the humming!) … was nice.

Homey.

I brought the cup to my lips, hoping the steam would excuse the heat I felt building in my cheeks. They were already a little sore from the strength of my smile. "What are you making?"

Sam pulled a whisk from a drawer and set to work beating the eggs. There was a half loaf of bread next to him and a finished cup of coffee beside it. He'd been up for a while, then. "French toast. At least, I'm attempting it, but I can't promise it will be very good. I'm better with dinner foods."

My smile widened, taking in his bedhead, the disheveled clothes (was his t-shirt inside out? Fuck, that was so cute), and the awkward way he eyed the pan like he was afraid of it. I'd never seen him unsure of himself before.

Throwing back the last of my coffee, I hopped up and sat on the free space along the counter. "What have you added to the eggs?"

A crease appeared in his brow. "Added?"

Fuck, I was about to start swooning.

"Ok," I said, biting back a giddy smile. "First question. Sweet or savory?"

"Sweet."

"Good choice. Second drawer on your right, you'll find the spices." I watched him open it. "Grab cinnamon, nutmeg, and vanilla."

He did, placing them next to the bowl.

"Just add a pinch of all three."

He opened the cinnamon, then paused. "How much is a pinch, exactly?"

I so desperately wanted to kiss him right now. "Just a little bit. Don't worry about getting it exact. It's not a science."

His dimple looked even better in the morning. "It's exactly a science."

"Shush. Just add them."

He did. I tried not to explode from happiness.

"Great. Now a little salt to bring out the sweetness." The salt was next to me, so I threw it in myself. "And now soak the bread and cook."

"It's that easy?"

"Yes. Just make sure the pan isn't turned up too high."

He checked the cooktop and made an adjustment. "Ok."

From my perch on the counter, I watched as he trialed a piece, quickly growing more confident as he cooked. After the third slice was placed on a waiting plate, he stepped over to the coffee pot and refilled both of our cups before returning to cooking.

As he relaxed, he started recalling an article about the rise in pre-mixed spritzers, but all I could focus on was how distracting his lips were.

Those fingers.

Those eyes.

I licked my lips.

"Tiffany." Hmm. The way he said my name ... "Are you listening?" That damn lopsided smile. I wanted to lean over and taste it.

"Mmm."

He chuckled, and my stomach flipped.

When the food was ready, I jumped down and picked up the maple syrup, gathered our coffees, and joined him on the couch, where we ate off our laps, side by side.

We groaned in unison at our first bite. I must have made this meal a hundred times, but it had never tasted this good before. Nudging his knee with my own, I asked, "If this is your favorite, how have you never learned how to cook it?"

"I've tried. I couldn't get it to taste right."

"What about this?"

"Incredible. Thank you."

"Don't know why you're thanking me. You did all the work. I just sat around looking pretty." And when I was rewarded (as I had hoped) with that stunning, crooked smile, I couldn't help but lean in to taste it.

An indiscriminate amount of time later (or perhaps five minutes, who knows?), there was a knock on the door, and Audrey's voice called out a hello.

"Shit." I'd forgotten what day it was.

"Everything ok?" Sam asked, and I laughed into his shoulder, feeling irrationally caught as if this was my parents discovering me with someone in my room past curfew.

"Yes. It's Audrey. We always hang out on Saturdays. Give me a second." I couldn't be more thankful that our clothes from last night were close by as we hastily redressed so that we were (at the very least) decent, even though we both looked like we'd wrung through. It was ridiculous, and I loved it.

I rushed to open the door, the same silly grin on my face that had been plastered there all morning. It was likely going to get stuck this way. "Hey, Auds."

My bright tone was as unusual to my ears as it clearly was to hers, and her eyebrows raised, almost becoming one with her hairline. "Wow, did you sleep at all yesterday? Why are you dressed in your work clothes? Did you only just get home?" she asked, her eyes darting past me into the apartment, and I caught the exact moment she saw Sam's face, her pupils dilating so wide her eyes looked black. "Oh—um," she stammered, and goddammit, I felt myself flushing.

Fuck.

This was ridiculous. I was a fucking adult, for God's sake. I opened the door wider, stepping back so she could enter. "Alright, you're lucky I've already had breakfast and coffee this morning and that we even bothered to put clothes on before I opened this door. Also," and here was where I was a bit remorseful, "I may have forgotten what day it was."

"Yeah, I kind of figured, Tiff," Audrey said, all too pleased.

She was silent as she stepped inside, biting the inside of

her cheek the way she always did when she was holding back a laugh. Following her line of sight, I saw Sam's rigid posture, his tight smile. Jesus, Mary, and Joseph, these two. I fought the urge to roll my eyes.

"Auds, you remember Sam. Sam, Audrey." I waved nonchalantly in the air between them before retrieving a fresh cup of coffee for myself.

Audrey coughed out an embarrassed laugh. "Hi, Sam. It's good to see you again."

"You, too, Audrey. How is your fiancé?"

"He's good. How are the renovations going?"

"We hit a road bump recently, but I'm confident we'll make the deadline."

"Oh, that's great news. I'm looking forward to it."

I resisted the urge to shake my head at them. How Sam managed to seem like the most pulled together person in the room while wearing rumpled clothes and a full head of bedhead, I didn't know. Another of his skills.

"Speaking of Jackson," Audrey awkwardly offered as a segue, turning to me. "He's got the day off today, so I thought we could skip our usual date, and I'd get some time with him while I could."

I smirked. "You came all the way over to tell me that?"

Her glare was challenging. Cute, but ineffective. "You seem to have your hands full anyway."

I pulled her into a hug and whispered, "Oh, you have no idea," enjoying the way it caused her to blush. "Fine, go be with your man. We can chat later."

After Audrey had left, Sam looked prepared to do the same. Phone in hand, apologetic expression in place, he said, "I should ... probably think about getting back to the bar."

But I wasn't ready for him to leave. Something about him, here, felt precious. "You could," I said, already removing my shirt, lips curling when I caught his eyes tracking the movement, "or you could stay. Weren't you the one who said you worked too much?"

He stayed. And okay, maybe my suggestion of showering together moved the needle in my favor, but once we were clean(ish) and back on the couch, he seemed happy where he was.

I was glad.

I synced up my Netflix to play the next episode of a Norwegian sci-fi show I'd recently started watching while Sam lounged beside me, one arm around my shoulders. I was practically purring as his fingers played with my hair. There wasn't anything I needed right now except this. If someone asked me at that moment what my future looked like, it would be this.

During a long stretch of exposition, I caught him eyeing his phone. "No work. It's the weekend, for christ's sake. You're not going to miss anything important."

"I could."

"Sam," I kissed his cheek as I pulled the phone from his hand and hid it behind a cushion, "it'll be fine."

"It's just. Since the whole thing with Pierce, I've been anxious about the re-opening. But you're right. I should take a break."

It was the mention of Pierce that set my teeth on edge.

Returning to the show, I sunk a little deeper into his side, basking in the soapy smell of his skin and recalling the surreal reality that only a few months ago, I'd been on this very couch calling him every name under the sun.

My small chuckle jostled him, and he said, "I didn't realize a foreboding forest could be funny."

"I was just thinking back to when we first met. I would not have guessed this was where we'd end up."

"You were very hostile. I was certain you were going to stage a revolt."

I poked his ribs where I knew he was sensitive. "You didn't

exactly make it easy on me. Who expects bartenders to be pleasant so early in the morning?"

He looked smug. "I needed to know who would show up."

"You were testing us? You asshole." I sat up to push him in the chest, careful of his shoulder. "What would you have done if we didn't show?"

"Fired you." He sounded serious, but the tiniest lift in his lips gave him away.

"Like you could ever replace me."

The teasing left his voice. "It has been difficult. You're one of a kind."

"You're not so bad yourself."

He laughed. "The highest of compliments."

"Oh, you want compliments, do you?" Ignoring the show, I straddled his lap. "In that case. You're sweet." I kissed one cheek. "You're loyal." I kissed the other cheek. "You're generous." I ran my hands up his chest, around his neck, nuzzled his nose with mine. The next words escaped, soft like a secret. "And even when you make me want to tear my hair out, you're still one of my favorite people."

I pressed one last kiss to his lips, soft but sure, with the conviction of an emotion I didn't want to voice but knew to be true in every fiber of my being.

Sam was quiet when we parted, and I had expected it (when was Sam not quiet?), but the silence still dulled the hope that had sprung up under my skin. It was fine, really. What had I expected? That I'd open the door with some sweet sentiments and he'd confess his love for me, and we'd live happily ever after?

I was too much of a realist for that.

Still, I'd hoped for *something.*

That wasn't selfish, right? To hope?

With a last chaste kiss, I pulled off him and stood, collecting our cups from the coffee table in an effort to explain my movements. Sam remained still, but his gaze was clouded with whatever was circling in his head. "Tiffany, I …" he broke off, and while he looked outwardly calm, the air was thick with possibility.

This was ridiculous. I didn't do tension, and I didn't do self-pity. If Sam didn't feel the same way, well, I was a grown-up. I could handle that. "Shit. Did I break you?" I forced a laugh out, as hollow as I'd ever heard myself. "It's alright, Cooper." Jesus, that name didn't sound right. "You still top the list of people who get under my skin." A truth that meant a hell of a different thing than it used to.

But it worked. Sam took a breath and smiled that small smile he always did when he was trying to make someone feel better before saying, "I guess some things never change."

It didn't surprise me when five minutes later, he announced he was going to head home so that he could change.

And it was only after he left that I let out a harsh laugh and realized that no matter how this ended (and it would end), no matter how it hurt (and it would hurt), the only person I had to blame was myself.

39

———

TIFF

My mama could tell you that I wasn't one to waste time. Not on bullies, not on indecision, and certainly not on wallowing. I'd decided a long time ago that if I wanted to be the kind of person who leaped without looking, I'd have to get used to a few bruises along the way.

And because I knew that I'd likely get bruised a lot, I didn't bother people with my problems too much. They had lives and their own shit to figure out. They didn't need me coming around every five minutes with whatever clumsy consequence I was up against now. And frankly, I was damn good at being my own savior.

So, I knew I'd be okay this time. I always was.

But even okay people liked a little comfort. I picked up my cell phone.

"Did you have a good day?" Audrey said, teasing, later that afternoon.

I watched my foot tap on the ground. "Hypothetically, if I told you that I had feelings for Sam, would you tell me it was a bad idea?"

A pause. "Wow. Uh … I thought it was just sex. I had no idea."

I shrugged, even though she couldn't see me. "It surprised me, too."

"When you say feelings ..."

My heart skipped. I hadn't said the "L" word to a person in years, always too aware of what I wanted it to mean to want to throw it around. Just the thought of meaning it, of saying it out loud, felt like those final few clicks of the uphill climb on a rollercoaster.

Tick tick tick.

"I like him. A lot." A fucking understatement for sure, but I didn't like the idea of saying it before I'd talked to Sam. He should be the first person to hear how I felt.

There was a light giggle from her end. "You know, it's kind of weird being on the other end of this conversation. Weren't we just here a year ago? Except it was me freaking out about Jackson."

"I'm gonna stop you there. I'm not freaking out about Sam."

"But you're still asking me for relationship advice, which is how I know this is serious."

"It is serious." That, at least, felt safe to say.

"What will you do if Sam doesn't feel the same?"

My head sagged back against the couch. Of all the things I'd been mulling over since Sam had left, this was the one I kept coming back to. But it was also the part I was most sure of. "I'll do what I always do. Pick myself up and keep going."

"You wouldn't want to fight for it?"

"And what? Convince him to stay with me if he doesn't feel the same? No, thank you. Besides, I want him to be happy. Fuck, Auds, he puts so much of himself into his work, like everything. And the last time he was with someone, they walked away with all of it. He's good at hiding it, but I can tell it's hurting him that he has to start over. I can't be another thing dragging him down. And I deserve way more than to be pining away for someone who doesn't want me back."

"I'm sorry, Tiff. I can't even think of what to say."

"That's ok. I just wanted to hear a friendly voice. Now, disgust me with some sappy story so I can remember that fairytales exist or whatever."

"I've got a better idea. Jace got roped into attending some promotional thing tonight. I could come over with ice cream, and we could watch that sexy demon show you like."

I burst out laughing. "It's called *Lucifer*, but yes, that sounds like a great way to spend tonight."

Audrey showed up a few hours later, and in that time, I'd watched two and a half episodes of something that I hadn't paid any attention to, baked blondies, gotten out some extra toppings that we'd need to make spiked sundaes (booze *and* dessert? What could be better?), and slipped into my favorite pair of super-soft sweatpants.

As Auds and I curled into opposite ends of the couch, our legs collectively huddled under a handmade blanket between us, desserts in hand, I knew that no matter what happened with Sam, I'd still have this. And I'd be okay.

"Do you regret it?" Audrey asked with a mouth half full of ice cream.

"Quitting or having sex with him?"

"Either. Both."

The answer was swift. "No. Definitely not." And why the hell would I? "I've spent the last few weeks having some of the most amazing sex of my life." The joke fell flat, so I opted for sincerity. "But even without that, I'm really glad that I met him. I didn't realize how stuck I was, and not just at work either. I knew something was feeling off. It's been years since I've gotten out of my comfort zone, and I'm excited now. Especially because I don't know what's next."

I twisted on the couch, my legs getting caught in the blanket and pulling it off Audrey. She rearranged it while I continued. "It's like …" I ran my free hand through my hair.

"I don't even know. Being with him … I feel exactly the same, and yet …"

"Different?"

"Yes! I mean, I'm awesome, right? You know that. I know that. And I'm completely capable of being happy by myself, but … I just enjoy everything better when he's around."

"I think that's called—"

"Uh uh uh uh." I stopped her. "I know what you're about to say, and I'm going to stop you right there. I don't even know how Sam feels yet. I don't want to get ahead of myself."

"Ok, now you're really scaring me. I don't know what you've done with Tiff, but if you wake up in the morning with a third arm, don't call me."

I threw a cushion at her, narrowly missing her sundae. "Oh, shut up."

We settled again, letting the next episode autoplay. I caught Audrey texting someone (who I could only assume to be Jackson) with a goofy smile on her face, and I playfully nudged her with a foot to get her attention. "Thanks for coming over tonight."

She put her phone down so that she could reach over and squeeze my hand. "Anytime. You know that. I just want you to be happy. And I still kind of owe you for getting Jackson and me together."

"Oh, right. You do," I joked as I leaned in and hugged her. She smelled of lavender and felt like home. "This makes me happy, too, you know. I'm really grateful you're my friend."

"Aww. You're going to make me cry."

"All your sappiness must be rubbing off on me. Now, let's rewind so I can see Maze kick that guy's ass some more."

40

SAM

"There should be another delivery this afternoon. Audrey added a crate of MacMillan's small batch release for us to taste."

"That's great, Sam," Tiffany said, finishing her coffee.

We'd migrated down from the apartment to finalize our supplier contracts. At least, that was what I was doing. Tiffany was enjoying free expressos while draped across the chair opposite me.

"Are you sure you didn't want to rethink getting the back bar done? Diego said that the article would be posted next week, and once Pierce sees it, they won't want to risk the bad press. You could get your deposit back."

I hummed, keeping my eyes trained on the screen, even if I wasn't reading anything. I hadn't yet told Tiffany about my comments in the interview. She'd gone out of her way to set it up, specifically so that I could smooth things over. I wasn't sure how happy she'd be once she knew I'd gone against her advice. Especially since I had, somewhat politely, told Stephen Pierce to mind his own goddamn business. Somewhat literally, I realized with amusement.

It had only been four months since I'd come home, and I was already burning bridges.

"Whether the interview changes anything remains to be seen, and I'd rather not put my hopes on Pierce's reaction." I'd rather not have anything to do with him ever again, but the likelihood of that was slim. "I'd feel better knowing that the bar is completed without any further interruptions."

She looked up from her phone. "It's your bar." A smile played on her lips. There wasn't any difference in her today, yet something felt different.

As I considered it, I admired Tiffany across the table. Strong, sparkling, kinetic. She lived her life boldly, in a way I'd always tried to attain but now realized was possibly out of my reach.

I'd wanted to tell her I felt the same. Because I knew, without a doubt, that I loved her. Was in love with her.

It was hard to be aware of anything else. Which worried me. Because here I was, repeating history, right back to where I was with Piper. Making the same catastrophic decisions that led me back to Chicago. Where I'd promised myself I would play it safe. That I wouldn't risk the bar's success. For anything.

A booming knock on the door of the bar surprised us both. Either someone wasn't aware that we weren't open today, or they knew and, what? Hoped someone was here?

The mystery lasted all of ten seconds when my cell phone rang, showing Jordan's name and number. He didn't waste time when I answered. "It's freezing! Are you going to open the door or leave me on the sidewalk all night?"

The call ended as I moved to let him in, and once I'd opened the door, I was immediately overcome by Jordan's strong hug. "Finally!"

I patted his back. "It's not even that cold. You could have easily lasted another hour out there." It had only been a year since we'd last seen each other, briefly catching each other between work commitments. He looked good if a little stressed. He was as sharply dressed as I'd ever seen him in light gray dress pants and a matching vest, the rolled-up sleeves of his pressed white shirt pulling the salt out of his beard, dashing against his dark skin.

"I'm a delicate man, Sam. Years under the harsh Nevada sun have changed me. I don't know how you do it."

"I'm cold-blooded," I responded dryly, enjoying his hearty laugh.

Jordan entered, and a flicker of nerves spiked in me as he surveyed the room. He didn't have to love it, but I'd always respected his opinion and knew that he'd give it to me honestly. "Not bad. The ceiling is a little bare. Probably would have been better with some molding or an accent color."

"That's what I said." Tiffany walked over with her hand out. "Hi, I'm Tiff."

"And I'm impressed." Jordan shook her hand, and I did my best to blink away a flare of jealousy. "Jordan. Lovely to meet you, Tiff."

"And you. I'm a big fan of your twist on the Manhattan."

"Thank you. I've heard you have a take on the Sazerac that I must try."

Her cheeks pinked, and a sharp pain in my hand caused me to release my fist before I broke the skin with my nail.

"It's nothing much, but I'd be happy to make you one if you'd like?"

"Wonderful." Tiffany started towards the bar to start on the drinks. Jordan hung back for a moment, keeping his voice low. "So that's the infamous Tiff?"

I shook my head—*not now*—and we each took a seat at the bar.

Tiffany quickly fixed up three cocktails, moving smoothly behind the bar, and I took the opportunity to watch her work. She didn't miss a beat, able to continue a conversation with

Jordan as she measured by sight, free pouring, and acting on instinct. She was mesmerizing.

If I hadn't let our professional relationship become muddled by my selfish desires, I would have been safe without the knowledge of how far her light went and all the ways she made me feel again.

If I hadn't been so distracted by my feelings for her, maybe the whole mess with Pierce would have gone differently. But I'd never know now.

If I weren't so selfish, I would put a stop to this. But it was hard to let go. I felt trapped between backing away from us and stepping closer, the pull to let myself have this insistent and undeniable. Reaching for her as she passed me, noticing her in any room, wanting to preempt her needs and be the one to provide them.

Tiffany poured the cocktail out into three glasses. "You know, this was the first drink I ever learned to mix."

"Really? That's not what I expected." Jordan reached for his glass, sniffing and examining the liquid with a keen eye.

"I know. It didn't make sense to anyone in college either. But my uncle is a huge whiskey nut, and I thought it made me cooler to serve cocktails no one had heard of." She chuckled.

"Did it?" He took a sip, not hiding his enjoyment, which I could tell was genuine. It filled me with pride.

Tiffany leaned against the bar, confident, enjoying her creation. "Hell no. I liked it, but everyone else just wanted Jägerbombs."

"This is good. Well worth the praise," he said, and Tiff nodded her thanks as he had a second taste. "Well, I would have thought you were cool. In my day, the closest I got to mixing a drink was having rum and coke."

Tiffany smiled. "It's a classic for a reason."

"True, but by the end of the night, we'd be drinking rum and whatever was left. And trust me, we were all lucky that we couldn't taste anything at the end of the night because they were not my best inventions."

I laughed, recalling my own horror stories of house parties and disgusting concoctions, only occasionally being surprised that two elements I'd never have otherwise paired went well together.

Huh … That wasn't a horrible idea.

"Uh oh." Jordan turned to me. "Sam's got his thinking face on."

I turned it over in my mind. Actually, if done right, it could work. "That experience is rather universal, don't you think? Drinks made up of odd combinations of leftovers. I was wondering if there was something in that."

His eyes narrowed, not yet convinced, but I could see he was intrigued. "Keep talking."

"There's an accessibility there, not to mention the nostalgia, and if kept to the standard 'booze plus mixer' combination, anyone you hired could make it." I felt my mind running a few steps ahead of me, lost in planning.

"Step back. What exactly are you saying?"

"I'm not exactly sure yet, but either some sort of dual selection gimmick,"

Jordan was nodding, "Pick your booze, now spin for a random mixer …"

"Something like that." I looked over to Tiffany to find her watching our conversation with amusement.

"Not that I want to disagree," she started, snorting a laugh when I added, "That would be a first." Picking up a fresh 18-28 shaker, she began a fresh cocktail. "But, I think I have a way to take that and make it better. There are too many variables for random selection to work, but what if you took the foundation of that—the different combinations—but anchored it in a style? Like a sour. Then, you could still use different infused bases and mix and match them with a range of juices."

Before us, apple brandy, egg white, lemon juice, and a colored lavender simple syrup come together with ease, and it was hard to tell if she'd made it a hundred times or if this is the first. "Dry shake, single strain, with or without ice …" The actions followed her words.

Finally, a single sprig of lavender garnished the coupe. "It would take seconds to pump out and give you a pretty solid lineup to keep year-round, plus room for changing things up if you wanted to." She slid the glass towards me, and I appraised both it and its beautiful creator. Tiffany's cheeks brightened with a small blush. "And sours are pretty classic, right—spirit, sugar, citrus—but not revolutionary either. This would be just different enough not to be boring, but also accessible enough to not be designer."

The drink tasted incredible, but that wasn't surprising. What floored me was the way Tiffany so effortlessly transformed the seed of an idea into something brilliant and marketable. Like a perfect combination of both of us.

On my left, Jordan looked pleased. Too pleased. He had that glint in his eyes that only meant trouble. "You two make a good team."

"We sure do," Tiffany added, the soft glimmer in her eyes causing my entire body to melt.

And that's when I knew.

No matter how much time passed, I would always have a weak spot for Tiffany. And that terrified me.

41

SAM

Today was the day the article would go live, Diego had warned me. And sure enough, when I fired up the site over my second espresso, there it was, my face and words shining back at me.

Diego hadn't twisted my words out of context and had even added some of his own thoughts to support my points. There was no question that Pierce would be pissed, but I had officially run out of patience with that blowhole, so he could think what he liked.

When I'd said the same thing to Jordan last night, he'd been supportive, if cautious ("I hope you know what you're doing."), and while I appreciated his concern, finally being able to defend my position was somewhat freeing. No risk, no reward, right?

It wasn't a tactic I'd engaged often, but how often had public statements been used as a veiled middle finger in business? It was practically the status quo. Besides, what was the worst that could happen? Pierce wasn't named, so he couldn't claim libel.

Making a public comment would only serve to identify

himself as part of the problem I was speaking about, and he was hardly going to do that.

A text message arrived from Tiffany. "Bold choice." An image followed, a screenshot of the article, and she'd circled one particular section:

"What statement are you trying to make here?"

"I want to speak against the gatekeeping and misogyny that I've seen, and while I agree that this town has proven itself a bastion of innovation, change moves in many different directions, and as he sees it, inclusion is key. There's a place for the over-designed wine bars of the world, just as there's a place for the local club or tavern. Each offers an experience."

"What experience are you offering?"

"In a word? Acceptance. Sick of feeling out of place at a wanky establishment? Nervous to order a cocktail because there are twelve ingredients you don't know in it? My mission is to offer somewhere you want to be and enjoy being. Good drinks, mixed by professionals, and an atmosphere that no matter your preference or poison, you're welcome."

The rest of the morning, I waited for a sign that Pierce had seen the article and, hopefully, understood my message. In truth, I knew that as a businessman, and a proud one at that, any grudge he was going to hold against me would be harbored in private and expressed through thinly veiled barbs to my face—not unlike how he'd treated Tiffany at the dinner those weeks ago.

Even so, I could picture his scowl in my mind, and I was happy enough for now that he would know without a doubt I was referring to him. His absurd play at interference with the contractor still pissed me off, but at least now he knew I wasn't going to fall in line behind him. If he needed someone to kiss his feet, he was going to have to look elsewhere.

It took two hours before he called.

"It seems you have something to say to me," he said, ignoring any form of hello.

"Nothing that hasn't already been said by my staff or me."

"I'm not sure what you hoped to get out of this, but I would have hoped that you were smart enough to talk to me in private before making a statement like this. Instead, I received a call two days ago from a friend at the paper, telling me to prepare myself."

"And yet you waited until today to call me."

"Oh, I tried to get in touch with you on Saturday, but you weren't around." That would have been when I'd spent the day at Tiffany's.

"You have me now. Is there anything in particular you want to say, or is this more posturing? Because I think I've made it quite clear that I won't tolerate you harassing my staff or me any longer."

There was a long drag of silence on the other end of the line, and I wondered if I'd pushed him too far.

"It's counterproductive to make an enemy of me when we could work together instead."

"I could. But as long as I dislike you, I know I've got good taste."

Pierce clicked his tongue. "I thought you would have understood after that business with Star Constructions, but apparently not. And now that you've aired your dirty laundry publicly, I'm going to say to you the same thing I said to your favorite bartender. You should have realized not to fuck with me. But if this is how you want to play it, so be it."

It was exactly the reaction I expected, but that didn't diminish the sense of dread that trickled down my spine.

"Have a good day, Sam," he said before hanging up, leaving me swallowing down the unfortunate fear that I'd just taken one risk I was absolutely going to regret.

———

A TALL MAN wrapped in a thick navy coat stood in the center of the bar room, sharp eyes trailing over every beam, each worn floorboard. Once in a while, he paused, making notes on his smartphone.

"Could I see your identification again?" Amid my confusion, I wanted as many details as possible. Because if what I thought was happening was real, then I could be in trouble.

With a nod, he reached inside of his coat and held out his I.D. Yep, there it was: special agent for the Illinois Liquor Control Commission. Shit.

This wasn't happening. It couldn't. Okay, it could, but hell, it didn't make any sense. It just ... What the hell was happening right now?

I noted his name on my phone, determined to take down as much information as possible in case I needed it later. Hell, of course, I would need it. "Thank you. Can you tell me why you're here? Is this a routine inspection?" I'd never heard of them doing these unannounced before, but maybe things worked differently here?

"It's been recognized that there is an error on your liquor license, and it was decided that a full review of the premises should be undertaken to determine any further issues."

It has been months since Harry had handed over the bar. Months. Why now? Who would suddenly think to check on the paperwork out of nowhere for a bar that had been running for years?

Okay, stop. I could feel myself getting worked up, my breathing erratic, my thoughts even more so. *Breathe. Think.* The local permit renewed every two years, the ILCC one annually. But we'd had an inspection earlier in the year when the ownership was transferred, so this made no sense. Why were they back for an unannounced visit now?

"The license was renewed back in July when ownership was transferred. Shouldn't this have been caught then?"

He pinned me with a sharp look. "Yes, it should."

Fuck. I hated not having all the facts. I needed to recheck the paperwork as soon as possible and work out what the error was. How the hell had I missed it?

"That signage isn't exactly visible from here," he said, pointing to the license that hung on the small wall by my office before making another note. I forced myself to maintain a calm expression, adding a nod of acknowledgment. This wasn't his fault. The ILCC conducted thousands of inspections a year. We were another item on his agenda.

Knowing that didn't lessen my frustration, though.

I followed him as he stepped behind the bar, taking notes as he reviewed the stations. Even though I'd watched as the team closed last night, and I knew that they cleaned everything, my nerves were on edge. *Please don't let anything be wrong.* "Can I ask how it got picked up now if it was missed before?"

"We've received an allegation that you're operating in violation of your liquor license. We've opened an official investigation and identified the error on your local tavern license, which will need to be rectified before you can reopen."

My stomach was in my throat. This was a waking nightmare. It didn't matter that we were operating to the letter of the law and that I knew that without a shadow of doubt. Violation allegations were serious. Go out of business, serious. Do not pass GO. Do not collect $200 *serious*.

"Where did the allegation come from?"

"I'm not allowed to disclose that information."

Of course, he couldn't. Shit. It could be anyone. One of our neighbors—although that seemed unlikely, as none of them had been unfriendly—or anyone with a grudge ...

And then it hit me.

Pierce. That dick. Of course, he would. Who else? Ever since that damn article put us against each other, he'd taken up a stance against me. But this just took the cake. The whole damn bakery.

How could he? This went beyond petty rivalry and veiled —although when had they ever been veiled?—comments to the press. This was underhanded. Vile. He'd gone from messing around with the contractor to actively trying to shut me down.

All because of … what? I was a threat to his profits? He'd made it clear we weren't in the same league, but maybe that had just been posturing. So what, I call him out in one article, and this was how he retaliates?

Dammit, I never should have made those comments. What had I been thinking? Every other time I'd been asked to comment, I'd deflected. I knew it wouldn't be a good idea to fight fire with fire.

The inspector continued to wander, taking notes. *Definitely not a good idea.*

In fact, it was easily the worst idea I'd ever had.

Faster than expected, he'd completed his notes, and my breath held in my throat as I waited for the verdict, my mind racing.

"There doesn't appear to be any validity to the allegation, and your other permits seem to be up to date and in order. Based on that, and the fact that the initial error is minor, I can see no reason to revoke your license at this time."

Sweet relief rushed through me, and I finally exhaled the breath I'd been holding.

"However," he said, and I felt my blood pressure spiking again, "I do have to issue a temporary suspension. It will take effect immediately." To his credit, he looked sympathetic to what he had to do. Goddamn, what a thankless job that must be. If I weren't currently swimming in my own misery at the idea of the bar having to shut down, I would have offered my condolences. Instead, I focused on keeping my cool. I didn't need to know what would happen if I blew up at him. Nothing good, I'm sure.

Pocketing his phone, he said, "You've got a week. If you don't supply the necessary forms by then, your license will be revoked and you'll need to appeal the decision to have it reinstated. In the meantime, we'll issue a formal report of the investigation and the suspension notice."

This was followed by a warning. "You should ensure all future renewals are completed correctly and on time as this will remain on file."

He left quickly, leaving me alone in a room too small for everything I was feeling. I barely knew where to start.

Dropping into the closest seat, I started with slow breaths. I needed to think clearly, get a plan in order.

Jesus, had this really all happened because of Pierce? Because of a single interview in a single newspaper? He turned out to be worse than I'd realized.

I knew this wasn't solely a by-the-books situation. This was a statement. A declaration. I'd stepped out of bounds. And I needed to be put in my place.

The sinking realization that this wasn't wholly Pierce's fault sat like lead in my stomach. Yes, this shit show was his doing. But it wasn't his fault.

No. That laid entirely with me.

For months I'd been poked and goaded into a grudge match with Pierce, but I'd refused to play that game. Why? Because I *knew* this was what it would lead to. The entire time, I'd stuck to defending the bar and myself but never made any direct remarks about Pierce or his bars—at least publicly—because you could never walk them back.

So, why had I? What a great question.

It had made so much sense at the time. Months of Pierce's snide personal attacks against me, the bar, Tiffany. Defending her came easy. I couldn't help it. And it felt like the right thing to do at the time.

It should be the right thing to do. But what was right didn't always factor into business, did it?

What a lesson to learn twice. That was what stung. Hadn't I already worked out that love and work didn't mix? That if I wanted to do this job and do it well, I needed to keep those two things as far away from each other as humanly possible?

What had I been thinking? The truth was, I hadn't been. Not like myself, in any case. In a moment of anger, I'd done something completely out of character. No planning, no strategy. Just a few choice words, aimed at the wrong person, at the wrong time.

Months of work, and now I was potentially facing losing the bar entirely. Another loss for the books. Another notch against my reputation.

My head hung heavy in the silent bar. There was a lot to do. Someone needed to tell the staff not to come in. Visit my lawyer. Check the paperwork. Call our distributors. Shit. Announce the closure publicly.

I should have …

Well, I should have done a lot of things. I should have *not* have done a lot of things.

Within minutes, I'd called Jordan, awaiting his arrival at the bar. If anyone knew how to handle this, it was him.

It was startlingly obvious now where I'd gone wrong. Coming home, this bar had been my priority. However, I'd gotten distracted by attraction. By Tiffany. Now, I was acting irrationally and upending everything I'd been trying to re-establish.

I needed to refocus. Get back on track. Put the bar before anything, and everything, else.

Breaking it off with Tiffany wasn't something I wanted to do, but the bar had to come first. Once this mess was sorted out, maybe we could see how to make it work.

By the time Jordan arrived, I had barely moved, too lost in the cavalcade of emotions running through me.

As he took the seat beside me, I let my head fall into my hands. There was no time to sugarcoat anything. "I've fucked up."

He faced me head-on, serious. "Talk to me. What's going on?"

"Where do I start?"

"The beginning usually works."

So, that's where I started. I told him about Pierce, the permit issue, the problems with the contractor, and then further back, to my first day at the bar, meeting Tiffany, the arguments, the growing respect, the attraction, the surprising night that she showed up at my apartment and announced she was quitting—"Ballsy move. I really like this one, Sam."—as well as my inability to stay away despite knowing I might be putting myself in the same position I'd found myself with Piper.

"You were there. You saw how I blinded myself with her. It's happening again. No matter what, I'm always going to put her first. And so far, all it's done is make things harder for the bar."

"You're allowed to have both, Sam. You don't have to choose."

"I do. Maybe if I'd waited until after the bar was a success, it could have worked out differently. But you can't tell me that I haven't been dropping the ball here."

"Fine. Yes, you've clearly let your emotions get in the way of work. And after seeing what you went through with Piper, I would be a hypocrite if I didn't warn you against making the same mistakes. I just want you to be sure that this is what you want."

It wasn't. But what choice did I have? How many more setbacks would I accept before I realized this relationship was a problem? "If we end it now, it's still recoverable."

"For you or Tiff?"

"She'll be fine. I've never met anyone as self-sufficient as she is. Not even you."

Tiffany was tough, perhaps not as tough as she acted, but tougher than anyone else I'd ever met. Or maybe tough wasn't the right word. Resilient. She would move on. Even though I knew I'd never meet anyone like her, it would eventually be fine. I would concentrate on the bar, which is what I'd come here to do.

I'd been so busy defending her against Pierce that I'd put her before anything else.

It was time to get my priorities in order.

42

TIFF

Shock was an understatement. The bar had been forced to close. For a week, at least, and (if what Sam was explaining to me was right, and knowing him, it absolutely was) potentially longer. It all came down to what his lawyer could do to turn around the discrepancy on the original paperwork.

Sam was … I didn't want to say confident because he looked like a wreck. But he seemed sure that once the week was up, the bar would be reopened.

From the moment I'd arrived at the bar, he'd been distant. I hadn't realized how familiar I'd become with having him close until he was standing in his kitchen, the breakfast bar between us. Like a barricade. Or a shield.

Something was very, very wrong. And I was pretty sure I was about to find out what.

"Jordan offered me a job."

Sam's eyes snapped up to mine, genuinely surprised, along with something else that I couldn't decipher. "He did?"

"Yeah, he, uh, asked me to head up his new bar in New York."

"Are you going to go?" Was that hope or fear in his voice?

"Maybe," I lied, hoping to get a reaction.

The need to be near him when he wanted space was eating at me, and I was really starting to hate having these *feelings*. Life had been so much easier when I only had myself to worry about.

Well, if Sam thought I would let a little thing like kitchen furniture stand between us, he'd learned nothing.

His body stiffened as I stepped close, wrapping my arms around his waist. I turned into the crook of his neck, breathing deep. Something about tonight made me want to catch every sense and bottle it up. Memorize it for posterity.

I had barely settled onto his chest before he pulled out of my arms, stepping back to increase the distance between us again. Ouch, okay. Something akin to a klaxon sounded in my mind.

My body entered defensive mode; one hip cocked against the counter, arms crossed. I continued to stall. Not my usual M.O., but once I crossed enemy lines, I knew tonight would be over. "Jordan is pretty great. Why have we never talked about how you used to work for him?"

Sam barely moved but allowed the subject change. "It never came up. He was my rock while I was figuring things out. Without him, my first bar would never have gotten off the ground. He saw something in me, mentored me, was the reason I believed I could open my own place. I learned a lot from him. After a rocky first month, we almost closed, and I thought I'd have to start over, but he came in, showed me where I could do better, and gave me the confidence to keep going. And it worked out."

"I can tell he really cares about you."

His nod was slow, his gaze locked on the floor. "He saw what happened with Piper, and I know he feels responsible for not seeing what was going on there, but there wasn't anything anyone could do."

"So, why do you still feel responsible for what happened?"

"Because it was my fault."

"You were in love. You can't blame yourself for that."

His next words were chosen carefully. "That won't be a mistake I'm willing to make twice."

Seconds felt like minutes as my emotions scurried and settled within me. I should have learned my lesson by now (especially when it came to Sam). My heart was practically screaming at me just to LEAVE. THIS. ALONE. But not knowing had never worked out for me. "What's going on with you?"

"You mean, on top of the fact that I might lose the one thing I really care about?" Not since we'd met had he spoken to me that way. *The one thing he really cares about isn't me.* My heart splintered, but anger rose to the surface first.

"Fuck you. I know you're upset right now, but you do not get to say that to me. Not now."

Sam's expression hardened, flexing his hands before he pounded a fist on the counter. I was immediately transported to my breakup with Hannah when I'd done the same. Unbidden, her words flooded back. *Some of us can't take the risks you do. Some of us have to face the consequences.*

"I'm not you. I can't say what I want and not care about the consequences."

My breath caught in my throat. "I care about the consequences."

"Do you? Because I'm not sure I've seen it. Not when you continually act without thinking." Shakily, he ran a hand through his hair. He was a mess. I wasn't faring much better.

"Christ," he continued, "Do you realize how lucky it is that you haven't been blacklisted?" I balked. Because it hadn't occurred to me. "No, you haven't. What consequences have you faced? Everything that has come out of your actions has affected me, not you. You're still able to find work. But this is my business, my life, on the line here."

"If you regret it so much, call Pierce. Take it back."

"That's not—" His brows were pinched. "I don't want to take it back. Pierce needs to be told where to shove his shit. But that doesn't mean I don't regret what I said. This isn't me. I don't make these decisions. I'm not acting smart."

"Meaning I'm not?"

"Stop twisting my words."

"Then stop talking around what it is you really want to say, Sam. If you don't want to be with me, then just say that."

"I do want to be with you. But I think we need some breathing room. We've spent every day of the last five months together, whether that was working or—"

"Fucking," I finished for him.

"Yes."

The air hung heavy. He continued. "I have feelings for you. You know that. And I want to be you. But …"

"You need to be sure."

"I do."

"Goddammit, Sam. You're not even going to try? Take this one little risk?"

"I … can't. I'm sorry."

"Fuck," I breathed into the quiet between us. I want to fight him, shout, convince him. But I was worth more than that. And he knew it. But he was still walking away. And I was not going to beg him. He needed to want this as much as I did. Otherwise, I'd always wonder, and he might come to resent me. He loved me, I was sure of it, but if he couldn't realize that and chose to put the bar before his heart, I couldn't stop him.

The fact was, what I wanted hadn't changed. I still wanted a partner who accepted me and was as committed as I was to making a life together. Making it work. It didn't matter how much I liked Sam if he wasn't going to be that person.

I couldn't resist one last chaste kiss before I left, my fingers ghosting his in an aborted hold before I pulled back. "Goodnight, Sam."

My steps fell heavy on the stairs as I left.

This was the problem with diving headfirst into everything. The risk was high, and the crash was hard. I had lots of practice picking myself up when things didn't work out. None of them had involved my heart before, so ...

Guess it never was too late for your first heartbreak.

43

SAM

It was done. Over. It was what I wanted. What I'd decided. The safer option. So, why did it feel like my heart just got up and walked out the door?

The apartment was cold and empty, and I was suddenly sure I couldn't spend the night there. Not alone. Not without her.

Everywhere I looked, there was a memory of her. The way she'd draped herself over almost every piece of furniture in the room, Luna curled up and purring in her lap. The sound of her laugh as she plucked a book at random from my bookcase and inevitably found some way of making fun of me for it. The lingering smell of cinnamon and coffee that followed her everywhere.

It was too much.

After I packed an overnight bag and put Luna in a carrier, I called Harry.

It was late, but he was still up and refused to take no for an answer when he offered to drive in and pick me up.

Imogen and the baby were fast asleep when we arrived, and I dropped my bag and Luna in the spare room before joining my brother for a beer.

"How are you holding up?"

"Fine."

"It's okay if you're not fine."

"Tiffany and I …" How did I phrase this? Broke up? We'd never acknowledged it as dating. "Decided just to be friends." It was not even close to what I wanted to say and sounded ridiculous, but there it was.

Harry had paused in raising his beer, decided to follow through, and was now watching me. "And how do you feel about that?"

"Fine." I sounded anything but.

"Liar."

I took a draw of my own beer, the cool liquid soothing my frayed edges.

"Will the suspension change your plans for the bar?"

"Probably, but I won't know for sure until it's fixed. I have to close for a week. But it should get turned over quickly, so hopefully, we can keep to the re-opening date."

"I'm glad. It's better in your hands."

"Look, Harry, there's something I've been wanting to say for a while. I'm sorry that I wasn't here after mom and dad passed. You had so much going on—"

"So did you."

"—and I should have come home sooner, or at least helped in some other way."

"Sam, you have nothing to apologize for."

"Funny. That's just what Tiffany said you'd say."

"Smart woman."

"She's a menace."

"I would offer the same critique of you." His hand stilled mid-air. "Holy shit, you're in love with her."

I wordlessly acknowledged it while taking a long drag of beer. There was no denying it, even if I wanted to. It would certainly make life easier if I weren't. But from the beginning, I'd been entranced by her.

Pinpointing the exact moment when I'd known would be impossible because the only timeline I had become aware of was before and after her presence in my life.

"No offense, brother, but what the hell are you doing here, then?"

"How I feel doesn't change anything."

"You're not making any sense, Sam. Of course, it does."

"Yes, I have feelings for her." I felt like a coward, fumbling around the word he'd used, knowing I wasn't ready to face those feelings yet. Not if I was going to move on. "You and I both know that what happened with Piper crushed me. I shouldn't be with anyone right now, let alone the first person I slept with after I've gotten back."

"You're acting like you weren't practically infatuated the minute you met her."

"Of course, I was. But isn't that how it started the last time? I let my feelings for someone get in the way of my work, and it bit me in the ass. I won't let it happen again."

"You have to let that go, Sam. Tiffany isn't Piper." Rubbing his hands on his thighs, he sighed, and I knew what came next would be a hard truth. "So, you had to hit the reset button on your life. Starting over isn't inherently a bad thing. The difference is that you have experience now. What would be a bigger mistake is throwing away something good because you're scared. Hurting Tiffany won't make up for how Piper hurt you."

"You don't think I know that? Tiffany is a hundred times the person Piper was."

"I'm not hearing the problem."

"The problem is that I should be focused on the bar right now. You remember? The whole reason I came back?"

"This has nothing to do with the bar and everything to do with you." He'd clearly given up trying to be gentle with me and so plowed on, exasperated. "Do you seriously think Tiffany gives a rat's ass about taking over? Has she indicated once while working for you that she felt she deserved it in some way? Has she mentioned once that that's even something she wants?"

"This is more than sex. I can't go through it again. When Piper ended it, the damn floor disappeared beneath me. I don't know that I'll be able to get back up a second time."

"Are you afraid she doesn't feel the same?"

"No, I know she does. That's the problem. If this doesn't work out ..."

"Then, it doesn't work out." He finished his beer and set it on the table, tired. "Look, you're going to do what you want. You always have. But life's too short to give up on something that clearly means this much to you."

Rationally, I knew that. I did. But it was a risk I wasn't sure I was willing to take.

"Jordan offered her a job. In New York."

"Has she accepted?"

"I don't think so. Not yet."

"Then, you still have time to figure it out."

"Figure out what?"

"I love you, but you're an idiot."

44

——

SAM

Waking early the next morning, I was halfway to the kitchen when I heard Imogen softly singing, accompanied by spurts of giggles. Following the sounds, I found my sister-in-law lounging on the floor of the baby's room, Gracie lying on a brightly colored mat before her, waving her hands and laughing excitedly.

"Morning, I hope we didn't wake you."

I leaned down to kiss her cheek. "Not at all." Taking a seat beside her, I looked down, halting when I locked eyes on Gracie. Deep pools of royal blue stared back at me in wonder, and I was helpless to do anything but look back.

What did she see, apart from a wary, confused man?

Then, slow and sparkling, she smiled, and my own smile followed. Warmth flared in my chest.

"She likes you."

Tentatively, I reached out, and Gracie's miniature hand grasped onto my index finger. I knew then that I'd tear walls down for her. "She's adorable."

"We think she's pretty special." Imogen tickled Gracie's stomach, resulting in more giggles. "You're our precious little penguin, aren't you?" Catching my curious look, Imogen explained, "It's an old nickname my pop had for me."

"It's very sweet." Mental note: I'd have to order some penguin toys later.

We sat together, watching Gracie as she rolled over onto her stomach, tapping her hands and feet on the mat joyfully. Imogen kept her eyes trained on the baby as she said, "Harry mentioned the shutdown to me last night. I can't believe it."

"Neither can I."

"What's next? What do you do in these situations?"

"I have a lawyer looking into it. He's confident we can re-open after the week is up, and then it's a matter of having the permit confirmed as valid. He's going to handle all the details. There's not much more I can do, unfortunately."

"I'm sorry." Gracie started to cry softly in frustration, so Imogen helped her roll back over, picking up a fluffy gray rabbit and passing it to her. I recognized it as part of the gift I had sent them when they had announced the pregnancy. "Your uncle gave you this. Say 'thank you, Uncle Sam'." She wiggled the toy at Gracie, who squealed in delight. Imogen turned to me. "I know it's not the best circumstances, but it's really nice having you here. And I don't just mean this morning."

Nodding in understanding, I said, "I know. It's good to be home."

———

HARRY WAS KIND ENOUGH to drop me back at the bar a short while later in exchange for me returning that night. It was sweet, something I hadn't experienced from my brother in a long time, and I enjoyed getting the added time with him.

I'd already given the staff the bad news, telling them that we'd be closed for the week but that I'd make sure their wages were paid for any shifts they had been scheduled for.

When I arrived to find the bar door unlocked, I panicked —had it been unlocked all night? No. I specifically remember locking it before I'd left. But the panic quickly dissipated when I walked in to find Devon, Jade, and a few others in the middle of various tasks.

Devon directed two others to clear out any of the fresh produce that wouldn't last through the closure. We arranged to donate it to a local food bank. "Easy done, boss," Nathan said when I'd asked.

Devon and Jade were taking inventory, checking the back bar and speed racks. "We wanted to make sure we're ready to go when we open up again next week."

"That's great. Thank you," I said, a little choked up.

My chest swelled with pride. This is why I loved my job. Why I'd kept at it for as long as I had. The opportunity to work with good people. Knowing that they had voluntarily given up their own time to be here, to help, it meant more than I could say.

———

Not wanting to stew in my thoughts after the team cleared out, I met up with Jordan at his hotel, enjoying a room-serviced espresso in his suite.

"Maybe I should cut my losses and head over to Manhattan with you." I was equally joking and not.

"Running away was never your style before."

"What do you call this, then?" I asked, gesturing to the view of Chicago.

"That wasn't running away. You got blindsided in a bad situation and came home to get a fresh start. That's different."

"No, that's the PR line."

"Then, what is the truth?"

I stared out the window at the city, considering. "That I wanted to be somewhere that didn't remind me of my mistakes. Somewhere I could forget Piper and how naïve I'd been."

"You could have done that anywhere. Why here?"

"Because it's home."

"I'm leaving tomorrow," he said abruptly. "Have to head back to NYC and finalize the last of the details before opening."

I nodded, silent. I'd known he wouldn't be in town for long but was still sad he had to leave. Having him here had bolstered my confidence. Reminded me that I had once been fearless. It felt so long ago now.

He straightened. "Can I say something you won't like?"

"I'm an idiot."

"Oh, you already knew that? Ok. In that case, I'll let you in on a little secret. Kind of an inside tip." He leaned in. "Us self-sufficient types can sometimes be the worst at sharing our feelings."

I shook my head. "Normally, I would agree with you, but you don't know her. There's no holding back with her. I've never known her not to say what she's thinking. Trust me, if she felt something, she would have told me."

He didn't look convinced. "Just be careful. If she's even half as clever as you've said she is, she's learned how to hide behind a smile. Don't let that fool you into thinking you can't hurt her."

Sighing, I rubbed at my face. Could Jordan be right? I'd seen Tiffany upset before when she'd broken up with her ex, and even then, she'd handled it gracefully. I'd watched as she'd picked herself up from that and kept going, never letting it interfere with her work. And they'd been dating. I didn't even know how to name what we'd been doing, beyond a mix of flirting, fighting, and fucking.

No. That was too cheap a way to describe it, and I knew it. In reality, we'd spent almost all of our waking (and some of our sleeping) time together in the last few weeks, and despite whatever reservations I had about crossing that line, I had enjoyed every second of it. I'd legitimately forgotten how much I enjoyed rising to a challenge, and there was no one more capable of challenging me than Tiffany. She was a competitor and cheerleader, all in one.

"I don't want to hurt her. If I could, I'd tell her that I don't want her to leave. That I can't think of anyone else I want to be with. But," my breath left me in one go, "I don't trust it."

"Why don't you give it a chance?"

"I don't take chances. I take calculated risks, but not chances."

"Love shouldn't be calculated."

"I don't know that that's what this is."

"Yes, you do."

"Maybe I've done the math and worked out that this isn't a risk I'm willing to take."

"Then, you're more stubborn than I thought. And you'd be missing out on something worthwhile. Which I know for a fact you never like to do."

"It's too soon. Piper and I—"

"I don't know much about Tiffany, but from what I've seen, I find it hard to imagine she's anything like Piper."

"She's not. But I'm," the word sat like ash on my tongue. I forced it out, "afraid."

"That's not a bad thing, my friend. The Sam Cooper I knew didn't let that stop him, either. Look. No one can guarantee forever. We know that better than most. But even if you seem to have forgotten, I know what you're capable of. And just because you made a mistake with Piper doesn't mean you're going to make the same mistake again. It also doesn't mean that you can pretend you can do this alone. You need people in your corner, Sam, people you can trust. Some might be in it for selfish reasons, but not all of them will be."

I thought about Tiffany helping me even after she'd quit, giving up her favor with Diego so that I could kiss Pierce's ass, and so much more. She'd proven time and again that she would help without needing anything in return.

"Piper might have walked away with the last four years of your life, but don't let her rob you of the rest of it."

He was right. I'd let my guilt consume me, attaching my fears to Tiffany when I could have easily seen that she was nothing like Piper. She'd never shown any interest in taking over. She'd only ever wanted to work *with* me. And I'd fought her almost every step of the way. Keeping my distance, putting a wall up, pretending that she hadn't already won me over the first time she stalked into my office.

Had she ever shown anything except generosity and loyalty and selflessness? Tiffany gave everything to this bar. To my brother. To the staff. To me.

Because she cared.

My head fell into my hands. "Fuck. I'm an idiot."

"That's what I've been trying to tell you."

45

———

SAM

Even though we'd only been away for two nights, Luna made short work of re-marking her territory the next morning.

As nice as it had been to spend time with Harry, Imogen, and the baby, I was glad to be back. There was still plenty to do, and I didn't want to waste any time. I left Luna to her wandering and put the coffee pot on, settling in at the kitchen counter to start a list.

- order stock to top up inventory
- confirm staff schedule with Devon
- Talk to Tiffany

The last one got underlined. Twice.

I had no idea what I would say beyond "I'm sorry" and "I love you," but I reasoned they were a good place to start.

When our usual opening time rolled around later that evening, I wasn't surprised to hear the knock on the door. Though Devon had updated our social media sites with the news of the closure, I knew news could slip through the cracks.

But it wasn't a confused customer at the door. Instead, it was Tiffany's friend Quinn, dressed in a flattering jumpsuit that accentuated her height. Her face was buried in her phone but snapped up at the sound of the door opening.

"A little birdy sent me this." She turned her phone around, where the tribute interview was open. "I don't know what I was expecting from you, Sam, but you and Tiff are two of the gutsiest sons of bitches I've ever known. You know you just killed whatever goodwill you had with Pierce, right? Of course, you do. You're not an idiot. Anyway, I think we can help each other out." She moved confidently into the bar, and I marveled at the similarity to Tiffany. There was a lack of airs about her, and it made me warm to her instantly.

"Oh?" I locked the door and followed after her.

"Absolutely. You're not the only one, you know. There are a lot of us who are sick of the Pierce's of the world holding their influence over our heads. We've been talking about a mutually beneficial arrangement, a coalition, to get around him. I wasn't sure you'd be interested, but after reading this, I've changed my mind." Without waiting for a response, she took a seat at the bar, swiveling the chair around to face me. "Sorry to hear about the permit situation, by the way. If there's anything I can do to help, let me know."

I took a seat beside her. "Tell me more about this coalition."

"It's not only bar owners. We're cafés, restaurants, retailers, all small businesses really, across town, and the idea is to get enough of us on board that we can pretty much support each other, try our best to keep our businesses alive, give new startups the best chance possible. Where we can, we supply to each other, cross-promote, mentor each other. Right now, it feels more like an all-hours support group." She laughed.

"It's not gonna be foolproof, but it's nice to know you're

not out here alone, you know? That when you're faced with a problem, there are people around, people who are in the same position, and who care, that you can talk to about it. That could maybe help with it. Silly idea in this day and age."

"But a noble one."

"Most businesses fail, and we're all just out here trying our best. It's utter bullshit not to help, in my opinion. Where one succeeds, we all do. All that jazz."

And there was something in that. A thread, itching under my skin. That coming together, working together, wasn't a result of giving something up but rather pooling resources together. It bubbled up alongside a jerk reaction of cynicism. I was once that naïve, believing wholeheartedly in the goodness of others.

Then, Piper took that hope and crushed it.

Ever since then, I've been holding on to what was mine with both hands and a chain-link fence. Never wanting to give any ground. Not wanting to give away any more of myself than I could spare.

Did I really want to let that become who I was?

What Quinn was talking about was a larger version of what I had with Jordan, and the idea that I could be that for someone else was thrilling. I wanted to be a part of it.

Immediately, I knew there was no one more suited for this than Tiffany. In the time that I'd worked here, could I even count how many stories I'd heard of favors she'd done for others?

"Can I ask you a question? It's a little left field."

Quinn nodded, her body language subtly shifting, readying herself for what I was about to ask.

"What has Tiffany done for you?" I heard the question and stammered to rephrase it. "I mean, uh. Hmm." Christ, this shouldn't be this hard. "Has she ever—"

Quinn, realizing that I was floundering, cut in with a laugh. "I think I know what you're getting at. She has a habit of helping out. I know a lot of people who owe her a favor or two, not that she ever keeps count or cares about collecting. It's just her way."

"I used to believe it was selfishly motivated," I said, not ashamed to show my regret.

She hummed, considering. "She's tough, but anyone who has spent more than a minute with her can tell she'll do anything for the people she cares about."

"Yes, I've learned that."

"What has Tiffany done for you?" Quinn watched me carefully as she returned my earlier question.

A good question with a difficult answer. Because what hadn't she done for me? Every memory of the last few months were colored with her presence. Every moment was an integral step to where we were now, to how I felt about her.

I loved her. I knew that without question.

Tiffany brought both the challenge of thought that I chased, as well as a sense of mindfulness, of being completely in the moment. It was gut instinct and empowerment versus my tendency for careful contemplation.

More than any one action, there were the small, subtle ways that Tiffany had done things for me. Cups of coffee and words of encouragement. Hell, even when we'd been at each other's throats at the beginning, she'd always made sure it never affected how the staff treated me, never let it interfere with her work. No matter how much she debated an idea or fought me on something, she would concede. Usually with a wave or a shrug, saying, "It's your bar."

Like a key finally clicking into place, I knew what I had to do. What I needed to do.

"Anyway," Quinn said, standing, and I realized I hadn't answered her, too lost in thought. The knowing look on her face said she hadn't minded. "I'm sure you have a lot of work to do, but I'm glad to have you on board. Tiffany was right about you. You're not like the rest. She's a pretty good judge of character, that one."

I smiled. "Yes, she is."

Quinn shook my hand, promised to be in contact with more information, and left me alone with my mind racing.

It was clear that the bar would be alright. Despite my recent efforts, it had the support of the people around me, and now that Pierce had used his trump card, we'd faced the worst and come out relatively unscathed. One call to my lawyer had confirmed it—we could re-open next week, and there would be no further issues with the permit.

All that was left was to move forward with the re-opening. And for the first time since I'd started, I could work free from distraction. Just me and the bar.

It felt bleak.

What was wrong with me? How had I failed so spectacularly at this again?

Flashes of it all came at me at once. Tiffany, agreeing to help me, hands locked in her shirt, voluntarily conceding. Over and over. Giving me control. She'd been upfront, challenging but never asking for more than what she wanted.

And I had reacted like a preschooler. *Don't touch my stuff.*

I'd acted as badly as Pierce. Selfish. Stubborn. I palmed my eyes until spots appeared. Fuck.

I wasn't an idiot. I was an asshole.

My fingers dialed the familiar number before I contemplated what I was going to say. Just that I needed to do this. I couldn't move on without talking to her.

"Sam?" Piper's surprise was evident.

"Hi, Piper."

"Is … Was there something wrong with the paperwork?"

"No. That should already have been it back to your lawyers." She would already know that, but it made sense that

that was where her mind had gone. "I wanted to …" This was harder than I expected. Not that long ago, we had shared a life together, and now, I'd forgotten how to speak to her. "Are you happy?"

Her sharp intake of breath cut through the phone, and there was another stretch of silence while I wondered if I'd pissed her off. When she spoke next, it was sadness that I heard instead. "I am. Is that horrible?"

I'd thought hearing that would hurt. And perhaps it would have months ago. Now? Nothing.

"No, it's not." And it was the truth. No matter how much I wished that things had gone differently, I didn't want her to be miserable. "I'm sorry for how things ended with us. For not telling you sooner what I wanted."

"Thank you, Sam. I think I needed to hear that." It was then that she nervously admitted she was seeing someone new. "We had the kids conversation upfront. I learned that much from what happened with us."

Afterward, I was struck by that thought. What had I learned? Underneath the bitterness and guilt, which were fading faster now, I'd told myself that I'd learned not to risk my livelihood with love. But that felt hollow.

"How are the bars going?"

"It's not the same without you, but profits are holding steady, and we've been approached for a local partnership. I'm exploring options right now. I want to make sure it's a safe bet before I make any decisions."

The statement was so cold and calculated that I was transported to how different our relationship had been. How different Tiffany was. It was unnecessary and yet grounding— Tiffany wasn't Piper. And perhaps, more importantly, I wasn't the same man I'd been.

Yes, I'd changed since I had arrived, but it was clear that I still had a lot to learn. I needed to be better.

46

———

TIFF

It was obvious that Sam's life before and the way his last relationship ended was a sore point. I'd seen Audrey deal with the same thing after her divorce. His defensiveness whenever someone (usually me) had an opinion about the bar. His reluctance to commit himself to anything outside of work. His half-answers whenever we talked about the future.

It was a shame. Much like Auds, he had a big heart. It wasn't right that one bad experience could shut that away. And even if his future didn't involve me, he deserved to be happy. To find love again.

He just needed to let himself.

God, I just wanted to prove it to him, convince him of everything I saw in him, what we all saw in him. It was a constant fight with myself not to tie him down and just talk until he realized what he was pushing away.

But that was the old me. No matter how much I wanted to fix this, fix him, that wasn't my place. And it definitely wasn't how I wanted our relationship to be. Sam was a grown-ass man. He was smart (most of the time). If he really wanted something, he'd figure out how to make it happen.

And if that wasn't me …

Well, I was a grown-ass woman. I'd be okay.

Eventually.

It's been two weeks since I'd seen Sam. He wasn't a big texter, but he'd occasionally respond if I sent anything.

Quinn sent me updates on the bar with some uninspired asides relating to Sam, but I'd told her that we were friends and nothing more.

I missed him, but I had a life to live, and he'd made his bed.

A whimsical (and rather complicated knock) sounded at my front door, and I was laughing as I opened the door to Wes. Olivia was beside him, and I was surprised. Like Wes, she was a co-lead of *The Guild*, the urban fantasy TV show Jackson filmed. And like Wes, I'd only met her briefly a handful of times. Although I'd invited Wes to help me with a new project, seeing both of Jackson's co-stars at my front door was amusing. "Should I be expecting anyone else?"

"Hey, you said you needed help, and Liv is the best person I know." I didn't miss the tinge of seriousness in his voice, and I resolved to ask him about it later.

"Tiff, right? We met—"

"A few times. Last was Audrey's birthday, back in February." I opened the door, stepping back to let them both in. "It's good to see you again. Unlike this idiot, who I can't seem to get rid of."

"I have that same issue. Every single day I go to work, there he is."

"Both of you are blessed with my presence, admit it."

Before I could say anything, Liv pushed his face away with one hand, turning to me. "Don't mind him."

"I never do."

"I hope you don't mind me tagging along. Wes was talking about the videos you were planning, and I got curious. Started pestering him with questions he couldn't answer—"

"Because I'm supposed to know what your lighting situation is, apparently."

She ignored him. "Anyway, we figured it was just easier if I came along." There was a split second pinch in Wes' smile at "we," and another puzzle piece slotted into place for me.

I returned her smile because I was more than grateful for the extra help. "Three heads are better than one, especially since I'm not even sure where to start."

Wes pulled out a camera, winking. "Oh, that's easy."

Liv had been assessing the room, nodding to herself, before she pointed to a spot in the corner, by the window. "I think we should set up over here. There's some natural light that should work for now. If you want to really do this, you might want to think of getting a studio light and a softbox, but we can think about that later."

Wes began setting the camera up, propping it on a box he found and then messing around with the settings. Liv watched as I touched up my makeup, offering the occasional suggestion before asking, "So, what made you think of this?"

I shrugged as best I could while adding some white liner to my waterline. "Funnily enough, it was something Jackson said. Then Jordan," and I realized they had no idea who I was referring to, "a well-known bar owner, offered me a job heading up his new place in New York."

"That's incredible."

"It was flattering, that's for sure. But it got me thinking that I know enough, and I love sharing it, so why not give this a go. What have I really got to lose? I've got some savings to get me through and options if it doesn't work out."

"Do you have a game plan? Where do you even start?"

Absentmindedly, I pointed in the direction of my home bar while admiring my highlighter (did I want to add more?). "I thought I'd start with the basics of a home bar but focusing on elevated options."

In the corner of my eye, I saw Wes walk over to it,

shuffling bottles to get a look at the labels. "I don't know half of these."

He was holding a bottle up when I glanced over. "Oh, that's my uncle's whiskey. He started making his own a year ago from his place in Kentucky. Went through a midlife crisis after his divorce and bought an acreage. Always trying to get me to visit." I wanted to. I couldn't remember the last time I'd seen him, but with work and … "Huh, I guess I could do it now. I could use a little R&R. You should see this place. It's practically a resort." I pulled up a photo my mama had sent, showing it to Liv.

"Wow. That looks amazing. What I wouldn't give to stay out there. I've never really seen the country."

"You should go." I chuckled at her surprise. "Trust me. He loves visitors. And he lives out there by himself. You'll get a whole wing and a guided tour."

"Sounds like a great idea," Wes added. "Especially if it means more of this." He'd taken it upon himself to pour some into a glass, tasting it.

"Okay," I said, happy with my makeup now and turning to Liv for a second opinion. "What do you think? Good enough?"

"Are you kidding? You look great. I wish I had your bone structure."

"Please. You're the star here."

"If you're going to fight over who is the prettiest, at least acknowledge that, next to me, neither of you stand a chance." Wes joked, twisting out of the way when Liv reached over to smack his arm.

"So, what's next?"

Good question. "Have either of you done this before?" I asked.

Wes wasn't bothered. "No, but there are literal children out there with millions of followers. How hard can it be?"

"That's the first thing someone says before finding out exactly how hard something is," I said, wondering how this became my life.

Wes clapped his hands together. "Don't worry so much, Tiffster. It'll be fine."

"If you value your life, that'll be the last time you call me that." But he was right. What did I have to lose? "Alright, then. I'm putting myself in your very capable hands."

Wes brightened. "Great. I've been told many times that I'm very good with my—" Liv's hand was suddenly cupped over his mouth, and I laughed at the indignant squeak that escaped him.

———

"ALL DONE!" Liv said afterward. "That was pretty fun, actually. Probably needs some editing, but you're a natural on camera."

"It's easy being myself, I guess."

"Can I ask you something?" Liv asked, tentative. Wes busied himself by hovering again at my bar until I gave him the ok to help himself, which he did with glee.

I turned my attention back to Liv. "Shoot."

"It's not really my place, but … Wes mentioned there was something going on with your boss?"

I pinned him with a glare. "Oh, did he now?" He had the grace to look uncomfortable, at least. Softening, I said to Liv, "There was, but there isn't anymore."

"Is that why you left your job?"

"No, I quit before that." *Barely*, I remembered with a smirk. There was an odd distance to my memories of that night. Of how long ago it felt. So much had changed since then. My reasons for leaving seemed so important, and now I could barely remember what they were.

I caught a flash of worry in Liv's expression and saw Wes' own concern as he watched her. *Oh.* "If you're worried about mixing work and pleasure, I don't think the two of you have much to be concerned about. Isn't the entertainment industry littered with couples who met on set?"

Two sets of eyes widened, and Liv broke into an embarrassed laugh. "Me and Wes? No! No. We're just friends."

One look at Wes told me that was likely far from true, but those puppy dog eyes of his were practically begging me to let this slide, so I did. "Boss, then?"

She blushed, a pretty pink brightly showing against her pale cheeks. "We're not telling anyone, at least not until the show ends."

"That has to be tough."

"Did your coworkers know about you and …"

"Sam," I said. "No. But I'm not sure they would have cared. Maybe if I was still working there, but now?" I shook my head. "Other people knowing wasn't the issue with us."

"Can I ask what happened?"

"We gave ourselves a used-by date. When we reached it, I wanted to continue. He didn't. Sam and I …" I sighed. "We both know what we want, and right now, his priority is the bar. I never told him how I felt, but Sam's a smart man. If he doesn't know already, he'll figure it out."

"So, you're just going to wait around for him? That doesn't seem like you."

"Who the hell said I'm waiting around? I've got my own shit to worry about." I smiled. "Or did you think I invited you here for my own amusement?"

Wes didn't budge. Damn those puppy dog eyes. It's like trying to lie to a Labrador.

"I'm not waiting around," I stated. Because I would never. "But I might be keeping busy and hoping he gets his head out of his ass."

"And if he doesn't?" There's a resigned acceptance in Wes' voice like he was doing his own waiting.

"Then … I keep going. There'll always be a part of me that loves him, but you can't change how other people feel."

47

———

TIFF

There was a decisive knock on my door, and I groaned. Who the hell was it now? This was getting ridiculous. I missed the days when only Audrey showed up at my place.

I half hoped it was Audrey when I opened the door, not expecting to be faced with Sam's arresting eyes instead.

Butterflies erupted in my stomach. *Traitors.*

"Hi, Sam."

"Jordan said you turned down the job."

That's why he was here?

He didn't wait for a response. "Why didn't you take it? You have so many options. You could go wherever you want, work anywhere."

"I don't want anywhere. I want to be here. I want ..."

"What, Tiffany?"

"Why are you here, Sam?"

"I ... Can I come in? Or are we going to have this entire conversation in the hallway?"

"And what conversation is that?" I was being a brat, but goddammit, he was standing there, looking as handsome as ever, maybe more so because I hadn't seen him in weeks, and I was fighting every urge I had to touch him.

"Tiffany, please." It was as much of a plea as I'd heard from him, and my grip tightened on the door handle as my body flushed.

And how could I say no?

I let him inside. "Can I get you a drink? Water? Coffee?"

"Water is fine."

I tried to distract myself by getting us both a glass, all too aware of him standing awkwardly in the middle of the room, a hand shoved into his pockets, the silence building between us.

"So," I said, feeling the echo of the last time I'd started a conversation that way.

"Why didn't you go to New York?"

"I told you, I want to stay here. My life isn't in New York. Jordan's offer was nice," I ignored his huffed disagreement, "but I'm not interested. He didn't seem to have a problem with it, so I'm not sure why you do."

"I don't have a problem with it," he said, cryptic as ever.

I studied him, trying to get a read on what the hell he was doing here. He looked nervous, which probably shouldn't have made me happy, but it was reassuring to know I wasn't the only one. He looked stressed—no, pained—and vulnerable, and I quickly drank the entire glass of water to soothe my suddenly dry throat.

Anticipation began warring with the hope stirring within me, and I felt a strange sickness, trying to fight it back. "What do you want, Sam?"

"Quinn came to see me about the coalition."

I'd hoped she would. "I'm glad to hear that. Are you going to be a part of it?"

"Of course."

Jesus, this was awkward. My empty glass felt heavy in my hands, but I had nowhere to put it without moving away. So, instead, we both stood at an odd distance from each other, catching and avoiding the other's gaze, like the world's most uncomfortable game of chicken. My entire body felt magnetized towards him, but I held firm. It didn't matter how willing I was to open up if he didn't feel the same.

That said, the awkward silence was excruciating. "How are the plans for the reopening coming?"

He opened his mouth, thought better of it, and closed it again. I shoved my hands into the pockets of my jeans, just for something to do. I was about to crawl out of my skin.

He took a step closer. "That isn't really why I came here." I suddenly realized he was holding a large envelope when he dropped his gaze to it, turning it over in his hands. "I have something to ask you."

My pulse picked up, even though I had zero clue about what the hell was happening. I was racing to figure it out, but every possibility seemed ludicrous.

"Actually," he said, looking back up at me, "I'm getting ahead of myself. I need to apologize first. I've been an idiot."

"I won't argue with that."

He didn't acknowledge my interruption, but I saw the smile he tried to hide. "I've tried to think of where I could have prevented this, but honestly, I think I was doomed the moment I met you. Maybe even before that." He paused, then, his expression complicated, and I could practically see him weighing what he wanted to say. He turned the envelope over in his hands. "I like you, Tiffany," he laughed softly at himself. "Which I know is a ridiculous thing to say when we've been sleeping together, but I want you to know that I do. Like you. And respect you. You're one of the most incredible people I've ever met. It frustrated me when we first met. I hate how blind I was back then. I completely misjudged you, and I was dismissive and—"

"You were a dick," I added helpfully.

He looked at me, pained, and I wanted to take it back, but he stopped me. "No, you're right. And I'm sorry. It's not an excuse, but I was too caught up in my own problems, what I'd left behind, and the bar." Another unimpressed look flashed across his face. "It's something I'm trying to get better at, but the point is—"

"What is the point, Sam?" It might be the most I'd ever heard him say, and yet, I still couldn't work out why he was here. What he was getting at. I knew what I wanted it to be, but damn, did he have to take so long to get there? I was aging here.

Sam took a tentative step forward, and my skin tingled in anticipation. "I was scared. After Piper, I was convinced that I had to do it all on my own, that if I let someone back in, history would repeat itself. And when I realized how much I felt for you ..." He rubbed the back of his neck. "I'd like to repeat, I've been an idiot."

"What you said really hurt me."

"I know," his hand reached for me, but I retreated, stopping him.

"No, wait. I need to get this out." Suddenly, I was nervous. "I know I look tough, and I am, but that doesn't make me invincible. All my life, I've been fighting other people's judgments of me. When it's coming from Hannah or Pierce, I can take it. But hearing those same things from you ... Sam, I love you, but I can't be with anyone who can't accept me for who I am. If you're here trying to make things right, that's great, but if you're here to try and change me, then you can take your apology and walk straight back out that door."

"I know I don't deserve your forgiveness, but I need you to know that I don't blame you for anything. I wouldn't want you to be anyone other than you. No exceptions. Because you're incredible. You have this light, a fire, that I don't think I ever felt before I met you, and it's addictive. From the moment I met you, you got under my skin, and I kept telling myself to stay away from you, and when I couldn't, I told myself that it was because I was letting how I felt override my sense, and then everything with Pierce happened and I just

…" His hand flapped awkwardly in the air, and I took pity on him.

"Pushed me away because it was easier than dealing with it."

"Yes, and I'm sorry. It's not enough, but I want to make it up to you. What bothers me the most is that I didn't tell you what I should have before."

"And what is that?"

"You're important to me. More important than the bar."

"Sam," I said, suddenly breathless. It felt like a question, but I had no idea what I was asking for. Just that I wanted it. I wanted this to mean what I thought it meant.

"What do you want, Tiffany? When I asked you why you didn't take the job, you said what you wanted was here." He continued to close the gap between us, and though my heartbeat was racing, my feet were stuck in place. "What do you want?"

My voice came out shaky. "You know what I want."

"Tell me." Another step closer, a dare in his eyes. Teal pools that I couldn't look away from. I'd almost forgotten how pale the color was. A shiver ran through my body, and I ached to reach out now, feel the warmth of his chest under my hand and the strength of his heart beneath it.

He took another step forward, now within reach. Convulsively, I pressed my palms to my thighs. It was either that or touch him.

Saying nothing else, Sam stood there, solid and stubborn, waiting. And I was done. I was so over being patient. Of holding back all the things that I'd been wanting to say. *Weeks.* Weeks of waiting. I should have won a fucking award for all the patience I'd shown.

But even I had my limits.

My hand reached out, slipping easily into place around his neck, and something settled deep inside of me. "You. Ok, you silly, stubborn asshole. I want you. God knows why when you drive me this fucking wild."

His lips broke into a smile. "If it helps, I'm not sure why either. I'm not—"

My hand slipped down to his chest as I cut him off, still high on the adrenaline of finally letting my feelings out. This dam had burst, and he was going to hear it, whether he liked it or not. "Not what? Enough? Perfect? Bullshit. I'm not going to say it'll be easy, Sam. We'll fight. We'll need space. But for the first time in my life, I have someone I want to choose over and over again. Who takes everything I am and amplifies it. Who makes me want to learn and grow and fucking compromise. And honestly, it would be great if you felt the same, but frankly, you can't change the way I feel. I'm going to love you no matter what. So, deal with it."

He captured my hand where it had landed over his heart, intertwining our fingers. "Why didn't you say anything before?"

I met his eyes, feeling laid out before him, anchored only by his grip in mine. "We both know you didn't want to hear it."

"When has that ever stopped you?"

With a mock scowl, I pressed our hands into his chest. "I'm trying something new. Sue me."

Watching his smile curl wider brought a fresh wave of butterflies. "The one time you don't speak your mind."

"Would it have changed anything?" I asked, but we both knew the answer. When he brought our hands up to his lips, I watched transfixed, the brush of his kiss scattering a burst of electricity through my body. Every inch of my skin felt alight. It wasn't enough. I needed more.

"Sam," I ventured softly, my eyes glued to the deep pink of his cupid's bow as it raised off my knuckles. "You have to tell me."

"It's difficult for me to express my feelings."

"Understatement of the century"

"I'm trying to tell you I'm in love with you. Do you have to interrupt?"

"Hmm. Not quite sure I caught that. Can you tell me again?"

"I don't quite remember it now."

"Sam," I said impatiently, slipping my hand out from his. Incredibly, it worked. Or maybe we were both just too far gone on each other.

"I'm in love with you."

My lips were on his before he'd finished speaking, catching him off guard, but I felt his grip close on my waist, pulling me in as I pressed closer, threading my fingers into his hair so I could deepen the kiss, hungry for him after our time apart. When I felt the tip of his tongue tease mine, I responded in kind, eagerly licking into his mouth, swallowing his soft groans as he stole the breath from my lungs.

"I'm in love with you, too," I finally said when we parted. Giddy, a laugh bubbled up out of me, light as air. Sam rested our foreheads together. "What?"

"Are you sure? I'm not an easy person."

He chuckled. "I know that. I'm not either."

"Yes, but which one of us pissed Pierce off?" I punctuated my statement by tapping my finger to his collarbone.

"I think that would be both of us now."

"Ok, I'll give you that one.

"Any other points you want to make, or can I go back to kissing you now?"

I gave him a look. "Sam—"

He pressed his lips to my cheek, "I know what you're going to say. And I'm, surprisingly, not going to disagree with you. Neither of us is easy. We're probably going to be wrong or argue or get sick of each other. But we're also going to understand each other and support each other and care for each other."

I bit back a smile. Honestly, I'd made my mind up the minute I saw him on the other side of the door, but I really liked watching him try to convince me. I'd always enjoyed the benefit of Sam's focus when it was directed my way, and now that I was hearing all the words I'd hoped for, I was hardly going to stop him.

"Whatever the future holds, I want to face it together." With that, he finally opened the envelope and held out a stack of papers, eyes hopeful but unsure.

Taking them with trepidation, I felt my breath catch when I skimmed the first page. *Co-ownership extended to Miss Tiffany Young …* I didn't read any further and thrust the papers back at him. "Sam, no. I can't take this. It's too much."

"You wouldn't be taking it. I'm offering."

"This is by far the dumbest thing you've ever done."

"Excuse me?"

"This?" I said, waving the papers in his face. "What made you even think I would want half of your business?"

"The two most important things in my life are you and this bar. What is so wrong about me wanting to combine them?"

I dropped my forehead to his shoulder with a groan. What a sweet, irrational, irresistible man. "This is your idea of a big romantic gesture, isn't it? Gifting me half of a bar that I don't want." Lifting my head, I let the papers flutter to the floor.

Sam's hands, those warm, soft fingers that I'd become so familiar with, cupped my face. "Everything that I want, I want with you."

"Dammit, Sam. You can't just say shit like that."

"Why not?"

"Because it makes it hard to say no to you."

"Then don't say no."

"You're impossible."

"I know. I think it's what makes us perfect for each other."

"Sam," I groaned, but he only smiled wider. He knew he

was getting to me, picking away at my resistance. "There's so much to work through. Talk about. We shouldn't rush into this."

This, finally, stopped him. "I don't think I ever imagined hearing those words from you."

"Trust me, I know. But it's your fault for teaching it to me."

"You're right. We should talk. We can talk all night if you want. I'm not going anywhere. But you're not going to change my mind on this. I want this, and I want you. And if you feel the same way, I don't know why we would let anything stop us."

"You're starting to sound like me."

"We make a good team."

I looked at the paperwork again. Noticed the name. "Your Bar?"

He shrugged. "I know it's a bit on the nose, but ... I like it. Like a mission statement. I want people to know that this is for them, a place of community, of enjoyment. It's not going to be like 'nothing they've ever seen before', but it'll be a comfort, a home, a common ground where all are welcome."

"You're such a sap," I said fondly. "But it's a good name."

"The second choice was 'complete fool', but I thought that might sound too self-referential."

I barked out a surprised laugh. "No, for that to be true, you'd have to call it stubborn bastard."

"I deserve that."

"Yes, you do."

My eyes skimmed over the words. I was in awe of what I was holding in my hands. At how monumental this gesture was. Just the thought of it, of what Sam was saying with it, overwhelmed me. I didn't need it. I didn't need anything but him, but I was tempted. I just needed time.

Catching his eye, I passed the papers back to him, pressing

through when I saw the disappointment show on his face. "I'm not saying no, but I need to think about it."

He swallowed, nodded slowly. "Okay. Anything you need."

Once he'd taken back the contract, I stepped closer, tentatively reaching up to caress his cheek. "As for us, there's no question for me. I'm all in if you are."

"Without question," he said, turning his head to kiss the palm of my hand. "I love you."

I pulled at the collar of his shirt, tugging him closer, speaking against his lips. "You love me."

Our smiles met, making hard work of our kisses, but neither of us caring. "More than you know."

"Oh, I'd say I've got a pretty good idea. But how about you show me." I hauled him towards me, walking us backward to my bedroom. "And don't spare a single detail."

"I wouldn't dream of it."

EPILOGUE
TIFF

I didn't sign the papers in the end. Not when I knew how much it meant to Sam to have something of his own. We were currently discussing opening a second bar, something we both had a stake in, and I was excited about that. Excited for all the possibilities of our future together.

We made a great team, something I delighted in reminding Sam at every given opportunity. He usually responded by sending me another five links discussing algorithms and analytics. I typically sent them back explaining in explicit detail what he would get if he read them and gave me the cliff notes instead. It worked about fifty percent of the time. The other half, he would bring me food (a proper meal, Tiffany) or a coffee with a promise of his own if and when I read them. I'd never had so much fun learning about statistics and growth ratios.

Outside of the channel, which was growing slowly, I'd started guest bartending at various bars around town, working with Audrey and Quinn to stage themed events which gave me the opportunity to craft unique one-off recipes. It had started small, but we were now consistently selling out, and I'd found my subscriber count rising as a result.

As for the channel, it probably helped that Wes, Liv, and Jackson had all volunteered to be taste testers on an episode series I had started, where I trialed new recipes on unsuspecting guests. Between sponsors, Patreon, and my bartending side gig, I was comfortable.

Above all else, I loved all the time I got with Sam. After a few weeks of commuting back and forth (and some persuasive arguments on my side), I moved into his apartment. Of course, he'd been very gracious about it, saying, "If that's not something you want, if you don't want to give up the freedom of your own space, I'll respect that." He then offered to move into my place instead.

Of course, I'd told him, "And make you trek across town every day for work? Sam, you're the smartest person I know, but sometimes you're a real dumbass. I want to be with you. Now, shut up and help me pack."

Moving my things in hadn't taken longer than a weekend (with some help), and I'd since turned the spare room in his apartment into a recording studio, and he would migrate downstairs to his office while I filmed or edited.

As for the bar, it was doing better than ever. Sam had expanded on my original idea and actually improved it (because, of course, he did). Using one of the recipes we'd created, he went to work with Audrey and one of her local suppliers to collaborate on "at-home cocktails," which let people purchase online a pre-mix of cocktail ingredients and the steps to make it at home. He'd even gone as far as sending free packs to a handful of online creators, some of whom loved the idea so much, he barely had to do a thing to promote it—it was spreading like wildfire.

But the best part was that the profits finally paid the way for his renovations, and now Your Bar was the sexiest damn drinking spot in town. I was not biased in the least about this.

We co-existed very well with my work and his work, living in parallel, and always choosing each other.

Sam, for his part, was getting better at taking my suggestions (though I still hadn't convinced him about the saffron).

Of course, some things didn't change at all.

"Would you like a coffee?"

Sam's voice carried through from the living room, and I paused the video I was editing to answer him. "Do you mean now or in five minutes when you remember you haven't made them?"

I heard him chuckle from the other room. "Now."

"Then, yes." Stretching, I ignored the mewl of protest from Luna, who had staked her claim on my lap. My back ached from at least two hours of editing, and while I hated to evict Luna from her cozy perch, I needed a break. Besides, I could picture Sam out there, hair rumpled from running his hand through it, probably wearing those glasses that made me want to jump him.

Fuck, had it already been a few hours since I'd kissed him? That absolutely needed to be remedied ASAP.

But first, coffee.

Six minutes later, Sam was so engrossed in his reading that I was certain he hadn't noticed the fact that I'd been standing in the kitchen, waiting for the coffee to brew but mostly watching him. The late afternoon light streaked through the window, adding a warm honey glow to his skin, catching on the soft whiskers of his beard and the unkempt ends of his hair.

Everything about him, from his gray sweater to his bare feet, looked relaxed and inviting. Sometimes, like now, I would catch myself lost in the wonder of him, of how much I loved him, completely in awe of how fucking happy we were.

It wasn't always easy, but it was always worth it.

Cup in hand, I finally made my way over to the couch, leaning over his shoulder to get a look at what had kept his attention all this time. "Actually, that study was disproven already. It's only twenty-five percent."

Sam startled at my presence. Fuck, he was adorable. "Huh?" He turned back to his screen, then did a double-take at the cup in my hands. "Shit, I'm sorry. I completely forgot."

I smirked, "It's ok." After another sip, I reached forward, tapping the screen of his laptop. "And this is just flat out wrong. What are you even reading this for?"

"Research," he replied, not taking his eyes off of me. I kept my eyes on the screen. "Did you make me a coffee?"

"Of course," I said, offhand, enjoying a long, drawn-out pull. "I'm drinking it."

When he reached for it, I considered moving it out of reach, but even I wasn't that cruel. However, he surprised me, taking it and his laptop and placing both on the coffee table before him, then laying his glasses on top before turning back to me and pulling me down into a kiss, the momentum carrying me over the side and on top of him. One of my favorite places to be.

"That coffee is going to go cold."

He kissed me again. "I don't care."

———

It was dark outside when my phone rang, and I debated ignoring it (I was busy, after all), but a devilish idea seized me, and I rose off of Sam to answer it, chuckling at his protesting groan.

"Hi, Auds, can't really talk right now. We're a little tied up."

Sam groaned again, pulling against the bindings on his wrists, the wooden slats of the headboard creaking under the familiar pressure.

"Do I even want to know?" Audrey asked.

"Probably not. What's up?"

"I was just making sure that you two were coming because we're all waiting outside."

I watched my fingernails trail over Sam's flat chest, saw him biting his lip as they caught on a dark nipple. "Oh, we're definitely coming."

"*Tiffany,*" Sam growled.

I chuckled, enjoying myself way too much.

Audrey cleared her throat, embarrassed. "You know what? We're all gonna get a drink down the street. Call me when you're done with … whatever you're doing."

Tossing the phone away after she'd hung up, I looked down at the incredibly sexy man under me. "Hmm …" I reached up to pinch Sam's nipple, then followed the move with my teeth and tongue because I adored the feel of him arching against my lips. "The way I see it," I purred, lapping at the salt of his skin. "You have two choices. Come now, or wait until later."

"I can wait, but I don't think you can," he said, his voice rough.

"Oh, really? Because I think," I said, using my thighs to slowly lift myself until just the tip of his cock was inside me, then holding myself there, "I think you're close. I bet I can last longer than you."

"You like losing, then." Each word was strained, and he pressed against the mattress, raising his hips in an attempt to get deeper, but I simply moved with him. He sagged back, moaning in frustration. Damn, he looked good like this.

"You seem to be struggling with something. I could help with that. If you wanted me to." My thighs were burning in this position, but I held firm, squeezing my pelvis around him, little pulses to tease and torment.

The binds were taut now; his knuckles white where he gripped them. "Please."

With a loud moan, I sunk down hard and fast on his cock, rolling my hips to get the angle just right. Bet forgotten, I chased my pleasure, fucking myself on him, getting off on the grunted, "Ah, ah, ah," streaming from Sam's lips and the wet slap of our bodies. His eyes were heated, laser-focused on mine, closing only as he came, the throb of him inside of me getting me one step closer.

Quickly, I reached for myself, rubbing my clit and panting his name as I fell over the edge.

———

WE EVENTUALLY MET our friends down the street, only twenty minutes late and not looking nearly as fucked-out as their smug expressions seemed to indicate. Sam joined Jackson at the bar, where he was ordering another round, and I settled in between Audrey and Wes, who was showing Liv a viral video of a cat in a toupée, lip-syncing to "Never Gonna Give You Up" by Rick Astley.

When the others came back with the drinks, I asked, "What should we toast to?"

I gently shoved my elbow into Wes' side when I heard him mumble, "You finally getting here."

My attention was caught by the shared look between Audrey and Jackson. Lord help me if they went and got eloped, I was going to kill them.

Blessedly, Audrey said, "We finally set a date."

There was a collective sigh of relief around the table, followed by a cheer. Finally.

Liv beamed at them. "That's great news. When will it be?"

"June 9th."

That surprised me. "That's only six months away."

Jackson nodded. "We didn't want to wait any longer."

"That'll be right before filming. You won't have much time for a honeymoon," Wes said.

"We'll have a week or two, which will be enough."

"I, for one, am glad you've finally picked a date! Does this mean you'll need to rush the preparations?" Liv really did look incredibly happy for them. It was sweet to see. I wondered if she were hoping her sort-of-secret-boyfriend would propose soon. From what Wes had told me, they'd been seeing each other for a while now, even if they were hiding it from the media because they worked together.

"No. Um, we kind of decided against something big," Audrey said tentatively. "I didn't want anything elaborate. All through the planning, something just felt off, and we worked out that we were trying to make it something neither of us wanted."

Jackson's arm tightened around her waist, leaning in to kiss her temple. *These two.* "Right. We'll still have a ceremony, but we're thinking of something small. Just close friends and family."

Audrey touched my arm. "It also means no more florists."

"Oh, thank God," I said, elated. Today couldn't get any better.

Sam's broad palm glided under my shirt, teasing the ticklish skin above my jeans. I shivered when his deep voice whispered in my ear, "I suppose now isn't an appropriate time to tell you that your Christmas present arrived early and that I don't know that I can wait another week to use it."

My mind raced, immediately sure of what it was that he must be referring to. There had been a few things we'd been discussing recently, mostly bedroom-related, and only one that he would have to whisper to me like a dirty secret. "Please tell me it's the—"

He cleared his throat, halting me, but the hungry look in his eyes gave it away. "Perhaps. If you're good tonight, maybe we can open it later."

Later would be hours away, which Sam knew, and he was doing this on purpose. Probably because of my comments to Audrey on the phone earlier. Oops. So worth it, though.

Leering, I curled a hand around his thigh, deliberately

brushing his length through his pants. I heard his sharp intake of breath and leaned in to catch one of his hoops in my teeth. Two could play this game. "I hate you," I said lovingly.

"I love you," he replied, then turned his head to catch me in a kiss.

"I know."

NEW BEGINNINGS
TIFF

I stood in the middle of the room, my boyfriend beside me, and had only one thought.

Fuck yes.

Paint peeled off the back wall, the floor was sticky with something I definitely didn't want to think too hard about, and it had the square footage of a trailer, but I loved it.

Sam's careful gaze catalogued everything in the room, no doubt crafting a pro and cons list in his mind, then turned to face me. He kept his expression clear, but I didn't bother. I was too busy smiling my ass off.

"This one? Really?" He asked, his nose twitching.

Yes, fine. It was a dump. But it was *our* dump.

"It's going to be great," I said, stepping closer and ignoring the sound of my shoes peeling off the floor with each step. "Don't you trust me?"

Finally, there was a crack in his expression, his lips curling up. His hands were hot as they grabbed my hips, and when he pulled me against him, my entire body responded.

Fuck, his lips were delicious. He tasted of black coffee and a little bit of sweetness. And maybe a bit of orange blossom?

So that's where the last cookie had disappeared to.

Luna, my ass.

I rolled my hips, purring at the grind of his thigh between my legs.

So you could imagine my disappointment when Sam pulled back.

"Despite its appearance, the numbers are promising."

"Ugh."

Only Sam Cooper, the love of my life and perpetual workaholic, could make me utter that phrase. He knew it too, the bastard, chucking as he kissed my cheek by way of apology.

"As hard as I am right now," he said, steering my hand toward his very sizeable erection. "I'm convinced this building is ground zero for at least three infectious diseases and possibly, one plague. So, you might not want to start anything we can't finish until later."

Sam was probably right.

I didn't have to like it, though.

And come on, if he didn't walk around being so motherfucking sexy all the goddamn time, we wouldn't be in this mess.

I enjoyed watching Sam struggle to keep his composure as I gave his cock a firm stroke through his trousers, but in the end, I knew he was right. Better for us to finish up quickly so I could get him home and really make him squirm.

Forgetting the smell and the stickiness, all I could see was potential. After a year of Sam's mutterings on cost analysis and profit margins, it had sunk in that if we really wanted to do something special, keeping it small would be the best thing.

And if this derelict shoebox had anything going for it, it was that it was small.

Remnants of some vulgar graffiti lingered on one wall. Even after we cleared out the mess, there would only be enough room for the bar, a storeroom, and maybe six seats.

It was perfect.

"I know that look. Would you care to fill me in?"

I'd lost myself again in thoughts of what this place could be. Sam fit his warm, lean body in behind me, one hand curling possessively around my hip. My shirt had ridden up, and his thumb and forefinger teased over the exposed skin. His steady breathing brushed over my cheek, calm and unwavering. Exactly as I knew him to be.

I smiled, leaning into him. A year ago, I couldn't have imagined myself here, staring at a poorly drawn dick and balls in neon green, picturing the best way to incorporate shelving without covering it completely. At the same time, the man I loved tried to pretend he wasn't rocking an impressive hard-on. Fuck, I loved my life.

"I want to keep the back wall, graffiti and all. New flooring, obviously." I wouldn't wish this Petri dish on Stephen Pierce himself, and that was saying something.

"Obviously." Sam's thick voice had deepened, but I could hear the trademark curl of his lips that told me he was teasing. I felt my smile widen, a joy wholly 'Sam' radiating through my blood.

200 proof and potent as all hell, kicking outward from my heart.

This fucking man, I swear.

It was challenging to stay coherent at the best of times, and any fleeting thought I'd had that these feelings would fade had been grossly wrong. So wonderfully, overwhelmingly wrong.

Was there any praise left that I hadn't heaped on him? Any part of my body, mind or soul that he hadn't already touched and made hopelessly in awe of him?

"A new countertop, maybe. Whatever is in your top three options right now."

Sam's chuckle rumbled from his chest through my back. "This is my first viewing. What makes you think I have a list already?"

I snorted, not dignifying that with a response. He definitely had a list. Multiple, guaranteed. He snuck his hand further around my waist, his fingers dipping under the waist of my jeans to caress my sensitive skin.

That sneaky bastard.

The hairs on his forearm were rough as I halted his movement. "Don't start something I can't finish."

Another chuckle and a playful bite along my neck. It was killing me not to jump him right now.

"The counter?" he supplied, putting us back on track. Or attempting to. But I was done talking.

I turned to face him. "Nuh-uh. You're taking me home."

"Am I?"

"Yes, you are," I said, getting impatient.

He watched me with a lazy smile, his eyes shrewd. "What's wrong?"

Even after a year together, I hadn't quite gotten used to Sam being able to read me. It was equal parts annoying and fucking adorable. Damn him. "Nothing's wrong."

He didn't budge. "Tiffany."

"Sam." And dammit, I cracked a little bit. I couldn't help it. He was looking at me all sweet and shit.

"You're nervous," he chuckled, and I fought to keep a poker face. "Wow." His smile widened, splitting his face, making him more gorgeous than ever, and setting off the butterflies in my stomach. "I might need to take a note of this."

"Okay, shut up now."

"No, no, this is too much fun. Wait." Sam grabbed his phone out of his pocket while I rolled my eyes, fighting back a smile of my own. Fuck, I loved this man.

"I'm looking for the mayor's number. We need to make this a national holiday."

"Fuck you," I said through my laughter, grabbing the phone from his hands. Sam didn't put up much of a fight, letting me take the phone and wrapping his arms around me. Between his teasing and his body, I started to feel a little less like a nervous wreck.

With his hand curled around my neck (his favourite spot), I shivered in delight as his thumb brushed over the design shaved behind my ear, a simple set of three lines in descending length.

He caged me against the bar, pressing his lips against the ink below my ear. The ink he'd inspired.

"You can't just distract me with kisses, you know."

"My research says otherwise," he said, kissing along my neck to my shoulder as I melted against him. He was so smug when he was right. "There's nothing to be nervous about."

"I think our experience last year says differently."

He stilled. "Is that what you're worried about? Pierce?"

I shuddered at the name but stayed silent. Sam was right, but I didn't have to tell him that.

"I've never known you to back down from a fight, even with Stephen. Especially from him."

I sighed, pleased and a lot relieved that Sam wasn't worried. I hooked my fingers back into his belt loops and tugged him closer, taking advantage of his good mood. "Maybe I'm trying to be more pragmatic."

And the look of amused disbelief on Sam's face only made me smile wider.

I rolled my eyes. "Fine. I'm not. I just want this to go well."

He leaned down, his lips capturing mine. I expected a light brush, but Sam expertly licked into my mouth, chasing my lips hungrily. I'd experienced a hell of a lot of Sam's kisses, but this one was insane.

His voice was gruff when he pulled back; course gravel contrasted against the soft stroke of his fingers in my hair. "There's nothing to worry about. I know a thing or two about business, and we both know how incredible you are. Not only is this going to work, it's going to be great." He tightened his hold of me. "Now, let's get out of here so I can fuck you properly."

*****

"Honey," I said softly.

Sam sat beside me on the couch, Luna curled up at his feet, her tail wrapped possessively around his ankle. He blinked, his attention locked on the paperwork in his hands.

"Sweetie."

This time there was a slow, laboured breath. I wondered how many times he'd tried to read the same sentence.

I smiled. I knew he wouldn't hold out much longer.

"Sugar Bear." The endearment was difficult to get out, but it was worth it to see the twitch of his lips. *Got him.*

"Tiffany."

There it was.

His deep voice was laced with amusement, and I practically purred in pleasure at hearing it.

"What?" I asked, with all the fake innocence I could muster.

Getting under Sam's skin was one of my favourite pastimes. Getting under his clothes was a close second.

That was plan B.

Sam turned his head toward me. "I'm trying to help you."

And bless him, he was. We were knee-deep in preparations for the bar's soft open, and he was triple checking the schedule to make sure we were on track. Meanwhile, I'd changed the menu twice in the last week, always making sure to wait until he was fuck drunk to mention it. I think he had caught on to my tactic.

"I know." I pulled the papers out of his hands, straddling his legs as I dropped them to the floor.

He automatically slid his hands up my thighs, licking his lips. Lust darkened his gaze even though his thick-rimmed glasses.

Every time he put them on, I wanted to jump him, and he damn well knew it too. His toned upper body was hard and hot under my palms, amplifying my need for him. I wrapped my arms around his neck and leaned in to get a taste of his lips.

Damn, he was sexy.

"You're not changing the menu," he said, leaving no room for argument.

"Yes. I am."

His short nails stroked a line up my spine, making me melt. Bastard. He knew what that did to me.

"No, you're not."

Two could play this game.

I ground down against his straining erection. We both moaned at the contact.

"How are you going to stop me?"

The grin he gave me was sin and sex and a promise all in one.

Fuck, I loved this man. I couldn't have made him more perfect if I'd grown him in a lab. Although if I had, I would have made two of him. Double the pleasure.

Our mouths met in a familiar frenzy of hunger and passion.

When his phone started to ring, I ignored it, sucking on his tongue as I pulled at the zipper of his jeans. If Sam had heard it, it didn't show; he was too busy pulling the cups of my bra down underneath my shirt so that he could pinch the peaks of my nipples. I moaned into his mouth and felt him smile against my lips.

I needed him inside of me. *Now.*

The ringing stopped as my top was stripped from me, the straps of my bra hanging uselessly by my side. Sam dipped down to tease with his tongue what he teased with his fingers. I had no room to remove his jeans, so I thrust my hands into his hair instead, arching into his mouth as I rocked against him.

The ringing started up again a second later, and I groaned in mutual pleasure and frustration. Sam chuckled against my skin as he kissed his way back along my neck.

Already I knew he was going to want to answer it. It was probably important. Possibly his brother.

I loved that Sam was intelligent and capable and busy; it made him more irresistible.

But they couldn't wait ten more minutes?

Before he could pull away, I recaptured his mouth with mine, wanting to enjoy one last kiss. Whatever this phone call was about, it would probably mean no sex until it was dealt with, so I was going to draw this out for as long as I could.

When I ran out the second call, I prayed they wouldn't dial back. But it was in vain.

At the third ring, Sam ended the kiss. His chest rose heavily with each breath, and his glasses sat eschew on his nose. And fuck me if he wasn't the sexiest damn thing I'd ever seen.

"You drive me crazy," I whispered.

"You're one to talk," he said, voice rough.

The ringing persisted.

Then my phone started to buzz, the vibration sending Luna away to search for peace and quiet.

I know the feeling.

Now I was worried.

Sam and I shared a concerned look before we both moved. Audrey's name was lit up on my screen, and I answered.

"What's going on? Is everything okay?"

"Are you seeing this?" She asked, and I couldn't tell if it was panic or excitement in her voice.

What the hell was going on?

"Seeing what?"

"Turn on the news."

Sam a step ahead. Whoever had called him had clearly told him the same thing. It took a second or two of channel surfing before we found it.

I stared. "Holy shit."

Stephen Pierce, douchebag and restauranteur extraordinaire, was walked out of a building *in handcuffs*.

"Is that…?" I asked, still not believing my own fucking eyes.

Sam made a noise of agreement beside me, as hypnotised by what was playing out on screen as I was. Then I remembered Audrey was still on the phone. "When was this?"

"An hour ago, apparently. Caught embezzling money from his businesses."

"Fuck."

"Is Sam with you?"

"Yeah, he's here. We're both pretty shocked. Can I call you back?"

"Of course. Go celebrate. I know you want to."

I would have been offended if it was anyone but my best friend. But Audrey knew me better than anyone else, and she was 100 percent correct. So I said an offhand goodbye, climbed back into Sam's lap and smiled down at him.

"Holy shit," I repeated.

Sam's grip was firm where he held my hips. I could see the surprise mirrored on his face. Underneath that, his cool grey eyes sparkled with relief.

Pierce, that scum-sucking, bigoted asshole, had just been arrested. Who knew if he'd face justice or not, but his rep was damaged, and no amount of money or friends would ever make Sam or I forget it. We'd gladly remind Pierce—and everyone else—of any chance we had.

It was the least Pierce deserved.

Now Sam could relax. We both could.

"I didn't dream that, did I?" He asked.

"Even if this is some bizarre collective hallucination, I don't care."

"You know what this means, don't you?"

I could guess. I pressed closer to Sam. "That we can get back to what we were doing?"

He raised his hand, brushing my long hair behind my shoulder. The gentleness of his touch sent shivers through me. My heart skipped its usual beat. The one Sam always inspired.

I felt my fingers clutch a little tighter in his shirt. Holding.

If anything was a dream, it was him.

"It means everything is going to be all right." With his fingers curled around my neck, he pulled me into a slow, tender kiss.

*****

It took a lot to make me speechless.

Despite what some people thought (*that's right, I am talking about you, Sam*), I didn't have to fill every silence. I recognised the art of holding back.

But being genuinely without words?

That was rare.

Sam had been the direct result of many of these moments, with his dimples and hidden depths.

Always surprising me.

But the paperwork in my hands wasn't a surprise. We'd been talking about it for months. Planning it. I knew it was coming. And still …

I couldn't resist raising a finger and brushing along our names where they're written side by side on the contract.

Owners: Tiffany Young and Sam Cooper.

"Wow."

I always liked the idea of having my own bar, but it felt like the kind of hope that is always in a far off future. Or a galaxy far, far away. Not stamped and witnessed and sitting next to my coffee cup at ten-thirty on a Thursday morning.

It was finally official. Sam and I were partners.

"Everything okay?" Sam gently brushed his fingers along the slope of my neck.

I blinked down at the paperwork, trying to rein in my emotions. It was silly. We'd been working towards this for months. Why now was I feeling so overwhelmed?

Sam's grip changed, his fingers sliding under my chin until he could tilt my head up and catch my gaze. His eyes looked pale green this morning, shining against the dark stubble on his cheeks. It was at a scratchy stage, where Sam would cast a dark eye over it in the mirror and want nothing more than to shave it off, but he didn't.

Because I liked the scruff, and he liked me.

Crazy, but true.

"You're not going to regret this, are you?" I asked, my eyes never leaving Sam, but my fingers still pressed into our names on the counter.

A year of living together and of planning this next step had brought us closer than I had thought we could be. I'd expected friction where there was balance, complacent where there was growth. Being with Sam was never stale, even in the quietest moments. His kisses were just as addictive, his taste just as enticing.

With a fond huff and a tilt of his head (that same one he always used when he said my name in the best kind of exacerbation), he curled a firm hand around my neck and set me straight.

I mean, not *straight* but ... No. Right. Not a time for joking.

"Tiffany."

There it was. My heart skipped a beat.

His grip was solid. Steady. Like always.

"I couldn't be surer of anything. I'll remind you that I've been waiting very patiently for you to agree to this for twelve months. I want to be your partner."

Tingles, I swear.

Being someone's anything had been another of those far away dreams.

I should have known it would be Sam who would make all my tomorrows come today.

———

THE END

THANK YOU!

I can't thank you enough for reading my book! Romance is so special to me, and if I was able to pass on a little bit of happiness to you, that makes me extremely happy.

If you enjoyed reading my book, please consider leaving a review on Amazon, Goodreads, etc. Even if it's just a sentence or two about what you liked most about my book, it will help my work to be seen by other readers.

I absolutely love to hear from my readers! Message me anytime, let's talk books! Or cocktails. Or coffee. Or how Rick and Evie from The Mummy are #couplegoals. Take your pick!

ACKNOWLEDGMENTS

Wow. Look, I know every author says this, but this book is my baby. This was the one that sat impatiently in my brain, poking at me until I wrote it. Tiffany and Sam - they just would not leave me alone, and boy do I love them for it.

I had so much fun with these two, and hopefully that comes across in the book. Tiffany is who I want to be when I grow up - someone so wonderfully strong and caring and generous - with a blue tongue and a cocktail for every occasion.

To my wonderful friends and family who continue to support me (and buy my books) and let me drag them to cocktail bars for book research.

To every single person who's poured me a drink in the last 12 months - I couldn't have done this without your help.

A special thanks to Mickey, the loudest cat in existence, for inspiring Luna.

To my beautiful bi's, who may have shared similar experiences to my own (and Tiff's), and especially those I've spoken to who have been so wonderful in supporting me in my journey. I'm not always a disaster, but when I am, I love knowing I have a loving extended family around me.

Another huge thank you to my incredible cover designer Bailey, who manages to always amaze and put up with my very picky comments but turns them into something beautiful every time.

And my eternal gratitude to my wonderful editor Olivia,

whose critique and guidance really turned this manuscript around from 80k of banter into a journey that I could really be proud of. Sam in particular benefitted greatly in the revisions, and I'm so happy with his story now.

And to every other writer who has listened to me ramble on about this story, and these characters, thank you and I'm sorry! This was the one I couldn't stop talking about! I love these characters so so much, and I know you all got sick of me but you stuck it out anyway.

ABOUT THE AUTHOR

Dani McLean is an emerging author of Contemporary Romance stories that feature kickass women who can't quite get their shit together, and the irresistible but confused men who fall in love with them.

Born in Melbourne, she now lives in Perth, Western Australia with two walk in robes and a linen closet that's full of wine.

Dani loves to read, write and travel (in her memories, these days). She loves Hallmark movies because they're unintentionally hilarious, she's been on enough terrible Tinder dates to fuel countless books; and when she isn't conducting unofficial wine tastings in her pyjamas, she's devouring all things romance.

instagram.com/danimcleanwrites
facebook.com/danimcleanfiction
twitter.com/dmc_lean
tiktok.com/danimcleanwrites
amazon.com/author/danimclean
goodreads.com/danimclean
bookbub.com/authors/dani-mclean

www.ingramcontent.com/pod-product-compliance
Lightning Source LLC
Chambersburg PA
CBHW021956130726
47903CB00014B/1467